Limited/Unlimited

Limited/Unlimited

সীমাবদ্ধ / আশা আকাঙ্ক্ষা

SANKAR

Translated from the Bengali by

ARUNAVA SINHA

BLOOMSBURY

NEW DELHI • LONDON • OXFORD • NEW YORK • SYDNEY

BLOOMSBURY INDIA
Bloomsbury Publishing India Pvt. Ltd
Second Floor, LSC Building No. 4, DDA Complex, Pocket C – 6 & 7,
Vasant Kunj, New Delhi, 110070

BLOOMSBURY, BLOOMSBURY INDIA and the Diana logo
are trademarks of Bloomsbury Publishing Plc

First published in India 2024
This edition published 2024
Limited was originally published in Bengali as *Seemabaddha* by Dey's Publishing, 1970
Unlimited was originally published in Bengali as *Asha Akankha* by Dey's Publishing, 1973

ISBN: PB: 978-93-56407-69-5; eBook: 978-93-56409-03-3
2 4 6 8 10 9 7 5 3 1

Typeset in Adobe Garamond by Manipal Technologies Limited
Printed and bound in India by Thomson Press India Ltd

For sale in the Indian Subcontinent only

FSC www.fsc.org MIX Paper | Supporting responsible forestry FSC® C010615

Contents

Limited 1
Unlimited 163

Author's Note 349
About the Author 353
About the Translator 355

Limited

The whole duty of life is implied in the question, how to respire and aspire both at once.

— Henry David Thoreau

1

The office was very close to where Kolkata's Chowringhee Road bifurcates, passing on its entire responsibility to Jawaharlal Nehru Road, with the lonely metal statue of Mahatma Gandhi as silent witness.

After a ritual viewing of Gandhi at dawn, if anyone were to walk along the Chowringhee Road pavement past this neat building of modern design, they would see, well before the business district had woken up properly, Jatadhar Das, armed with a tin of Brasso, polishing two brass nameplates with great concentration, one of them in English, and the other Bengali. Using a soft cloth, the bearer rubbed them—with the same attention and care that beautiful women apply while doing their makeup before accompanying their husbands to a cocktail party—so that the engraved words became even brighter.

Hindustan Peters Limited
Incorporated in India
Shareholders' Liability Limited

If Jatadhar had to polish the nameplates at this hour of the morning, it was because some of the bosses arrived early. The top boss was from Blighty, his punctuality was unshakeable. No sooner did the clock strike nine than his imported Impala was seen gliding in from the direction of Alipur to stop directly outside the foyer. Barqat Ali, Mr Ferris's personal bearer, took up position near the entrance five minutes ahead. Marching up to the door of the car in military style, he opened it dexterously. Mr Ferris came out with his jacket draped over his arm. Barqat Ali offered a mighty salute, after which Ferris disappeared through the door, his head bent. Gathering his bag and other things, Barqat Ali followed him. The small hand of the clock touched nine, and the big hand twelve, at that very moment. This was the true Englishman. The word of a man, engineer's plan, iron lock, Englishman's clock.

Jatadhar's father used to work in the same company. He would say, 'The British ruled the world on the strength of the clock. If they defeated even the formidable Germans in war, you must realise it was also on the strength of the clock. If work starts at nine for them, it means one minute past eight fifty-nine.'

Neither the British of yore nor the India of old remained. If his aged father were to travel from his village in Orissa to Calcutta now, reflected Jatadhar, he would be flabbergasted. These days nine a.m. meant any time between eight-fifteen and nine-thirty. You were allowed to be late three times every month, so Mukunda-babu, Jadu-babu, Nagen-babu, and others like them made sure to be at work no earlier than nine-thirty three times a month. Just the other day Ramesh-babu received a gold watch from Mr Ferris for completing twenty-five years with the company. No one knew what getting the watch did to Ramesh-babu, but now he was late every day. Working twenty-five years here meant full immunity. Ramesh-babu was believed to have secured special permission to come in late.

Those who came in late were still tolerable. The troublemakers were the 'fast passengers'. Mr Ramalingam from the salary department arrived at three past eight every morning. He had sandalwood paste marks on his forehead. Only on Tuesdays he arrived at eight-thirty instead of three past eight. Mr Ramalingam was a warm, friendly person. He came later than usual on Tuesdays because that was the day of the week he had to offer a hundred and one red hibiscuses to the god Venkatesh. Mr Ramalingam sometimes gave Jatadhar a flower or two from the holy offering accepted by the god. Not just him, Mr Ramalingam gave flowers to anyone in the company who was in trouble, saying, 'Worry no more, now that you have a flower accepted by Venkatesh himself, He will protect you.'

On the other hand, Mr Ramalingam was an incredible miser. He never spent any money, he had not even bought a new tie in the past ten years, he had the same one around his neck every single day. But even a tight-fisted man like him bought the best hibiscuses in the market, making sure to choose them personally. He *had* to have large red hibiscuses—no matter how expensive. And he took casual leave on only one day a year, the day on which his requirement was a thousand and one flowers. Most of this day passed in offering Venkatesh the flowers, to the accompaniment of incantations.

Apart from Tuesdays, then, three past eight on all other days. Jatadhar wasn't particularly afraid of Mr Ramalingam, but the moment he spotted Mr Ramalingam at the gate, he knew he had to hurry, that he didn't have much time.

Today Jatadhar was actually late, because the blue Fiat had rolled in and stopped in front of the office. Its driver Srishtidhar Bera was Jatadhar's brother-in-law. They were great friends and even smoked a chillum or two on holidays. But Jatadhar had mixed feelings about the person seated behind Srishtidhar in the car.

The man in the back seat didn't let anyone open the door for him. Mr Chatterjee, S Chatterjee. Not very old, really. Thick black spectacles, with dry but disciplined hair. Mr Chatterjee might not have been as fair-skinned as Mr Ferris, but he certainly couldn't be said to have a dark complexion. His nose was pointed, in a fashion, and behind the thick glasses his eyes appeared wistful. As though, even if he was physically here at Hindustan Peters, his gaze was elsewhere.

Mr Chatterjee opened the door and got out of the car without taking anyone's help. Jatadhar had noticed there was something stylish about this movement. He hadn't dared tell anyone about it, but he felt he must discuss it with Srishtidhar one of these days. Mr Chatterjee always stepped out of his car like a film star. Jatadhar had been to watch a Bengali film once with Srishtidhar, the hero had got out of his car the same way, slinging his jacket over his shoulder and holding it in place with his left thumb.

After getting out of the car, Mr Chatterjee picked up his briefcase in his right hand, using his thumb to hold on to his lighter and packet of cigarettes. These cigarettes—they were called Rothmans or something—weren't even made in India. They came directly from England. But if one had to smoke, it ought to be brands like this. Mr Chatterjee had on one occasion left behind an opened packet in the car by mistake. Srishtidhar had secretly passed on a sample to his wife's brother. There were just two cigarettes. But oh, the flavour, the aroma—the taste still lingered. Jatadhar hadn't been able to smoke a bidi for an entire day after that. It was Jatadhar's plan to buy a packet of Rothmans with his bonus before going back home on his annual holiday—why, on the pavements of Park Street you could get all kinds of imported cigarettes and perfumes and soaps and condoms, if you had the money.

Jatadhar leapt off his stool to offer a salute to Mr Chatterjee. Exactly like Barqat Ali's salute for Mr Ferris. Jatadhar was a little worried, too. On paper his duty hours began at eight a.m., but he hadn't put on his uniform yet. He climbed back on the stool. Mr Chatterjee threw a sidelong glance at two words on the nameplate: 'Liability Limited'.

Closing the door of the automatic lift, Shyamalendu Chatterjee switched on the fan. Then he pressed the button lightly with a fingertip and leaned against the gleaming wall. Shyamalendu mused on the two unusual words he had caught sight of again after a long time. Of all the places in the world, why was the phrase 'limited liabilities' engraved at the entrance to this British company?

It wasn't just today, the words had caught Shyamalendu's attention the day he had entered the office of Hindustan Peters for the first time. Back then, too, several questions had occurred to him—who were the shareholders of this organisation? What were their liabilities? Could any liability possibly be unlimited in this ever-changing world? And why did the fact that the liabilities were limited have to be trumpeted from the rooftops? Later, however, Shyamalendu found out that it had to be written for legal reasons.

But there was no more time for reflection, the automatic lift had stopped on the second floor with a loud jerk. Shyamalendu Chatterjee was no longer standing on the ground. A very interesting expression was used these days in advertisements for Otis lifts. Not 'atmosphere' or 'stratosphere', just 'Otisphere'. Opening the collapsible gate of the lift, Shyamalendu emerged from Otisphere into Petersphere.

Shyamalendu savoured these early morning hours in the office. They were like a blemish-less maiden. Perhaps the English word virgin was even more appropriate. No matter what the dictionary said, a virgin and a maiden were not the same. In Bengali families the idea of spinsterhood was strongly contained in the word maiden, but virgin implied sacred, untouched, unspoilt—something that was not yet tainted by touch or usage, which could still be offered to the gods.

Shyamalendu Chatterjee chuckled. Why were these juvenile ideas from his college days intruding on his thoughts? It was college students and professors who split hairs like this when analysing the intricacies of language. Does the vessel hold the oil or the oil the vessel? They pored over thick books to answer such questions as though the future of the universe depended on it. Those who lived in the modern world of commerce were straightforward in comparison, there could be no luxury of ambiguous conundrums here, everything needed to be prefixed by 'with reference to'. The world wouldn't run on celebrations of Shakespeare and Socrates. The Isaac Pitmans and Peter Druckers revered by management specialists had proved more beneficial to mankind.

Shyamalendu tap-tapped his way across the empty office to the glass-walled room at the southernmost end of the hall. No sooner had he opened the door with his foot and entered than the door closed slowly behind him. Putting his briefcase on the desk, Shyamalendu reflected that this was how the world ran. Opening the door to one's career needed all the persistence and hard work in the world, but the road to growth thereafter was inevitably congested, even without anyone blocking it deliberately.

Shyamalendu put the flask of water hanging from his shoulder on his desk. This was a recent annoyance. Ever since Shyamalendu had worked here the office bearer used to bring him water to drink, but as soon as he was promoted to manager, Dolon said, 'You have to take a flask of water along with your briefcase from now on.'

At first Shyamalendu had protested vehemently. Besides kindergarten children and neurotic foreign tourists, who carried their own drinking water around Calcutta? But his objections were overruled. 'You don't even look around you,' Dolon had said, 'you're still a small-town boy from Patna. None of the managers in your company drinks the office water.'

Shyamalendu had stared at Dolon, who said, 'I observe everything from this ninth-floor balcony of Blue Haven. Your Chief Accountant Chopra, Deputy Finance Manager Harris, Technical Manager Hartley, even the Company Secretary Sengupta all take water bottles to work.'

Shyamalendu couldn't object anymore. A close examination of the arrangements for water actually revealed the hierarchy in the company. He didn't know how those on the lowest rung, the bearers, got any water to drink. He had never actually seen any of them drink water in all his years in this job. He had heard a couple of glasses were hidden behind the filing cabinet, which they used when needed. Then came the clerks. Each of them had glasses on their desks, numbered in red, so that the bearers could put the glasses back in their respective places after washing them every morning. The glasses for the senior clerks were one-and-a-half times larger than for the junior clerks. The next level was occupied by local assistants, referred to by some as Indian assistants. Their glasses were not very large, but they were slender and pleasing to the eye, with floral patterns and colourful enamelled covers. The next rung was that of junior officers. Their desks had red containers within which the glasses were kept, they had to lift the lid to drink their water. The senior officers had embroidered covers for their glasses, and if you were a manager, office water was completely ruled out, you had to have your own flask. The directors had two flasks, one filled with chilled water, and heaven knew what the other one held. Some said it was hot water for coffee, some claimed it was whiskey, and some said it was empty. But being a director meant you had to have two flasks.

Placing his jacket on a hanger, Shyamalendu put it in the wardrobe and shut the door, but not before taking out several slips of paper from one of the pockets.

Then he lit a cigarette—these Rothmans were becoming more expensive by the month. Apparently, when there were no guests at home, many of the managers had begun smoking Indian cigarettes on the sly. Not that they were bad—India Kings was quite a good brand. But that didn't mean a Hindustan Peters manager could smoke Indian cigarettes in public. Nilambar Sengupta was an uncomplicated man, and not a smoker himself. 'You have no idea what's going on these days,' he had told Shyamalendu. 'Forget India Kings, many managers are smoking even Scissors. Ask your wife to discreetly check with the Blue Haven sweeper. They sweep all the managers' flats, they know everything.'

Shyamalendu began unrolling the little slips of paper. He would have to write to the manager of the Delhi office—sales were growing but so was the money owed to the company. Outstanding payments were on the rise in Madras too these days. They should put up prominent signs in the offices—cash today, credit tomorrow. He would also have to write a polite but tough letter to Shivshailam, the Bombay manager. All the big promises at conferences, but why weren't sales going up in proportion to development in Maharashtra? The area manager in Ahmedabad was a bright young man. He had crafted an innovative plan to sell fans to farmers in Gujarat before the onset of summer. The plan would have to be finalised this week.

There were some more slips. Shyamalendu had learnt this technique from the marketing director, Davidson. Davidson's memory was like an IBM computer's—he seemed to remember perfectly the tasks he had assigned and to whom, what promises he had made and to whom, what additional supplies he had to ensure and to whom. But how? Shyamalendu could never make out. He finally learnt the secret at a meeting of area managers. All the sales people were gathered around Davidson like leeches, led by Shyamalendu's dearest friend Runu Sanyal. Runu had won over Davidson effectively—the marketing director had begun addressing him as Runu. And Runu also called him John.

Shyamalendu made no attempt to break through the cordon thrown around Davidson, standing instead in a corner of the banquet room of Grand Hotel. From a distance Dolon expressed her displeasure at her husband's reticence with a sharp look that said, 'What's the point of passing the ball to Runu and looking on?' Turning his eyes away, Shyamalendu went up to Mrs Davidson instead. The wives of the top brass of commercial firms were not as powerful as ministers' wives. Only chauffeurs, clerks and, at most, Indian assistants could expect to flatter a director's wife to secure something for themselves—but for higher-ranked employees the directors took their own decisions, they didn't defer to their wives' wishes.

'Your husband's efficiency seems miraculous to me,' Shyamalendu told Mrs Davidson. 'I have no idea how he remembers every single thing. He comes to the office at nine in the morning and discusses a dozen different matters as though he's just read the files.'

Mrs Davidson, who was nursing a gin, took a drag on her cigarette and said, 'Thanks very much, you've just given me an idea.'

'Have I?' said a bewildered Shyamalendu.

'Yes, whenever he has an idea about work at home, John notes it down on a slip of paper and stuffs it in his left pocket. When he goes to work he refers to it straightaway. But when he's at work he doesn't remember a thing about home. Now I'm going to put down important things on slips of paper and stuff them in his right pocket. Let's see if it works.'

Shyamalendu had applied the Davidson technique since then. Just as there are two kinds of people in the world, there are two kinds of managers as well, those who learn from example and those who learn from experience. But only one of them—learning from example—leads to career growth. So Shyamalendu also used the left-pocket–right-pocket strategy. He just remembered that when he got home he would have to go over the speech he was scheduled to deliver at the Calcutta Management Seminar tomorrow. At least the main points. There was no time for things like this at work. Shyamalendu made a note on a slip of paper and put it in his right pocket.

Then he took several files out of the drawers and made some points in his scribbling pad. He would dictate the letters as soon as Mrs Anderson came to work. Shyamalendu looked at his watch. He had asked her to come in a little early today, he wanted to finalise the note he had dictated to her yesterday as quickly as possible.

Mrs Anderson must have arrived now, the lights came on in her cubicle. There was a strict rule in this office that the lights would not be switched on unless the room or cubicle was occupied. Ferris had circulated a notice as soon as he was appointed managing director—'Every employee of Hindustan Peters must cooperate to meet the challenges of the future and help India progress further. Costs have to be curbed. Come, let us keep an eye on every naya paisa, and the rupees will automatically take care of themselves. I would like us to economise from the ground up. Let there be no lights burning unnecessarily in any of the rooms or cubicles.' Ferris didn't write the circular himself, of course. He had summoned Shyamalendu and said, 'Chatterjee, you have a flair for speaking informally with everyone. I've noticed the buggers in this office wasting electricity. Can you please draft a suitable circular to remind the buggers that every light has a switch to go with it?'

Ferris was an engineer by profession, who had worked in factories for many years. So he was prone to profanity.

Reading Shyamalendu's draft, he said, 'Good job. Even to switch off the lights you have to remind these blighters of India's five-year plans. India is your country, after all, you know it best.'

From senior to junior employees, everyone was very pleased with Ferris's circular. 'He really does love India,' the clerks said in the lunchroom.

The fact was that every managing director wanted to leave something memorable among their accomplishments. The previous head of the company, Graham, had apparently issued instructions as soon as he had taken charge to close the taps in the bathrooms properly. But the language of the circular had made everyone livid. The company had been on the verge of a strike.

Mrs Anderson came in. 'Good morning, Mr Chatterjee.'

''Morning,' said Shyamalendu.

'Sorry, Mr Chatterjee, I couldn't keep my word, I couldn't get here on time.'

Blowing out a mouthful of smoke, Shyamalendu said, 'I need the note I dictated yesterday. Immediately.'

'I'll have it with you in ten minutes, Mr Chatterjee.'

Mrs Anderson returned to her desk. Creases of irritation appeared on Shyamalendu's face. The woman was turning into a cabbage now that she was married. Her name had been Miss Wood earlier. She used to type like lightning and kept all the papers and files flawlessly up to date. Now she wouldn't stay back even a minute after office hours. That Mr Anderson of hers walked into her cubicle as soon as it turned five. It really irritated Shyamalendu sometimes. One day he had told Dolon casually, 'I'm thinking of asking him why he lets her work if he's so attached to her.'

'Poor thing, he's still under the trance of the honeymoon, don't say anything to him. Not everyone is so obsessed with work like you that they don't care whether their wife is alive or dead.'

Today, though, Shyamalendu was genuinely annoyed, because he did need the note early this morning. But there was no way to tell her anything. She was pregnant on top of everything else. This business of having children was something of an animal instinct for women. From empresses to film stars, from female scientists to directors' wives, from lady secretaries to lady sweepers, there was no difference between them and cats when it came to reproducing. This wasn't Shyamalendu's own observation, however, it was Runu Sanyal who'd said this. This was back in the days when Shyamalendu and Runu would get together quite often. Shyamalendu would visit Runu at home with Dolon whenever possible, and Runu would also go over to Shyamalendu's home on Townsend Road with his wife. He used to be full of his trademark one-liners then.

Shyamalendu had actually told Runu's wife Anindita, 'If Bernard Shaw overheard some of your husband's lines he'd definitely use them.'

'And what good would that do me? The company wouldn't increase my salary by a single rupee because Bernard Shaw has quoted me. Just that Bernard Shaw would earn more from royalties,' Runu had said after a sip of coffee.

And no, Mrs Anderson might be pregnant, but she hadn't become inefficient, she brought the typed note to Shyamalendu very soon. He was embarrassed, there was no need to have been so annoyed with her, she was expecting a child, after all. No one went to work out of choice in this condition.

Shyamalendu scanned the note quickly, then jumped to his feet and got his jacket from the wardrobe. It was a quarter past nine on his watch.

Davidson had been in England for some time. Shyamalendu was in charge of one of the two divisions under him.

Shyamalendu stopped outside the managing director's room, knocked lightly on the door twice, and entered.

It wasn't as though you had to open just the one door to meet the MD. Before that there was his secretary, Mrs Dick. Her physical appearance was hotly discussed at all levels of Hindustan Peters. No one had seen her come to the office in the same outfit on successive days. These days this evil genius had taken to wearing near-transparent chiffon saris and matching blouses. And the very next day she might wear a miniskirt. Those who dressed in miniskirts had to face certain difficulties, especially the typists. From a foreign fashion magazine Mrs Dick had learnt how to cover the front of her desk with something known as a modesty board. This kept the eyes of visitors from troubling her lower half.

It was said that Mrs Dick was extremely conceited, and that she behaved badly with everyone. But with Shyamalendu her relations were friendly, and they even exchanged banter. Shyamalendu would say, 'You can fight with your boss, but never with his secretary.'

Giving him an arch look, Mrs Dick would say, 'Don't kid with me, Mr Chatterjee.' Using the word 'kidding' had become something of a mannerism for her.

Shyamalendu would say, 'There are two types of secretaries in the world, Mrs Dick—good secretaries and good-looking secretaries. But in all of Calcutta there's only one who's both.'

'There you go, kidding me again,' Mrs Dick would complain, quite pleased.

'There's just the one thing that I'm worried about,' Shyamalendu would say. 'Mr Crifford from the Home Board is coming to India on a tour. Don't blame us afterwards if you end up with a home posting.'

'England! Spare me, Mr Chatterjee, I can't possibly work in England. There's a dearth of secretaries there, getting a job is no problem at all. But I have decided I shall go nowhere but Canada.'

But there was no banter today. Shyamalendu saw the MD had the red light switched on outside his room.

Mrs Dick said, 'There's no one inside, he's preparing for the board meeting.'

'Will you send this note in, please? He needs it for the board meeting. He asked me to prepare it after our meeting at four o'clock yesterday.'

'Do you want to meet him?'

'No need. I'm going back to my desk, will you send word if he asks for me?'

Emerging from the room, Shyamalendu walked down the corridor solemnly. He never looked left or right when walking. High-ranking officers mastered this skill after dedicated practice. You're walking in a crowd, but nobody can tell where your eyes are. Shyamalendu's first head clerk Abani-babu had said a long time ago, 'Finally, sir, a Bengali in this company. We're so happy, all of us. We may be clerks, but when a Bengali prospers we are pleased, we feel confident.' He had also said, 'You're a born officer, sir, you must behave the way the Englishmen do. Don't be involved in petty matters like these petty officers who've risen through the ranks. Never look around when you walk through the office.'

Shyamalendu had found it funny then, the things Abani-babu had told him. Could anyone be an officer from the moment they were born? How was he supposed to walk in a crowd without looking at anyone? But Shyamalendu didn't consider it funny now. Shyamalendu Chatterjee had acclimatised himself completely to the environment at Hindustan Peters.

Soon after he returned to his room Shyamalendu's internal telephone rang. It was the company secretary, Nilambar Sengupta. 'Are you free, Mr Chatterjee?'

'Always free for you, Mr Sengupta,' Shyamalendu answered.

Nilambar Sengupta entered with a bunch of files.

'What time are you starting the board meeting, Mr Sengupta?' Shyamalendu asked.

'Eleven thirty sharp. After the meeting the directors will go to Sutanuti Club for lunch. That's always been the tradition. Lunch after the meeting, or the meeting after lunch.'

'Please take a seat Mr Sengupta, have a cup of coffee with me at least,' Shyamalendu requested.

'Company Law and the board of directors are driving me mad. These British directors don't understand how complicated Company Law here is, one slip and the Company Law Board will come down on us like a house of bricks. And then, as you can imagine, everyone else will go scot-free but the company secretary will be in the line of fire.'

'What's going on, Mr Sengupta? Why so many board meetings and so frequently?'

'Nothing in particular. The board of directors is the supreme authority, after all, so they have to be consulted from time to time. And besides, unless we hold meetings the external directors will not get their fees.'

Sipping his coffee, Sengupta continued, 'The marketing director isn't here, as you know. I believe you've given the MD a note, so he's asked you to wait outside the boardroom. He'll ask for you if he needs anything.'

Shyamalendu had never been to a board meeting. He had no idea what the directors might ask.

'You've got me worried, sir,' Shyamalendu said with a smile.

'You've got the managing director eating out of your hands, you have no reason to be worried,' Sengupta responded.

'I know the full-time directors well enough, Mr Gordon from finance, Mr Murthy from Delhi, Mr Ferris, I have worked with them, I can manage them. It's the external directors I'm afraid of, who knows what they might ask. I don't even know if I should answer them candidly. Mr Davidson handles these things himself usually. Give me some advice, sir.'

'Don't make me laugh, Mr Chatterjee. All right, can you answer this question? How many types of boards do you think there are?'

'Why are you getting me into trouble again, Mr Sengupta? According to the Indian Companies Act there's only one kind of board, and its directors are elected at the shareholders' meeting. You're the one who writes the announcements, aren't you: so and so is retiring by rotation, and, being eligible, offers himself for re-election.'

'My answer is that there are two kinds of board,' said Sengupta, 'hard and soft. Our Delhi resident director and our finance director constitute the hard board. As for the rest, you can imagine. One of them is the company solicitor Panchu Boral. Then there's Sir Baren Ray of Camac Street, whom everyone used to call Sir Brian Ray during the British raj, and Kumar Sengupta.'

Sengupta didn't linger after finishing his coffee. He would have to get his papers in order for the board meeting.

Shyamalendu also arranged his documents in a clear plastic folder, and then set off for the visitors' room on the ground floor.

The floor of the room was fully covered with an expensive carpet. It was like entering the most elegant of theatres. Ferris kept an eagle's eye on these things. 'As in love, first impressions are crucial in business too. Anyone who sets foot in the Hindustan Peters head office must realise it's not a run-of-the-mill establishment.'

A great deal of thought had gone into the design of this room. Ferris had sent for both Shyamalendu and Runu on that occasion. 'I'd like you young men to put some thought into this waiting room,' he had said. 'Consult your wives if needs be.'

The story of how the room was decorated was a complicated one. There was even a bit of conflict between Dolon and Anindita. Runu had consulted some of the most renowned interior designers of Calcutta and Bombay.

The budget was drawn up after this. Perhaps a little on the high side considering it was just one room. Two lakh rupees.

Someone must have tipped off the workers' union, but Ferris didn't budge. 'You do your work,' he told the union leader Sujoy Mitra, 'and let me do mine.'

'I had assumed it would cost three lakh,' Ferris had told the finance people. 'This means we're saving a hundred thousand. Even if our company isn't the biggest now, it will be much bigger one day. Our annual sales will cross a hundred million next year. And don't forget we have begun exporting our products. What will foreign buyers think when they visit our office? How can we impress them? How will we convince them that they're buying from one of the most renowned companies in the world?'

The point about foreigners hadn't occurred to Runu Sanyal, it was Shyamalendu who had included it in his note. As a matter of fact, the expenses had seemed a little exorbitant to Shyamalendu, especially for a company whose annual sales amounted to barely sixty or seventy million rupees. But Runu's wife was adamant. Anindita told her husband, 'Never be a miser on these trivial matters, don't set your sights low like middle-class people do.'

'But darling,' Runu had said, 'I have to explain it to Mr Ferris, we need to justify the expense.'

She answered him at once, 'Didn't you say the other day Shah Jahan would never have been able to build the Taj Mahal if he had been asked to justify it financially?'

The tightest of fists were loosened these days if exports or defence was mentioned. Everything was permissible for these two. But the funny thing was, although Runu had proposed splurging on the room, it was Shyamalendu who had brought up exports. He was effectively in charge of the company's entire exports, since the division that Runu looked after had no scope for exporting its products at all.

When she saw Shyamalendu enter the visitor's room, the receptionist Srila Chakraborty said, 'Good morning, Mr Chatterjee.'

Shyamalendu reciprocated in his usual style. Two vases of fresh flowers adorned Srila's desk. A shop from New Market delivered a variety of flowers every morning. And Srila, too, dressed in new ways every day. It was the managing director who had made the plan to hire a sari-clad woman as receptionist. He had personally told Harihar Talukdar, the personnel officer, what sort of person he wanted.

Poor Talukdar turned into a wreck over the next few weeks. Every day he interviewed and rejected a dozen beautiful women. 'I can't take it anymore, Mr Chatterjee,' he confessed to Shyamalendu one day. 'Imagine having to do something like this at my age. The boss won't approve of any of them. If the candidate looks right her voice doesn't please him, and if the voice passes muster her physical appearance is not to his liking.'

Shyamalendu listened, smiling indulgently. 'He wants to kill two birds with one stone,' Talukdar continued, 'She must look like a purebred Indian, but sound like an Englishwoman. We might still find a real Indian beauty, but the convent-school accent is where we run into trouble.'

They had finally found Miss Srila Chakraborty. Now Talukdar's concern was, what if she didn't last? 'The times we live in, women like these get married overnight. And I don't know what happens to Bengali women after marriage, they become stale and soggy, completely useless. Say what you will, look at the Anglo-Indian girls—married or not, always crisp and fresh.'

'Are you attending the board meeting?' Srila asked Shyamalendu.

'No, I'll wait outside. Are the directors here already?'

'Not yet, but any moment now,' said Srila, arranging the flowers.

Sengupta arrived with his papers. Murthy, the company's resident director in Delhi, appeared too. 'Hello Sengupta, hello Chatterjee,' he said, extending his hand.

After the handshakes Sengupta said, 'Did you fly in this morning?'

'Absolutely not, I came last evening. Can't take a risk with a board meeting.'

Jagannath Venkatachari Murthy went into the boardroom.

'A real piece of work,' Sengupta commented.

An old Bentley came to a stop outside the foyer. The scrawny old man in the back seat was all but asleep. The chauffeur got out, opened the door, and said, 'Sir!' quite loudly.

The gaunt occupant of the car, dressed in a three-piece suit tailored in London, said, 'Tomlin company?'

'Hindustan Peters, sir,' said the chauffeur, 'this is where you asked me to drive you.'

'That's true, I did ask you to drive me to Hindustan Peters.'

The man ambled into the office with his file. Srila had never seen him before—who had this old man come to trouble this morning, she wondered. When the man went up to her, shaking his sleeve, his shoulders bent, Sengupta whispered to Shyamalendu, 'Sir Brian is here. A member of the Ray family of Colootola. ICS, now retired. A formidable man of the British era.'

'Good morning, Sir Brian,' Sengupta said deferentially. 'How are you?'

'Ah, Nilambar. How do I look?'

'Like garden-fresh tea from the best company.'

Sengupta's answer pleased Baren Ray, the former canny ICS officer of Delhi. 'I'm quite active,' he said, 'I go to the Golf Club regularly, I drop in at Gobindopur Club, I attend board meetings, I digest everything I eat. What else can I ask for? You know of Henry Ford. So much money and fame, couldn't swallow a boiled egg. I still follow the Viceroy Lord Linlithgow's advice and still eat two-quarter boiled eggs at breakfast.'

Sengupta's response was prepared. 'You're a classic Rolls Royce, sir, the older you get, the more valuable you become. Not one of these new-fangled made-in-India cars.'

Glancing at his watch, Baren Ray saw he was early, and began to hold forth. 'You're right, Nilambar. And besides, we're fighters, we've fought all our life. The fights nowadays are nothing like they were in the British era. What do today's IAS officers have to do anyway? This lot would have been head assistants in our time, one or two might have trickled upwards into the BCS. How can you expect the country to develop with such people in charge?'

'Of course,' echoed Sengupta.

'These IAS fellows can barely handle half-a-dozen MPs in caps, and maybe a minister or two. In our time we had them under our thumbs, whenever necessary we sent them where they belonged, which was prison, and then we went toe to toe with ferocious Englishmen.'

'Legendary stories,' Sengupta egged Baren Ray on.

'As you know, the public thought we supported the British, but to the British we were hard-core freedom fighters. Fire off the stiffest notes against the British, that was our policy.'

Sengupta and Shyamalendu gazed at Sir Brian. 'Didn't you have a conflict with Field Marshal Auchinleck once?' said Sengupta.

Baren Ray of Colootola was delighted. 'I see you don't forget things. The war was in full swing. And while the battles raged I held back Auchinleck's TA bill for three full days. The note I wrote almost led to his TA being refused altogether. Long story! It went up all the way to the viceroy. In the end, at the personal request of the finance secretary, I softened, considering the war effort. Auchinleck's bill was passed. Come home one of these days, I'll tell you the entire episode. You'll be astonished. But look at the greatness of the British, even after this incident they gave me the knighthood.'

Now Brian Ray asked, 'What time are you starting the board meeting?'

'Eleven-thirty sharp.'

'I was about to go to Tomlins by mistake, you know. Then I remembered theirs is at three-thirty.'

'We don't let you rest even after retirement,' Sengupta sounded regretful.

Sir Baren Ray nodded. 'I can't tell you, Nilambar, there's a board meeting almost every day. Not one or two, I'm a director of twenty companies, so you can imagine.'

'Fortunately the Companies Act doesn't allow more than twenty, or else many more companies would have requested you to join their boards.'

'What use would that be? I can't grow ten arms for your benefit.'

Sir Baren entered the boardroom, mumbling under his breath.

'The ideal director,' whispered Sengupta. 'Seventy-two years old, nods off in his chair all through, never asks a question. When it's time to vote, says, "I agree with Mr Ferris." These days, though, he's not keeping well. Last time he actually fell asleep during the meeting, and there was a rumbling in his throat.'

The person who followed Sir Baren Ray into the boardroom almost immediately afterwards was Kumar Jagadish. He seemed to have been appointed to the board as a match for Sir Baren. As corpulent as Sir Baren was thin, Kumar Jagadish was extremely correct in his behaviour. Greeting Sengupta formally, he marched solemnly in. 'Everyone has to agree that our board has become more important because of him. His father was Raja Haridas of Uluberia. But this gentleman was too much of a scrooge to contribute to the

War Fund and make the other necessary payments to take on the title of Raja. He remained an eternal prince in the books of the British. Spends most of his time in Uluberia, travels when he needs to.'

The other members of the board were meeting Ferris now. Giving instructions about coffee to Miss Chakraborty, Sengupta disappeared inside the boardroom.

Shyamalendu had seen the empty boardroom many times, but he had never witnessed a board meeting. Today in the visitors' room he felt particularly curious about it. After all, the post just above his was that of a whole-time director of the company. And it was this board that decided the company's fortunes—the board was all-powerful.

'Good morning.' It was Runu Sanyal.

Runu appeared with a clear plastic folder in his hand and sat down next to Shyamalendu. Taking a packet of cigarettes from his pocket, he offered his colleague one. Then, stroking his lighter with his own cigarette, he said, 'Don't ask, summons from the board. Had to drop everything and run. Mr Ferris's secretary said, "Wait outside the boardroom, they might ask about the note you put in yesterday."'

'I was called here for the same reason,' Shyamalendu said.

There was not much conversation after this. Both of them sat there smoking. As she was sending the coffee into the boardroom, Srila asked if they would like some too.

They finished their cigarettes and coffee at the same time—the two young heads of the two sales divisions of Hindustan Peters, Shyamalendu Chatterjee and Ranabir Sanyal.

However, they were not summoned in the end. Sengupta emerged briefly to tell them, 'The board is discussing other matters today, Mr Ferris sends his thanks and says there's no need to wait any longer.'

'Thank goodness.' Both of them sighed with visible relief. An unwelcome responsibility had been lifted off their shoulders. They got into the lift together, and then, holding their plastic folders casually, marched towards their respective rooms in executive style.

Shyamalendu sat in his chair quietly for a few minutes. No matter what he had said, he was disappointed. A sweet expectation had been building within him. There was honour and a certain drama in facing the board of directors to answer questions, an acknowledgement of critical responsibility. The opportunity had slipped through his fingers.

Runu Sanyal booked an urgent call. 'My residence please.'

'Hello, Bibi? It's me.'

'Yes, how did it go? Is the board meeting over?'

'Listen, it doesn't seem that important. I'd told you as soon as I heard from Mr Ferris. I just got back. I thought I'd let you know right away so that you don't worry.'

'Naturally I was worrying. I couldn't even join the ladies' coffee meet at Ferazzini. I've been waiting by the telephone ever since you told me. Anyway, tell me the details when you get home. But it's a matter of honour, you know, being sent for in Mr Davidson's absence.'

Runu Sanyal sounded anxious now. 'I thought they'd called me alone, Bibi, but I found Shyamalendu sitting there. They must have called him too.'

'Let them, don't worry. I can ring Ranga Mashi if you like, so she can ask Meshomoshai what's going on when he's back from the board meeting. I'll let you know after that.'

'Sir Baren won't be back home early. I'm sure they'll go for lunch after the meeting. And besides, ringing them isn't a good idea.'

'Why can't I ring my mother's sister? I may be your wife but it's still my fundamental right.'

'Let me think it over, Bibi. A company director, after all, and not of any old company either but Hindustan Peters.'

'He may be a director for you but for me he's my aunt's husband.'

'Yes, but ...'

'What's the but about?'

'Your aunt's husband is old school ICS. Steel frame. You know what that's like, don't you? He may not take kindly to it.'

'Oh all right, darling, since you're so hesitant I'll just give her a courtesy call. Just how are you, how's Mesho, etc., etc.'

'That's not a bad idea,' Runu agreed.

'By the way, darling,' Anindita said, 'tell the driver I'm out of cigarettes. Can he get five packets of Benson & Hedges as quickly as possible? Bye now.'

Shyamalendu had meanwhile finished dictating some letters and answered several telex messages as well.

This was a new nuisance, the telex. Telegrams could still be ignored, since the sender would never know when it had reached the head office. But now there were telex machines at every branch office, which the people were using to send messages at will, since it was like dialling a number. And they were printed out immediately in the telex room at the head office. The messages ended with 'awaiting your response', so there was no choice but to take decisions quickly. Many of the managers had given up writing letters altogether, sending telex messages for all requirements. A circular had to be sent out, the telex bill would run into hundreds of thousands this year. The facility shouldn't be used except for very urgent requirements, or else the posts and telegraph division would keep increasing the bill.

Now Shyamalendu's phone rang too.

'Chatterjee,' announced Shyamalendu.

'It's me.' He had no trouble identifying the voice.

'I rang earlier too,' said Dolon, 'Mrs Anderson said you'd gone to attend the board meeting. Anything special? You didn't tell me anything.'

'I didn't know myself, Dolon. The MD issued orders this morning. Mr Davidson isn't here, so ...'

'That's good news. The boss sent for you because Davidson isn't here.'

'Not just me, Dolon, the MD sent for Runu too.' Shyamalendu reluctantly doused Dolon's exuberance.

'Listen, I have some good news,' Dolon said. 'Just got a telegram. Sudarshana's coming. Morning train tomorrow. She's asked us to meet her at the station.'

'Really? She didn't write or anything.'

'You know what they're like. But I'm so happy.'

'So you should be, Dolon. We'll have fun for a few days.'

2

Shyamalendu had forgotten how beautiful Howrah station was at dawn. He hadn't had anything to do with a railway station in a long time. All travel nowadays was from Dumdum Airport. Nobody at Hindustan Peters except the young salesmen took trains these days.

Smoking, Shyamalendu said, 'Do you remember, Dolon, how we had pretty much memorised Jajabar's *Drishtipat* in college? There was something in it about trains versus planes, science has given us pace but snatched away grace.'

Dolon smiled. 'I remember very well, you gave it to me for my birthday. Must be lying somewhere in Patna. Should have told Sudarshana to bring it. Your first gift to me, after all.'

'If Jajabar were to revise the book now he'd definitely amend that line. Taking a train now means thousands of worries. Getting reservations, negotiating traffic jams on Howrah Bridge, arguing with porters. On top of which you have strikes, theft of copper wires, removal of fish plates, missing staff, Bengal bandh, Bihar bandh, among many other things. Where's the grace in any of this, for heaven's sake? Airplanes aren't as bad as this.'

'Do you remember?' Dolon said. 'You'd just joined your company, I was in Patna, you were supposed to go to Delhi. You decided to take Delhi Express so that we could meet for a while at Patna Junction station. But you didn't show up. I was so embarrassed. I took Sudarshana with me without telling anyone where I was going, and then there I was walking from one end of that long train to the other, but not a sign of you. I can't tell you how upset I was, I had tears in my eyes. Sudarshana said, why are you crying, Didi, it's only been two weeks since you came from Calcutta. I answered her in my head, just wait till you grow up and get married, you'll know then what two weeks can mean. How would a girl of fourteen know why her sister was crying because she couldn't find someone?'

Shyamalendu smiled. 'Wasn't my fault though. Mr Davidson said, no, you must fly. The train may be cheaper, but it takes too much time. And time is valuable. In this age of the jetplane, officers' time is not meant to be wasted sitting in trains.'

'I'm terrified of taking the train now thanks to all these newspaper reports,' Shyamalendu continued. 'But Dolon, I'm enjoying Howrah Station today.'

'Is that because of the station or your sister-in-law?' Dolon joked.

'My sister-in-law isn't here yet, Dolon,' Shyamalendu answered.

The electric engine was visible now near the signal in the distance. The train was on time.

Shyamalendu didn't care for the electric engine, it seemed a bit of a snob, strutting in arrogantly and coming to an abrupt stop. But the older steam engines used to pant for a while afterwards—much like marathon runners after the race. The latest issue of *Business Week* had carried a brief biography of the chairman of England's biggest company. His hobby was repairing train engines. He had bought a second-hand steam locomotive for his home, which he tinkered with on weekends. Of all the machines that humans had built since the beginning of the industrial revolution, the steam engine, in his view, was the most captivating as well as humane.

Howrah station seemed to suddenly wake up from slumber. Silent so far, Platform No. 6 rang with the laughter of children.

'Dolon, do you want to wait somewhere? Let me go find Sudarshana,' Shyamalendu asked.

'Never. You think I can't find my sister?' Dolon answered solemnly, like a child. Then they both burst into laughter.

Sudarshana Bhattacharya appeared outside the door to the third-class sleeping compartment. She was a little taller than the average Bengali woman, her complexion even more golden than her sister's. Added to this was a radiance that came from living a healthy life away from Calcutta, which the women of the big city always envied. A charming tenderness was combined with the glow of intelligence in Sudarshana's expression, but it was not a blinding glare, more like the milk-white Peters lamp which spread light but was not painfully harsh.

Sudarshana waved when she spotted her sister and brother-in-law, and then, sidestepping the porters, hugged Dolon. 'How are you, Didi? Haven't seen you in ages,' she said.

'Shyamal-da is standing next to Didi,' Shyamalendu reminded her with feigned seriousness. 'He should now be greeted the same way.'

'As if a sister and a brother-in-law are the same.' Sudarshana wrinkled her face, and then offered a sweet smile before bending over to touch his feet respectfully.

To outdo her, Dolon said, 'For unmarried girls, brothers-in-law are far more lovable and valuable than sisters.'

The brother-in-law in question said, 'Let me take care of your luggage first, or it'll disappear.'

'This leather bag is what I have by way of luggage,' Sudarshana said, pointing at it with a smile. 'And this bag on my shoulder.'

'These Santiniketan sling bags hold a lot, but they're no longer in fashion in Calcutta,' Dolon said.

'Back home, Didi, this bag isn't out of fashion yet,' Sudarshana replied.

'It wouldn't have been here either,' her sister whispered, 'but you know ...'

'Know what?' Sudarshana asked.

'You know all the girls here who're into politics, the ones who march in processions and shout slogans, they all carry these bags. And the others who use them are American hippies. Naturally, middle-class women get a little nervous seeing them.'

Handing the bag over to a porter, they walked towards Cab Road. That was where Shyamalendu had parked.

'You didn't have trouble on the train, I hope,' said Dolon.

'Trouble? I slept like a king.'

'That's grammatically incorrect—you should say queen,' Shyamalendu quipped.

'The third-class compartments are quite good these days, aren't they?' said Sudarshana. Dolon had quite forgotten the interior of a third-class coach. She had taken the train one or two times after getting married, but in air-conditioned class. The very thought of a third-class compartment frightened her, to be honest.

When they reached the car, Shyamalendu put the luggage in the trunk and held the door open.

'Wait, let me take a good look at the two of you,' Sudarshana said. 'Shyamal-da, I feel like I'm watching a film. You look just like Uttam Kumar, you've kept your movie-star looks, and then the white shirt and shorts!'

'These are not for movie-star looks, though, I went for golf this morning. I was up at five for practice. The Merchant's Cup is starting soon, Hindustan Peters' future depends on our performance.'

'His routine is too complicated for me, but your Shyamal-da does look like a film star in this sports outfit, doesn't he?' Dolon said to her sister. 'The hero's come to Howrah station to receive someone.'

Sudarshana turned her attention to her sister. 'If Shyamal-da is Uttam Kumar, you're Suchitra Sen.' Scanning Dolon closely, she continued, 'But Suchitra Sen has put on some weight. She'll have to be slimmer to match the hero.'

'You'll know once you're married,' Dolon laughed. 'God hates married women, doesn't matter how careful you are or how little you eat, you're bound to put on weight.'

'I don't know about that, Didi. You just have to remember that your name is Dolonchampa, the flower that sways in the gentlest breeze.'

'Honestly, what a peculiar name I've been saddled with,' said Dolon.

'Peculiar! Sweet, you mean. Isn't that right, Shyamal-da?'

'Sweet and uncommon,' Shyamalendu said.

'How could it be common?' Sudarshana said. 'You have to remember who named her. Bibhutibhushan Bandyopadhyay himself. Didi, the other day I saw the photo of him cradling you in his arms, we found the album unexpectedly. Baba said Bibhutibhushan had stayed with us when he visited Patna, and Baba requested him to name you. You were sitting on the floor rocking back and forth madly, so he suggested Dolonchampa.'

'Enough, Tutul, get in the car now.' Dolon looked embarrassed as she bundled Sudarshana in.

'No, let me finish. You used to rock yourself to sleep earlier, now you rock Shyamal-da.'

'Not just rock, your sister shakes me, too, when she's angry.'

'Do I have a choice? Haven't you seen how it says on medicine bottles, "shake the bottle before use"?'

Dolon's words caused much laughter. Sudarshana got into the car. Getting into the driver's seat, Shyamalendu said, 'You're asking Sudarshana to sit next to the driver, what if the driver loses concentration and causes an accident?'

'Oh come on, Shyamal-da! Why don't you just say you won't be inspired to drive unless Didi's next to you.'

'Executives at commercial firms don't need inspiration—press the button and they start running like machines,' said Dolon, taking her seat at the back.

Shyamalendu heard her but didn't respond.

They were on their way. 'It's been so long since I saw you both,' said Tutul. 'Didi at least came to Patna a couple of years ago, but you're a rare bird, Shyamal-da.'

'It's true, I haven't met any of you in ages,' admitted Shyamalendu.

'You think your sentence will be commuted just because you've confessed? No way. I'd made up my mind not to talk to you at all.'

'What's the point of being alive if such a beautiful and well-educated sister-in-law hovers nearby without talking?' Shyamalendu said, turning the steering wheel.

'You never think of Patna since you married Didi and left with her, do you?' Sudarshana accused Shyamalendu sweetly.

'It's not that, Tutul, it's just that I haven't got round to visiting. I can barely keep track of how time passes at Hindustan Peters.'

'I'd have liked to see you keeping away from Patna if Didi had kept you hanging instead of marrying you.'

'I'm not joking, Tutul. I don't have official work in Patna, I have to do the rounds of the metros, Delhi, Bombay, Madras.'

'Are you saying no one buys Hindustan Peters fans in Patna? I bought one myself last month with my scholarship money. The shopkeeper was trying to push some other brand, but Baba is blind with affection for his son-in-law, and Ma is full of pride. Both of them instructed me to buy nothing but Peters. I'm telling you the truth, I was so angry I'd have happily bought another brand, but paternal orders, so I had to spend extra and get your fan.'

'Nothing good in the world is cheap, Tutul.'

'Being more expensive doesn't necessarily mean it's good, Shyamal-da,' Sudarshana parried. 'Value and price are not the same thing.'

Shyamalendu grinned. 'Since Peters fans work the best they should be priced the best too. That's what I keep telling our workers.'

'Oh please, Shyamal-da. The web of illusions you people weave with your advertisements has turned innocent customers in a free society into slaves. The winds of socialism are blowing through Patna University too. Please don't forget that your sister-in-law didn't abandon Patna before taking the MA examinations that followed two years of concentrated studies in economics.'

'Oh my god! You're talking like a revolutionary who opposes capitalists, Tutul. What's your point?'

'Very simple. Businessmen are making extra money by dangling the temptation of acquiring the best things in the world, but in fact the actual best things in the world, like sunlight, wind, and moonbeams, are still available free of cost. And humans still give away the best things they have, just as you gave your heart to my big sister Miss Dolonchampa Bhattacharya. Don't you remember Rabindranath's song, "To her I shall give whom I can give for free".'

'We haven't yet thought of giving away Peters fans free of cost, but we're considering a plan to sell them in easy instalments in villages and the suburbs,' Shyamalendu answered.

'You've just given your brother-in-law an undeserved certificate, Tutul,' Dolon exclaimed. 'He certainly did not give his heart to me free of cost, he sold it to me in instalments, under an enjoy-now-pay-later scheme. I didn't know then that I had fallen into the clutches of a canny salesman. Now it's a slow, burning death—I'm paying principal plus interest.'

The other two laughed at Dolon's wit. 'You've developed quite a sharp tongue, Didi,' said Tutul. 'In the old days you didn't say a word. None of your friends could fathom how you began dating Shyamal-da.'

'All that was once upon a time, you were a little girl.' Dolon changed the subject. 'How are things at home? How are Ma and Baba?'

'Baba's very well. As soon as he gets his salary he buys more books on English literary criticism. And Ma flies into a rage, where am I supposed to store these, she asks. Baba couldn't care less. That apart, Ma's fine too. She just gets grumpy when you don't write, she feels hurt as well, my elder daughter's become so distant now that she's married. Doesn't even visit me, she says.'

'She's not wrong, but what do I do? Couldn't go last year, your brother-in-law had a sales conference in Kashmir, then we went on a holiday. And we're supposed to be going to England at the end of this year.'

'What, you're taking home leave?'

'Don't be silly. The Englishmen get home leave to go to England, but the Reserve Bank reserves its wrath for Indian officers. They won't give you foreign exchange if you say it's home leave, it has to be overseas training or an assignment abroad.'

'Shyamal-da's been to Europe on official work five or six times already. Why don't you just tell them you're accompanying him this time?'

'You're right.'

'Oh how lucky you are, Didi. What a stroke of fortune to have met Shyamal-da.'

'Tell her, please, Sudarshana. Not only does your sister not acknowledge this, she actually tells me, "It was only after you married me that your fortune turned and your career took off."'

'You can argue about this in bed,' Sudarshana quipped. 'My plea is this, will you take no one but your wife abroad, Shyamal-da? You have just the one sister-in-law, what wrong has she done?'

'Nothing at all. To tell you the truth, the sister-in-law is even more beloved than the original wife. Why do you think the poet wrote these lines:

Neither mother nor aunt nor girl nor child
Art thou, o sister-in-law ever mild
Whenst thou redden thy lips and wear flowers
Gazing at thee lengthens with longing my hours
Oh why was I not the emperor of Delhi by plan
Or at least highborn, so as to marry the entire clan
And liveth my life in eternal, endless joy
For none of my mistresses wouldst then be coy'

It was the sisters' turn to burst into laughter. Sudarshana's lovely face grew even redder. 'Really, Shyamal-da,' she said, 'you are such a flirt.'

'When did you add this poem to your stock?' Dolon asked. 'You have never recited it to me.'

'Come on, how could I? You're not the alluring young sister-in-law as pretty as a nymph, you're the wife.'

Their new home on Lord Sinha Road was visible now. Dolon pointed out the high-rise to her sister from a distance. 'That's where we live.'

'Such a lovely name, Blue Haven,' said Sudarshana. 'Blue Heaven wouldn't have been out of place either, rather appropriate, in fact.'

'We're on the ninth floor,' Dolon told her. 'The building came up about a year ago, thirty flats in all. The company owns ten of them.'

Depositing the car in the care of the doorman, Shyamalendu ushered his wife and sister-in-law into the lift. Sudarshana gazed in wonder at the fountain outside the building. 'Looks just like America, Didi, this is how they show America in the movies.'

'Now that you're here I'm not letting you go back soon,' Dolon told her. 'I'll show you everything there is to see in Calcutta.'

'This is part of Calcutta too,' said Sudarshana, 'but all they talk about in the newspapers is filth, bombs, and processions.'

'Hush now, Tutul, don't remind us of these things on a holiday. Your brother-in-law works so hard Monday to Friday that I don't let anything unpleasant enter our conversations on the weekend.'

'So your office is closed on Saturdays too?' asked Sudarshana.

'We work an hour extra on the other days to compensate,' said Shyamalendu. 'That's why Saturdays are holidays. When we were young, though, only girls' schools had holidays on Saturdays.

Dolon smiled. 'Girls' schools and multinational companies in Bombay and Calcutta belong to the same category now.'

Shyamalendu pressed a button in the automatic lift, which began to whoosh upwards.

Sudarshana looked astonished. 'I've never been in a lift without an operator.'

'No one in Patna has,' Shyamalendu assured her. 'I was in the same boat a few years ago. You might not believe this, but the first time I went to Hindustan Peters for my interview, I didn't dare take the lift. I was under the impression you had to pay to ride in it.'

Dolon chuckled. 'Don't make us laugh now. Are you trying to say you were a dolt nine years ago?'

'Not just nine years ago, Dolon, I'm still a dolt,' Shyamalendu answered.

'What if the lift breaks down midway?' Tutul asked innocently.

'We'll pass the time chatting till the fire brigade people turn up with ladders,' laughed Shyamalendu.

'What are you scaring the poor thing for?' Dolon scolded her husband. Then she reassured her sister. 'Nothing will happen, mechanics are available round the clock, they will rush here to repair it.'

Shyamalendu wasn't ready to stop his jokes. 'What if there's a power failure suddenly like it happened in New York? Didn't you read the report in *Time* magazine? A large number of people were stuck in their elevators for hours. They had no idea what was going on outside, it was pitch dark. Some people thought someone had dropped an atom bomb nearby, or that the Day of Judgement was here.'

'And then?' Sudarshana asked. She didn't read *Time* magazine regularly.

'And then?' A naughty smile appeared on Shyamalendu's face. 'You're an adult now, I can tell you. Calculations revealed that there was a mini baby boom in New York hospitals at the right time nine months later.'

'You and your dirty jokes.' Dolon wagged her finger at her husband. 'Nothing but the Americans pulling off a publicity stunt. Never mind other problems, imagine calculating how many extra babies were born because of a power cut.'

'Very well, I withdraw my statement,' said Shyamalendu, scratching his head.

The lift stopped on the ninth floor. The door opened automatically, and they stepped out into the landing. On the door to the left, in shiny steel letters, it said: S CHATTERJEE.

Dolon took the keys out of her bag and unlocked the door.

Taking Sudarshana's bag inside, Shyamalendu said, 'You'll have to excuse me for some time. I'm going to make a quick trip to the office. There's some pending work, I'll be done with it and back by lunch.'

'Don't you want a cup of coffee before you go?' his wife asked.

'Not now, I had coffee with Mr Gordon at the Golf Club. And besides, Mrs Anderson will be waiting, I've asked her to come for an hour.'

'Who knows whether it's work or the secretary he's going for,' Dolon complained to her sister.

'What's this I hear, Shyamal-da?' Sudarshana glared at Shyamalendu.

'You'll hear a lot more from your sister while your brother-in-law's away,' said Shyamalendu and left, laughing.

3

'This is your sister's home,' said Dolon, hugging her sister. 'The total covered area of this flat is two thousand seven hundred and eighty square feet.'

Sudarshana was stunned by the drawing room alone. 'You call this a room, Didi? This is an auditorium! You can set up microphones and have a meeting.'

'That's true. Everyone loves it. It's easy to have a music recital here.'

Sudarshana was addicted to music. 'Calcutta is a centre of music,' she said. 'You must be inviting famous singers to perform here. Shyamal-da used to be devoted to Rabindrasangeet. And you were mad about the sitar.'

'That was a long time ago, Tutul. I'd meant to organise small recitals at home, but too many things come in the way. Your Shyamal-da is so busy, and then there are all these cocktails and dinner parties. I'll tell you everything now that you're here. Let me take you to your room first.'

Sudarshana was about to pick her bag up, but Dolon said, 'Let it be, I'll tell Abdul.'

'After two university tours I'm used to carrying my own luggage, Didi.'

'Rubbish. Let them do some work. What's the company paying not one but two of them for every month?'

So Tutul left her bag behind. 'This is such an unusual carpet, Didi. As though it has springs in the material.'

'It's not a Persian carpet, of course, but a genuine one from Mirzapur. Made to order specially after taking wall-to-wall measurements. There's a Dunlopillo underlay beneath it. The company paid for it.'

'How nice!' Sudarshana couldn't suppress her amazement.

'The directors get authentic Persian bukhara carpets. You have to set foot on one to know the difference,' Dolon said, arranging the keys in the ring tucked onto her waist.

Then she continued, 'There are two bedrooms, one for us and one for Raja when he comes home from his school in Ajmer. And a guest room. Besides these there's his study, the dining room, the kitchen, the pantry, a covered balcony, and the box room. The servants' quarters are outside, a hundred and twenty square feet. Plus parking space.'

Sudarshana was truly dumbfounded by now. She knew Shyamal-da had a good job, she had heard he had been promoted several times, but imagine living in a flat like this! It was a fairytale house.

Now her sister led her into the guestroom. Two beds lay side by side. 'This will be your bedroom,' said Dolon. 'As you can see, we can accommodate a couple. So once you're married both of you can come.'

Adjusting the end of her sari, Dolon said, 'The wiring is all concealed, of course. All the piano switches are near the floor, so that you can turn everything on or off without getting out of bed. Only one thing in this room is ugly, the colour of the piano switches doesn't match the plastic emulsion on the walls. A horrible colour. I hadn't noticed earlier, but it came to my attention when I was doing up the room for you. I rang the maintenance department immediately, they'll change the switches by Monday. I'll have to remind your brother-in-law too so that he can follow up with them.'

Dolon scribbled something on a slip of paper. 'What are you writing, Didi?' Sudarshana was taken aback.

'A slip. I'll put it in the pocket of your brother-in-law's jacket, a reminder about the switch when he goes to office on Monday morning.'

Sudarshana looked around the room. 'Try the bed,' her sister said.

'Oh Didi, I'm sinking in it.'

'Don't be silly, the six-inch foam rubber mattress makes you think you're floating, your body feels weightless.'

'You've become used to these beds haven't you, Didi?'

'Why do you say that?'

'I'm thinking of how difficult the ten-year-old mattress was for you when you came home to Patna last. That was probably why you couldn't sleep. I used to sleep next to you, and one night I woke up suddenly to discover you were awake. I didn't realise then, I thought you were pining, aching for Shyamal-da, even more so at night.'

Dolon smiled. 'You girls know too much now. You've discovered even before marriage what it is to ache for someone.'

'Smile again, Didi?' Sudarshana said.

'But why?' Dolon asked.

'You get a lovely dimple when you smile. Hasn't Shyamal-da noticed?'

'He doesn't have time to notice these things nowadays. So much to do at work, so many responsibilities.'

'I'm not taking that for an answer, I'm going to give him a lecture today. I don't care how busy you are, if your wife has a dimple you have to spare the time to think about it.' Sudarshana laughed as she conveyed her opinion.

'See that switch on the right?' Dolon said. 'Press it in the morning, Gomes will bring you bed-tea from the pantry. He used to make the tea at six in the morning earlier and knock on the door. But I've created this system now. Sometimes I feel lazy in the morning and don't feel like getting out of bed too early.'

Dolon pressed the switch. Gomes knocked on the door. 'Come in,' she said.

Gomes entered and offered a salaam.

Dolon introduced Sudarshana and added, 'My sister, she'll be staying with us for some time.'

'What would you like now, Tutul?' Dolon asked. 'Tea or coffee?'

'We don't drink anything but tea at home, Didi, you know that.'

'You're not at home, you're visiting your sister. So have some coffee. I'll ask for an espresso with milk and sugar. We've put a machine in the kitchen, many of your Shyamal-da's guests like espressos with foam.'

'Espresso!'

'Why, coffee shops with espresso machines must have come up in Patna too.'

'Yes, whistles like a steam engine and the coffee is covered in foam,' Sudarshana said.

'You have an attached bathroom. It has fresh towels, a toothbrush, paste, hair-oil, shampoo, soap, mouthwash, Dettol, everything. You can keep your clothes in this built-in wardrobe.'

After a pause Dolon continued, 'If you want to see the world outside, draw the curtains open on the south. You get a wonderful view here, Calcutta will feel like fairyland. And if you don't like it you can draw the curtains shut again.'

Sudarshana gazed at her sister, who said, 'I don't like the colour of these curtains very much. It was different when I chose it, but one visit to the laundry changed it completely. We'll have to tolerate it for another three months, managers are allowed to change their curtains once a year. No such constraints for directors, they can ask for a change anytime.'

'It's not a bad room,' Dolon continued, 'but it doesn't have an air-conditioner. Only one of our rooms is air-conditioned.

Directors can have their bedroom, children's room, and guestroom air-conditioned. It's a bit odd actually. Even your Shyamal-da's colleague Mr Sanyal's wife was saying the other day, this is mean-minded of the company, as if only the directors' guests are guests, not ours.'

Gomes came in with the coffee. 'Do you want it here, or do you want to see my room?' Dolon said.

'Let's go see your room,' Sudarshana said. They walked into Dolon and Shyamalendu's bedroom with their coffee. It was quite large, with a door leading into the adjoining room. 'It's planned so that the children can sleep in the next room, see?' Dolon said.

'See these beds?' she continued, 'They have a history. This kind of bed doesn't suit the room, it's also a bit too high. Tell Baba to give you a low bed for your marriage. Okay, no need, I'll make the plans.'

'Here you were showing me your house, now what's it got to do with my marriage?' Sudarshana protested.

'So I was saying your brother-in-law's very sentimental about these things,' Dolon said. 'Your father gave us this bed, he said, and then we spent our first night in it too, no need to change it.'

Sudarshana looked at her sister. 'But that only means we're losing out, because the company would have paid for the bed.'

'You'll sleep on it but the company will pay?' Sudarshana was surprised.

'Yes sir, that's the rule. They wring all the blood out of these covenanted managers with work all day, shouldn't they ensure the managers can sleep peacefully at night with their families?'

'Really Didi, you could have been a superb labour leader, look at you arguing for your husband.'

'You have no idea, Tutul,' Dolon smiled. 'There are one or two really selfish directors, they want everything for themselves, who cares for the managers? The covenanted officers shed blood sweat and tears but they cannot speak up.'

'That reminds me, Didi, I've long wanted to know what that word covenanted means.'

'So you've heard it before.'

'I see it quite often in matrimonial ads in the papers. My class-friend Lalita was asking me about it, her mother has put it in the ad for her marriage. She's very pretty, so they want a covenanted groom. Lalita had asked her mother, who said I don't know exactly, but must be something very good, or why do the parents of pretty girls spend money to ask for doctors or CAs or covenanted managers for their daughter?'

'Don't joke, Tutul, he'll die laughing if he hears.'

'It's the truth, Didi. We know about CAs. We used to shout slogans against the CIA in college, we don't want the CIA but we're ready to marry CAs. The CIA may be American spies, but take the I away and you get Chartered Accountants, ideal husband material. Even better if it's a British degree, but an Indian one isn't bad either, although our friend Nandita's husband did say the other day an Indian CA is a shattered accountant.'

'In simple terms, covenanted refers to very high-ranking officers in mercantile companies. Your brother-in-law is covenanted—there are only seven or eight of them at Hindustan Peters. A covenant is a contract, renewed every three years or five. I'll show you his document one day, it's in the locker. Says so many things, I don't understand all of it.'

Four photographs stood on a small table near the bed. Shyamalendu's parents and Dolon's parents. Tutul had met Shyamalendu's father, he used to be a teacher of English at Danapur School. He had made a name for himself writing a book on English grammar. Shyamalendu's mother, who had passed away, she had been Dolon's mother's childhood friend.

There were two other photographs, facing each other. One was of Dolon and Shyamalendu, taken a few days after their wedding in a Patna studio. 'This photograph of yours is so funny, Didi,' Sudarshana couldn't help saying. 'You were as unsophisticated then as I am now. You don't look like the wife of a covenanted manager of Hindustan Peters. Imagine covering your head! Even Shyamal-da looks so strange.'

'Small-town studio, what do you expect? I've told him so many times, let's go to Bourne & Shepherd or Ahmed Ali or Bombay Photo, and get our photographs taken. Your brother-in-law refuses. He looks at this photograph and says a picture needs two things, photographer and subject. You can always get a good photographer, but no one can bring back this moment in our life ten years ago.'

'Oh my god. You flirt even now whenever you can. I have to talk to Shyamal-da about this.'

Dolon's face brightened, but she protested at once. 'No chance, your brother-in-law only thinks about work. Wife and son and family are secondary. Can't blame him either, the bosses at Hindustan Peters keep adding to his responsibilities.'

'They do it because he's capable,' Sudarshana consoled her sister.

'Rubbish. The Britishers are poring over the form book now on Saturday. Everyone who lives here, Runu Sanyal, Hargovind Chopra, Mr Pillai, Mr Nigam, Mr Jain, they're all getting ready to go to the racecourse with their wives. They'll meet the bosses there. And your brother-in-law? Office on Saturday.'

'What happens at the racecourse, Didi?'

'Heaven knows. All of them memorise the names of horses all week from those small booklets. Our company secretary,

Mr Sengupta, he likes your Shyamal-da very much. One day he said, what do you think you're doing, Mr Chatterjee? I'm not taking no for an answer, you have to become a member of the Turf Club. Your brother-in-law said, I don't care for these things. Mr Sengupta told him, not everything seems pleasant at first. And anyway not everything we do is because we like doing it. Horses for courses.'

'And then?'

'He goes to the racecourse sometimes, he's become a Turf Club member.'

Sudarshana's face fell. 'Doesn't it frighten you, Didi?'

'Why should it frighten me?'

'You keep hearing about people becoming bankrupt at the races.'

'Only in novels. As long as you stay within your limits there's no need to worry. He never bets more than fifty rupees and, besides, it's also a sport. Haven't you seen the results being published in the sports pages? The Governor visits too sometimes, surely he wouldn't have gone there if it was bad?'

Sudarshana turned to Raja's photograph. 'It would have been so nice if Raja were here too. Haven't seen the naughty little boy in so long.'

'He'll come home for the summer holidays, visit then if you can.'

'Calcutta has so many good schools, surely you could have sent him to one of them? Just the one child, and if you keep him so far away from this age, what's the point?'

Dolon was partly in agreement with this. Her eyes filled with tears when Raja came up in the conversation. After some thought she said, 'It's not as though I don't feel that way sometimes. After all, this is the time of their children's lives that parents enjoy the most. I read somewhere there's no sweeter experience as parents than seeing your child grow up. But ...'

'But what?' Sudarshana asked.

'You have to be prepared to sacrifice a lot if you're married to a commercial executive, Tutul.'

'Why? Has anyone at the office said you can't keep your child with you?'

'Not that. But the job involves transfers. Your Shyamal-da was transferred to Delhi after we got married, then to Madras, then Bombay. Now of course there's no possibility of being transferred out of the head office. But we were transferred from Madras to Bombay at twenty-four hours' notice. Would you believe it, Mr Davidson made a trunk call and said, Chatterjee, what if I posted you in Bombay? He answered, with pleasure, if it helps the company. Tell me when I should move. Mr Davidson said, I'm sorry for giving you very little time, what if I said the day after tomorrow? He was ready. I will report at the Bombay office the day after tomorrow, he said at once. I was furious. I said you could have easily asked Mr Davidson for ten days, he likes you very much. Do you know what your brother-in-law told me? Never forget you're the wife of a commercial executive, Dolon. We're like the military, always ready for marching orders.'

Sudarshana put down her cup of coffee and stared at her sister in amazement. 'Really? You were so hopeless when it came to managing luggage.'

'Tell Ma your Didi is no longer who she used to be. Under pressure and after being disciplined constantly she's learnt to toe the line. Your Shyamal-da couldn't care less, he left me behind and dashed off to Bombay the very next day. And I had to get an entire mountain of things packed, put them away in the company godown, and then go to Bombay in search of my husband. Where we had to stay at the Taj Mahal hotel for a month and a half. The company paid, but footing the bill isn't everything. These Britishers have no idea how painful it is to live in a hotel.'

'I've never stayed in a hotel, you know, Didi.'

'You will. Your life lies ahead of you. And you'll come to hate them, you'll realise home is everything. So, as I was saying, I told your brother-in-law bluntly, I'm your wife, you can torment me as much as you can, but you can't do any such thing with my Raja. Send him to a good boarding school the first chance you get.

'Mrs Davidson had said she would ensure admission to a famous public school in England, Renton. But nowadays you have the government to overrule God himself. They refused to provide foreign exchange. So the children of foreigners can thrive but ours can go to hell. But who's going to argue with the government? So we had to send Raja to an Indian public school.'

Still Sudarshana wished Raja were there, what fun it could have been. He had been born in Patna, how worried everyone had been for Dolon then. Both her father and Shyamal-da were waiting outside the hospital. Then Raja arrived. How naughty he was as a child. His cheeks were plump like apples. 'Do you remember, Didi, how enraged Raja would get when I pinched his cheeks?' said Sudarshana. 'He'd be so angry when I called him Gabbu.'

'He's no Gabbu anymore, even I have to talk to him respectfully. He often writes to his father in English.'

'Really?'

'Yes, I'll show you. Do you want to rest now? You were on the train all night. Maybe have something to eat and then a bath? Your brother-in-law will be back by then. He will be ecstatic to see his beautiful accomplished freshly-bathed electric spark of a sister-in-law.'

'Just you wait till Shyamal-da comes back, I'll take care of you.' Sudarshana went into her room.

Closing the door, she sat for a while on the bed, then opened her bag and arranged her clothes in the wardrobe. Then it was time for a bath.

The bathroom was stunning too. The white tiles seemed to have been put in only today, they glittered as though they were absolutely new. There was a bathtub in a corner. But Sudarshana couldn't possibly bathe in it. She had seen the heroine of an English film in a bathtub, there was so much foam that her body was entirely covered. Suddenly the bathroom door had opened, it was terrible, the idiot hero had wandered in. But the foam protected the heroine's modesty. These scriptwriters could certainly be imaginative. Stay on the right side of the law and yet leave very little to the imagination.

Sudarshana had brought her towel and soap in, but found her sister had made all the arrangements already. There were four or five towels in different sizes. What could one person do with so many towels, for heaven's sake? Dolon had also laid out fresh soap, a new bottle of egg shampoo, a new toothbrush and tube of toothpaste, a new bottle of Jabakusum hair oil. There were several bottles too that Sudarshana had never seen before. Bath salts, deodorant, cleansing milk, and many other things.

Sudarshana visualised the family home in Patna. At least their bathroom floor was made of mosaic. There was an ancient shower overhead, which was often not working. It was crazy—sometimes there was a torrent of water and, at other times, not even a drop. At other times, a couple of minutes after turning it on, the water would start flowing. Sudarshana recalled Shyamal-da's house too. His father took great care of her when she visited. What they had in the bathroom was a tank of water into which you had to dip a mug with a hole and pour the water over yourself. There were a few nails in the wall to hang clothes from. It was a difficult business, on one occasion Sudarshana's frock fell into the water. Her sister had only just moved there after her wedding, and Sudarshana hadn't taken spare clothes. Dolon couldn't say anything out of embarrassment.

It hadn't escaped Shyamal-da's eyes though. 'Your frock seems wet, Tutul,' he had said.

Both Tutul and her sister had turned red with embarrassment. 'Splashed a bit of water on it when I was bathing,' Tutul explained.

Shyamal-da had figured out what had happened. 'Must have fallen on the floor, those nails are useless, have to put up a rack.'

Did Shyamal-da remember those days? Did Didi? Tutul wondered.

Tutul used to really like Shyamalendu. In fact, perhaps even Dolon didn't love him as much as her sister did. Shyamalendu was immersed in his studies all day, and, besides, he had an ideology. He made a sincere effort to know and understand the problems of people.

'A handful of people in Delhi cannot eradicate the poverty of hundreds of millions of people in this vast country,' Shyamalendu would say. 'We've only got political freedom, the freedom to fly the tricolour instead of the Union Jack. The real work is still to be done. Who knows when Kumbhakarna will awaken. But it will be a day of transformation. From the Himalayas to the Indian Ocean these hundreds of millions will demand to know why they have no food, no clothes, no health, no happiness, no comforts. Then the dance of the apocalypse might begin. So we have to accomplish a great deal before Kumbhakarna wakes up.'

Tutul took the telephone shower and turned the tap. The nozzle could be turned in any direction. It fell like rain on her face, and Tutul could see Shyamalendu Chatterjee from all those years ago, the student of English Literature at the university. How beautifully he would recite Shakespeare in his deep voice.

Shyamalendu's first visit to their house was with his mother. Tutul's mother had been overjoyed to see

Shyamalendu's mother. 'Kamala! What brings you here? It's been so long. Even though you live just around the corner.'

Kamala said, 'You know what it's like running a schoolteacher's household. The day ends but my work doesn't.'

'Who's that with you?' inquired Tutul's mother.

'My one and only Shyamal,' Kamala had answered.

'Oh but he's like my son too, how can you keep him waiting outside, that's terrible.'

'I told him to come in. But he's so shy, he insisted on standing there.'

'We can't have that, we're childhood friends after all, how can he stand outside?'

Dolon and Tutul were playing. Their mother said, 'Go get your Shyamal-da, bring him inside.'

Dolon was embarrassed. 'You go,' she told Tutul.

Tutul didn't agree. 'As if I'm not embarrassed.'

So the sisters decided to go together.

Tutul still dressed in frocks, though Dolon had graduated to saris. Running out, they saw a young man with curly hair and thick glasses standing in the veranda, gazing wistfully at a lamppost.

It was just before dusk, the rays of the setting sun were bathing Purbachal in golden hues. (Dolon and Tutul's father had named the house Purbachal.) When Tutul grew up she learnt this was the time of day at which prospective brides were presented to the boys' families. That was the light in which Dolon and Tutul set eyes on Shyamalendu for the first time.

'You call him,' Dolon poked Tutul.

Tutul wasn't willing. 'You're a grown-up. If you don't have the courage to do it, how do you expect me to?' she said.

Afraid of being looked down on by her little sister, Dolon went up to Shyamalendu and said, 'Excuse me.'

Shyamalendu probably wrote poetry or something at that time. Why would anyone stare at the sky like a fool otherwise? He didn't seem to register what Dolon had said. Besides, she must have spoken very softly, her voice was low in any case. Tutul was annoyed. Going close to Shyamalendu, she said, 'Excuse me?'

Finally returning to his senses, Shyamalendu looked at them. 'Did you say something, little girl?'

'Yes. My sister Dolon is calling you, can't you hear?'

Tutul had not yet forgotten the foolish expression on his face as he turned to look at Dolon.

'Not me,' said Dolon hurriedly, 'my mother's calling you. You're Kamala-mashima's son, aren't you?'

Who knew then that Dolon was opening the door to the devil.

'Don't be shy,' Kamala told her son. 'Come sit here.'

To Dolon and Tutul's mother, she said, 'You haven't seen my son in a long time, Asha.'

'Yes, your son's grown-up now. Your troubles are behind you. You can sit back and enjoy your son's income and daughter-in-law's care.'

Poor Kamala-mashima. She didn't live long enough to enjoy any of this.

'What's your son studying now?' Asha asked Kamala.

'Thanks to everyone's blessings, he's a good student,' Kamala answered. 'He's just completed his BA Honours in English, he came first.'

They were all stunned—Tutul, her sister, their mother. Shyamal-da's light was switched off all this while, Kamala seemed to have switched on a 100-watt bulb.

'You were first in English? Didn't your name come out in the papers recently?' Dolon asked.

Shyamalendu nodded.

Dolon was normally tongue-tied, but now she shot to her feet in excitement. 'Wait, don't tell me, I'll tell you your name.'

In utter surprise Tutul found her sister doing just as she had promised. After a pause, Dolon said, 'Your name is Shyamalendu Chatterjee.'

Shyamalendu had not yet overcome his embarrassment. But Kamala said, 'You're right, Dolon, how did you know?'

'Oh we discuss these things at Patna Women's College. We were talking about it in the common room today. You're so solemn in the MA classes, you don't talk to anyone.'

Still Shyamalendu was silent. 'Is that so?' said Kamala. 'And why do you do that? That's not good, surely. How did you find out, Dolon?'

Like a detective in a story, Dolon had regained her confidence. She had said, 'You know Ashima Jha? She was second-class first in your batch. Ashima told her sister Sita, who studies with me. That's how I know.'

Dolon's mother was astonished. 'You see what it means to get good results?' she told Shyamalendu. 'Everyone discusses you. Dolon's studying English honours too. She'll take her finals next year.'

Making arrangements for tea, she told Kamala, 'So you can't accuse your husband of neglecting the family anymore. He's teaching students, but he's also looked after his own son's education.'

Tutul remembered Kamala-mashima as an uncomplicated person. 'I'm not educated, I don't understand these things. But Shyamalendu studies on his own, and, as for his father, he's obsessed with his grammar book. He keeps correcting things in it so that the next edition is even better. And, I won't lie, he's got me some jewellery, the grammar's selling well, apparently.'

'And why didn't you put on your new jewellery, Kamala?' said Asha. 'We could have had a look.'

'I'm too old to flaunt jewellery. I've put it away so the polish doesn't get dull. It's for my daughter-in-law when my son gets married.'

Now Asha told Shyamalendu, 'You must have met Tutul's father since you're studying for an MA. He's a lecturer in English.'

'He teaches us Shakespeare,' Shyamalendu said.

'Yes, he's ruined his life with Shakespeare. How many books did the man write anyway? But Tutul's father has a library full of books to explain Shakespeare. The tail's bigger than the dog.'

Shyamalendu and Dolon laughed in unison. Then Dolon warned her mother, 'Who do you think you're talking to? Shyamal-da scored record marks in the Shakespeare paper.'

'So, Didi, from Shyamalendu-babu to Shyamal-da in an instant?' said Tutul archly. 'There are great benefits to coming first, I see. No joy in life if you don't.'

Kamala replied, 'Shyamalendu didn't want to come at all. I said, Asha is my childhood friend, come with me, I'll introduce you to Botu-babu.'

'Maybe we'll see more of you now, Kamala, because of your son,' Tutul's mother said joyfully. Then she had said to Dolon, 'Tell Shyamalendu about your father.'

'Baba's gone to Bhagalpur,' Dolon said. 'Some work at the university there. He'll be back yesterday.'

Tutul went off into peals of laughter. 'Yesterday, Didi? Don't you mean tomorrow?'

Dolon's ears were red with embarrassment. 'Please don't mind.'

'Didi gets confused between these two days quite often, Shyamal-da.'

Shyamalendu probably couldn't bear Dolon being taunted. To protect her, he told Tutul, 'When you grow up you'll discover a school of thought that denies the presence of yesterday and tomorrow. Everything that there is is in the present—at this moment.'

'We'll tell Baba about you the moment he's back,' said Dolon.

'Consider this your own house,' Asha said, 'come over whenever you like.'

She took her childhood friend into the kitchen for an intimate chat. Tutul and Dolon took the new guest into their father's study. Tutul was very precocious, she wasn't going to spare Shyamalendu, who had destroyed a golden opportunity to harass her sister. So she began an argument with him. 'What's that you said? If there's no yesterday and tomorrow why do the grammar books talk of three tenses, past, present, and future?'

'Well said.' Shyamalendu smiled.

Dolon was gazing at Shyamalendu. He looked at her too and said, 'Have you read Christopher Fry? He said somewhere there's no such thing as the present, it's only a point between the past and the future.'

Shyamalendu used to be a real intellectual back then, with razor-sharp intelligence and memory. No wonder Tutul's father was so fond of him. 'Knowing English well is no guarantee of understanding Shakespeare,' he would say, 'you have to be a good person to go deep into Shakespeare. Without a golden mind you cannot mine the gold in Shakespeare. And if this gold is mined properly humans will no longer be immature. I'm telling you Shyamalendu can do this, you'll see for yourself.'

Did her sister and brother-in-law remember these things, Tutul wondered, turning off the shower. No one knew. The towel Dolon had left for her was huge—it could have been a sari.

There was a knock on the door. 'It's me, Tutul. Don't put on any of your saris, I'm leaving one here for you.'

Sudarshana put on the sari Dolon had laid out for her. 'Comb your hair at my dressing table,' her sister told her.

'Is Shyamal-da back?

'Yes,' said Dolon.

Shyamalendu was lying flat on his bed without having changed his clothes. 'Go sit outside,' said Dolon, 'Tutul will do her makeup.'

'Are you going to deprive me of the opportunity to gaze at the freshly bathed sister-in-law's manoeuvres with her hair?'

'You're talking rot these days, Shyamal-da,' Sudarshana answered with a smile.

'Say what you will, I'm thinking of the Tutul of the past, whose nose always ran. Wert thou ever a weak-livered crybaby, o ever-smiling sister-in-law?'

'Stop, Shyamal-da,' Sudarshana feigned anger.

'Very well, I shall not rake up the past. About the future, let me declare,

When my eyes gaze upon you they can only tarry,
For my brother-in-law, your husband, I can only worry,
I weep for the day you marry.'

'Why are you irritating the poor thing?' said Dolon.

Sitting in front of the mirror with her comb, Sudarshana said, 'Weren't you the one who once said there is neither past nor future, only the present?'

'I said that? When?' Shyamalendu looked surprised.

'You seem to have become one of those ministers who can't remember what they've said, Shyamal-da.'

Sudarshana glanced at her sister. 'Remember, Didi?'

Dolon plunged into the depths of the past to recover the memory of that first day. Her face lit up suddenly.

'When did I say it?' Shyamalendu asked.

'It was a matter of survival that day, Shyamal-da, that's why you said it. Pleasing Dolon was a life-and-death problem then. It's not anymore, so you're denying it flatly.'

Dolon and Shyamalendu burst into laughter at this. Both of them joyfully recollected the scene from all those years ago.

Dolon had bathed already. Now Shyamalendu went into his bathroom. 'Why does one room have two bathrooms, Didi?' Sudarshana asked.

'This is the latest trend. Separate bathrooms for husband and wife. The foreign women at his office say I can't imagine sharing a bathroom just because we live together. Next thing you know he'll be demanding we share a towel too. So all the master bedrooms in the flats here have separate bathrooms for him and her.'

'You have so many bathrooms that even if thirty people stayed here bathing wouldn't be a problem,' said Sudarshana.

'No chance of that,' Dolon said sadly. 'These white men have strange rules.'

'What do you mean?' Sudarshana asked.

'No one apart from your wife and children can live with you permanently in this flat.'

'What are you saying, Didi?'

'It's the truth, Tutul. Not even your own parents. They're not part of your family.'

'So what are they, just the outer skin of the family?'

'Many of these companies have the same rule.'

'Doesn't anyone protest, Didi?' asked Sudarshana.

'Far from it, most of them are quite happy about it. The wives say our companies are so strict they don't allow parents to live with us.'

Sudarshana gazed at Dolon as she went on, 'Take Mr Chopra on the sixth floor. He told his father bluntly, the company has forbidden it, you can't live here. The poor old man lives in a semi-slum in Bhabanipur. Sometimes he brings his grandchildren pickles made by his wife.'

Sudarshana was silent. Dolon continued, 'Your brother-in-law gets furious when the topic comes up, his eyes start blazing. I'd have created a furore if my parents were alive, I'd have liked to see who'd dare stop me.'

Tutul was silent. 'There are other rules too,' Dolon continued. 'The servants cannot use the lift if they're carrying heavy loads. Women are not allowed in the servants' quarters. Our poor Gomes's wife was ill, he had brought her to Calcutta to take her to the hospital. The property officer rang after three days. Your staff member has a woman in his quarters. I explained, but he wasn't pleased, said it ruins the discipline. I said what's wrong with sharing your room with your wife. He said, you don't know the servant class well enough, Mrs Chatterjee. How will I or the gateman know whether she's really his wife or not?'

'Why didn't you ask how they know whether the woman who lives with a manager is really his wife?'

'I didn't create more trouble, fortunately Gomes's wife's treatment ended that day.'

Shyamalendu was done with his bath. They sat down to eat together. 'Why didn't you bring Ma too?' Shyamalendu asked.

'Who'd look after Baba then?' Sudarshana answered. 'He's reached a point where he can't manage a minute without her.'

'Could have brought them both,' said Dolon.

'And where would that have left me? Ma would have discussed groceries with you, and Baba would have immersed himself in talking about Shakespeare with his dearest son-in-law. He has no idea that there are many peers other than Shakespeare in this world. I would have been left high and dry.'

Shyamalendu laughed at this. 'What sort of results are you expecting?' he asked.

'What you achieved, I can't emulate. No chance of a first-class first.'

'It was much easier in our time, Tutul.'

'I don't know about that, but you've raised my parents' expectations. They're not satisfied with anything other than first.'

'And after the exams?' asked Shyamalendu.

'Why don't you get me a job at Hindustan Peters? I'll travel around different towns selling your Peters fans.'

'If beautiful women like you hawk our fans we'll be able to sell them in Gulmarg too.'

'Never mind all that nonsense,' Dolon told her sister, 'Jobs are not the most important thing for women.'

'What's this reactionary talk, Didi?' Sudarshana stopped eating and stared at her sister with a smile.

Shyamalendu made a joke playing on the Bengali word for wedding, 'Even after an MA, women have to sit for their BA exam.'

Dolon glanced at the clock. 'You'd better not be late for the Turf Club.'

'What if I don't go today?' Shyamalendu said.

'Aren't all the directors going?' Dolon asked.

'Yes, Mr Murti is in Calcutta, he's bound to be there.'

'Then you'd better go too.' Dolon looked at the clock again. 'Runu Sanyal must have left by now.'

'Runu is addicted to betting, I'm not,' Shyamalendu informed his sister-in-law. But paying heed to his wife's wishes, he got up.

As in England, horse races in Calcutta were also a social affair. Half-sleeved shirts were unacceptable. So Shyamalendu followed the Britishers and put on a dark blue jacket and a matching tie. Then he left wearing dark glasses and carrying a pair of binoculars.

Dolon wished her husband best of luck and shut the door. Sitting down on the sofa for a bit, she asked her sister, 'Where do you want to sleep? Come to my room, we'll lie down and chat for a bit.'

Switching on the air conditioner, the sisters sat side by side on the bed. With the curtains drawn, the room was almost as dark as at night. Tutul got used to the constant groaning of the air conditioner after a while.

Leaving her made-in-Hong Kong slippers on the carpet, Dolon sat with her legs tucked beneath her. Picking up a jar of face cream, she said, 'Want some? This is a very good cream, made in Paris. Imports aren't allowed, but Rahim from New Market manages somehow. Terrible name though.'

'What's it called, Didi?'

'See for yourself. Bourgeoisie.'

Dabbing a little on her cheek, Dolon said, 'I don't know, the word scares me. Considering what's going on in Calcutta. Anyone can be labelled a capitalist or bourgeoisie or something.'

Rubbing the cream carefully into her skin, Dolon said, 'You have dry skin just like me, so you need Bourgeoisie No. 1. Those who have oily skin need Bourgeoisie No. 2. So as I was saying, people in Calcutta don't understand things. Let's say someone is working hard all day, is thinking of work even at night, can't sleep because of the pressure, and makes more money because of all this, and that makes him a capitalist? What kind of logic is that? Why don't you try too, why don't you earn well too? You know how much your Shyamal-da used to earn as a college professor when he married me. Now he makes five thousand one hundred a month, all with his own effort. The bosses don't pay him for his looks.'

Sudarshana stared at Dolon. 'Apply the cream very lightly, or else your skin will turn rough like Mrs Sanyal's. And rotate your fingertips clockwise.'

Tutul copied her sister to move her fingertips across her own face. 'Feels very cold, doesn't it?' Dolon said. 'That's the effect of Eve-22. It's a special chemical that no other brand besides Bourgeoisie can use.'

Now she brought two absorbent paper towels from her drawer. Handing one to her sister, she pressed the other one to her own cheek. 'Very lightly, don't rub it, just pat.'

Dolon went on talking. 'Sometimes you know, it feels terrible. They've put up these posters, the day is not far away when the poor will wear shoes made with the skin of the rich. I'm horrified. How many rich people are there in all of India? How many pairs of shoes can you make with the skin off their backs? It won't ensure a pair for every Indian. And then Mr Sen was here the other day, he goes to the Bata shoe factory in Batanagar every now and then, he said tanning human skin is very troublesome, it's doubtful whether the shoes will be sturdy.'

'You think a lot about things these days, don't you Didi?' Tutul asked.

'I don't have much to do. Your Shyamal-da is engrossed in work. What do I do all day? I read the fashion magazines, go to New Market, look at Calcutta from the ninth-floor window, write to Raja, think of Ma and Baba, of you. This is how I'll grow old.'

'Time for a nap.' Dolon lay down.

Tutul followed suit, spreading her hair across Shyamalendu's bed. 'Use the sheet at the foot of the bed if you feel cold,' Dolon told her.

'Ma and Baba would have been so happy if they could have seen your home, Didi. Ma sings Shyamal-da's praises every day.'

'Must persuade them to visit at least once.'

'You know what Ma says? There's much more happiness in being a rich man's wife than in being successful yourself. I argue with her. Does this mean there's no point in women becoming scientists and writers and prime ministers like they do now?'

'What does Ma say to this?' Dolon asked her sister.

'She says, you'll know when you're older. Success and happiness are not the same thing.'

'I can't go deep into things anymore,' Dolon said. 'Can't read fat books either, I get tired. I didn't carry on with my studies like you did. My only concern now is, when will your brother-in-law become a director at the company? And I worry about Raja too.'

'You could have completed your MA, Didi. You did study for two years.'

'Impossible, I can't be a youngster at this age. And, as I told you, I can't think beyond magazines and detective novels these days.'

'That's rubbish, Didi, you were pretty good at studies. It was just that you got married and couldn't take your exams.'

'Fate didn't have academics in store for me. Your Shyamal-da ruined it all.'

'Do you remember those days, Didi? Shyamal-da would come home to discuss things with Baba and you'd stand near the door listening to them talk. Then you asked him for his notebooks. He was so serious then, wasn't he?'

'He's serious about everything he does,' said Dolon. 'Take this job of his. So many of his colleagues have a good time, golf, cocktails, Turf Club, and a bit of work. Not him. When I get angry he says, this body is all we have, Dolon, we have to compete with the others using physical labour.'

'As dedicated to labour as to love, you mean?'

'Are you making fun of your elder sister?' Dolon smiled.

'Tell me, Didi, you used to be so shy and Shyamal-da was so serious. How did you fall in love?'

'I liked him the first time I saw him.'

'Both of you played hide-and-seek that first year. Once you passed your BA and went from college to university things became easier,' Tutul said.

'You won't believe this, Tutul, but your brother-in-law was so very serious about studies. All he mumbled about when we met was Shakespeare and Shaw and Hardy.'

'Nothing else?' Tutul asked her sister with a covert smile.

'I swear on you! Shakespeare and Bernard Shaw, that's all he ever muttered about. And he'd give me advice, concentrate on your studies, doing well in exams is not difficult at all. And besides you have so many facilities, look at that library you have at home. I used to be terrified, I didn't dare tell him I don't care for studies.'

'Are you saying the romance flowered on its own?' Tutul teased her sister.

'More or less,' said Dolon innocently. 'But I won't lie, sometimes he'd gape at me through those thick glasses of his.'

'You're a smart girl, Didi, that was good enough for you. You realised you had a chance to get the best fruit on the tree.'

'Don't bug me, Tutul. You think I knew then that your Shyamal-da would end up at Blue Haven? All he had then by way of a house was the rented place in Kadamkuan. All I knew was he'd at least get a college professor's job if he got good marks. I liked his eyes and his intelligence during conversations, especially with Baba.'

Tutul grinned at what her sister said, which didn't escape Dolon's notice. 'You know, Tutul, there was an article in the papers a few days ago where it said when Harold Wilson was prime minister of England reporters had asked his wife, what is your opinion of the prime minister? Mrs Wilson told them solemnly, I want to remind you, my friends, that I never wanted to marry the prime minister of England, the man I married was a professor at Oxford. If someone asked me as well, I'd tell them to their face, I didn't marry a covenanted officer of Hindustan Peters, I married a young professor at Patna University, whose monthly salary was a hundred and ninety rupees, who commuted to and from college on a cycle.'

Why wasn't Tutul answering? Had she fallen asleep? Turning to her side, Dolon discovered she had indeed, with her arm across her face. Tutul looked very sweet. Let her sleep, poor thing, she had borne the brunt of an overnight journey in a third-class train compartment.

But Dolon couldn't sleep. The bosses of Hindustan Peters were busy blowing up money at the racecourse. Mrs Ferris was taking pinches of snuff from her ivory snuffbox. Women smoking was a common sight these days, but not snuff! And yet many of the wives of managers had acquired snuffboxes with Mrs Ferris as their role model. No one had the nerve to ask the managing director's wife directly, but Mrs Sanyal had applied her detection skills to find out where Mrs Ferris got her snuff and what kind it was.

Dolon put her foot down at taking snuff. She had told Shyamalendu as much the other day. 'If that means you won't be made a director, so be it. Drinking is bad enough. Can you imagine what my parents will think if they find out?'

'Why do you say that? Does drinking make people bad? Is every officer at Hindustan Peters bad?' Shyamalendu had asked.

'I'm sure they're not. But when I was a child I'd be terrified when I heard someone drank. Sanatan in the slum next door would drink and beat up his wife. My god, I can still smell the alcohol.'

'That's country liquor, these are imported drinks,' Shyamalendu had answered.

Runu Sanyal had once said at a party, 'The Bengali race is going to be finished because of its middle-class sentiments. Drinking is bad, betting on horses is sinful, women shouldn't smoke, only men can take snuff. Why? What are women being punished for? Imagine how much sales would go up if women took snuff. Tobacco farmers would make more money, the unemployed would get jobs at snuff factories, industry would thrive, and the government would get more funds for social improvement from excise duties. Slums would be developed, education would be improved, workers would be needed to build roads, more jobs for everyone. Chain reaction.'

Runu Sanyal's imagination had turned colourful that evening under the influence of alcohol. 'You know what,' he blurted out, 'we're not ready for the industrial revolution in our country. One more thing. For the industrial revolution to be successful, you need executives. But you cannot beat an ass till it becomes a horse. It needs an entire generation to create commercial executives. These are high posts in merchant offices, these are not exactly jobs. This is a unique culture, a distinctive way of life.'

Taking another swig of his whiskey, and his arm around Mrs Chopra, Runu said, 'To put it bluntly, first-generation executives are bound to be sickly sentimental and stodgily ideological. There's no option. They'll torture themselves, they'll torture everyone else too.' Turning to Dolon, he continued, 'You're a well-educated lady, Mrs Chatterjee, you believe in evolution. There's no such thing as leapfrogging in nature. One cannot get a cut-price degree from an ordinary college and jump to the level of an executive. Yes, one can start trying now so that one's son or grandson can get there. That's possible.'

His wife joined the group suddenly. Shushing her husband, she said, 'What's all this nonsense.'

'Look, darling, what I'm getting at is that I'm not a first-generation officer, my father was one too, at Shaw Wallace.'

Anindita Sanyal drew her husband away and apologised. 'He's a little distraught today, he's had too much to drink. Please don't mind.'

Back home, Shyamalendu asked Dolon, 'Did something happen between Runu and you?'

'How did you know?'

'He came up to me and apologised. Please don't mind, his wife told me.'

'I didn't quite get it. He began babbling out of the blue about first generations and second generations.'

Shyamalendu looked grim. 'Don't you get it? I belong to an ordinary family, son of a schoolmaster. A first-generation officer. And Runu is a second-generation one.'

Perhaps Dolon shouldn't have told him. Shyamalendu changed after that incident. He seemed driven by some sort of obstinacy. He no longer skipped the golf club or cocktail parties. He showed up regularly at Gobindopur Club, not to mention the races.

For a while Dolon had felt these things did not suit Shyamalendu. He was superior to these petty people in merchant offices. But Shyamalendu told her, 'It's not like I care for these activities, but I refuse to lose. You need to do a bit of this, even though cocktail managers can't get the real job done anymore. The bosses have realised the days of monopolies are over, the company has to work in the face of competition if it is to keep its business going in India. So the Englishmen want efficient people now—they have learnt to pick and choose.'

Dolon turned over to the other side. Poor Shyamalendu, he could have taken a nap, he really needed some rest. Instead he was out chasing horses under the mid-day sun.

4

No one noticed when afternoon had turned into evening. Both the sisters were fast asleep.

Shyamalendu didn't ring the bell when he came home, letting himself in quietly with his duplicate key. It wasn't as though he would have minded a nap, but on entering his bedroom he saw Tutul.

Shyamalendu retreated, sat on the sofa in the drawing room, and lit a cigarette. Mr Ferris had had bad luck today, losing all of the one hundred and fifty rupees he had wagered. His own horse hadn't done well either. Mrs Ferris had won a bit of money though. Thank heavens Shyamalendu had lost, the managing director of Hindustan Peters was fuming at anyone who had won today.

A nap would be very nice, actually. Shyamalendu went into the guestroom.

He wiggled his toes as he smoked. A set of Shakespeare's Complete Works gleamed in the bookcase in the corner. Ten volumes with the titles embossed in gold letters. Dolon had got them for him with the money from his first salary after joining Hindustan Peters. Seems funny?

But it's the truth. Believe me, this expensive edition had been bought with Shyamalendu's first pay. Before that his monthly college salary had been a hundred and ninety rupees. And his very first month at Hindustan Peters had earned him eight hundred rupees. Dolon was in Patna then. She had written a letter sent in a blue envelope, 'I won't take no for an answer, I'll just assume you're a professor for one more month. You must buy the new Shakespeare series, swear to me you will.'

This afternoon, the bearded gentleman from Stratford-on-Avon seemed to be glaring in fury from his glass-enclosed prison at the rising star among corporate executives, Shyamalendu Chatterjee.

'Why do people read Shakespeare with so much attention? Why did Dolon's father always tell him, 'Immerse yourself in Shakespeare, Shyamal. It's a wonderful world'? Students have been cashing in on Shakespeare for ages to score high marks in examinations. Reading Shakespeare over and over again meant knowing him well, and knowing him meant good marks, and good marks meant it was easier getting a good job. And that was the end of Shakespeare. After that it was all about the house, the car, the wife, the club, cocktails, contracts, bridge, dinners, dances, Perry Mason, and *Time* magazine. You can stay where you are, poet of the world from a foreign land. The fact that I have kept you here as furniture to decorate our home, that I haven't asked Abdul to throw you out while spring cleaning. More than enough!

'Mr William Shakespeare,' Shyamalendu said, 'don't look at me like that. The truth is that all those things you have written with such flamboyance do not help us sell either fans or lamps at Hindustan Peters. There was a time when I pored over your words, but can you tell me a single line that I can use to forecast how many electric fans I can expect to sell in India in the next three years? Or what the market share of the forty-eight-inch fans and the fifty-six-inch fans will be? Tell me, will the sale of fans go down in West Bengal because of the economic decline? Why are you silent, Mr Shakespeare? Your fame is worldwide, you have presented your opinion on all significant human problems—love, separation, jealousy, ambition, murder, death, there's not a subject you haven't touched upon. But are you in a position to tell me about the impact on the market of summer arriving a fortnight early? Questions like these may seem laughable to you, but to us they're a matter of life or death. Wrong answers might mean having to take my wife's hand and leaving this ninth-floor flat to beg on the streets. The invisible wires of Peters fans are intricately tied to this happy household, these air-conditioned rooms, this carpet, fridge, and telephone, this servant and cook, this house and car. But here you are, drunk on philosophical luxuries, earning cheap applause with enigmas like "to be or not to be" from those who do not remember the kind of effort that peasants have to put in to extract crops from the soil, the suffering involved in prising out iron and coal from the womb of the earth, the agonising toil of refining steel in the blast furnace, the cumulative hard work of hundreds of people that takes to manufacture a single Peters fan, or the backbreaking labour we have to undertake to sell it. Please don't mind, Mr Shakespeare, but there's no room for you in this industrial age. It's only out of pity that you still have a place in schools and colleges, but don't imagine, as our clerk Sudhanya-babu did, that just because you've been given an extension we have great need for you, that we cannot do without you.

'Shakespeare sahib, don't smirk at me. Behind that faint smile on your bearded face there's a faint Mona Lisa arrogance. I'm telling you the truth, I used to enjoy reading your work. You wrote so many interesting things, some of it true, some of it imaginary. These things can make one a good actor on the stage, or solve crossword puzzles, or be an excellent teacher of English. I was one. But even after regurgitating all your catchphrases, it was impossible to go higher than a hundred and ninety rupees a month, and if you took away eight and a half rupees for provident fund and ten paise for the revenue ticket, you were left with a hundred and eighty-one rupees and forty paise. Deduct thirty-one rupees for rent, which was low only because the house was originally taken on rent in my father's youth. How much did that leave? A hundred and fifty rupees and forty paise. And with this amount of a hundred and fifty rupees and forty paise left over, if you were told that your father was ill and couldn't work anymore, that he needed an X-ray immediately, and that your wife was pregnant, the wife whom you had lovingly induced to abandon college and marry you, what state of mind would you be in? I don't know what doctors prescribed in your age, but nowadays when they see damaged lungs in an X-ray they prescribe milk and butter and cheese and eggs and fruit along with medicines. To husbands of pregnant women they urge the use of vitamins, and warn them, make sure your wife doesn't lack for nutrition, that she has plenty of fish and meat and milk and eggs, don't forget she has to eat for two.

'In this situation, when someone finds a British company advertising in the papers for people in its marketing department, with the salary being commensurate with abilities, and additional benefits like house-rent, free medical treatment, an annual bonus, and so on, should they sit back and do nothing about it? Put your hand on your heart and tell me what you would have done if you'd come across an advertisement like that, even if it meant not writing *A Midsummer Night's Dream*.

'So now you understand why I sent off an application that day to the box number mentioned. The sales manager Mr Davidson was in Patna on work, that was when he interviewed me.

'I had classes to teach that day. I'd never appeared for an interview in my life. Still I raced off on my cycle to Davidson's hotel. What's your master's in, he asked me. English, I said, first-class first at the university. Your favourite author?

he asked. So I named you. I had no idea Mr Davidson is devoted to you. He had studied Shakespeare closely at Balliol College, Oxford, before turning his attention to selling fans and lamps in India. He asked me many questions about your works. My memory isn't bad and, besides, Dolon's father had conveyed to his future son-in-law the essence of all that he had come to understand about your works after a lifetime of devoted scholarship.

'The theme of ambition came up in the course of conversation. "As ambitious as Lady Macbeth." Forgetting he was interviewing me, Mr Davidson delivered from memory the famous line from your play *Henry VIII*: "Cromwell, I charge thee, fling away ambition: By that sin fell the angels." I had discussed this in great depth with Dolon's father on one occasion. I said, the theme of ambition comes up forty-six times in Shakespeare's complete works, but the word 'ambitious' has been used thirty-six times, I don't know why.

'Davidson was astonished by my answer. How much does your college job pay, he asked. He was taken aback by my answer. Is this what teachers make in India, he said. Yes sir, I replied, and glanced at my watch. Why are you checking the time, Davidson asked. From one o'clock I have to teach the honours students *Hamlet*. It's twelve forty-four now. I was thinking, if I ride my cycle fast enough I can take the class, the students won't have to miss a lecture.

'Davidson asked, did you cycle here? Yes, I answered. He was from Oxford, after all, and my command over English and my small-town dedication to my work must have made a mark on him. He said, you'll get the job, Chatterjee, I promise you. But we can't pay you more than eight hundred and fifty right now.

I thought I hadn't heard right. But it turned out he was talking about a salary of seven hundred, and house rent of one hundred and fifty.

'He's a strange chap, our Davidson. He walked me out of the hotel. As I mounted my cycle, he said, but what about Shakespeare, Chatterjee? This job involves selling things.

'I was worried, what if the job slipped through my fingers? I said, don't worry, Mr Davidson, Shakespeare will always be my guiding light. Can one who has tasted Shakespeare ever forsake him?

'You could say it was a bit of a lie. But Mr Shakespeare, since no human mystery baffles you, you should know I was willing to do anything to get the job. And besides, I hadn't imagined at the time that I would turn out this way—that, like shareholders' liabilities, I too would become limited.

'Well? Why are you still staring at me as though I've borrowed money from you without returning it? I told you already, at first I thought I'd have the cake and eat it too. My wife Dolon, daughter of Batukeshwar Bhattacharya, Reader in English Literature, wanted the same thing. Otherwise why would anyone not demand jewellery bought with her husband's first salary and insist instead that I buy an expensive edition of your complete works?

'I had so many more plans. During training I even wrote in some of my reports, love's labour lost, or much ado about nothing. You can check the old records of Hindustan Peters if you don't believe me. It's a British company after all, they'll show you even the most secret of notes if they know it's none other than you who wants to read them. And besides, as you know, the British have many flaws, but they aren't swindlers. At worst some of them might be crooked, but they can't be rogues and robbers like the fat-bellied bloodsuckers of our country who are known as businessmen. Look, British companies do business honestly, don't cheat their customers, don't besmirch their reputations with black-market dealings, pay their employees well. Anyone who proves their talent can rise up the ladder without having to be fat-bellied bloodsuckers. But that's a different matter. As I was telling you, I had made a name for myself using quotations from Shakespeare in my notes.

'The director of our department was N.K. Menon. A Christian from Kerala, highly intelligent. His one flaw was coming under your spell in his youth. He invited me to coffee one day. You cannot imagine how a greenhorn salesman might feel when asked to join a director for coffee. You have no direct experience of the industrial revolution, after all. Mr Menon praised me and said, you have a future in this company, but you must make your goals sharper. As pointed as a needle.

'Mr Menon said, I hope you are aware of the history of our Hindustan Peters. John Peters was a coalmine worker in Wales. He was at home recuperating from an injury when a miraculously rare phenomenon for the UK took place. It suddenly became impossibly hot in Wales. And this was the house of a miner. You can imagine what it was like, there was no breeze at all. Rotting in that heat, Peters suddenly had a brainwave. How about making a wheel rotate with the help of electricity to generate a breeze? A simple idea that gave rise to the invention of fans, Peters fans. From an ordinary patent to a company operating globally. Wherever in the world you go, you will find Peters Limited, Peters Incorporated, Peters Industries. After fans, Peters began manufacturing electric lamps too. The founders of the company were distantly related to Thomas Alva Edison, who invented electric lights. They haven't looked back since then. Never. They came to India too, as Hindustan Peters, although we're not a very big company here. But remember, according to the census report, there are ninety or ninety-five million households in India. As soon as they're a little better off the members of these households will install electric lights and fans at home.

'There you go again, Mr Shakespeare, staring at me. You think I'm rambling? Not at all. Now listen, Mr Menon had then asked, tell me, what is the objective of your enterprise?

I said, doing good for people, as it says in John Peters' illustrated biography. Mr Menon told me bluntly, listen to me, Chatterjee, we have only one objective. To manufacture more Peters fans and lights, to sell more Peters fans and lights, and not just to sell more but also to make more profits. I asked, and then? To which he replied, manufacture even more, sell even more, and then make ... I gazed at him ... He said, we'll do whatever is necessary to reach these goals, and we won't do anything that is not necessary.

'Now tell me how Mr Menon or I could have included you in this way of life. And let me tell you, genuine executives are like suicide squads in wartime. They can commit suicide in their effort to reach their targets. Now don't think of suicide in the literal sense, what it means is that you can kill your real self and insert a new person into your body. It's even better if you can amputate your heart and mind and install an IBM computer in their place. As you know, no matter how intelligent an IBM computer might be, it cannot do anything on its own. Those who have bought or rented it give commands and the computer spouts out answers.

'I hadn't quite realised all of this yet. In the excitement of going from a hundred and ninety to eight hundred and fifty, sales was all I thought about all day. Like the devotee who tries to lose himself in God, I too tried to merge entirely into Hindustan Peters. Let me tell you, this had good results.

'I was sent to Delhi. I sold twenty thousand fans when not even ten thousand used to be sold earlier. Believe it or not, I sold fans even during Delhi's extreme winter. Mr Menon asked me how I did it. I said, when you can get to God if you try hard enough, why can't you sell fans in winter? After this I went to Rourkela, Bhilai, Durgapur, Jamshedpur, Burnpur. I prepared our now-famous sales forecast, in which I predicted how we could take advantage of the government's steel plant initiatives in those towns to increase the sales of Peters fans there in the next ten years.

'You have no idea how this company rewards performance. At the end of my first year Mr Menon said, how much of an increment will make you happy?

'I managed to overcome my embarrassment and say, if you could add a hundred and fifty and make it a round thousand, all my expectations would be met. He chuckled and said, here's your letter, read it. I was stunned. Has anything like this ever happened to you? My salary had been increased to twelve hundred.

'A long chain of events followed, I have no wish to bother you with details. All I want to say is, there was no looking back after this, all roads led forward. One responsibility after another came my way, I took them all. People said it was a meteoric rise. S Chatterjee only kept climbing.

'But Mr Menon said, this is nothing, Sanyal and you have to rise even higher.

'He could have mentioned me alone, why did he have to bring Sanyal into it? Sanyal is also in sales, he's in charge of lamps. No, you don't know who he is, let me tell you about Mr Menon instead. He fought grimly, but you ensured the downfall of this Keralite Christian.

'Mr Menon possessed a certain quality, it's called a conscience or something. You're a specialist in that particular subject. Tired of selling more fans and more lamps, he resigned from his job one day. He said he would teach in a college somewhere and do something that would benefit the people of the country.

'Have you heard of Siddhartha, the prince of Kapilavastu? He was a bit older than you. When he renounced his huge kingdom and beautiful wife, no one knew why he did it. Our Mr Menon didn't abandon his wife, but he gave up his kingdom. You think it was because of a dispute at work? Absolutely not. Some great grief, perhaps? Not even that. Just like that. Thanks to what he read in some abstruse work of yours named *Macbeth* in which you condemned ambition.

'But look, Mr Menon's father was a rich man. I'm a schoolteacher's son. My own salary was a hundred and ninety rupees. I have to work hard for a living. It's all very well for Mr Menon to have you as a friend, but for me a relationship with you is a luxury, you know what I mean?

'Why do you smile still? If you smile again I'm going to say you're a fraud. There was no one named William Shakespeare. There's plenty of evidence that you didn't write your books, what if I accept this evidence? What are you going to do then?'

'Shyamal-da!' Someone poked him. Shyamalendu sat up with a start. Sudarshana was calling his name.

'Lovely, you sneaked in and fell asleep,' Sudarshana said. 'Why didn't you wake me up? I'd have come out, you could have slept next to your wife.'

Dolon had come up to him too. Shyamalendu hadn't collected himself yet. 'Something terrible was about to happen, you know. William Shakespeare himself appeared in my dream. We were having a bitter argument, it might have led to fisticuffs, but Tutul woke me up.'

'What? Did you drink too much?' Dolon asked.

'Not especially. Three gins at the club. Mr Ferris took us.'

'Three gins don't usually affect you. Something must be the matter with your health,' Dolon said worriedly.

'Coffee now? Or do you want to sleep some more?' Sudarshana asked.

'Not sleeping anymore. What slumber is this you wretched soul when you do not awaken even with your sister-in-law by your side.' Shyamalendu tried to laugh at his own oratory.

5

Jatadhar Das had barely finished polishing the English nameplate and begun with the Bengali one when Mr Chatterjee's car drew up in front of the Hindustan Peters office.

Climbing off his stool to salute Mr Chatterjee, Jatadhar spotted one more woman in addition to Mrs Chatterjee inside the car. The similarity in the two women's appearance made it obvious to the quick-witted Jatadhar that this could be none other than Mrs Chatterjee's sister. So he offered Mr Chatterjee's sister-in-law a salute first and then turned to Mrs Chatterjee, before hopping back onto his stool to resume his polishing.

Sudarshana got out of the car with her brother-in-law. 'How lovely this building is, Shyamal-da,' she said. 'Heaven on earth.'

'Do you think employees are likely to concentrate on work unless the office is heaven on earth? All of them will be hankering to go home,' Shyamalendu said, smiling.

So Mr Chatterjee is not serious all the time, he can make jokes too, Jatadhar told himself, polishing the nameplate with Brasso.

Sudarshana's eyes were drawn to the nameplate. 'This is so unusual, Shyamal-da, so you do use Bangla? I see the name of the company written in Bangla here.'

Examining the plate carefully, she continued, 'But what's this riddle? The liabilities of the shareholders are limited. What are you trying to say?'

Even the military soften when it comes to sisters-in-law. Jatadhar was vastly amused to hear Mr Chatterjee speak so gently. 'It was a puzzle to me too the day I began working here. Then I asked the company secretary, Mr Sengupta. He said this is a legal requirement. We're a limited company, so the liabilities of the shareholders are not unlimited, as in a partnership. Simply put, the Companies Act says some essential information must be displayed at the entrance in English and in the local language.'

'So there's something interesting about merchant offices too. And yet people say they just amount to accounting for every penny and a tedious existence,' Sudarshana said.

Dolon let her views be known from the car, where she was still seated. 'That's what they tell their wives when they go back home. Actually they have quite a good time at the office.'

A man in a suit and tie, with an enormous white mark on his forehead, was seen in the distance. 'Mr Ramalingam, he pays their salaries,' Dolon whispered to Tutul. 'The oldest employee here.'

Ramalingam was a little late today. 'Good morning, Mr Chatterjee,' he cried affectionately from a distance. He was in fact a junior officer compared to Shyamalendu. But the old man that he was, he had been witness to all the top bosses starting work on their first day here. Besides, Ramalingam didn't care about others very much. He would say, 'Kings, emperors, managing directors, how long do they last? The main thing is your parents and lord Venkatesh.'

Ramalingam said, 'The stellar positions are propitious today, Mr Chatterjee. Venus has entered Capricorn at seven forty-five in the morning. So I offered fifty additional flowers to Venkatesh today, that's what kept me.'

Now he noticed Tutul. Studying her carefully, he said, 'The young lady has a very bright future.'

'My sister-in-law,' Shyamalendu introduced her.

'Take my word for it,' said Ramalingam, 'your sister-in-law will make all of you proud one day.'

'Take this,' he added, handing Tutul a hibiscus he had offered to the deity earlier. Tutul touched her forehead with the flower.

'Can you check her marriage prospects, Mr Ramalingam?' said Dolon.

'Excellent fortune when it comes to a husband, but not in the next twelve months. You can offer lord Shiva a pair of jasmine leaves every Wednesday if you like.'

Dolon wanted to know a couple of things about her own future as well, but she was too shy to ask Ramalingam in the presence of others.

'Come into the car, Tutul,' she called out to her sister. She wanted to take Sudarshana to New Market.

'You don't need the car now, do you?' Dolon asked her husband.

'No, you can show Tutul around,' Shyamalendu answered.

As soon as the car left, Ramalingam and Shyamalendu entered the office together.

'Did I miss you at the finance director's party the other day?' Shyamalendu asked Ramalingam.

'I'm trying to withdraw,' Ramalingam said loudly. 'It's time to retreat, Mr Chatterjee, just three months to retirement.'

'Just three months!' Shyamalendu expressed surprise.

'Do not be deceived by appearances, Mr Chatterjee, I'm getting on in years, I came to Calcutta from Madras in the year nineteen thirty-five. Where were any of you at the time?'

'I wasn't born yet.'

Ramalingam walked with Shyamalendu to his room. 'Here's my story, Mr Chatterjee. On the seventh of March in nineteen thirty-five I took a seat in a third-class compartment of Madras Mail with my father's blessings and a promise to make an offering to lord Venkatesh. You know how things were like then, we were in a recession. Everyone said, you're going to Calcutta in search of a job at this time? Mad! I said, I have my father's blessings—I have no worries.'

Shyamalendu was fascinated by Ramalingam's story. There were nearly twenty minutes to go before working hours began.

'I had twelve rupees in my pocket, given to me by my mother who had sold her jewellery. Of course, twelve rupees was a lot of money those days. Three months later, when I returned to Tamil Nadu, it was with two lakh thirty-five thousand seven hundred and thirty-six rupees. You know I never lie.'

This was true. Ramalingam was an unusual man.

'My vital statistics then were forty-five by one-twenty.'

'What! In Madras men's statistics are also measured like women's?' Shyamalendu was not aware of this.

'No, no, Mr Chatterjee, I'm talking about my typing and shorthand speeds. These were the vital statistics for unemployed young men in Madras, it was a matter of life and death, as you can imagine.'

'There was no breakthrough in Calcutta in the first fifteen days,' Ramalingam continued. 'I wrote to my father, asking for fresh blessings. But no results. After three weeks I was quite nervous. Finally, I decided to fast after bathing in the holy Ganges. I prayed to lord Venkatesh, cast your benediction on me at this sacred moment, lord. If you can kindly find me a job, I will worship you with offerings of hibiscus flowers every day. Young men today do not believe in prayers, Mr Chatterjee, but I got a job with Peters that very same day. Those days the company had a small office on Bowbazar Street. It brought in fans from England and sold them here. I was doing the rounds of offices as usual, on that particular day the first company I visited after my prayers was Peters. Mr Miller was the head of the company then and Mr Vasudevan was his clerk. Mr Vasudevan heard me out, read my application, and asked whether I was married. I said, I can barely survive myself, how will I support a wife? Vasudevan took me to meet Miller, who tested me with dictation. I got the job. Those days were different.

'A few weeks later Mr Miller told me, Ramalingam, you know I hired you on Vasudevan's request, you're not confirmed in your job yet, meanwhile poor Vasudevan is very worried about his elder daughter's marriage. I realised what Mr Miller was getting at. I have no objection, I said, as long as my parents don't refuse. I wrote a long letter to my father, explaining the state of my employment. Mr Vasudevan's elder brother met my father. Finally the wedding took place—but only after I was confirmed in my own job.'

'So lord Venkatesh gave you both the princess and half the kingdom,' Shyamalendu said with a smile.

'Which is why I offer flowers to Venkatesh every day despite the price, Mr Chatterjee,' Ramalingam said.

After a pause he continued, 'Look, I'm happy, I have no regrets. I joined as a stenographer, I even pasted labels on fans at one time. It was a small company then, selling a hundred fans a month meant a celebration, Mr Miller would treat everyone to cups of tea. The company has grown since then, and so have I. Now my salary is nearly three and a half thousand. Both my sons work here too, so does my son-in-law. What else can I ask for, tell me.'

Then he complained, 'Young men today won't believe it, but all of this is because of Venkatesh's blessing and the fact that I didn't disobey my father. When my father heard I'd got a job, he wrote me a letter which I have kept with me ever since.'

Taking his moneybag out of his pocket, Ramalingam retrieved a faded piece of paper from it. Written in Tamil, the letter had a smear of vermilion on it. Unfolding it with great care, Ramalingam said, 'My father wrote, remember your superior officer is like fire. If you're too far away you will not get the warmth, but if you're too close there's a strong possibility of being singed. So, with Venkatesh's blessing, maintain a middle distance.'

Putting the letter back in his moneybag like a valuable document, Ramalingam said, 'I have followed my father's advice at work all my life. So many have come, so many have risen dramatically, so many have left too—but I've remained, constant.'

Glancing at his watch, Ramalingam changed the subject. Looking closely at Shyamalendu, he said, 'You've got even better times coming up, Mr Chatterjee. I know you're thinking, I make five thousand at just thirty-three, how can it be even better, but I am telling you a lot more lies ahead. But Mars might play some games with you, you'll have to put in some effort. Wear a coral.'

'What's that?'

'A coral ring, red coral, pick a large stone.'

Shyamalendu smiled to himself after Ramalingam had left. Whoever said merchant offices are drab and boring, he wondered.

Perhaps it would have been good to feel the kind of satisfaction Ramalingam did. The progress that Shyamalendu had made in barely ten years was already like a fairy-tale. He had been promoted to the post of commercial manager at the age of just thirty-three. But even this had brought no satisfaction. It wasn't as though Shyamalendu was greedy, money was not everything. But an addiction to climbing the corporate ladder had set his blood on fire.

Publicity officer Mithu Sen came in. 'Would you like to take a look at the media list for our new ads for our fans, Mr Chatterjee? The list of newspapers is ready, we also have radio jingles and cinema shorts.'

Mithu Sen was usually dressed in drainpipe trousers and had large sideburns running down his cheeks. His name was actually Lalit Sen, but everyone in the profession called him Mithu. Shyamalendu signed the media list, and said, 'Nice name we've got for the new fan, don't you think? Urvashi.'

'What do you mean nice? It's wonderful! Ms Nargolwala from the agency is very excited. She admitted there hasn't been such a creative name for a fan in a long time,' Mithu said.

'Especially since we want to position it as a wedding present, right Mr Sen?'

'Most certainly. If the market research done by our ad agency is worth anything, Ms Nargolwala says we won't be able to meet the demand.'

'But what about the export market? Foreign markets are becoming vital now,' Shyamalendu commented.

'Are you thinking of the American market by any chance? It will be a sensation there Mr Chatterjee, Indian Ravi Shankar, Indian ganja, and now India's eternally mysterious society girl Urvashi. In her creative note, Ms Nargolwala has said this aspect has to be highlighted more in our ads for America. For instance, she's suggested that instead of labelling them fans made in India, the ad could say made in the land of the Kama Sutra.'

But Shyamalendu didn't seem as excited as Mithu Sen. Lighting a cigarette, he said, 'But you must have seen in the brief that for our fans we have no market to speak of in America. If we can offer fans free on board at seven-and-a-half rupees they might pick up a thousand. I'm thinking of countries like Thailand, Korea and Malaysia now.'

Mithu Sen spoke like an expert, 'Ms Nargolwala and I will have to visit these places before I can say anything about the markets there. But the desk research team at the agency says, thanks to our forefathers, almost everyone in Thailand is aware of Urvashi and her exploits. So it won't need heavy advertising to establish the name.'

To please Shyamalendu, Mithu Sen continued, 'Ms Nargolwala is amazed at the way you're casting the net far and wide in India and abroad. We were having a creative discussion at the Las Vegas bar yesterday, she said the agency is convinced if we increase our advertising budget next year we'll have to increase the factory output—the company will have to apply to the government for permission soon for substantial capacity expansion.'

Shyamalendu didn't allow the conversation to be prolonged. Gravely, he said, 'We can think about advertising for exports in greater detail. Prepare a note. Meanwhile, let's see what happens.'

'We're taking solus positions in the biggest newspapers. Twice as expensive, but it means no other ads on the page.'

'Good idea, take solus positions.' Shyamalendu managed to get rid of Mithu Sen.

The solus position. What everyone in the world was fighting for. Shyamalendu Chatterjee also wanted the solus position. The post of director. Solus. But even there the shadow of Runu Sanyal was in pursuit. Runu had joined Hindustan Peters in the same year. Both of them had been climbing the ladder at the same pace since then. It was like an 800-metre race, after several turns in the track the others had fallen behind. Now just one turn remained, and there were only two contenders—Shyamalendu Chatterjee and Runu Sanyal.

A little later there was a knock on the door. Runu peeped in and asked, 'May I come in?'

Shyamalendu didn't like the way Runu knocked. If someone opens the door, pops his nose in, and then asks if he can enter, how can you tell him not to come in?

Shyamalendu never did this himself. If he had business with Runu he always checked beforehand on the internal phone.

Suppressing his feelings, Shyamalendu said, 'Of course, come in.'

Carrying a file, Runu sat down opposite Shyamalendu. 'I had some points to discuss with you.'

'You're always welcome,' Shyamalendu said. 'How's your market? I am frankly having a harrowing time selling fans. The salespeople say once you buy a Peters fan it lasts a lifetime. So replacement sales are zero.'

'The lamp market was supposed to have been dismal according to our market forecast. We thought we'd have to sell our hundred-watt bulbs at a discount of ten paise. But it turns out every Peters lamp is selling at a premium of fifty paise,' said Runu. No one used the word black-market in this business—the common parlance was premium. When the price rose it was a premium, when it fell it was a discount.

'Congratulations, brother, were it not for your marketing genius, this wouldn't have been possible,' Shyamalendu told Runu.

Runu accepted the compliments without protest, as though he was indeed deserving of them. Blowing out a mouthful of smoke, he said, 'Mr Ferris also congratulated me today. It's like flies swarming around stocks. I can barely sit at my desk for a moment before some dealer or the other rings me for more lamps. But to be honest, I didn't have to do anything, although Mithu Sen is jumping up and down claiming that it was because that fatso Ms Barbellwala or whatever her name is released some ads last month that our sales are up. The fact is two other lamp companies are on strike, they cannot provide stocks at all.

'So I've taken the opportunity to turn the screws on wicked dealers. That goddamned Mandal and Company was talking big even a couple of months ago because there was a little oversupply in the market. Now they're sir this and sir that. I've told Khosla not to give Mandal a single lamp.

Better to support Chokhania Brothers, who're always prepared to pay in advance when they pick up stocks.'

Chokhania Brothers also sold Peters fans. Hiranandani, the sales manager for the eastern region, had told Shyamalendu just yesterday that Chokhania offered no additional support, for they knew there would not be a lack of fans in India in the near future. Without bringing this up, Shyamalendu said, 'So there's no pressure at the moment, you're quite free now?'

'Yes, since I have no work I thought I'd prepare for the challenge of the decade. You know, what the MD keeps harping on. I decided to do some advance planning for the next ten years and discuss things with Davidson once he's back.'

'Wasn't Davidson supposed to have been back by now? What's keeping him?' Shyamalendu asked.

'Can you ring the bell and ask for some coffee? Bibi and I came home at three in the morning. There was a dinner at my friend Surinder Lal's place, the Higgins director. Informal party. But you know, everyone got so tipsy they wanted to dance. I had a headache by the time we were done. Didn't sleep at all. Surinder Lal went to Doon School with me. He had nothing but pure cowdung in his head. But look how he's vaulted ahead of everyone to become a director at Higgins.'

Shyamalendu summoned the bearer and asked for some coffee. 'Please get my bottle of saccharine from my desk,' Runu requested the bearer.

'Saccharine? Why on earth?' Shyamalendu asked.

'Bibi's annoyed, says I must get rid of the belly. Apparently all the whiskey I drink collects at the centre of the earth.' Runu pointed to his stomach.

Sipping his coffee, Shyamalendu said, 'What was that you were saying about a rumour?'

'I don't know how much of it is true. I went to meet my father yesterday, he said everyone was asking about Davidson, they've heard in Sutanuti Club or somewhere, the doctors are suspecting stomach cancer. Who knows? And besides my father's claims have to be discounted, he was down two and a half pegs of whisky first thing in the morning. He's retired and idle, so while Ma's busy with her deities he gets hold of cheap whiskey from the army canteen through the good offices of his son-in-law and downs it every day.'

'Cancer? Davidson?' Shyamalendu was unhappy to hear this. For a moment he recalled the scene in the Patna hotel—Davidson escorting an unknown young college teacher to his cycle.

Runu stirred his coffee after adding his saccharine. Suddenly Shyamalendu noticed it on his finger—a ring with an enormous red coral.

Runu realised Shyamalendu had seen the ring. 'The wife insisted,' he said, 'I have no idea why. But madam is leaning towards all this stars-and-planets business of late. She keeps visiting an astrologer in Baghbazar.'

Now they began operational discussions. Runu wanted some of the salesmen to sell both fans and lamps, this would lower the costs of his department. Shyamalendu said, 'As you know, selling fans and selling lamps are not the same thing. And besides, production in my division will increase twenty per cent from next year. I'll have to work much harder to sell Peters fans.'

'Come on, Shyamalendu. The company might find it difficult to sell its products—but not your Urvashi model.'

'Even the common people of India are not fools anymore. Neither Urvashi nor any other heavenly nymph can win the customer over if there's oversupply without quality.'

After further discussions it was decided to try the system of one salesman for both products in one region. 'But I have the freedom to withdraw if I find my sales being hampered,' Shyamalendu told Runu candidly.

'All right,' said Runu. 'I'll send a note to the MD.' He left, but not before Shyamalendu's eyes were drawn again to the new coral ring on his finger. If he told Dolon about the astrologer she would run to him at once and force Shyamalendu to wear a coral ring too. But Shyamalendu refused to walk down this road. If he had to rise up the ranks it would be through his work. Not through an uncle's influence or hereditary connections or even appeasing the stars and planets.

Meanwhile a summons came from the managing director's room.

Ferris was reviewing the company's financial health with Gordon. 'I've read the note about your fan division, Chatterjee,' said the finance director. 'I think your planning has been excellent. You've sold nine months' worth of production in India—the factory wouldn't have been operating at full capacity had you not exported the winter production.'

'How *are* your exports doing?' asked Ferris.

'Not too bad,' said Shyamalendu. 'We will begin shipping to Thailand and Korea in ten days. It's not as though these exports will be greatly profitable, but the brand will be built. The government will be pleased. We will be able to get more import licences for the subcomponents we still have to buy abroad for the lamp division. And our home market won't suffer.'

'I hope the factory is cooperating fully. Let me know if there's any trouble, we'll talk to Hartley,' said Ferris.

Glancing at a sheet of paper in front of him, the finance director said, 'These figures are fine, but if we could make another million in profits from your division, we'd make record profits this financial year.'

'Home office has sent a telex,' said Ferris, 'asking for an all-out effort to make more profits.'

'Can't we do something from exports, Chatterjee?' Gordon asked.

'Exports are all a matter of contracts, they were signed much earlier,' Shyamalendu answered.

'Review your plans, Chatterjee,' Ferris said. 'If you try I'm sure you can push up profits.'

The red light was still on outside the managing director's room when Shyamalendu left. It occurred to him that no one was all-powerful, even Ferris and Gordon had to show results to the home office. Ferris had said the other day, 'The home office evaluates us on the basis of the returns we generate on their capital.'

No sooner had Shyamalendu returned to his room than the bearer handed him a piece of paper. Tutul! Just look at her, imagine sending in a visitor's slip. 'Please send Miss Bhattacharya in,' Shyamalendu told Miss Chakraborty on the phone.

Miss Bhattacharya was accompanied by a smiling Dolon. Holding his hand out to shake Tutul's, Shyamalendu said, 'Why this little game, Tutul? You could have just walked in.'

'Tutul wanted to have some fun, so she sent a slip,' said Dolon.

'But hats off to you,' said Tutul. 'We've been waiting for ages, I was about to walk off in a huff.'

'Terribly sorry, Tutul. The managing director had sent for me.'

'Who comes first, your wife or your managing director?' Tutul asked with a covert smile.

Dolon provided the answer. 'The top brass of merchant offices know very well there will be no lack of wives as long as you don't lose your job.'

Shyamalendu said, 'There are some carnivorous executives who are so ambitious they will send their wives into exile if the MD so orders. But as you know, my dearest, your husband is a domesticated Bengali.' Turning to his sister-in-law, Shyamalendu said, 'Placate your sister, I have begged pardon.'

Laughing, Sudarshana said, 'Very well, you are forgiven this time.'

Looking at her sister, she said, 'You can smile now, Didi. Didn't you say husbands of peevish women end up stumbling.'

'Would you like some coffee?' Shyamalendu asked.

'Look at your watch,' Dolon said. 'It's five to one.'

'How beautifully your room is done up, Shyamal-da,' Sudarshana said admiringly. 'You look just like a film star in this setting.'

'Film stars don't have to sell fans,' Shyamalendu told her.

'What's that photograph on the wall, Shyamal-da?'

'They've just got it from England. I want to use it in an ad. Our air laboratory, set up at a cost of a million pounds.'

'Your company has spent a million pounds so that people can give themselves airs,' Sudarshana retorted at once.

'That's exactly what I want to inform the public about. We create different environments in separate chambers there—June in India, September in Ethiopia, March in Spain, anything we need. Different kinds of breezes are induced—sea breeze, river breeze, winter breeze, spring breeze. Computers prepare reports on these, then famous scientists read these reports to design new models of Peters fans. Get it?'

'Wonderful! You really are a supersalesman, Shyamal-da,' Sudarshana declared in admiration. 'Now I see why you've risen so much in just nine years.'

Someone peeped in through the glass door. 'Come in,' said Shyamalendu.

A slim and handsome young man entered. A management trainee, Atanu Ray had studied in the English medium all his life. People like him spoke Bangla mincingly. 'Were you looking for me?' Atanu Ray asked with great deference in Bangla. 'I was in Radhabazar for market research. I interviewed five people who came from small towns to buy electric fans. You're right, Mr Chatterjee, they may have seen the ads put out by various fan companies, but when it came to purchasing a fan, they took the advice of their friends, relatives and colleagues.'

'We'll talk at length about this later,' said Shyamalendu. 'Try to interview at least a hundred and fifty buyers. Get their addresses if necessary, visit them at home, study their buying habits and psychology. I didn't send for you for anything in particular, I just wanted to find out where you were.'

Atanu left. Dolon had been surveying him closely. 'I've seen him before, haven't I?' she asked.

'Yes,' said Shyamalendu, 'at the MD's annual tea party. That's the one day of the year we can meet the junior officers and management trainees socially.'

'What are the prospects for management trainees?' Dolon asked.

Smiling, Shyamalendu said, 'Bright, to put it briefly. Earlier the jobs in merchant offices went to idiot sons of wealthy Indians who cosied up to the English. Immediately after independence senior government officers pushed their sons and sons-in-law into these posts. The company authorities were gratified at the opportunity to please bureaucrats in Delhi, they considered it the easiest way to safeguard the future of the industry. No one wants the company their sons and sons-in-law work in to wind up. But now these companies have learnt the hard way, they've realised that if they are to survive here in the face of competition, they need people who are intelligent and hardworking—those who know and understand the people of the country. That's why the industry is now trying to attract the best college students. Management trainees go through two years of training here, after which they start climbing the ladder rapidly. In a couple of companies in Bombay, management trainees have already risen to the post of managing director.'

They went out. The clerks noticed out of the corners of their eyes that today Mr Chatterjee was leaving with Mrs Chatterjee and a beautiful young woman at thirty seconds before one o'clock.

'Where are we going now?' Tutul asked when they were seated in the car.

'To the club,' answered Shyamalendu.

'The club? Now?' Tutul asked.

'We'll have lunch at the club, Tutul,' Dolon said.

'You get food at the club?' Tutul was genuinely astonished.

'Don't confuse it for our Kadamkuan Club, Tutul. Here the clubs have restaurants, bars, swimming pools,' Dolon explained to her sister.

Tutul's surprise knew no bounds when she saw the enormous building of Gobindopur Club. Dolon said, 'Your Shyamal-da's a member, but the company pays for everything. You can meet many well-known people at these clubs, so it helps the company. They've learnt the hard way that you can't do business with strangers simply by turning up on their doorstep. Networking is very important for the company.'

Several women were playing cards in the cardroom, smoking and drinking beer. Dolon said, 'The wives of the members come here to play cards in the afternoon. They can have lunch too if they like. You don't have to pay on the spot, just sign. Nagen-babu from the club sends the bills to their husbands at the end of the month.'

Dolon added in a whisper, 'This club has made a huge contribution to securing independence for India, you know. Calcutta had just the Sutanuti Club earlier—only for white people, Indians weren't admitted. In protest, Indian nationalists under the leadership of Sir Haren Pal made great sacrifices to found this club.'

'And then?' Tutul asked.

'What do you suppose? The white people couldn't believe their eyes. But Sir Haren Pal taught them a lesson they wouldn't forget, he said Gobindopur Club wouldn't follow the example set by Sutanuti Club—whites would be allowed to join.'

Tutul's eyes were fixed elsewhere. A frail, ageing man was seated silently in a corner of the hall with a mug of beer. Just like an Egyptian mummy. 'Look, Didi!'

'Shh,' Shyamalendu warned her. 'That's our director, Sir Baren Ray, a retired ICS officer. His wife is a shrew, his son a simpleton. The poor man has no choice but to sit here quietly and drink beer.'

They went into the lunchroom. Taking a table, Shyamalendu asked, 'What would you like Tutul, Chinese or continental? There's tandoori too. Also a cold buffet, if you'd prefer that.'

'This is too confusing for me, Shyamal-da,' Tutul blurted out.

'Let's get Chinese food today, Tutul won't mind that. Send for the Chinese steward Mr Hua, I'll place the order myself. The Chinese cook at Gobindopur Club is very renowned you know, Tutul.'

Tutul looked around in wonder, noting everything carefully. Dolon said, 'Each of the restaurants in Calcutta has its speciality. I'll take you to all of them. Sizzling steak at Blue Fox, bekti mayonnaise at Skyroom, fried fish with tartar sauce at Firpo's, roti-kabab at Amber, chicken tandoori at Mocambo, Bengali dishes at Madira. Lido Room makes a superb smoked hilsa, but it's not the season now, so it isn't available. Sometimes we don't cook at home and go out for dinner.'

'What have you been doing all morning?' Shyamalendu asked.

Dolon reeled off a list. 'First stop, the calico shop. From there to Hasem's tailoring shop to get Tutul a couple of body-fitting blouses. She was too shy to accept anything I bought her, but I told her Hasem is world-famous, you won't get blouses like these in Patna.

'Then I took her around Lindsay Street and New Market. We bought four petticoats. Remember they said in the papers the other day that petticoats from New Market are famous all over India? Tutul refused to believe me. Let me tell you, you won't get another wife like me. I bargained hard and saved six rupees of yours.'

'Well done!' Shyamalendu expressed his gratitude.

Then he said, 'You know, Tutul, our company would do even better if only the people in our purchase department were more like your sister. They don't care about the company's money.'

Paying no attention to Shyamalendu's comment, Dolon continued, 'From New Market we went to Jenny Tudor's, where we got Tutul's hair done. Mine too. So crowded. You have to book a slot a week ahead. I don't know why all of you claim business is down in Calcutta. Once we were done at Jenny Tudor's we went directly to Mrs Ferris's coffee party at Mocambo.'

'All right,' said Shyamalendu.

'You know, I was waiting in the car,' Tutul said. 'But Mrs Ferris is such a wonderful lady, when she heard about me from Didi she came out herself to escort me in.'

'Who else was invited to the ladies' coffee meet?' asked Shyamalendu.

'Only the wives of the covenanted officers,' Dolon said. 'You can see the state India's poor people are in. All of us must help as much as possible. Flag day for Siliguri Homes is coming up next week. All of us have to go out on the streets with boxes to collect money.'

'Lovely woman,' Tutul said. 'The wife of a managing director, but no airs. She had tears in her eyes when she was talking of the orphans in Siliguri.'

Dolon added, 'Seeing which our Mrs Sanyal also promptly began to dab her eyes. I believe she's joined the dog-lovers' society too. Apparently, Mrs Ferris is going to be the honorary secretary there this year.'

After lunch they went and stood under the portico. Sristidhar brought the car round in a flash and Tutul got in. Taking the opportunity, Dolon said to her husband, 'Listen.' Then she whispered something to him.

'What are you telling him, Didi?'

'Nothing,' said Dolon, signalling to her husband with her eyes.

6

Dolon's whispers rang in Shyamalendu's ears. As soon as he returned to his room, he called out, 'Mrs Anderson!'

Mrs Anderson rushed in with her notebook. 'No, it's not to dictate a letter. I'd like to have a look at Atanu Ray's personal file, please.'

Mrs Anderson brought it within a minute. On a sheet of paper Shyamalendu noted down, 'Atanu Ray. Father Sudhamoy Ray, retired district judge. Age 25. B.Sc (Tech) in electronics from IIT Kharagpur. First division in ISC from St Xavier's School. Joined Hindustan Peters a year and a half ago as a management trainee. Good track record. Earning eight hundred already. Excellent prospects. Five feet seven inches tall, Tutul was five-feet-four. Well-matched.'

Shyamalendu asked to be connected to his phone at home and passed on all the details about Atanu Ray to Dolon. 'Smart and cultured. Works directly under me now. Our Delhi resident director Mr Murthy wanted to visit Santiniketan recently and had asked for a guide. I asked Atanu to do the job. Mr Murthy was very impressed, praised him to the skies.'

'Then will you find out if it's possible?' Dolon said immediately. 'I got a letter from Ma today, she says we have to find a boy for her. What I suggest is we invite him home to tea, let them meet, after that we'll figure out how to get things going.'

'Let's see,' said Shyamalendu, and disconnected the call.

Sending for Atanu, Shyamalendu made a plan with him. 'We can discuss the market research over tea at home. Market research is ruling the roost in England and America these days. The companies that study their markets closely to anticipate what customers want, what kind of tastes buyers have, and where their own weaknesses are, will be the winners.'

The conversation would have continued, but Rao, the technical officer at the factory from sales, arrived.

'Are you very busy, Mr Chatterjee? I have to talk to you urgently, I just came back from the factory.'

Shyamalendu asked him to sit down.

'It's absolutely confidential, sir.'

The red light outside Shyamalendu's room went on.

The red light outside another room in the office was switched on too at exactly the same time. Mr Murthy used this room during his visits to Calcutta. He had sent for the Company Secretary.

Sengupta found the formidable representative of the company's business matters in Delhi somewhat subdued today. Murthy usually had an air of superiority and aloofness, never speaking more than he had to, and frequently dropping the managing director's name when he did. But then, why not? The strings on which the business danced were pulled in Delhi, and it was Murthy's responsibility to ensure these strings were not severed. Import licences, licences to expand capacity, permission to repatriate money, all of it depended on the orders issued by the courtiers of the emperor of Delhi. So Murthy's power as well as responsibility were unlimited. But today he seemed to have softened quite a bit as he said, 'There's a problem, Sengupta.'

'For you?'

'For me, and for the company, too.'

'The directors' problem is effectively the company's problem, since they steer the company,' Sengupta said.

'Let me tell you the whole thing. You've met my daughter Ragini.'

'Of course, more than once. We talked a lot with her during the week we spent in Delhi. Very sweet girl. My wife loves her too. Is Ragini studying in college now?'

'I don't know if she's studying, but she's enrolled for a BA Honours course at Miranda House. I doubt if she studies.' The normally daunting Murthy sounded rather helpless.

'But she's a very intelligent girl. I don't think you have to worry.'

Murthy said, 'My wife may be married to a company director, but she still makes dosas herself, she still wakes up at four in the morning to get the household going. But Ragini doesn't give a damn about any of this. She's perpetually in mini-skirts or bell-bottoms, she's absorbed in herself.'

'Times are changing, Mr Murthy.'

'I wouldn't have worried about it, but Ragini has put us in a difficult position.' Murthy was quite worked up now. 'I'm embarrassed to tell you she has fallen in love with someone. She's barely nineteen, but she wants to get married already.'

'What can we say about this Mr Murthy? As parents of children ourselves we can only pass on our sympathy. It's entirely your affair.'

'Exactly, that's what I'd thought too. It's a personal matter for me, my wife, and my daughter. Considering how adamant Ragini is, I have no choice but to agree to the marriage. But this is where there's a big but.

'I had invited Mr Ferris to drinks yesterday. My wife let him know casually. But he said it's a serious matter, you'd better consult Sengupta before agreeing to the marriage.'

'Your daughter can marry anyone she wants, what business is it of the company's?' Sengupta said.

'Quite. Isn't that so?' Murthy seemed a little reassured. 'I wouldn't have bothered if the boy worked anywhere else, but the problem is that he's one of our employees.'

'Our employee? That *is* a problem then Mr Murthy. The Companies Act comes in the way of this marriage.'

Murthy swelled with indignation. 'Are we company directors not human beings?' he said. 'Are we second-class citizens? Do we have to beg the government for permission to get our own daughter married?'

Well versed as he was in Company Law, Sengupta said, 'Not permission from the government, but permission from the shareholders. As far as I remember, Section 314 of the Companies Act 1956 was amended, so that a special resolution must be passed at a general meeting of shareholders to allow a relative of a director to hold an office of profit.'

'My god! But Mrs Murthy has finalised the date!' Murthy almost broke down. 'Do you see what a dangerous girl Ragini is—did she have to fall in love with someone from my office? Mr Ferris will be very annoyed with me when he hears of Section 314.'

After some thought, Murthy said, 'What if I don't give my consent to this marriage?'

'That doesn't matter. Even if your daughter marries without your consent, to the law her husband is still your son-in-law, and according to Company Law a director's son-in-law is a relative. Not just him, if your daughter has a daughter, the person she marries will be a relative too.'

'My god!' Murthy invoked the almighty again.

'I'm sorry, Mr Murthy, the Companies Act includes a list of thirty-eight kinds of relatives, and sons-in-law are one of them.'

Murthy asked what might ensue if the wedding took place without permission from shareholders.

'We'll have to take legal advice,' Sengupta said. 'But as far as I remember, unless a resolution is passed at the first general meeting of shareholders after the marriage, the son-in-law will lose his job. He will also have to return all his earnings from the company. Things are slightly better now. If this had taken place before the 1965 amendment, even the director would have been dismissed, according to the Companies Act.'

'What!' Murthy all but shouted.

'But there's no need to worry so much. The general meeting of shareholders is coming up in July. We can get a special resolution passed there.'

'No other way out?' Murthy's plea was wretched.

'It's not right for me to suggest this—the other way out is to sack the son-in-law-to-be before the marriage.'

'No, that's impossible. You have no idea how sentimental my daughter is.'

'Then you can have his monthly salary reduced to less than five hundred rupees.'

'Five hundred rupees won't pay for my daughter's saris, Sengupta,' Murthy said tragically.

'There may be other routes. Let me study Section 314 Subsection 2 carefully. It would be helpful to have a look at Ragini's fiancé's file.'

'You want to know his name?' Murthy hesitated briefly before scribbling the name on a slip of paper.

It was getting on for five o'clock. The red light outside Shyamalendu's cabin went off finally.

Shyamalendu looked extremely anxious. He stared at the ceiling with a frown on his face.

Sengupta came in. Always jovial himself, he asked, 'What's the matter, you look very worried.'

'Huge problem, Mr Sengupta.'

'No point being upset about it. If there's a problem, there's a solution. Don't you remember Rabi Thakur's song—"no need to bear the world on your shoulders, o timid one, the helmsman will take you across the river".'

Shyamalendu chuckled. 'We're in big trouble, Mr Sengupta. Don't tell anyone. A huge consignment of the new Peters Urvashi fans is ready for export at the factory, and now the technical experts from sales have discovered the fans are defective. It's a serious flaw. One of the small components was supposed to have been imported, but the factory heads were lax and ordered the part from an Indian company instead. The quality's not good at all. All the fans are ready in the godown, and now we find they're defective.'

'I'm in trouble too,' said Sengupta. 'I have to rush now for a consultation with barrister A. K. Chowdhury. Could you give me management trainee Atanu Ray's personal file, he works under you.'

'Atanu Ray? His file?' Shyamalendu was surprised.

'Yes, sir. You're to blame for this.'

'Me?'

'Of course. You're the one who set the trap for this royal romance. Mr Murthy's daughter Ragini and Atanu Ray. I'm told you're the one who chose Atanu as the guide for Mr Murthy and his wife and daughter on their visit to Santiniketan.'

'I did, but that was just two days, a weekend.'

Sengupta laughed. 'When you can have love at first sight, can you imagine what two full days can do?'

Taking Atanu Ray's personal file, he said, 'You'll be rewarded for matchmaking. And an invitation card too—chi Atanu and sou Ragini. Those are the words Madrasis use when they're getting married. But I have to take care of Company Law first. There's a problem with a director having someone from the same company as his son-in-law. Your daughter's husband is your relative according to the Companies Act Section 6, as amended by Act 31 of 1965.'

Shyamalendu turned grave. Then he asked, 'What about the wife's sister's husband?'

'Difficult question. The bible is with me, let me look it up.' Opening the fat volume of the Companies Act and poring over it, Sengupta said, 'Saved by the bell. The older version of the law said the wife's sister's husband is a relative, but the amendment says only the wife's sister is a relative, not her husband. Still, you never know. Some people are pressurising the government to expand the list of relatives.'

As soon as Sengupta left Shyamalendu picked up the internal phone.

'Is that Ray? It's Chatterjee. I'm afraid I'm a little out of sorts today, would it be all right if we cancelled the meeting I'd planned at home?'

'Of course, not a problem at all,' said Atanu.

'I hope it's not too much of an inconvenience?'

'Not at all, it's perfectly all right.'

7

Dolon had got tickets for the night show of a film after dinner. Shyamalendu wasn't very keen on going, but Sudarshana was here for only a short visit, and poor Dolon seldom had the chance to have a good time with her own family. So Shyamalendu didn't want to be a wet blanket.

They arrived at Metro a little early. The evening show had just ended. That's where they ran into one another. Atanu was coming out of the cinema. With Ragini. So Mr Murthy was visiting Calcutta with his daughter.

Shyamalendu felt a little embarrassed. But Atanu said, 'Good evening, Mr Chatterjee. All of you will enjoy the film.'

'Not feeling on top of the world yet,' Shyamalendu said. 'But it was depressing at home.'

Atanu didn't have a company car, but it was an unwritten law at Hindustan Peters that officers shouldn't travel on public transport. So Atanu commuted to and from work in taxis. But now Shyamalendu saw from afar a company car parked outside the cinema, with a uniformed driver in attendance. Mr Murthy himself was inside.

Dolon had a serious expression, she sat silently as the film began. Shyamalendu only whispered to her, 'You didn't say anything to Tutul, did you?'

She answered, 'Are you mad?'

Tutul went out briefly during the interval. 'Why so serious?' Shyamalendu asked Dolon.

'I was hoping Tutul's would be lucky, that she might hit the jackpot at the first chance.'

'The first chance is not the last one. Everyone can't score a century in their first test match,' Shyamalendu consoled her.

Nestling closer to Shyamalendu, Dolon said, 'Just feels like Tutul isn't as fortunate as you and me. We were married at first sight, you got your job on the very first interview, and now if you become a director at the first opportunity it'll be a hat-trick.

Director! The very word was like a thorn in his side. He had happily forgotten about it during the film.

'How much do directors earn?' Dolon asked.

'Seven thousand. Then there's commission on profits. And many other perks and benefits. All told, a hundred and twenty thousand a year.'

'What does that work out to every month?' Dolon began to calculate. 'Twelve tens are one twenty, so ten thousand a month.' She was very pleased—it was like she was having a dream. Rabindranath Tagore had won a hundred and twenty thousand rupees for the Nobel Prize. 'How many directors' posts are vacant?'

'Just one. To appoint more directors the company will have to change its articles of association,' Shyamalendu answered.

'Honestly, I don't feel bad for Tutul anymore.'

'And what made you change your mind?' Shyamalendu asked, smiling.

'Just as well things didn't go too far with Atanu. You might have got into trouble because of your sister-in-law's husband. You'd have also started fretting about the Companies Act like Mr Murthy as soon as you became a director.'

Shyamalendu took Dolon's hand in the dark and pressed it lightly.

But Dolon didn't stop. 'Why do you think the government has made a law like this?' she whispered.

'So that there's no nepotism. But, as you know, the tighter the laws in our country, the more the loopholes.'

Now Dolon began asking questions like a child. 'Listen, that Section 314 or whatever it is you told me about, can it prove difficult to get shareholders to pass a resolution about relatives?'

'Nothing is impossible these days. Ours is a public limited company, anyone can buy a share or two at the stock exchange and create trouble at the shareholders' meeting. The trade union people do this quite often in Bombay. And then you have the institutional shareholders like the Life Insurance Corporation and the Unit Trust of India. Mr Ferris fears them greatly, although he knows he can get any proposal passed by a majority vote, since seventy-five per cent of the shares are still owned by the British company.'

Tutul's return ended their conversation. The sisters were sitting on either side of Shyamalendu. The ad reels began. Suddenly Tutul poked Shyamalendu. 'There, hymns of praise for your Peters fans.'

Shyamalendu nodded. At the end of the one-minute-long film, Tutul said, 'Really Shyamal-da, you people can turn day into night and night into day in these ads of yours. I feel like running out and buying an Urvashi fan right now—so that its breeze can blow away all my sorrows and suffering.'

The ad ruined everything for Shyamalendu. The lights came up briefly before the main film was resumed, but all Shyamalendu could see was the factory godown stacked to the ceiling with boxes of fans, with the words 'For Export Only' stamped on them. Each of them defective.

And he recalled what Gordon had said. The finance director's face was superimposed on the heroine's on the silverscreen. Asking for one million rupees in profits this financial year.

Apparently Gordon had asked Runu too, who it seemed had planned to reduce his costs by five hundred thousand. Okay, if Runu Sanyal can save five hundred thousand, Shyamalendu can certainly save a million. He had a large budget for advertising, he would save five hundred thousand from it. He had also provisioned three hundred thousand for emergencies, he'd return this amount too. That was eight hundred thousand. He could always cut another two hundred thousand from other expenses. Instead of sending fans to villages he'd try to sell more in the big cities. This would reduce costs since the salesmen wouldn't have to travel quite as much.

A romantic scene was playing on a foamy Hawaiian sea beach. The heroine, almost completely disrobed, was about to fall into the hero's arms. Excitement ran high in the cheap front seats, there were a couple of wolf whistles. Dolon pressed Shyamalendu's foot naughtily. Locked in an embrace, the hero and heroine proceeded to kiss. The massive screen was filled with just their faces. 'So indecent, these white-skinned people,' Dolon said.

But all that Shyamalendu could see was a pile of defective fans. He couldn't hear anything at all. He might still be able to deliver the one million, but what about the exports to Thailand and Korea?

8

Shyamalendu was back in the office the next day with the anxiety about exports still clouding his mind. No one in Hindustan Peters knew of the crisis yet. He had to let the managing director know.

Shyamalendu wrote the note by hand, he didn't dare give it to Mrs Anderson to type.

A few minutes after he had got the note, Ferris rang Gordon on the internal phone. 'Can you come over for a few minutes please, John?'

The red light outside Ferris's office went on. A few minutes later Shyamalendu was sent for. He knew this would happen, so he had already got on his jacket.

Shyamalendu went to the MD's room as soon as Mrs Dick rang him.

Runu Sanyal came by several times to meet Ferris on another matter, only to be thwarted. 'What's going on?' he asked Mrs Dick. 'Will the meeting go on all morning?'

Applying a second layer of lipstick, Mrs Dick said, 'Heaven knows, and Mr Ferris. But I think it will go on. The technical manager has been sent for.'

The head of all the factories, Hartley the technical manager, entered the MD's room with a smile. But when he came out fifteen minutes later it was with a dour expression. He returned a few minutes later with a sheet of paper.

The three men in the cabin were still looking grim. 'So where do we stand?' Ferris said.

'It's obvious we can under no circumstances export these fans. They will be rejected.' Drawing on his pipe, Hartley continued, 'It's a minor defect though. All we have to do is replace the component we bought from a third party, Urvashi will again be the best fan in the world. I'm sending a telex to Sheffield at once, to send the parts by air.'

'Do we have an import licence?' asked Gordon.

'We'll use the blanket quota for now so that exports aren't held up.' Glancing at the paper in his hand, Hartley went on, 'If Sheffield sends everything by air-freight, the fans will be ready in three weeks.'

'We are sorry, Peter,' the technical manager said. 'I'll institute an enquiry to find out who's responsible for this ghastly mistake. And I admit we should have discovered the flaw much sooner. But at least the company's prestige has been saved because the sales inspectors found out in time.'

Hartley rose to leave. Gordon told Ferris, 'The company's prestige may have been saved, Peter, but you and I are in deep trouble.'

'Why?'

'The value of the exports to Thailand and Korea was ten million rupees. And the government gave us a grant of another million for exports.'

'But John, we'll send the consignment before the end of the financial year, won't we?' the managing director said.

'Read clause number ten, Peter,' Gordon said grimly. 'The last date for putting the entire consignment on board a ship is the fifteenth of this month. The fresh components from England will be here by then, but the fans won't be ready.'

'What's the upshot then, John?'

'Read the next paragraph, you'll find out rightaway. The clause that brought Chatterjee running to us. Unless the cargo is on board by midnight on the fifteenth of the month, we have to pay five million as compensation.'

'What! Why on earth did we agree to such a condition?' Ferris wailed.

It wasn't as though the directors hadn't read the clauses before the contract was signed. But there was no point reminding them. Tapping his palm with the back of his pen, Shyamalendu answered, 'Neither Thailand nor Korea was ready to import fans from us without this particular clause.'

Gordon said, 'You and I approved the contract before it was signed, Peter. And look at it from their point of view too, what will they do with the fans if they arrive after summer?'

'No country trusts India to deliver on time yet,' Shyamalendu said regretfully.

Gordon made some calculations in his notebook and said, 'Five million compensation, export subsidy loss to the tune of one million, that's six million. Add nine million as fresh manufacturing cost for the defective fans. We can't sell them in India either, because they're made to run on 110-volt power supply, it's 220 in India. We would have made a profit of eight million from the whole deal. We'll end up losing several millions instead. Brilliant.'

Ferris's red face grew redder. 'Let me see the contract,' he said.

Shyamalendu took the document out of his file and passed it to the managing director.

Ferris read every line carefully. Then he said sombrely, 'I see no way out. All I can say is send the factory manager home on the next ship.'

'We may have to send more employees home from the factory. But I don't see any way to save this six million. Hindustan Peters will make a loss for the first time in history, the first stroke of red ink on the ledger,' said Gordon.

'Let me read the contract too,' he said and went over it. Handing it back, he stated, 'I don't see a way out either.'

Shyamalendu was extremely perturbed. 'I'm very sorry,' he said.

'No, you have nothing to be sorry for,' Ferris said. 'The factory is responsible.'

'Let me examine the documents closely once more, in case there's a way out.'

'I don't have to remind you not to let a soul know,' Gordon said. 'The stockmarkets are expecting bonus dividends and an additional share issue. If word gets out we'll have a catastrophe on our hands.'

Ferris shook hands with Shyamalendu. 'I wish you all the luck, young man.'

It was a transformed Shyamalendu who emerged from the managing director's office. Vastly different from the Shyamalendu Chatterjee, commercial manager, who had entered Ferris's office. He had a much greater responsibility now. It was as though he had to save Hindustan Peters himself, along with the directors.

The word 'manager' is part of your designation, Shyamalendu told himself, you are a leader on the battlefield of trade and industry, everything depends on your strategy. There might be many crucial problems in the world, but at that moment the possibility of losing six million rupees was the greatest challenge facing Shyamalendu Chatterjee of Hindustan Peters.

He read every word of the contract carefully till lunchtime, going to a restaurant nearby for a quick sandwich before returning to the office. Ferris and Gordon were out for lunch. Mrs Dick had told Shyamalendu that the managing director would be playing golf in the afternoon, he had an appointment with Haddow, the chairman of Dickinson and Company, at the golf course. The responsibility was squarely on Shyamalendu's shoulders.

Maybe the two directors were testing Shyamalendu, perhaps they wanted to see whether and how he could survive this trial by fire. No one could say they had forced the responsibility on him, but then nothing was imposed on anyone at these levels, you had to take the initiative on your own. This was the rule in the private sector, it had been in operation since the dawn of the industrial revolution in the west.

Immersed though Shyamalendu was in the contents of the export file, a thought played at the back of his mind—no one had told James Watt to invent the steam engine, no one had ordered George Stephenson to come up with the railway locomotive, no one had warned John Boyd Dunlop that he wouldn't get an increment unless he developed the pneumatic tyre, it wasn't anyone's instructions that had made Henry Ford get down to constructing an automobile, Alfred Nobel had received no reminders to invent dynamite, Anton Philips was not threatened with dismissal from his job unless he could secure an enormous order from the czar of Russia for electric lights. All of these things had come about without anyone asking for them—capable people had stepped forward in times of need, during emergencies, taking on challenges and had risen to the top in the process. Their names had been written in gold letters in the worlds of science, technology, and industry. Hindustan Peters was a puny little enterprise in comparison, what could anyone expect of its even punier officer, Shyamalendu Chatterjee.

Shyamalendu seemed to be in a daze. He began reading the documents yet again—the way top barristers read their brief, or Sherlock Holmes considered the evidence, or Dolon's father pored over Shakespeare. With a red pencil he underlined passages which could yield interpretations that hadn't been extracted from them before.

At times a faint light seemed to appear at the end of the tunnel, only to turn out to be a will-o'-the-wisp.

Suddenly Mithu Sen barged into Shyamalendu's room.

'Just got your note, Mr Chatterjee. You've reduced the budget by five hundred thousand. Ms Nargolwala is down in the dumps, she wants to meet you.'

'I'm very busy now, Mr Sen,' Shyamalendu told him seriously. Not that his face revealed what was going on in his mind.

'Please give her some time, if you don't mind. To tell you honestly, Ms Nargolwala is very sensitive.'

'I am sorry, please explain to her I can meet her only after two or three days.'

Depositing a giant image mounted on hardboard on Shyamalendu's desk, Mithu Sen said, 'The ad for our exports. It'll come out in the papers the day the ship with Urvashi fans sails from Kidderpore dock. Ms Nargolwala and I wrote the copy together. She's very excited. The first line says, Urvashi is off on a foreign tryst.'

'It'll take me some time to get back to you on this too, Mr Sen.' Shyamalendu conveyed his decision grimly.

A disappointed Mithu Sen about to leave turned back at the door. He was perturbed by the commercial manager's attitude. In a tragic tone he said, 'You'd said the exports ad is very urgent, Mr Chatterjee, it has to be released across India on the fifteenth. Anyway, let me at least ask the agency to shoot some beautiful models for Urvashi.'

'Go ahead, I have no objection.' Shyamalendu was desperate to get rid of Mithu Sen.

He sank back into his thoughts.

Mrs Anderson sat outside quietly. She had no assignments except preventing anyone from charging into Shyamalendu's office.

9

Sudarshana had written a two-page letter in Bangla. 'Want to read it, Didi?' she asked her sister.

'You're grown up now, it's not right for me to read your letters,' Dolon said.

'Nothing confidential in there—just a joint report to Baba and Ma on what's going on here.'

'You haven't written about alcohol, have you? You know how old-fashioned Ma is,' Dolon said anxiously.

'Are you mad? But I did say the place where your elder daughter and son-in-law live is nothing short of a fairyland. And what makes all of us proud is that Shyamal-da has secured this position in his own right, with his own efforts.'

'Effort is putting it mildly. The English are a nation of shopkeepers, they really make your Shyamal-da slave, you know.'

Glancing at her watch, Dolon continued, 'See what's happening today? All the top managers of Hindustan Peters are back home, except your brother-in-law.'

Footsteps could be heard even as they were speaking. 'Hmm, gossiping about other people?' Shyamalendu joked.

'Not other people but our own, Shyamal-da. Subject: Shyamalendu Chatterjee, commercial manager of Hindustan Peters, who never comes home on time,' Sudarshana responded at once.

'Your sister's been complaining, hasn't she. But my hands are tied, I wish I knew why God invented this thing called responsibility.' Shyamalendu sat down on the sofa.

'Women have no regard for men who have no sense of responsibility, Shyamal-da,' Sudarshana said.

But Dolon jumped in at once. 'It's one thing to talk of real responsibilities, but look at what your brother-in-law does. While the directors play golf and Runu Sanyal throws parties and Mr Chopra is immersed in gambling with cards, he just keeps working. And yet Mrs Sengupta keeps telling me no one can climb the ladder in a merchant office through hard work alone.'

'It's not enough to work hard like a fool, you need learning and acumen too,' said Shyamalendu, lighting a cigarette. 'And, besides, I hate losing. It's the responsibility of new-age Indian managers to demonstrate that we are as capable as white men. Those of us who have risen from humble backgrounds to the ninth floor of Blue Haven must prove we're no less proficient than anyone else.'

'Of course,' Sudarshana said in support. 'Baba would be so happy to hear you say this.'

They were done with their tea very quickly. Today, Shyamalendu wasn't able to entertain his wife and sister-in-law with stories and conversation. Dolon said, 'I took Tutul around the other flats this afternoon, we dropped in on Mrs Sanyal too.'

'What did you think of her, Tutul?' asked Shyamalendu.

'She maintains herself so well, Shyamal-da. But Ma would faint if she saw a Bengali woman taking snuff and smoking and referring to her husband by his name.'

Shyamalendu was slightly embarrassed. Then he said, 'Your sister and I didn't like it at first either. But now we tolerate it. The thing is, their culture is different, it's been imported directly from the UK and the US, packaging and all.'

'Your Shyamal-da used to fret about these things earlier. I gave him a scolding one day. The educated Bengali middle-class has remained obsessed with culture while others have bagged the top jobs. When in Rome, I say. If the Englishmen are paying your salary, you have to do as they ask. Criticising them has become a fashion, but could anyone else have given us such a comfortable life? I've seen how the Indian bosses behave, they're the meanest of the lot, they consider the officers in their companies their servants.'

Shyamalendu didn't prolong the conversation. He sat down at his desk and began to read the clauses in the export contract yet again with the same attention with which he used to pore over Shakespeare once upon a time. It was a long document, twenty-five or thirty single-spaced pages. Shyamalendu remembered Dolon's father, who used to underline his favourite passages from Shakespeare with colour pencils in various shades. Each colour had a unique significance. Shyamalendu, too, underlined passages in his copy of the contract.

With Shyamalendu absorbed in work, the sisters decided not to disturb him. Going into the other room, they bared their hearts to each other.

10

The next morning the red light went on again outside Shyamalendu Chatterjee's office. And yet there was no one else inside. Shyamalendu was still reading the documents with great concentration.

Soon after lunch, Mrs Anderson saw Shyamalendu hurrying out, looking quite excited, without even putting on his jacket.

The red light outside the managing director's room went on again. No one knew what the discussion was about.

When Shyamalendu emerged half an hour later, Mrs Dick went in. It seemed to her Ferris was not looking as worried as he had been before lunch.

Instead of returning to his own room, Shyamalendu looked in on personnel officer Harihar Talukdar. Talukdar had not made much headway in the company, but he made sure to be deferential to both Shyamalendu and Runu Sanyal. For he knew one of these two pillars would make it to the boardroom, at which point he might prove useful to him.

'Come in, come in, Mr Chatterjee, to what do I owe this honour?' Talukdar welcomed Shyamalendu.

'Just came by to find out how things are.'

After a long conversation about work matters, Shyamalendu asked about the situation in the factory. 'How many workers are in the fan factory right now?'

'Only eight hundred,' said Talukdar in exasperation, 'but sometimes it feels like eight hundred million. You'll find a sample of every single problem in the world in our factory. God alone can explain how I've kept things under control.'

'We're very fortunate to have someone as experienced as you,' Shyamalendu told him.

'The company doesn't appreciate it, sir. Else they would have made me a covenanted officer by now.' Talukdar couldn't contain his despair.

Shyamalendu was silent. Harihar said, 'I can tell you because you're a Bengali. We've named the lamp factory and fan factory Hiroshima and Nagasaki.'

'What do you mean?'

'Can I be honest, sir? Atom bombs.' Talukdar burst into laughter.

Shyamalendu couldn't join in. Embarrassed, Talukdar said, 'I hope you didn't mind the joke, sir, I only told you because you're a Bengali. Look at what I have to deal with, there are three trade unions in the fan factory. If union A says go north, union B will say go south. And union C will take the opportunity and ask for the moon. Then you have the company-run canteen. The workers will dutifully eat any rubbish their wives feed them at home, but in the factory everyone's an emperor—the slightest of problems with food will lead to a demonstration.'

Shyamalendu was back in his room, where he sat quietly. It was almost five. Mrs Anderson rushed in and said, 'Here are the names and addresses of the suppliers to the factory canteen that you'd asked for.' Shyamalendu saw that the names of all the suppliers were listed—fish, vegetables, oil, eggs.

The small hand on the clock had touched five. But Shyamalendu didn't prepare to leave. It was the fifth of the month. Not many days to go till the fifteenth. The date was getting larger, the digits growing till they seemed to swallow the calendar. So numbers could be cancerous too. If not, how could they be expanding on the wall like tumours?

11

Dolon and Tutul were dressed up and waiting. Dolon kept checking her watch. There was a cocktail party at Ferris's house this evening.

'Just look at this man,' Dolon grumbled to her sister.

'He's your husband, you look at him,' Tutul laughed.

The cars downstairs were visible from the ninth floor. All of them left—Mr and Mrs Sanyal, Mr and Mrs Chopra, Rao, Varghese. Varghese went alone, though, since his wife was pregnant.

Dolon had almost given up hope when Shyamalendu rushed in. 'Extremely sorry,' he said.

'That's your pet phrase you've learned from the English—to be used like penicillin for all diseases,' Dolon said with great irritation.

'Responsibility is a terrible thing, Dolon.'

Dolon grimaced. 'All the responsibility is yours alone—not the managing director's, not the finance director's, not Mr Murthy's, not Chopra's, not Runu Sanyal's.'

'I seek thy pardon, goddess,' said Shyamalendu, joining his palms in supplication and laughing.

'I rang you twice in the office. No reply,' Dolon said.

Tutul said, 'Didi's just worried about Mrs Anderson. We're thinking of asking the MD today to replace her with Didi.'

'Excellent idea,' Shyamalendu said. Then he went into the bedroom without prolonging the conversation, saying, 'Give me exactly three minutes.'

He came out soon afterwards, dressed for the evening. But Dolon exclaimed at her husband's outfit, 'Really, this is too much. How can you wear a lounge suit? Look at the card, dress formal.'

'So sorry, I forgot.' Shyamalendu went back into the room.

'What's this, Didi? Do the bosses even give orders on how you must dress?'

'Of course. It's the managing director's party—not to be taken lightly. A man named Pandey lost his job a few years ago because he wasn't dressed in a dinner suit. Mr Boylan was the MD then. His family had several peerages, he couldn't stand a breach of etiquette.'

Shyamalendu emerged from the bedroom once more, this time in his dinner suit. White jacket, black bow tie, black trousers whose bottoms were not rolled up, black pointed patent-leather shoes. Tutul could barely keep herself from laughing.

'Why dost thou laugh, beauteous sister-in-law?' Shyamalendu asked.

'The Jaiswals had hired a band for a family wedding in Patna. The man with the drum on his back was dressed exactly like you,' Tutul said.

'Is that supposed to be funny?' Shyamalendu widened his eyes.

In the car Tutul said, 'Your Mrs Ferris is very nice though. When she heard I'm still in Calcutta she rang me herself to invite me, though I have nothing to do with the company.'

'What do you mean nothing? You're the company's sister-in-law, after all.' Shyamalendu tried to lighten the mood.

'The company's sister-in-law? Whatever for? I'm *your* sister-in-law.'

Dolon obviously wasn't angry anymore. She said, 'You've said nothing about how your sister-in-law is looking in this sari.'

'I dare not say it in your presence,' said Shyamalendu, 'I shall offer my opinion in private.'

'Stop joking. Have you noticed how lovely Didi is looking? She could easily get married again. Give us your opinion about her.' Tutul's response put everyone in a good mood.

'I can,' said Shyamalendu, who was driving, 'if your sister permits.'

'I am giving you permission on her behalf, sir,' Tutul said at once.

'My own words are inadequate, so I shall resort to the poet's.

'You are my love from Avanti
Your skin is like golden magnolia
Your voluptuous arrogant breasts
Can be contained by no bandeau
Laden by the weight of your loins
Your pace is gentle and indolent
Your blue lotus eyes throw glances
Fragile and torpid with desire.'

Tutul blushed but smiled. And Dolon, caught unawares in the presence of her sister, said in mock anger, 'Do you want me to push you out? These merchant officer people are really indecent, you know, Tutul.'

'Who wrote this Shyamal-da?'

'Guess.'

'Rabindranath?'

'Sharadindu Bandyopadhyay. I used to read him voraciously once upon a time. Everything has gone down the drain after turning into a hawker for a merchant office. I survive on memory alone, passing off quotes from the books I read years ago.'

In front of the managing director's house was a lawn with high walls around it. It was as though the lawn had a carpet of soft, fresh green grass laid on it. Tiny lights twinkled like fireflies all around. Soft lights. The specialists in Runu Sanyal's lamp division had put in a great deal of thought into the arrangements. Runu had said, 'The lights at cocktail parties are not meant to illuminate, they're only supposed to keep the darkness at bay. Soft sweet lighting allows people to get intimate.'

Runu was probably discussing just this with Mrs Ferris. Many of the guests had arrived. Spotting Shyamalendu, Ferris came up to him with his wife and shook his hand. Mrs Ferris welcomed Tutul warmly. 'I'm very happy you could make it.'

Shyamalendu disappeared somewhere in the crowd. Accepting a glass of tomato juice, Tutul said, 'How strange of Shyamal-da to run away.'

'That's the rule at these parties,' Dolon said. 'Everyone laughs at you if you stick to your wife. Your better half isn't going to vanish, they say, concentrate on drinking.'

Runu came up to them, as did Mrs Chopra with a glass of whiskey. Runu told her, 'Spare a glance for us too, Mrs Chopra, you look exquisite.'

'Don't lie so blatantly, Mr Sanyal.'

'I'm ready to submit an affidavit to a High Court judge to the effect that you look as dazzling as a hundred-watt Peters lamp. Wait, let me fetch Mr Chopra. It's impossible that he hasn't noticed.'

Runu did in fact bring Chopra, saying, 'Is it possible you haven't noticed how much lovelier your wife has become of late, Mr Chopra?'

Melting in delight, Mrs Chopra said, 'I might as well tell the truth, for the past six weeks I've been going to the new figure salon on Middleton Road. I know Mrs Kaur, who runs it, she has a beauty diploma from London. Very reasonable, just twenty rupees for half an hour.'

'I'm sure Mr Chopra has no objections, even though he's got us chained when it comes to office expenses. Mrs Chopra, please recommend us to your husband so that he relents a little at work.'

Everyone laughed, including Mr Chopra.

The Chopras drifted towards Gordon. From a distance Mrs Sanyal observed, 'What's the matter with her? She's wearing the same violet sari she wore to the last party. Violet may be the MD's favourite colour, but still.'

Many of the women had noticed this. Tutul was astounded at Mrs Sanyal's memory. 'These parties are tests for the officers,' Dolon whispered to her sister. 'The bosses examine how social each of them is. The wives help their husbands as much as possible.'

'But Didi, how can anyone remember the dresses the guests wore the last time?' Tutul asked.

'The wives of those who are ambitious and want to rise quickly have special notebooks. They have to maintain a list of the top bosses they have met socially and note down the colour of the saris they wore on each occasion, so that they don't repeat their outfits.'

'Good god, Didi!' Tutul couldn't contain her surprise. Dolon said, 'If you throw a party at home, you also have to note down the names of the guests and the menu. Let's say Mr Davidson goes to Runu Sanyal's place for dinner and has mulligatawny soup, tandoori chicken with naan, and fruit salad. The next time he's invited, you have to be careful not to have the same menu. Or take, for instance, the fact that Mrs Gordon is allergic to prawn but Mr Gordon loves it; so you have to be sure that Mrs Gordon is in the UK when you invite Mr Gordon home for dinner.'

'Stop, Didi, my head is spinning. I have to tell all my friends in Patna they have no chance of marrying covenanted officers. It needs special training.'

'Don't be silly, there's nothing women can't do under pressure. Everything turns out fine, you just have to be eager enough to learn,' Dolon reassured her sister.

Mrs Sengupta had come up to them. The poor thing was in trouble, for she didn't know English very well. The older, well-meaning woman felt uncomfortable at these gatherings. Now she breathed a sigh of relief on being able to join Dolon. 'Big mistake not to have learnt English. They don't respect you.'

'Why do you say that, Mashima?' Tutul said, 'You know your own language perfectly well. Why, Japanese women are not embarrassed because they don't know English!'

'I understand Mrs Sengupta's difficulties,' Dolon said. 'You know, Tutul, India will never be Japan.'

'Might have helped if it did, Didi. All these important Americans and Britishers and Germans would have apologised for not knowing our language,' Tutul said bluntly.

'We're slightly different from the others in the company,' Mrs Sengupta said, 'we don't go to too many parties because it will affect the children's studies.'

Dolon said, 'Mr Sengupta can afford to avoid parties because he knows his subject inside out. And every boss fears Company Law. But it's different for the rest, they not only have to do their work but also have to pander to the bosses. That's the unwritten law in merchant offices.'

'I'm ready to work hard,' said Tutul, 'but why do I have to pander to them?'

'This is why Bengalis are such failures,' Mrs Sengupta said. 'Most of them are so sentimental that they refuse to consider this aspect of employment.'

'Everyone's worried when a new white man turns up,' said Dolon. 'What does he like eating? What's his favourite colour? What are the things he's interested in?'

'What business is it of yours?'

'What do you mean? What will our husbands talk about at parties? The previous MD Mr Boylan was interested in architecture. What do the managers in a merchant office know of architecture? So they bought expensive books right away and started reading up on India's temple architecture. Then things became difficult when Mr Boylan was replaced by Mr Ferris. It was impossible to tell what he was interested in. Everyone was anxious. One day we found Mr and Mrs Jain discussing dogs with the MD. I found three or four books about dogs in the Jains' seventh-floor flat. But I had never known them to buy books. Mrs Jain is a special friend of mine, so I cornered her. She told me in confidence that both Mr and Mrs Ferris were keen on dogs. How did you know, I asked. Mrs Jain said it was her sister's husband who had suggested how to investigate. Ask to use the toilet, he said. Women are usually taken to the bathroom attached to the master bedroom. As you're passing through the bedroom take a quick look at the books arranged near the head of the bed, that's where white people keep their favourite books. It was very easy after this, there were at least three or four books about dogs on the bedside table.'

Mrs Sengupta exclaimed, 'Oh! I was wondering why all the officers of Hindustan Peters had suddenly developed an interest in dogs.'

Their conversation was interrupted by Mrs Jain herself joining them. Gordon followed soon after. Lighting Mrs Jain's cigarette, he said, 'Splendid weather today.' He announced he was enjoying every moment of the party and hoped that the beautiful ladies were doing the same.

Having spotted Gordon from afar, Janardanam from accounts made a beeline for him. 'How are you, Janardanam?' Gordon said.

'Very well, thank you, Mr Gordon. But I'm in trouble with our new invoicing system.' Janardanam was about to launch into a detailed discussion to demonstrate how conscientious he was about his work.

But Gordon wriggled out. 'I have no objection to talking about work outside the office, but I charge ten rupees a minute for it,' he joked.

'In which case may I meet you tomorrow?' Janardanam said.

'Whenever you like. Do check with my secretary on the phone whether I'm available.'

But even if their white bosses were averse to the idea, the Indians discussed their work to their hearts' content. Many of them were not especially aware of the world beyond the office, other than the racecourse and clubs. Their wives, however, discussed prices of food, the poor quality of made-in-India cosmetics and, in one or two cases, English films. And servants! Where were things headed, given how lazy the servants in Calcutta had become? There was no difference of opinion among them that discipline among domestic servants was going to the dogs.

Mithu Sen had probably had a drink too many. Coming up to the ladies, he said, 'I must have got out of the wrong side of the bed this morning, Mrs Chatterjee, I've had nothing but tongue-lashings. I was at the Las Vegas bar in the afternoon for a creative discussion with Ms Nargolwala from the agency. Khokon Basu, the artist, was several drinks down, you know what he said in his drunken haze? That the high-ranked officers in flats have acquired the qualities that were exclusive to the lowlife in slums, who don't go to school or college, use foul language, play on the streets, get drunk, and beat up their wives. Khokon Basu had the audacity to scream that the people in suits in the new industrial society do exactly the same thing. I would have punched him if Ms Nargolwala hadn't stopped me. Then Mr Chatterjee didn't clear the ad for exports. And here, too, no one's got time for me. Even my wife has disappeared somewhere in the crowd, I can't find her.'

Dolon probably felt sorry for Mithu Sen in his tipsy state. She said, 'I'll go look for your wife, she was chatting with Mr Sanyal just a short while ago. I don't know about the ad for exports, but I'll ask my husband. And that Khokon Basu is really uncivilised, of all people in the world, imagine finding fault with high-ranked officers. It's all this jealousy that's holding our race back.'

They left the cocktail party around ten-thirty. 'Did you enjoy that, Tutul?' Dolon asked in the car.

'I didn't feel like I was in India, I felt transported far away to England or America,' Tutul answered without smiling.

'Your colleagues' wives have many qualities—they're pretty, they can drink, they can dance,' Dolon told her husband.

Shyamalendu smiled. Tutul asked, 'Didi, why was everyone fawning over Mr Ferris and Mr Gordon and Mr Murthy?'

'They're directors, after all. If they're appeased the world is appeased.'

'You didn't point out Mr Sharma to me though, Shyamal-da. The one who locked his father in a room during a party so that his image wouldn't be spoilt,' Tutul said.

'Oh he was there, all right, sticking to the MD like a leech,' Shyamalendu said.

'Locking your father in a room or introducing your mother in English as a maid are things that many people do. It was just poor Sharma who got caught,' Dolon added.

Changing the subject, she asked Shyamalendu, 'But what's happened to you? You were in a good mood when we went to the party, but then you got into a huddle with

Ferris in a corner and began to look grim. Like you weren't enjoying yourself anymore.'

'Nothing like that.' Avoiding giving an answer, Shyamalendu began to drive.

12

At the office, Shyamalendu had been immersed in work since the morning. But his eyes kept drifting to the calendar, where the number fifteen reminded him of the date on which the company would have to pay a compensation of five million rupees.

But who would know from looking around the office? From the celebrations and dancing at the managing director's party last night, who could say that Hindustan Peters was confronted with a crisis that could explode like a time bomb on the fifteenth and shake the very foundations of the company?

Around three in the afternoon, Harihar Talukdar came out of the managing director's room looking quite worried. His expression changed as he walked along the corridor. Two and two were beginning to add up to four.

Entering Shyamalendu's room, he sat down in a chair. The beads of perspiration that had appeared on his bald pate despite the air-conditioning showed how agitated he was. Shyamalendu said calmly, 'Take it easy, Mr Talukdar, why do you look so worried?'

'Serious trouble, sir. Tension in the factory. There was an uproar in the canteen during lunch—apparently the pieces of fish were smaller than usual. Since we are the fire-brigade, I had to rush to the spot—no time for my own lunch.'

Expressing his regret, Shyamalendu asked whether Talukdar had managed to eat later.

'Forget about eating. The workers' attitude didn't seem right to me. So after returning from the fan factory I went straight to the MD to give him a report. But he said he'd be busy—that I should report as all matters of the fan factory to you. Has he told you something like this?'

'Yes, I've got the order,' Shyamalendu answered gravely.

Harihar Talukdar crumpled in despair. Sighing, he said, 'All my life I've worked directly under the MD. And now fate has this in store for me a year and a half before I'm about to retire. Please don't mind, sir, I'm telling you only because you're a Bengali. After all, one Bengali will never eat the flesh of another.'

Talukdar had all but broken down. Shyamalendu gave him some time to recover. Talukdar said, 'Is there going to be a formal order, sir?'

'Not at the moment, you mustn't worry,' Shyamalendu answered.

'We go back to the British era, sir. Disciplined soldiers, all of us. Whatever else you may accuse me of, it can never be of disobedience.'

''Tell me about the factory now,' Shyamalendu said, signing some letters.

'That business of the size of the fish, sir. The workers swore at me in filthy language. My father had chosen Harihar as my name, but you know what they called me? Hardhearted bastard Talukdar.'

'Keep your eye on the situation. For all you know it's a temporary matter, everything will be all right tomorrow.'

'May your words come true. I will keep you informed constantly. But Ramalingam has already told me Venus is in Capricorn, the sun isn't beneficial for me. Still, because Mercury and Saturn are powerful I won't come to harm, Mercury protects me, Mr Chatterjee.'

The news spread soon afterwards. Whispered discussions erupted in glass cubicles, 'Is Shyamalendu Chatterjee's new responsibility a reward or punishment?'

Everyone expressed their opinion on the matter—the Indian officers over the internal phone network, the clerks in the bathroom, and the bearers near the staircase.

Runu Sanyal made a phone call immediately. 'It's me, Bibi, hot news.' Then he reported the whole thing in detail to his wife. 'What do you think?'

'I think it's the beginning of the end.'

'So do I. They'll probably give him some meaningless work related to labour and slowly take him away from marketing. I told you, remember, it's one thing to have been first-class first in English at Patna University, and quite another to be a marketing executive at a British company. As for the white men, they've also been touched by socialism. Imagine hiring any Tom, Dick or Harry's son for the management cadre without checking on his family background. Socialism is one thing, running a merchant office quite another.'

Mrs Sanyal concurred with her husband on the matter of blue blood. Her father was the No. 2 at Williamson Magor's tea gardens before retiring. 'My father used to say it's management policy to ensure every Indian is threatened by another one. They like you so much but still they've put a monkey on your back.'

'You should have worked as an attorney, Bibi. Your legal acumen is remarkable.'

'I didn't get around to telling you last night, Runu. Chatterjee had some disagreement with Mr Ferris. After that your friend was down in the mouth all evening.'

'What do you think will be the outcome if he's moved out of the fans division, Bibi?' Runu Sanyal wanted his wife's opinion.

'You will have to take on more responsibility. You're the sponge who can absorb all the pressure.'

'It's still top secret,' Runu warned his wife.

'I can talk to Ranga Mashima if you like.'

'Not yet Bibi—after all, she's the wife of a retired ICS officer.'

'All right, all right. And listen, please don't get food on your coral ring.'

The next day brought even more drama. Harihar rushed to Shyamalendu's office, panting with excitement. 'Switch on the red light, sir. Incendiary situation.'

'What do you mean?'

'Things might explode at the fan factory any moment. Apparently the fish pieces were even smaller today. Some of the fish was smelly.'

'Smelly?'

'They're alleging the fish was rotten. We denied it vehemently.'

'And then?'

'They're doing horrible things, sir. They ate the fish and then deposited the bones on my labour officer's desk. It's enough to make you throw up, sir. And the slogans—down with the company, take the hardhearted bastard's head.'

'What about production?' Shyamalendu asked.

'Lower than usual, sir.'

'Go-slow?'

'Not exactly go-slow, it's still go-medium. I can consult our attorney Mr Boral of Lion and Boral if you'd like me to, sir.'

Shyamalendu looked grim. 'Do whatever you consider necessary, but I want to make it clear that it is not the company's policy to tolerate any breach of rules.'

'I agree a hundred and ten per cent with you, sir. I have asked for a list of those who said take the hardhearted bastard's head—if required, I'll file a police report tomorrow. I've prepared the chargesheet. Their leaders are so foul-mouthed they refer to chargesheets as shitcharges.'

Over the next few days things became even more dire. Harihar rushed into Shyamalendu's room again and said, 'Switch on the red light, sir. This fish supplier is going to cause the downfall of the company. They've made the pieces so much smaller that this afternoon, after lunch, in protest, the workers smeared the walls of the manager's office with their food-soiled hands.

'I consulted Mr Boral of Lion and Boral. He said it's a clear breach of discipline. And, besides, the trade unions are making absurd demands. Union A wants two-hundred-gram fish pieces every day, at which Union B has asked for two pieces. And Union C's demand will drive you up the wall, they want meat and eggs in addition to fish.'

'What about production?' Shyamalendu asked grimly.

'Very bad. I'll give you the precise figures in a minute. And the slogans, I don't know where to start. Down with the company. Which is fine, workers say these things. But I'm in trouble. My wife already suffers from high blood pressure, she will collapse if she hears. Take both head and tail of the hardhearted bastard, they're saying.'

Expressing his concern on hearing that Harihar's wife was not well, Shyamalendu asked whether the company doctor was examining her regularly. 'Send her to a nursing home, if necessary, at company expense.'

'Never mind a nursing home, not even staying in paradise will reduce her blood pressure unless she stops worrying about me.' Glumly Harihar added, 'Young labour officers can't get married these days, sir. The girls' fathers turn away as soon as they hear of the boys' jobs.'

'Do you want to inform the police?' Shyamalendu asked.

'I went to them, sir. After all, taking a human being's head and tail amount to murder. But the police did not cooperate. They said, we know you're Harihar Talukdar; you have to prove you're Hardhearted Bastard. I asked them why they were adding legal complications. Everyone in the world knows I'm a hardhearted bastard. You know what the buggers said? Go make an affidavit in court stating you're Hardhearted Bastard.'

After a pause Harihar said, 'I suggest we serve the leaders with chargesheets. I've got them typed out, all ready.'

'Do that, what other choice do we have?' Shyamalendu conveyed his decision.

13

'Poor Tutul's visiting us for just a few days but you're doing nothing special for her,' Dolon complained. 'You're not even back home on time.'

'Now don't go saying I am sorry,' Tutul butted in.

'The sisters have conspired to shut me up,' Shyamalendu said.

'See the state I'm in, Tutul?' Dolon said. 'Never marry a commercial executive.'

'Is it right to blame the entire race of executives for the sins of one of them?' Shyamalendu said, laughing.

Tutul sided with her brother-in-law with feigned solemnity. 'Really Didi, you're confusing me completely. Don't marry a doctor, always messing about with pus and blood, devotes his time to patients, doesn't care for his wife. IAS sounds wonderful, but poorly paid. Besides, you'll spend the best years of your life rotting away in the boondocks. Now you're ruling out a covenanted officer too. Whom should I marry then, a lamppost?'

Shyamalendu burst into laughter. 'Excellent answer, Sudarshana. No matter what they say, every sister-in-law nurtures a constant flame of passion for her brother-in-law.'

'You've given Tutul no time, but I've been showing her around Calcutta as much as possible. My own sister after all, I can't use the office as an excuse to neglect her,' Dolon said without smiling.

'And what do you think about this life of ours, Tutul?' Shyamalendu asked.

'I read about it in a book from your shelves.'

'I can't read much nowadays, Tutul. I don't have the patience to go beyond five pages. I have no idea how I passed my MA examination. What did you read, Tutul?'

'I was reading some poetry. By Alan Dugan.'

'She didn't just read it, she translated it too.'

'He's written rather well about a tedious existence. Let me read it out to you:

Oh I got up and went to work
and worked and came back home
and ate and talked and went to sleep.
Then I got up and went to work
and worked and came back home
from work and ate and slept.
Then I got up and went to work
and worked and came back home
and ate and watched a show and slept.
Then I got up and went to work
and worked and came back home
and ate steak and went to sleep.
Then I got up and went to work
and worked and came back home
and ate and fucked and went to sleep.
Then it was Saturday, Saturday, Saturday!
Love must be the reason for the week!
We went shopping! I saw clouds!
The children explained everything!
I could talk about the main thing!
What did I drink on Saturday night
that lost the first, best half of Sunday?
The last half wasn't worth this "word".
Then I got up and went to work
and worked and came back home
from work and ate and went to sleep,
refreshed but tired by the weekend.'

'Fantastic!' said Shyamalendu. 'Send your translation to a magazine, call it "On seeing my brother-in-law".'

Dolon yawned. 'Let's go to bed.' She didn't care for the poem, it was quite vulgar.

In bed, Shyamalendu couldn't sleep. Dolon, however, had fallen asleep immediately.

Shyamalendu got up and went to the window. In the distance, far in the distance, the commercial neon lights on Chowringhee winked shamelessly at passers-by. The huge neon advertisement put up by Hindustan Peters was visible even at this distance. The word 'Peters' in indigo letters glowed steadily, beneath it the words 'fans' and 'lamps' lit up alternately. Fans lamps fans lamps fans lamps ... on, off, on, off.

'Not sleeping?' Shyamalendu was startled.

He hadn't noticed Dolon standing beside him.

'Headache?' Dolon asked.

'Funny feeling in my head.'

Dolon lovingly led Shyamalendu back to bed. 'Come, I'll massage it for you.'

Dolon ran her fingers over his forehead so well. It reminded Shyamalendu of his mother doing the same thing when he had a fever as a child.

Stroking his head with her soft fingers, Dolon said, 'Don't work so hard for the office, sweetheart.'

'I needn't, actually, Dolon,' Shyamalendu confessed like a child. 'But that Runu Sanyal pursues me like a bad star.'

'Let him be, don't worry about it.' Dolon soothed her husband.

'But I don't want to lose, Dolon.'

Shyamalendu could feel his eyes getting heavy with sleep.

14

Shyamalendu stared at the calendar on the wall. The fifteenth was four days away. The date glared back at Shyamalendu Chatterjee.

Harihar Talukdar rushed in to the room. 'The news from the factory is very bad, sir. Look where a small piece of fish has brought us. Fights breaking out between the two main workers' unions. The labour commissioner had sent for them. No one's going. Meanwhile, we just got the news—things have taken a serious turn. The third union, whom we don't recognise, the ones who want meat, eggs and fish, are squatting inside the factory now.'

'Production?' Shyamalendu asked grimly.

'Stopped. Do you want to talk to the factory manager?' Harihar asked.

'Get him on the phone, please. Since Mr Hartley is in Haryana, I might as well talk to him myself.'

After a conversation with the factory manager, Shyamalendu said, 'Let me discuss the situation with the MD. Give me a note quickly, Mr Talukdar. How many injured, what sort of damage to machinery, how much we're losing per day.'

'I'll send the note at once.' Talukdar added sadly, 'But they're so well paid. And very few factories have service conditions like ours.'

After a pause, he continued, 'Starting with the bearers and sweepers, no one at Hindustan Peters can put their hands on their hearts and claim they're worse off than employees of other companies. But look at what they've done for such a trivial reason. What is this age we're living in, sir? I don't blame anyone, but sometimes it feels like the entire race is suffering from malaria—even in the heat of summer they get bouts of shivering, the patients black out sometimes.'

Shyamalendu threw a glance at Talukdar but said nothing.

He went to meet the managing director as soon Talukdar's note arrived. The signal turned red outside Ferris's office.

Fifteen minutes later Shyamalendu came out and went directly to Talukdar's room to discuss the next steps and issue necessary instructions. 'I knew something like this would happen the moment Venus entered Capricorn,' a hapless Talukdar said. 'My Venus is descending.'

Talukdar's phone rang. He seemed shocked at what he was told. Covering the mouthpiece, he told Shyamalendu, 'Just what I was afraid of, bombs hurled at the factory gate. Our watchman Hira Singh has been injured.'

Shyamalendu could recollect Hira Singh. He would stand motionless outside the gate. An army man, he was discharged after injuring his leg in Bomdila during the 1962 war. He used to limp, and never spoke a word.

Hira Singh was an innocent man. Why was he attacked? 'The attempt was on the labour officer's life. But Hira Singh was injured.'

'What about arrangements for his treatment?' Shyamalendu asked. 'Get him the best possible medical care, money is no concern.'

'Don't worry,' Talukdar reassured him. 'He's been hospitalised. But it's not looking very hopeful yet.'

Shyamalendu wasn't feeling well. He suddenly felt dizzy. Talukdar looked at him. 'You are a well-educated gentlemen. You entered the world of industry by accident, you are bound to feel bad. I've been working with labour forces all my life, these things make no impression on me. This too is a jungle, sir, just that it's made of iron and steel instead of trees. No tigers here, but plenty of snakes and baboons and moles.'

Still Shyamalendu didn't respond. But Harihar didn't stop. 'Hold meetings, shout slogans, put up posters, file cases with the tribunal—but why resort to bloodshed? The poor are drinking the blood of the poor, you know, Mr Chatterjee. Our Major Thornie had grasped the situation long ago. The country was raging with the revolt of the Azad Hind Fauj. Major Thornie had told me, Talukdar, you're asking the English to leave the country, we probably will, too. But you won't be able to run this country, you'll be reduced to tears. But we won't return then, even if you beg us to.'

'Please find out about Hira Singh's treatment,' Shyamalendu said, getting Talukdar to leave.

He needed a drink. It was better to have a sip of whisky from the small bottle in his drawer rather than torture his nerves. Shyamalendu did just that.

Just then Mithu Sen burst into his room. 'We've found a beautiful model for our Urvashi fans. Both Ms Nargolwala and the photographer Victor Biswas are very excited. Plenty of sex appeal. The only question is, do we dress her like the Urvashi of the epics or in modern clothes like they show in the movies. Would you like to see a photograph?'

'No need to see any photographs, Mr Sen,' Shyamalendu said gravely. 'No need for the ad either, because the fans aren't going to Thailand now. We need a different ad instead—the fan factory is going to be closed from tonight. Because of violence between two factions of workers and acts of destruction, the authorities have been forced to announce the closure of the factory out of fear of damage to the machinery. Wait, let me send for Mr Talukdar.'

'I'll prepare the ad at once, it'll be in all the papers tomorrow. But we're very sorry about this. Ms Nargolwala is right, India has no future, especially West Bengal.'

Harihar came in with his file as soon as he received the call. He was in fine form today, the military was never valued unless war broke out.

'What are the points to be included in the ad for the lockout?' asked Mithu Sen.

'Not lockout but closure,' Harihar told him. 'Huge difference. One's temporary illness, the other's a death certificate. Works like an elixir. Lion and Boral had suggested a lockout. I refused. If it needs strong medicine, let it be the most powerful dose.'

'Let me send for Ms Nargolwala then, we'll have to write out the copy at once,' said Mithu Sen.

Harihar said with a big smile, 'Please don't mind, sir, but writing these advertisements is no child's play. The most formidable attorneys and barristers start sweating when they have to draft them. Mr Boral of Lion and Boral is a specialist, having ensured the closure of over a hundred and fifty companies. You don't have to worry. We've finalized the copy. They'll be printed in English, Bengali, and Hindi. Now listen.'

Harihar began to read.

'Workers and labourers are aware of the present circumstances prevailing at the fan-manufacturing factory situated at No. 510, Taratala Road. For some time now, workers and labourers have deliberately adopted go-slow-on-production tactics and have been indulging in destructive activities for trivial and irrelevant reasons. Workers and labourers are unwilling to follow the terms specified in their contracts. Security and discipline at the factory have been severely compromised.

'In view of the circumstances having gone beyond the control of the authorities, the directors have decided to close the factory with immediate effect.'

There was more. For instance: 'According to the provisions in Section 25FFF the Industrial Disputes Act of 1947, workers and labourers have the right to receive compensation in case of retrenchment; their other pending dues, if any, will also be cleared, etc.'

Mithu Sen was about to leave with the sheet of paper when Shyamalendu said, 'Oh yes, Mr Sen, please send me five clippings of the ads from the newspapers tomorrow morning. I will have to file them.'

Runu Sanyal rang his residence soon afterwards. 'I have news, Bibi,' he said. 'Massacre in the fan factory. No sooner had he taken on the responsibility than the factory's shut down. And Shyamalendu seems to have made a mess of exports too. The products are ready but they're not going on the ship. The ad that was to announce the exports has been cancelled.'

'Will they keep him on in sales?' Bibi asked.

'First let's see whether the wicket lasts,' Runu Sanyal said with great joy.

15

'Shyamal-da?' Sudarshana was calling him. 'What are you thinking about? Why haven't you switched on the balcony lights?'

'Sit down,' Shyamalendu said gravely. 'Nothing in particular—I'm not in fact thinking of anything, Tutul.'

'When we came in and found the apartment dark we thought you weren't back yet,' Sudarshana said.

'I was disappointed not to see you here when I got in. Just managed to take a shower and now I'm sitting here chain-smoking,' Shyamalendu said.

What he didn't reveal was the fact that he had been to the hospital on his way home.

Talukdar had tried to stop him, but Shyamalendu didn't pay attention. Bandaged from the neck downwards, Hira Singh recognised him immediately. He tried to raise his hand in a salute but was prevented by his bandages. He was being given a blood transfusion. His wife sat near the door with their young son in her arms.

'What's that in the glass? You weren't like this before. I've never seen you drinking alone,' Dolon said, sounding hurt. She had lost face with her sister.

Shyamalendu evaded the question. 'Where did you go?' he asked.

'It was flag day for Siliguri Homes, remember? That's what we were doing in the morning, I got Tutul to collect money too. She collected more than me, you know.'

'No wonder, who would say no to someone like her?' Shyamalendu tried to lighten up.

'Then we deposited the box and went to the special jam session at Trincas in the afternoon. Tutul should see what today's young people are up to.'

'Oh Shyamal-da, you can keep your young Park Street society. Boys turning into girls, girls into boys. And some of them made me want to laugh; they're neither girls nor boys.'

'Finally you're getting an idea about Calcutta,' Shyamalendu said solemnly.

'Yes, we went to College Street and the Coffee House. Saw bombs exploding in Bowbazar. Outside Sealdah Station I saw how people squat the whole day under the blazing sun with pumpkin slices or spinach bundles to earn thirty paise. On Council House Street outside the employment exchange I even saw the queues of unemployed young men. Saw how people go back home hanging on for dear life from trams and buses. And then the jam session, swinging Calcutta of the seventies.'

'And what do you make of it?' Shyamalendu said.

'Far from making anything of it, I'm only more confused, Shyamal-da. It's like a body suffering at the same time from both high blood pressure and low blood pressure, tuberculosis and cancer, obesity and malnutrition. Our economics textbooks have nothing on such cases. Have you made anything of it?' Tutul said.

'Trying to make sense of it is bewildering, Tutul. Merchant office employees like us are safe, Tutul, we don't even try to understand. Our vision and responsibilities are limited, we only supply goods according to orders. Some of us say that those who are trying to bring about a revolutionary social change are actually envious, that they would have joined us had they got the opportunity, what's causing them heartburn is that they cannot be like us, which is why they say we're useless, that the capitalists are keeping us happy with lollipops.'

'I'm taking your glass away,' Dolon admonished Shyamalendu. 'Instead of drinking alone why don't you start reading and writing again? You were such a good student, you wrote so well, I remember all the new ideas you had, Baba had such expectations from you.'

Shyamalendu sat silently for a while. Then said, 'My mother used to say drinking milk after eating meat isn't safe. It's best not to have original thoughts when you work in a merchant office.'

Tutul and Dolon drew up wicker stools and sat down. 'We are sorry, Shyamal-da,' said Tutul, 'we heard about your factory.'

'Where did you hear the news?'

'From your chauffeur,' said Dolon. 'Apparently there's another rumour too, that they'll move you out of sales.'

'All this talk of ill luck! I scolded him,' Tutul said.

'You're unhappy about what's going on, aren't you Tutul?' Shyamalendu asked her.

'Naturally,' Dolon said. 'Remember how cheerful she was when she came to visit us? On top of the world. And now you come home late every day, you keep brooding.'

'Do you see me brooding? Not at all,' said Shyamalendu. 'My guru Mr Menon used to say the ideal officer will never be overwhelmed, neither by joy nor by sorrow. I'm a first-generation executive, so adjusting to this is causing me some pain. Raja won't face this problem.'

'Should I tell Shyamal-da then, Didi?' Tutul asked.

'Yes, do,' Dolon said.

'I got a letter from Baba, Shyamal-da. I've passed the IAS examination. They've called me to Delhi for an interview. I'm thinking of going directly from Calcutta.'

Shyamalendu leapt to his feet. 'Cruel, cunning woman, you hid it from me all this time!'

'I rang you as soon as we heard,' said Dolon. 'But you were with the MD.'

'Wonderful news! Tutul, my dearest, I feel like dancing with joy,' Shyamalendu said. 'When is the interview?'

'Still a few days to go,' Dolon said.

'Very well, you shall go from Calcutta. But you must keep my request, dear girl. You will fly to Delhi at my expense, and your sister will escort you. I'd have come along too, but I won't get leave right now.'

'Why waste money, Shyamal-da? The Public Service Commission will pay my train fare,' Tutul said.

'I don't want to hear another word, Tutul. I'm so happy, you must allow me to celebrate.'

'Oh, all right then,' Tutul said. 'Baba's so blind about you he's already written, do as Shyamalendu suggests.'

'Now it's time to fight.' Shyamalendu was back in his element. 'When did you take the exam secretly, you didn't tell us? We talked about so many things, but not a leak! Who says women can't keep secrets?'

'I took the exam on a whim,' Tutul said. 'I didn't expect to get through, which is why I was embarrassed to tell anyone. Other than Ma and Baba, nobody knew.'

'You'll be a district magistrate, won't you?' Dolon said.

'Followed by deputy secretary, joint secretary, secretary, and even governor. When she's posted in Delhi, our Mr Murthy might prostrate himself at Sudarshana Bhattacharya's feet. So much power. The king might change but the king's officers don't. Surely Rabindranath wrote that line, 'They work on the ruins of hundreds of kingdoms', about civil servants. He certainly didn't have labourers in mind.'

After a pause, Shyamalendu said, 'I'm feeling really happy, Tutul.'

'Wait, let's not count our chickens ...' Tutul said.

'I'd love to go to Delhi with her,' Dolon said. 'But considering your situation ...'

'What situation? This is par for the course now. The usual sequence of events will unfold. The factory's closed down—some will starve, some will sell their wives' jewellery, some will go to moneylenders, one or two sensitive people will hang themselves because they cannot feed their children, some will go back to their villages and start farming again, some will deliver provocative speeches at the factory gates, some will get into trams and buses and hold collection boxes under passengers' noses, some will get into fights and die, and then one day everything will be all right again. The factory will reopen its doors.'

Shyamalendu realised he had lost control after a few drinks. Slamming on the brakes, he said, 'Don't worry, Dolon, there's still time.'

The doorbell rang. Dolon went to the door to discover Runu Sanyal and his wife.

'How nice to see you,' she welcomed them.

Shyamalendu joined them. 'What a lovely surprise,' he said.

'What would you like?' Dolon asked.

'Coffee, please,' said Mrs Sanyal.

'And you?' Shyamalendu said. 'Gin? Whiskey? Rum?'

'A gin and lime, please, in that case.'

Taking a sip of his gin, Runu said, 'What's all this I hear, my friend? Has your fan factory really closed down?'

'No choice,' Shyamalendu replied.

Runu said, 'I felt very bad when I heard. There's just the two Bengalis, you and I, surviving in this huge organisation, and now this. I didn't want to bother you in the office, people would notice and assume the Bengalis were being clannish again. So we came here directly. Bibi also said Mrs Chatterjee must be very worried, let's pay them a visit.'

'There's not much I can do,' Dolon said.

'That's not true, Mrs Chatterjee,' said Bibi Sanyal. 'The wives of executives in commercial firms have tremendous responsibilities. Didn't Mr Ferris say the other day at the party, behind every successful officer there is undoubtedly a great woman.'

Dolon said, 'At the wedding he swore to provide food and clothing for me with the sacred fire as his witness. Why should I poke my nose into his affairs?'

'Oh my god,' Shyamalendu exclaimed.

'I'm not joking, Mrs Chatterjee,' said Bibi, 'but many companies also interview the wives of candidates for senior positions. It's essential.'

'In that case no one will hire you,' Dolon told her husband.

'We should be paid too,' Mrs Sanyal said. 'They make our husbands slave all day and return these irritable creatures to us in the evening. And then we nurse them back to health to ensure they're fit for work the next morning. Aren't we doing it for the company?'

'What do you think will happen now?' Runu asked Shyamalendu.

Shyamalendu didn't divulge any information. 'Whatever has to happen will happen, speculation won't help.'

Before the guests left, Dolon said, 'Thank you so much. It's only in bad times that you know who your friends are.'

'If we don't even do this, what's the point of identifying ourselves as Bengalis?' Mr and Mrs Sanyal said on their way out.

16

The news had spread everywhere. Mithu Sen was even getting phone calls from newspapers. Like a gramophone record he kept saying, 'A terrible thing to have happened. It's not just the lost production—our fans were about to be exported when this happened. A loss of valuable foreign exchange. Our fans are useful for defence too—not on the battlefield, of course, but in military offices and barracks.'

Everyone rushed about. Shyamalendu was seen entering and leaving the managing director's office several times.

There were all sorts of rumours. Chandranath, the typist in Runu Sanyal's department, told the others in the bathroom, 'The news isn't good at all. An important wicket is about to fall. You can guess who. Those who want to score quick runs at Hindustan Peters are more likely to get run out. You know what I mean?'

Harihar Talukdar was extraordinarily busy. He was not to be found at his desk most of the time, he was more likely to be in Shyamalendu Chatterjee's cabin.

With a triumphant roar he told Shyamalendu, 'They've softened. As the disease, so the medicine. The leaders weren't expecting us to drop an atom bomb. They must have gone crying to the minister. There's no other reason for these constant requests from the labour commissioner for tripartite discussions.'

'The company's always ready for discussions, as I've told you,' Shyamalendu said.

'World War II would not have taken place if Chamberlain hadn't buttered up Hitler so much,' Talukdar told Shyamalendu. 'It's the policy of appeasement that's taking India backwards. Even Napoleon installed cannons on the streets of Paris to control the crowds. Pay heed to what this poor man says, sir. Let the closure go on for another month. We shall not join discussions so easily.'

'That won't seem right. You must go for the tripartite discussion. You can say we will continue to serve one piece of fish, and we'll ensure it's not small or rotten. But everyone will have to maintain discipline; production must not fall.'

During the next few days Talukdar whirled about between the labour commissioner, the office of Lion and Boral, the counsel's chamber, and Shyamalendu's cabin.

Dolon rang Shyamalendu. 'Any news?'

'Looks like things will be settled. The unions have refused to discuss things with Harihar. So I'll have to join the tripartite talks.'

'See if you can get it settled, we leave the day after tomorrow. I'll be so relieved if things are sorted out by then.'

'I'm off to the meeting right now, let's see what happens.'

The agreement was finalised the same afternoon. The company was withdrawing the closure of the factory unconditionally, but the workers had also given their word to maintain production levels. No action would be taken against any of the workers. For now, one piece of fish would continue to be served, but the demand for two pieces would be sent to the tribunal if necessary. The union leaders shook hands with Shyamalendu, but not with

Talukdar. 'He's the root of all trouble, there wouldn't have been such a quick settlement if you hadn't stepped in,' they told Shyamalendu.

On the way back in the car Talukdar said, 'I don't care whether they shake hands with me or not, but my wife's blood pressure will drop at least. Even yesterday they rang her at home and said we want both head and tail of the hardhearted bastard.'

Meanwhile the factory workers took out a victory march. Harihar Talukdar burst into laughter at the sight. 'Have you seen a bigger joke? Even after a resounding defeat they're trying to convince their people that they've won.'

'No individual or group or nation can survive once they lose their self-esteem, Mr Talukdar,' Shyamalendu said solemnly.

'If you don't mind, Mr Chatterjee, you're spouting these lines from books written by white men. What I have realised from spending my entire life in this jungle of rusted iron is that human beings are swine. The pig within must be fed sometimes and beaten up at other times. That's the only way to keep humans under control.'

Although he was annoyed, Shyamalendu said, 'How will I live if I hate my fellow humans so much, Mr Talukdar? We can talk about this in detail one day.'

Suddenly he recalled the injury to the watchman. 'How is Hira Singh now, Mr Talukdar?'

'All these meetings left me with no time to enquire. I'll pay a visit to the hospital today since you're asking. I believe the doctors have found he has diabetes, or else he would have recovered and returned home by now.'

Dolon was delighted to hear of the settlement. 'I'm going to Kalighat to offer prayers right now. Oh, I'm so relieved.'

17

Sir Baren Ray's car came to a halt outside Hindustan Peters soon after lunch. Sengupta welcomed him in the visitors' room. 'How are you, sir?'

'Very well, thank you. Frequent board meetings these days.'

'The company's growing, we need your advice constantly,' Sengupta said. 'We're lucky you could attend at such short notice.'

Kumar Jagadish also arrived, all the way from Uluberia. Then Ferris made an appearance, flanked by Gordon and Murthy. All of them went into the boardroom.

The meeting began. The first ten items were passed easily. Then the subject of worker disaffection at the factory came up. 'Fortunately, we did not suffer great losses. Factory operations will return to normal from tomorrow.'

It was Ferris himself who brought up the final item of the meeting.

'I propose that Mr Shyamalendu Chatterjee be appointed a whole-time additional director of the company, subject to government approvals, etcetera etcetera.'

Sir Baren Ray had nodded off, but he sat upright on hearing this. Then he followed the others in raising his hand in approval.

Sengupta escorted the newly appointed director to the room. Ferris rose from his chair to shake hands with Shyamalendu, and then formally introduced him to the rest of the board.

Shaking his hand, Sengupta said, 'Remarkable! You must know magic. Mr Ferris gave me the news this morning, I was astonished. I've never known anyone to become a director so young at this company.'

Now Ferris got hold of Shyamalendu and took him into his room.

Far from bubbling with joy, Shyamalendu looked as though someone had smeared his face with ink when he emerged from Ferris's office. He felt as though he had been bitten by a poisonous insect.

Ferris had dictated the circular about Shyamalendu's elevation to the board. The news would be all over the office soon. But instead of receiving congratulatory handshakes and phone calls at his desk, Shyamalendu couldn't bear to be in his office. He rose to his feet, collecting the key to the bathroom.

Shyamalendu locked the door. He was alone in the bathroom now. The fluorescent light above the mirror was on, he switched it off.

He had not been unhappy before all of this happened. He was a director of the company now, which was all very well, but Ferris had reminded him of the ugly circumstances in which it had happened. What Shyamalendu had done in secret, what he had not even allowed himself to acknowledge, was just what the managing director had brought up.

Shyamalendu could see Ferris now. He was saying, 'You have saved the company from a calamity, Chatterjee. It was you who discovered the clause that the company was not bound to pay compensation if the factory was shut down due to a strike or lockout or closure. When you suggested the plan I had no idea we could close the factory honourably by fomenting worker trouble through the simple expedient of serving smaller pieces of fish and winning over a few of the labourers. We have saved six million rupees, the components have arrived from England, and we can despatch the export consignment this month.'

Ferris was holding out his hand to shake Shyamalendu's. He could hear the managing director saying, 'No one can say we have done anything illegal. We only took advantage of a situation in which anyone can spark trouble among factory workers.'

Legality isn't everything, Shyamalendu reflected to himself, soaping his hands. Not everything that's just or unjust in the world lies in the domain of the courts. There's something else besides the law. What Mr Menon used to call morality.

What had happened to Shyamalendu? Not even the touch of cold water on his face could bring him any relief. He wished he could plunge his face in ice so that no one could see him.

Dolon had to be informed. She jumped with joy as soon as she heard. 'Really! Director!'

'The resolution was passed today, the application will go to the government tomorrow.' Shyamalendu couldn't speak anymore, he disconnected the call.

Another phone call was booked to Blue Haven from the Hindustan Peters office. It was Runu, saying wretchedly, 'Disaster, Bibi.'

His wife was shocked to hear the bad news. 'What? What are you saying? Should I go visit Notun Meshomoshai?'

'What can your uncle do. Should have got hold of a sister-in-law and pushed her into the arms of the bosses. It's too late now,' Runu sighed.

Bibi knew how her husband was feeling. 'Listen, darling,' she said, 'don't let anyone know how you feel. Go congratulate Chatterjee.'

'Over my dead body.'

'Don't be childish. When you're back home we'll go meet them together. I'm ordering flowers from New Market.'

Shyamalendu sat like a rock, silent. Menon's face kept floating up in front of his eyes. He was in Calcutta, Shyamalendu rang him. 'My first inspiration during my working life came from you, Mr Menon, so you're one of the first to know. I have become a director at Hindustan Peters. I request your blessings.'

Menon's voice sounded heavy. 'No blessings are necessary. Congratulations.'

'My father isn't alive, Mr Menon. You're like my father. I have a question. Is ambition wrong?'

Mr Menon laughed. 'You're still sentimental even after all these years of working at a merchant office. Why should ambition be wrong? Don't you remember what Joseph Conrad said? "All ambitions are lawful except those which climb upward on the miseries or credulities of mankind." The chariot of your ambition must not drive over the shoulders of the weak, the helpless, the ignorant.'

Shyamalendu ended the call. He was not feeling well at all, he kept asking himself why he couldn't have been like the people who were promoted to the post of director on the strength of their talent and efforts. What a horrifying thing he had done in his infatuation with his career, in his blind obsession!

Shyamalendu was about to leave when Harihar Talukdar burst in. 'Just got the good news. Please accept my sincere congratulations.'

Shaking his hand, Harihar said, 'I would have come with you to Blue Haven for sweets for Mrs Chatterjee, I wouldn't have taken no for an answer. But there's some last-minute trouble as always. Haven't I told you, even if there's peace in the industry there's never peace in the labour officer's life. That man who was in hospital, Hira Singh, died an hour ago. I've sent Das. What a time he chose to die, just when I have tickets for Metro cinema.'

Shyamalendu felt a cold hand gripping his heart. Hira Singh had died! The man who came away from Bomdila limping, here in Calcutta we ensured the rest of him perished too.

'Nothing to regret from the company's perspective,' Harihar said. 'We took full care of his medical treatment. But what can we do if he has diabetes, that's not our fault, after all.'

Harihar hadn't imagined Shyamalendu would be so distraught at the news. How will this man run the factory administration, he wondered. To Shyamalendu he said, 'Hira Singh himself admitted nobody arranges for such royal treatment.'

'But he is dead,' Shyamalendu said, his voice stricken.

Talukdar tried to make things easier for Shyamalendu. 'Of course it's a matter of great sadness, sir. His wife and children will be reassured by your feelings. But you know, those who take on the job of a watchman, who've been in the military before that—they know very well the risks they're taking. They pawn their lives to earn a living, their wife and children know it too. For all you know his grandfather and father also died in the first and second world wars. Dying is a habit for them.'

Shyamalendu wanted to go to the hospital at once, but Talukdar protested vehemently. The dead body would be sent for a post-mortem, after which the watch and ward staff would arrive. You never know, what if they began protesting? The sight of a company director would infuriate them further. When Shyamalendu insisted, Talukdar said, 'Very well, if it comes to that, I'll take you to the crematorium tomorrow. Meanwhile, I've ordered a wreath at New Market to be delivered on your behalf. In deep sympathy from Mr S Chatterjee, Director, it says. Since you're so upset, I'll make it a hundred-rupee wreath. And you can write a letter to his wife tomorrow, I have a draft approved by Lion and Boral. If the other watchmen are in a militant mood I'll declare on the spot that we'll hire Hira Singh's son as a bearer. All the cremation costs are ours too.'

Shyamalendu had no response to this. His powers of judgement seemed to have stopped working temporarily.

Dolon and Tutul were ready to leave for the airport. As soon as Shyamalendu entered, Tutul said effusively, 'Give me your hand, let me shake it. Are you a magician, Shyamal-da? A company director at this age! What will you do next?'

Even the innocent Sudarshana wanted to shake his hand. The same hand that the leaders of the workers had shaken. The same hand that Ferris had shaken a little while ago. Shyamalendu couldn't hold his hand out, it was too dirty for him to knowingly offer it to everyone.

Sidestepping Tutul, he went into his bedroom briefly. Dolon followed him inside and said, 'Let me give you something.' Then she kissed him passionately.

'But why do you look so pale? You're not ill are you?'

'Of course not, why should I be ill? We should leave, else you'll miss your flight.'

As they sped along VIP Road towards Dumdum Airport, Dolon said, 'I'm so happy, first your news, and then if things work out for Tutul.'

'No one can come in the way of things working out for Tutul,' Shyamalendu said.

'My first choice is the foreign service,' said Tutul, 'then the administrative service, then the IRS.'

'Why on earth do you want to leave the country? Doesn't the foreign service mean living abroad?' Dolon said. 'Aren't you going to marry, Tutul?'

Gazing at the Calcutta she was leaving behind, Tutul said, 'I've seen for myself the problems of being the wife of a merchant office executive. If I marry a teacher I'll starve. Far better to be self-sufficient and run away abroad. As a woman, my slogan is liberty, equality, fraternity.'

Shyamalendu felt there was a tinge of pain in Tutul's amusing response. At this point she may not have been joking at all, she may have been saying this specifically for her brother-in-law's benefit. Sadly, Shyamalendu said, 'Forget about Indian managers at merchant offices, to us liberty refers to Liberty shirts. Like the Peters fans, all of us are suspended from the ceiling, endlessly going round in circles in a limited space.'

Tutul was silent in response to her brother-in-law sounding so bitter suddenly.

But none of this could keep Dolon from being worried. 'Don't be childish,' she told her sister. 'IAS or company executive, women aren't complete without marriage.'

'And men are?' Tutul asked.

'You're arguing again, Tutul.'

'There's nothing preventing an IAS officer from getting married, Didi,' Tutul consoled her sister.

'Just as well you haven't chosen to marry anyone from the world we live in, Tutul. You have the freedom to choose someone from a new world, from a new environment. Don't forget to invite us for the wedding feast though.'

Tutul blushed in embarrassment. She realised Shyamalendu was not joking either. Turning to him, she said, 'Calm the director's wife down, Shyamal-da. Your sister-in-law promises not to do anything that will disgrace either of you.'

'You've turned so serious as soon as you've become a director,' Dolon said.

She couldn't keep still in her happiness and excitement, she didn't know what she should do first. In the airport lounge she said, 'Where will we live, Alipur Road or Burdwan Road? I like Burdwan Road more.'

The flight was announced. 'Time to go, Shyamal-da,' said Tutul.

She walked on ahead. In the corridor Dolon said like a little girl, 'I'm going to write to Baba tonight. He's always known you'd be successful on the strength of your own talent and hard work. How come they made you a director so quickly? You must have done *very* good work.'

Shyamalendu suddenly felt dizzy. About to say something, he stopped. 'Something you wanted to say?' Dolon asked.

Shyamalendu couldn't say what he wanted to. He stood like a statue, his entire body turning numb. 'Listen to me, Dolon,' he wanted to shout. But where was she? She had disappeared on the tarmac.

Shyamalendu's right hand felt as though it had been singed by a red-hot iron bar. He felt isolated, orphaned. But what had he done that was so wrong? And no one besides Ferris had realised anyway. From the union leaders to his sister-in-law, everyone wanted him to give them his hand, his right hand. No one wanted to know what was on his mind.

But the bearded English poet William Shakespeare had made an appearance again, glaring at him. Shyamalendu could have got rid of the intruder, but he said, you cashed in on me one day to get your job with Hindustan Peters.

Sipping a whiskey in the airport restaurant, Shyamalendu whispered to the invisible man, 'Please don't mutter your lines in my ear. Don't disturb me. I'm sitting in a corner of the morgue looking at Hira Singh. The doctors have cut open his body to investigate the cause of death. His newly widowed wife is weeping on the floor back home.'

Still the bearded man refused to hear. He had come up even closer to mumble something. Distinctly annoyed, Shyamalendu said, 'Your impertinence knows no bounds, how dare you violate the privacy of a Hindustan Peters' director? If you want to recite lines from your plays go to my former teacher Batukeshwar Bhattacharya.'

Still the man declaimed dramatically in Shyamalendu's ear, 'Cromwell I charge thee, fling away ambition; by that sin fell the angels.'

'Just you wait, I'm calling everyone. Waiter, waiter!' Shyamalendu screamed. A waiter ran up and said, 'You've been here long enough, sir, time to go home.'

Shyamalendu's chauffeur Srishtidhar had been waiting for hours outside the airport with the company car. Now he saw Shyamalendu return staggering. He has had one too many at the airport restaurant, Srishtidhar thought to himself.

Driving at high speed along the dark, deserted VIP Road, Srishtidhar discovered his sir was sobbing.

With his hand on the gear shift, he considered asking what the matter was. But the very next moment he remembered that Shyamalendu had become a company director today. Srishtidhar wasn't highly educated, but he knew people wept sometimes in joy. He decided not to disturb Shyamalendu.

Consumed by the primal desire to overtake the car in front of him, Srishtidhar flashed his headlights and stepped on the accelerator.

Unlimited

1

The chapter that began a short while ago in Kamalesh Roychowdhury's life could easily be titled 'Just After the Wedding Night'. Barely a few hours had passed since the long-awaited electrifying and radical experience. There could be no logical reason to see him shifted from a bed of pleasure to a train compartment in Howrah Station.

But it was a fact that the handsome, thirty-two-year-old Kamalesh Roychowdhury was sitting in a first-class comparment of the Howrah–Chandanpur Express, looking out of the window. He had been enriched by a novel experience last night—why then was his face creased in exasperation?

Kamalesh was taller than the average Bengali. Once Sutapa had rung him to ask, 'What's your height, Kamalesh?'

'How strange, did you actually make a trunk call from Calcutta to Chandanpur just to find out my height?'

'You talk too much, Kamalesh. You know very well we have only three minutes. Tell me quickly,' Sutapa requested from Calcutta.

'Why do you need to know my height?' Curious, Kamalesh asked with some surpise.

Finally, Sutapa let the cat out of the bag. 'I have to pass on some information about you to the mother of a beautiful girl, mister. The girl is adamant about not marrying anyone who isn't tall.'

'All right then, one point eight metres,' Kamalesh told Sutapa.

'Come on, Kamalesh. How do you expect a soft-hearted young girl as sweet as ice-cream to gauge her future husband in metres and centimetres?'

'Then write it down in kilogrammes, I weighed myself yesterday,' Kamalesh joked. 'Sixty-six kilos. You do know that Imperial measures have been replaced by the metric system?'

Sutapa said, 'You have no idea what you're missing out on with your kilos. The girl is a master's student of history, she doesn't get mathematics. Tell me your height. Five-eleven?'

She was right. 'How did you guess?' asked Kamalesh.

Ever-ready with her repartee, Sutapa said, 'Simple enough. I just had to compare you to my husband. He's five-eight, and you're about three inches taller.'

When Sutapa returned to Chandanpur, Kamalesh had told her, 'Hats off to modern women. In the olden days girls didn't even know their husbands' names before the wedding, they didn't dare ask. These days they're checking up on their vital statistics. And after marriage, you people don't even allow your husbands to grow.'

'What do you mean?' Sutapa feigned anger and demanded an explanation.

Pointing to Subhashish, Kamalesh had said, 'He's the same height that he was before he married you, five feet eight.'

'And has the world come to an end because of this?' The debater in Sutapa tried to corner Kamalesh, whom she thought of as her brother, as she placed a cup of tea in front of him.

Taking a sip of his tea, Kamalesh had said, 'My dear Sutapa-di, the sages have told us that staying in bed is Kalyug, sitting up is Dwapar, getting on your feet is Treta, and walking is Satya. And in our times management science says ...'

'You can put your management science back in your pocket.' Sutapa gave Kamalesh a piece of her mind pleasantly.

'Very well, you can get it straight from the horse's mouth then, your husband also partook of Digambar Bonarjee's seminar today.'

'We're being told growth is life,' Subhashish said. 'Not growing is a sort of death. All companies, even our state-owned Hindustan Agro Chemicals, must grow at least ten per cent annually just to survive.'

'Which means you must also inspire Subhashish-da to grow ten per cent annually,' Kamalesh said with a laugh.

'Indeed, I will,' Sutapa contorted her lovely face and warned her husband, 'You can contribute all you like to growth in your company's revenues, but contribute to growth in your weight and divorce will follow.'

Defending the beleaguered Subhashish in this domestic battle, Kamalesh rapped on the table and said, 'What's marriage got to do with weight?'

Sutapa smiled engagingly without paying any attention to the question. Meanwhile the very person Kamalesh was fighting for supported his wife shamelessly. 'It has everything to do with marriage, the weight of the couple is closely related to their conjugal life. You're still a bachelor, we can discuss this in detail once you're married.'

Even Sutapa, normally quick to respond, was embarrassed. Suppressing her laughter, she looked away expressionlessly, as though she had heard nothing.

Sitting in his train compartment, Kamalesh recalled what Subhashish had said. 'Actually, what women want is something in the middle, not too little, not too much. Not too thin, not too fat.'

Subhashish was a student of geology. He had gone to the same college as Kamalesh—though he was a few years ahead. But they had known each other at the college hostel. And then their paths had crossed again here in Chandanpur. Kamalesh had got an MTech degree meanwhile, and then acquired a 'Doctor' before his name. Subhashish too had been to a university abroad and picked up a couple of rubber stamps of additional degrees. Now he was well-established at Hindustan Agro-Chemicals. His wife Sutapa Majumdar often invited the unmarried Kamalesh home for a meal.

'How long do you mean to wander about as a bachelor, Kamalesh?' Sutapa had asked.

Her affection always put Kamalesh at ease. Smiling, he had said, 'I accept I'm a bachelor. But why are you giving me the bad name of a wanderer?'

Sutapa was too modern to be flustered. Wagging her finger at Kamalesh, she had said, 'I don't trust bachelors at all.'

Trying to prove his innocence, Kamalesh said, 'Where's the time to wander, Sutapa-di. I'm fully involved with my work, my laboratory, and my director Digambar Bonarjee.'

'You may be busy,' Sutapa had mischievously countered, 'but I don't know if you're involved. Didn't Satyen Dutta write "I want a breeze involved with nectar".'

'You're a brillant talent-spotter, Subhashish-da. Look how you picked an MA in Bangla, now you have perfect quotations on tap.'

The Majumdars had laughed uproariously at this. Then replacing the end of her sari on her shoulder from her lap where it had fallen, Sutapa had said, 'Beautiful women with MAs in Bangla are not endangered yet. A hundred or more emerge from Calcutta University every year. Not to mention the half dozen other universities in the state. If you show the slightest interest I can get into the business of matchmaking. Fathers of girls with MA degrees will queue up outside if I can find them such a groom.'

Kamalesh injected even more levity into the proceedings. 'Don't forget your're a senior public sector officer's wife,

Sutapa-di. You cannot run a private business from a government bungalow without the HAC's permission. I know Dasappa from the Vigilance Department quite well.'

'Try stopping me.' Sutapa adjusted the end of her sari again. Once she was certain her breasts were properly covered, she continued, 'I'm not going into the business for money, it's piety I'm after. Arranging matches for unmarried girls and boys is a ticket to heaven.'

Smiling slyly, Kamalesh said, 'Shout all you want, but Dasappa knows matchmaking is a lucrative business these days, plenty of people are making money from it. Dada will be in trouble because of you.'

'I can put three of your Dasappas under my arms and go into matchmaking,' Sutapa said with fearless nonchalance.

'Far from being a punishment, that would be a matter of fortune for Dasappa. But you'll never be able to give the poor man this opportunity, Sutapa-di. You haven't seen him. If you put him on a normal weighing machine the needle will go all the way to the end and the spring will collapse. It's a very weighty post, you see, so they've found a hundred-kilo person for it.'

Sutapa wasn't one to be cowed down by such wit. 'Never mind the nonsense,' she told Kamalesh, 'You're not exactly getting younger. If not now, then when? If you don't take the regular route you'll find yourself in the hands of a shrew who'll make your life miserable.'

Sitting in the train, Kamalesh recalled what Sutapa had said that day. And along with it, what had happened last night. The night had in fact turned thirty-two gentle years of Kamalesh's life upside down.

Kamalesh had no material proof of being married now. He had already ripped off the yellow string tied around his left wrist. All he had was a photograph in his pocket that Sutapa passed on to him some time ago. Mr Bose at Bombay Photo Studio had taken this photograph of Chandramallika himself. Several studio lights had lit up Mallika's face with a chiaroscuro effect. She looked excessively fair-skinned in it, just like a heroine who could be asked to act in a film any moment.

When Sutapa had shown him the photograph and asked Kamalesh's opinion he had said, 'Get it published in a film magazine. Any director will give her a chance.'

At this Sutapa had said, 'I don't know about films, but make her the heroine of your life—you won't be let down.'

Kamalesh had smiled. Sutapa had said, 'A very sweet girl. Such a tender face, and with the mischievous eyes of a doe. Surrender and she'll have you on a rope all her life.'

'My goodness, are you saying boys are bulls?' Kamalesh had said in mock-concern.

'I don't know about others, but you are definitely one. You've just been handed the photograph of a beauty in full bloom. Whether you marry her or not, I'd have expected you to examine the photograph carefully. Instead of which you just gave it a cursory glance and put it back in the envelope.' Sutapa didn't mince her words.

'Wait, what do you think you're doing? How can you haul my college cousin and colleague over the coals?' Subhashish was back from work. And though he was familiar with his wife's ways, he took Kamalesh's side. 'We hold responsible jobs in government establishments, after all—our prestige is at stake here. We can't have our tongues hanging out even if the proposal is for marrying Noor Jahan.'

'Oh really?' Sutapa put on a display of anger and glared at her husband.

'Give the poor boy a little time,' Subhashish had said. 'Ask him to take the photograph home. Let him view it in private in his own room under a light. Let him see it a hundred times if need be, just the way I looked at yours ...'

Sutapa had a beauty spot above her lips on the right. When she grimaced in anger the mole shifted position and looked most alluring. 'These Calcutta boys are clearly not of sound mental health.'

'You're a Bengali from UP, so you bad-mouth those of us from Bengal at every opportunity. But I won't lie, I looked at your photograph eighty-one-and-a-half times that first day.'

'Why half?' Kamalesh asked, laughing.

'The only reason was that Ma burst into the room without notice,' Subhashish had said. 'But I was a cricketer—I tossed the inflammatory material under the pillow at once.'

'And then?' Kamalesh was encouraged by the prospect of needling Sutapa.

'Ma didn't catch on,' Subhashish said solemnly. 'She assumed I was lying in bed because I was tired after work—and that I didn't like the girl. Son, don't say no, she told me, she may be Hindustani but she's a good girl. Be a dear, please say yes. I said, don't nag me now, let me think it over. Then she got me into trouble by asking for the photograph. I'll have to look for it, I said, I don't know where I've put it. But Ma wasn't going to give up, so finally I had to play my trump card. Come back later Ma, I have a terrible headache.'

At once Sutapa delivered a honeyed barb, 'Oh please. The love of men is no different from the butcher's for the chicken. You don't even look at me now.'

Subhashish picked up the envelope from the table in an effort to prevent the conjugal squabble from getting worse. It worked like a charm. The beautiful Sutapa was pleasantly disposed towards her husband once more. 'You haven't seen Chandramallika before,' she told him, 'What do you think? Can you give your disciple some good advice?'

Shubhashish's face lit up. 'If you want my frank opinion, then what I'll say is: Coca-Cola.'

His listeners were confounded. A sceptical Sutapa told her husband, 'Don't you dare crack your cheap factory jokes about a member of my family, I'm warning you.'

Jumping to self-defence, Shubhashish said, 'You call this cheap? This was fulsome praise. Haven't you seen the ad: Things go better with Coke.' Turning to Kamalesh, Shubhashish continued, 'Let me tell you, my boy, it's not because she's a distant relative of the wife. The name's a bit of a mouthful, but you'll get along well.'

Sutapa checked with Kamalesh on the phone a few days later. 'Well, Kamalesh? Did the photograph intimidate you so much that you aren't coming to our house anymore?'

'You have no idea, Sutapa-di,' Kamalesh said. 'The boss is in a trance, talks of nothing but work. You know all these hypnotic spells; can't you use one on N.D. Bonarjee?'

It was no secret to Kamalesh that Sutapa thoroughly disliked the HAC director Noel Digambar Bonarjee. Grimly she said, 'Couldn't the company find anyone else in all of India? They had to get this toothbrush moustache and install him in Chandanpur. A cold fish if ever there was one.'

'He may not have any emotions, but everyone at the company knows only too well he's always in motion, Sutapa-di.'

'Never mind your company,' said Sutapa-di. 'I'm fed up of listening to your office hymns day in and day out. Tell me what you think of Coca-Cola.'

'She isn't as cold as Coca-Cola, I hope,' Kamalesh said shyly.

No matter how affectionate sister-in-law figures can be, as messengers of love they don't hesitate when they have to be cruel. Who else would have passed on the quip about being ice-cold?

Kamalesh was in Calcutta on a short holiday. Sutapa seized the opportunity and followed him to the city, taking the intiative to set up a meeting between Chandramallika and Kamalesh. First at Metro Cinema, then at Kwality restaurant on Park Street. Only Sutapa was present. Controlled romance, in her words.

Chandramallika had dressed beautifully, without appearing to have made any effort. Modern educated women had adopted this art with great skill. There was no conscious effort to show it, but that she had it all was reflected in Chandramallika's face, gestures, and demeanour—they radiated her confidence.

'Let me make the introductions,' Sutapa said. 'This is my cousin's youngest daughter, Chandramallika Chatterjee—Mallika. We call her Jhumjhumi. She was born in Allahabad and spent her childhood in Bombay. Now her father's posted in Calcutta, so she's followed him here. You can say she's been convent-educated—a student of St. John's Diocesan. Then a BA Honours from Ashutosh College, and now she's taken her MA exam at Calcutta University. The results haven't been declared yet, so I can't tell whether she's cheated and created trouble for herself.'

'Mashi!' Chandramallika tried to control Sutapa with a show of displeasure.

'This is Kamalesh Roychowdhury,' Sutapa continued. 'A well-known scientist at our project. His life is fertilised by fertiliser. An M.Tech from IIT, followed by a doctorate. Then he caught the eye of mad Digambar and has been climbing swiftly up the ladder at the state-owned Hindustan Agro Chemicals. You must have read many novels about scientists, but I don't know if you've ever seen one for yourself. That's why I'm introducing you.'

Sutapa made them sit face to face in the low-lit Kwality restaurant. Then she said without a hint of a smile, 'Where's this you've brought us, Kamalesh? It's like a night with no moon.'

It wasn't as though this was Sutapa's first visit to Kwality. Kamalesh realised she had seized the opportunity to have a little fun at his expense.

Kamalesh and Chandramallika were silent, stirring their coffee. 'Both of you usually talk your heads off, what's the matter now?'

Kamalesh had no choice but to break the silence. 'History belongs to the past,' he said. 'And, as for science, our director Dr Bonarjee says, the future is what we deal with.'

Chandramallika listened without a word. Sutapa poked her. 'Scientists are full of pride these days; they behave as though they own the world. Don't give in, Jhumjhumi, give him as good as you got.'

Chandramallika widened her wide eyes further and summoned a quiet smile to her face. Then she said, 'You know, Mashi, the head of our department often says humans don't have the power to influence the past. The present is already here in its own form. That leaves only the future. You can create the future when you're standing in the present only by the light thrown by the past.'

'Excellent answer,' Sutapa said.

Then she made an excuse and went off to the toilet. 'Have your coffee, talk, I'll be back in a minute,' she said.

Kamalesh and Chandramallika sat facing each other. 'Should I pour you some more hot coffee?' Kamalesh had asked.

Rather gravely, Chandramallika had responded, 'Didn't you say "ice-cold"?'

After a discussion with Kamalesh's family, Sutapa said, 'Take my advice, Kamalesh, marry her. We live all alone in Chandanpur, no one here to spend time with. All of us can have a lovely time together. From boudi I'll be promoted to shashuri, you'll get the royal treatment a son-in-law deserves.'

But maybe this was not God's will. Soon after the wedding was finalised, Shubhashish left Chandanpur for another job after a run-in with the director. Chandanpur was unimaginable without Sutapa. But Sutapa didn't believe that. 'Forget the grand talk. On the contrary, this is more convenient for you. It's much nicer not to have familiar faces around during the first year of marriage.'

'But don't forget I played the role of the hyphen,' she added. 'Once the two halves come together, people usually get rid of the hyphen.'

'What are you talking about? The wedding cards haven't even been printed!' Kamalesh protested.

'Oh, are you interested in a little pre-marital romance? Then you'll need Sutapa as chaperone.'

It wasn't as though Kamalesh was averse to the idea. Getting away from Chandanpur at weekends to meet Chandramallika wouldn't be a bad thing at all .

Sutapa had no objections. She made an elaborate plan to get them together at her house in Calcutta. But Chandramallika's mother came in the way, and Sutapa had to tell Kamalesh, 'Very sorry, Kamalesh, Nihar-di hasn't caught up with modern ways yet.'

It was true that Kamalesh was a little disappointed.

But Sutapa said, 'It's not necessarily a bad thing not to meet before the wedding. One is more attracted to the unseen, you understand, my boy?'

'Is that so?' said Kamalesh.

'You're a man, I cannot speak for you. But our girl has already set up a twenty-four-hours-a-day-seven-days-a-week shrine in her heart for her future husband.'

The subject of the honeymoon came up. Sutapa asked, 'I hope you've made arrangements for the honeymoon. Make sure to elope with your wife as soon as the rituals are done—disappear from the face of the earth, as they say.'

'But where do you suggest I disappear?' Kamalesh asked for advice. He had applied to Digambar Bonarjee for four weeks' leave.

'You have to discuss the honeymoon with Chandramallika, you fool,' Sutapa reminded the young man who was still an amateur in the game of love.

'How will I discuss it with her? She's vanished, thanks to your family,' Kamalesh complained laughing.

'Oh my God, listen to you! I'm informing Nihar-di at once: "Your son-in-law is about to file a police case to rescue Mallika."'

'Please find out Chandramallika's views on the honyemoon, I beg of you, Sutapa-di. But in complete secret.'

Sutapa said, 'You haven't even decided on the compensation for matchmaking. Yet you're making me work round the clock. And you even want post-wedding advice.'

'Don't leave me in the lurch now,' Kamalesh made a desperate plea.

'I'm not your run-of-the-mill matchmaker,' Sutapa said with a smile. 'Rather than waiting for Kamalesh-babu to bring up the honeymoon, I've already had extensive discussions with the heroine.'

'Where does she want to go?' Kamalesh asked shyly but eagerly.

'We'd like our girl to have her honeymoon on Honolulu's Waikiki Beach in Hawaii. But what about you?'

'I don't have any wish; whatever she says.'

'The lady said the same thing, whatever mister wants. My God, the ideal couple already.'

Scratching his head, Kamalesh said, 'What about Khajuraho? As a history student she's sure to like it.'

With a covert smile Sutapa said, 'You will take your wife wherever you want to, who are we to stop you? Our girl is simple and pure; it's your choice if you want to make her lose her innocence by exposing her to the shameless acts of stone men and women in the Khajuraho temples.'

Shubhashish wasn't in Calcutta, or he would have taken up the cudgels for Kamalesh. He had a theory: 'College girls in Calcutta have changed a lot. They don't hesitate to buy obscene books and magazines from that kiosk near Hedua Lake and stash them away in their bags.'

Shubhashish wasn't present on the wedding night. He couldn't get leave from his new job. But many of Kamalesh's friends were there.

Camera flashes kept going off as the newlyweds were photographed repeatedly. 'What do you think?' Chandramallika's mother asked everyone.

'Just like the ad: "Made for each other,"' her brother told her.

Several of Kamalesh's colleagues in Chandanpur sent telegrams with blessings and good wishes. Sifting through them, Kamalesh's father suddenly turned grim. He put one of them in his pocket and passed on the rest to his son.

'No telegram from your director?' Sutapa-di asked.

'Not yet, maybe it'll come later,' Kamalesh said.

Kamalesh's father Sudhanya glanced at the clock soon after pocketing the telegram. 'It's almost ten-thirty,' he urged the people at home, 'make the arrangements.'

Sutapa was with them till they entered the bedroom for their wedding night. 'Should I check your pulse, my boy?' she whispered to Kamalesh. 'Maybe check your heartbeat? You'll soon have proof our girl isn't ice-cold.'

Taking his hand, she had added, 'This night comes only once in life. Use it well. Let there be no regrets later.'

The electric train had begun moving. Chandanpur Express sped past a small station in a flash. An old goods train heaved on a siding, having abandoned the main line in its unwillingness to humiliate itself after observing the triumph of the Chandanpur Express.

Kamalesh Roychowdhury glanced at this watch. Not even twenty-four hours had passed since he had stepped into the flower-bedecked bedroom last night. He touched the thick frames of his glasses, still feeling Chandra's caress. When Kamalesh had taken them off, she had wiped the lenses with the end of her sari.

What an extraordinary sensation it was! The disciplined disciple of science, Kamalesh Roychowdhury, had been swept away by last night's wild flood.

The women had led Chandramallika, dressed in wedding finery, into the room already. Kamalesh had hesitated before entering, but his father had said again with a glance at the clock, 'It's getting really late.'

Chandramallika saw a five-foot-eleven-inch-tall figure come into the room and lock the door. The frosted glass windows had been shut tight already, but Kamalesh examined them carefully once more. Trying to keep her floral ornaments in place, Chandramallika watched the preparations through a gap in the veil of her red Benaras silk sari, but felt no apprehension. Reassured, she began to play with the long nails on her left hand instead.

And yet only ninety-six hours ago this very woman had not been permitted to sit with the same Kamalesh Roychowdhury even in full view of everyone in a tea-shop on the main road. Even forty-eight hours ago, till fourteen minutes past ten in the evening, there was a sea of diffidence and distance between them. But everything had changed as soon as the wedding rituals began. Not superfically, but a chemical change, the way coal was converted to energy in Kamalesh's factory.

Kamalesh had noticed this chemical change in his sister-in-law from close quarters when his elder brother had got married. Until the wedding rituals were completed, women had their own identity, however gentle and reserved—she was still her own person. It wasn't rare to come across incidents where a crisis erupted on the eve of the wedding, which was then called off—after which the bride went on to marry someone else afterwards. But something happened when the marriage was solemnised. Following a long tradition, the women were transformed in a flash, with the catalysis taking place in the presence of hundreds of people under bright electric lights. But no one noticed it, no one was surprised either. They didn't realise that the woman who had sat down for the ceremony was not the woman who rose to her feet afterwards.

Kamalesh held Chandramallika's right hand lightly—this was how wedding night scenes began in films. Chandramallika didn't stop him. 'Not ice-cold at all,' he said. 'On the contrary ...'

'On the contrary, what?' Chandramallika asked, her eyes widening.

'As hot as a cup of coffee,' Kamalesh said with a smile.

'Coffee's too hot, you can't hold the cup for very long.'

Smart answer, thought Kamalesh. He was tempted to say, 'Hold not in one's hands but to one's lips,' but he applied the brakes at the last moment. He had heard that not proceeding with caution on the first night had ruined conjugal pleasures for many people for the rest of their lives.

'Your name's too long, Chandramallika,' said Kamalesh, playing with his new bride's hand.

'You don't like it?' Chandramallika asked fearlessly.

'I love it. But it's as valuable and heavy as a Benaras silk sari.'

The drops of sandalwood paste on Chandramallika's forehead shone. The thick streak of vermilion in her parting brightened too. 'A loving everyday nickname, as light and breezy as you are, would be so good.'

Far from shrinking in embarrassment, Chandramallika accepted her husband's demand and said enthusiastically, 'I'm yours now, give me any name you like. Just don't call me by it when my parents are around, that'll be awkward.'

This latitude from his wife made Kamalesh crave for more. He pushed her bangles up her wrist to where they sat tightly around her arm. Pausing his handiwork, he said, 'You do have a sweet nickname. Jhumjhumi. But Jhumu isn't romantic enough. I think I'll use whatever name I want to—Chandramallika, Chandra, Jhumu.'

Kamalesh took his wife's right hand in both of his now. Comparing her fingers with his, he said, 'What you see is a labourer's hand—if you spread the fingers it will be monstrous. No tenderness anywhere, there are even some calluses. And this is the hand of a princess in a fairy tale, soft as cottonwool, a little warm, a little cool.'

Chandramallika didn't protest at all. Having given herself to him, there was no sense in trying to release her hand.

Kamalesh took out a red box from his pocket. The ring was in it. He slipped it on his wife's finger gently, with deep love. Kamalesh hadn't realised how beautiful the ring was when buying it. It had come into its own now.

'Thanks,' said Chandramallika with a shy smile.

'You didn't ask how I knew your size,' Kamalesh said.

'I know already. You asked Sutapa-mashi, and you told her not to tell anyone.'

'Then how did you know?' Kamalesh complained.

'Obviously I'd know; it's my finger, after all. But Sutapa-mashi told me one of my boyfriends has asked.'

Kamalesh held the hand with the ring on it against his forehead and then his cheek. Chandramallika said calmly, 'You've given me a beautiful ring, but I have nothing to give you.'

Kamalesh hesitated for a moment before shedding his inhibition. 'Actually, you have a lot to give me,' he said. He glanced at her lips, and Chandramallika had no trouble reading, agreeing to, and granting his demand.

The first touch, followed by a long one, of the velvet-soft, moist lips were still fresh on Kamalesh's own lips. That particular part of his body was still in paradise.

Then they fearlessly boarded their raft of dreams to voyage across an Atlantic Ocean of turbulence, and then to sail on a Pacific Ocean of tranquillity, alternately losing themselves and drawing close to each other in fear.

Kamalesh realised that this primordial desire to become one was very much like a chemical revolution—the fusion in the laboratory at whose climax the elements lose their own identities, the revolution after which the old is nowhere to be found, when it extinguishes itself completely and gives birth to the new.

But they were neither tired nor impatient after their voyage, for this was just the beginning and they had all the time in the world. For a whole month Kamalesh didn't even have to think of work.

Drawing his wife close, he said, 'I've made all the arrangements for Khajuraho, Chandra. We'll finish the last of the rituals and take the train the same day. I've got the tickets and reserved a coupé. I believe the new hotel there is perfect for newlyweds.'

His wife, a modern woman, was excited. 'It'll be fantastic, we'll go everywhere, see everything.' She spoke slowly, for her body was still numb after the overwhelming waves of pleasure.

Without releasing her from his arms, Kamalesh said, 'And what if I don't want to leave the hotel room at all?'

'Then we won't. Whatever you want.' Chandramallika was ready to meet every one of her husband's demands unquestioningly.

Then night entered the playroom of the newlyweds stealthily and without permission and took them away to the land of sleep. Chandramallika had realised that their tired bodies, satiated with this new experience, were about to sink into exhaustion. 'Wake me up early in the morning if I'm still asleep,' she whispered to Kamalesh.

Mallika wanted to go to sleep with complete dependence on her husband. 'Why do you have to be up early?' he asked.

'It looks terrible for a new bride to sleep in. Everyone laughs.'

'No one here will say anything, no one expects the new bride to be up at five the morning after the wedding night.'

'No, please, listen to me, wake me up if I'm still asleep. Ma told me again and again, sleep in the afternoon if you must, but don't even think of staying in bed till eight in the morning with the door locked.'

Considering no one objected to the door being locked at night, Kamalesh couldn't tell why it was unseemly to be a litte late opening it in the morning. But he didn't want to argue with Chandra right now—what Chandra wants, she will get.

When the time came, though, Kamalesh was fast asleep. His long-nurtured habit of waking up at dawn had betrayed him. But Chandra didn't have to be embarrassed, she had woken up on time.

The first thing she did was to straighten the rumpled sheets, gather the torn flowers and put them in the wastepaper basket, and tidy her dishevelled hair with a comb in front of the mirror without allowing her bangles to clink. Then she opened the door and sat in a chair in the corner, covering her head with the end of her sari. To dispel her slight awkwardness in an unfamiliar environment, she picked up a book. But despite her efforts, not a single word in it made sense.

It was clear from Chandra's face that she considered herself unendingly wealthy now—she had so much of her own after the wedding that there was no fear of bankruptcy even if she were to be profligate not just one night but every night. Mallika had heard from her married fellow-students that many revered husbands behaved like gluttons on the very first night—but her own husband hadn't behaved that way. Many many more nights to go, Kamalesh had said. He had neither soiled the first opportunity for intimacy with shameless lust for Mallika, nor ravaged her privacy and independence.

Mallika's sister-in-law, who was married, was awake. She was surprised to see the door open. 'The new bride up already? No one's out of bed yet.'

Chandramallika didn't reply. She tried to look solemn, but she was embarrased too—her inexperience had allowed the vermilion to be smeared all over her forehead. She really should have wiped her face properly.

Her sister-in-law scrutinised her in silence from head to toe with a knowing eye. When her glance paused at her breast, Chandramallika felt very uneasy—she adjusted the end of her sari over her shoulder, even though it covered her adequately.

Inquisitive women can abandon all decorum and ask mercilessly uncomfortable questions at these times. Chandramallika had heard that many suggestive comments are made with no regard for the difference in age. But her sister-in-law did none of this. She had only asked, 'I hope you managed to sleep? It's often hard to sleep in a new place.'

Shrinking back from lying explicitly, Chandramallika conveyed with her silence that she had slept undisturbed. 'The bathroom's free,' her sister-in-law said.

Changing into fresh clothes, Chandramallika emerged from the bathroom to find her father-in-law pacing up and down impatiently in the veranda. He asked whether Kamalesh was up.

Chandramallika was not at all in favour of her husband snoring in bed till the afternoon after the wedding night. At eight she pinched Kamalesh lightly on his foot, but Kamalesh only gave her a glance before grabbing his bolster again.

'Baba's looking for you,' Chandramallika said in a low voice.

Kamalesh jumped out of bed and was about to go out when Chandramallika rushed to block his way. 'Wipe your face. Check in the mirror for any marks.'

Kamalesh's father was sitting quietly in a chair in the veranda, the telegram from last night lying in front of him. Not a congratulatory wire but a very important message.

'Who's this Bonarjee in your company?' he asked Kamalesh.

'Our technical director, Noel Digambar Bonarjee,' Kamalesh said.

'Does he know you're in Calcutta for your wedding?' his father asked again with great seriousness.

'Of course he does. I gave him the wedding card myself. He congratulated me the day I left and said he'd definitely be here for the ceremony unless something came in the way.'

Kamalesh's father handed him the telegram without saying anything further. It said: 'REGRET YOUR LEAVE CANCELLED STOP RETURN TO CHANDANPUR AT ONCE STOP BONARJEE'.

The telegram had come yesterday. His father had chosen not to ruin his wedding night.

Kamalesh discovered that his father had taken the whole thing in his stride, without making a fuss about it. 'I've sent Jodu to the booking office at Fairlie Place,' he told his son. 'He'll get a first-class ticket on Chandanpur Express.'

The news spread swiftly among relatives. No time was lost in ringing Chandramallika's family. No one was ready for this unexpected turn of events. After a few rounds of discussions between both sides of the family, it was decided to expedite the remaining rituals.

No one but Kamalesh accompanied Chandramallika on her way back to her parents. Poor Mallika was quite distraught at this unpredicted separation. Kamalesh wasn't ready for this bolt from the blue either. The mystery wasn't going to be unravelled till he was back in Chandanpur.

A sudden brake caused the train to stopped with a jerk. Kamalesh felt he had been jolted unfairly. He wasn't the only employee in the world—thousands and millions took leave from work to get married—but their bosses didn't send telegrams on their wedding nights to ruin their celebration.

Everyone at home was unhappy, most of all Chandramallika's family. They had meant to have a few days of festivities before seeing the newlyweds off on their honeymoon. What they were faced with instead was darkness at noon. Chandramallika was flustered—she was the one most upset, but the poor thing was also afraid people would blame her.

They spent an hour at Mallika's house before retuning home. Kamalesh's father issued another edict in the afternoon. 'Khoka has a long train journey ahead. Let him eat quickly and rest a little.'

Kamalesh knew what this 'rest a little' meant. His father wanted him to spend some time alone with his bride before the unexpected separation. They certainly deserved the opportunity, and no one was opposed to it. But Chandra was extremly embarrassed and refused to go into the room with Kamalesh. She was practically forced. Her sister-in-law shut the door, but Mallika didn't lock it.

Kamalesh drew her close at once. But she was stiff with apprehension. 'I'm unlucky for you,' she declared.

Kamalesh was deeply annoyed with his company. 'We weren't prepared for this separation in the very first round,' he admitted. 'But I'm not giving up so easily. I'll find out the reason in a few hours.'

With several hours gone, the train was approaching Chandanpur now. Kamalesh's thoughts turned to his work-life. He had all but forgotten Chandanpur for a few days because of the conspiracy hatched by the god of marriage.

2

Chandanpur was a picture-perfect town set amidst low hills. Till 1945 no one knew about this part of India. What it had was a huge military base. One square mile surrounded by barbed wire where secret equipment was stored—apparently essential for the war.

After the Second World War a huge fertiliser factory came up here—the first project of Hindustan Agro-Chemicals was in Chandanpur. In the first decade after Independence, Chandanpur was a showpiece, the smartest of them all. Starting with the prime minister, all the powerful people from the capital of the country brought heads of state to Chandanpur. From Zhou Enlai of China to Queen Elizabeth of England, no one was left out. Chandanpur had charmed them all.

What a beautiful name it was, Chandanpur. But the beauty and independence of local names could not be preserved thanks to red tape. In a fit of peculiar enthusiasm for abbreviating, an unpoetic but dedicated office superintendent had scrawled 'CP' on an official file. Imprisoned as CP, the Chandanpur project never gained freedom thereafter.

At a short distance from where the factory ended, visitors could see a large, long two-storeyed building of streamlined modern design. It bore no resemblance to the twenty-five-year-old factory. Public-sector offices seldom had such tasteful office buildings. This one could be mistaken for a contemporary auditorium from a distance. Actually, it housed the research department of HAC.

A guard always stood like a statue with a gun at the gate. Behind him a red gravel path stretched to the entrance. The words inscribed on granite at the front door were a reminder that the prime minister had inaugurated this research laboratory on a July morning a few years ago, dedicating the sacred temple of knowledge to the nation.

The reception hall was a short distance beyond the entrance. Here the indistinct figure of a relatively unknown foreigner cast in relief on a copper plate attracted the attention of visitors. There was a quotation beneath in Persian, which said: *Seek and ye shall find.* The immortal French scientist Nicolas Leblanc was said to have believed in this maxim.

Digambar Bonarjee had this timeless quotation beneath the glass on his office desk. Whenever doubts appeared, whenever despair threatened to cloud his faculties, Digambar Bonarjee went out to gaze at Nicolas Leblanc's portrait. The scientist sprang to life and reminded his intellectual disciple to seek, and only then would it be possible to find.

It was eight in the evening. Although the rest of the laboratory was dark, four neon lights shone in Digambar Bonarjee's office.

He was hunched over his desk, closely scanning a set of X-ray reports by the light of a table lamp. Then, reading a report on the powder defraction patterns yielded by these X-rays, he scribbled a reminder to himself in a small notebook to talk to B.S. Iyer from the X-ray department first thing the next morning. He wanted a report on all six states of ammonium nitrate. Why wasn't a corrugated layer visible in the structure during phase three?

Digambar Bonarjee stopped scribbling abruptly. Why waste another day needlessly? To save time, he picked up the telephone and dialled Iyer at home. Officers at any other company would be worried if the director rang them at eight at night, but in Chandanpur everyone was used to it.

'Were you having dinner, Iyer?' Digambar Bonarjee asked. 'I'm very sorry. I was looking at the X-ray data from your department, and it suddenly occurred to me that these boys are working like menial labourers without putting their minds to it. Ask them to read Benham and Bestrick's paper on the influence of structure on behaviour that we've procured. The paper came to the documentation division a month and a half ago, but I'm told no one from your department has consulted it.' Digambar Bonarjee ended the phone call with a 'good night'.

Then he sent for his assistant, Adhar Sinha. 'You did send the telegram to Kamalesh's address in Calcutta yesterday, didn't you?'

'Of course, sir.' Adhar never made mistakes when it came to such things.

'Express?' asked Digambar Bonarjee.

'Yes, sir.'

'The Howrah–Chandanpur Express should have arrived by now, shouldn't it?' Bonarjee asked Adhar with a glance at his watch.

'It's an hour-and-a-half late, sir,' Adhar informed him.

Digambar Bonarjee was annoyed. *We're a nation of laggards*, he told himself, *we won't allow anyone to keep pace with time. For thousands of generations we have kept our eye on timescales like millions and billions of years, the Vedas and Upanishads and the Mahabharata are vociferous about the eternity of time, so no one is embarrassed about wasting such mere things as minutes and hours and days.*

Digambar Bonarjee glanced at his watch again. Giving his assistant permission to go home, he said, 'It's time you left, Adhar. Why don't you drop in at Kamlesh's place on the way, my driver will take you. Leave word that Dr Roychowdhury can meet me this evening if he likes.'

'Aren't you going home, sir?' Adhar asked.

'Let the car drop you and come back here. Then we'll see.'

Fifty-two-year-old Noel Digambar Bonarjee was the lord and master of the fates of this gigantic building, the equipment that it housed, worth millions, and about four hundred employees. When he was appointed as director at HAC, many of the officers had expected him to be posted at the Delhi office, like the other directors.

But Digambar Bonarjee had done the impossible. He had told the managing director bluntly, 'You're welcome to appoint me as a director. I will attend board meetings if I'm asked. But a research director cannot be separated from his laboratory. I have to remain here in Chandanpur.' The managing director had no choice but to give his permission.

Leave alone Delhi, everyone in Chandanpur knew that N.D. Bonarjee wouldn't be at peace even in heaven if it meant leaving the HAC laboratory.

He looked once more at the quotation beneath the glass on his desk. *Seek and ye shall find.*

'Seek where? For what or whom?' Digambar Bonarjee asked himself.

He gazed out of the enormous south window. In parallel with the unbelievable progress in fertiliser science in the past twenty years, the importance of the Chandanpur factory had been diminished greatly—it was long past its prime. But the aged plant looked beautiful tonight. Who could tell from this view that the members of the expert committee at the head office had already decided there was no point pouring more money into this factory ridden with many illnesses? The days of the Chandanpur project were numbered.

And yet it was here that HAC had begun its journey. Those days, the authorities did not expend their energies on agriculture in India. Only country yokels were involved in farming, their harvests being sent to the cities on bullock carts or in lorries for the benefit of the masters. The illiterate peasant would rot in the village and the gentry would make merry in the city—that was as far as the expectations of society went.

Digambar Bonarjee recalled being one of these city-bred gentlemen. He had never been to a village, nor felt any desire to. The idea behind setting up a fertiliser factory in Chandanpur was not so much the improvement of agriculture as it was the impulse to put recently discharged soldiers from the army to work. And if some fertiliser was manufactured in the process of employing unemployed soldiers, that was far from unwelcome.

Thank heavens we had Chandanpur, mused Digambar Bonarjee. Circumstances led to even city-dwellers facing a scarcity of food. It was clear that if there was a famine it wouldn't be just villagers but also the urban population that would be vulnerable. In addition to which there was the humiliation heaped upon the country by foreigners. Considering Indians couldn't produce enough food for themselves, considering half the ships in the world had been commandeered to deliver grains sent as charity, who would tolerate the bombast of these people? Independent India might be a champion at oratory, but it turned into a target of derision and mockery for the rest of the world.

Eventually the leaders of the country were deeply affronted. Digambar Bonarjee knew the humiliation had yielded results. Waking up from their post-prandial slumber, the urban elite rubbed the sleep out of their eyes to ask: *Why aren't farmers farming? Even with plentiful land and unstinting effort, why is the earth proving so miserly? Where are the crops?*

Finally, India's bureaucrats learnt what the people of the world had known all along. We had extracted everything cruelly from the soil of this land for hundreds of years—and given nothing in return. Even Mother Earth experienced hunger and thirst. Rain could quench the thirst, but where was the nourishment for the hunger? It would need huge quantities of fertiliser to grow enough crops to feed everyone.

Digambar Bonarjee was an ordinary scientist at the time. He had written at least a dozen times to New Delhi, reminding them that what the soil yielded in the form of crops had to be returned to it. It was impossible to grow so much naturally—chemical fertilisers were necessary. It would be a big mistake for India to lag behind in the global flurry of activity around fertiliser.

Digambar Bonarjee remembered only too well how Hindustan Agro-Chemicals began to grow once the Dilli durbar shook off its somnolescence. The company was to operate at every level of the manufacture of agricultural chemicals. Beginning in Chandanpur, it would spread to every corner of India. There was a map in Digambar Bonarjee's office with several red and green pins placed at various spots in the north and the south, the east and west. The red pins marked the locations of proposed factories, while the green ones indicated the places where factories had begun operating.

HAC's headquarters had been moved to Delhi for the convenience of managing things across the country. But the research and development continued here in Chandanpur. Digambar Bonarjee believed that the pursuit of knowledge was impossible in big cities, especially Delhi. A multitude of temptations offered by the civilised world constantly invited the innocent to tread on the wrong path. A disciple of science could well find their dedication destroyed by the sight of swindlers posing as businessmen and equally undeserving political leaders living in royal splendour.

At this moment, looking back on the trajectory of his own life, Digambar Bonarjee is extremely surprised. How the twists and turns of circumstances led him to HAC when he was in no way connected to it to begin with.

Digambar Bonarjee was not very sociable. And he also had a foul temper. But he didn't feel like getting angry these days because the HAC management had not put fetters on him. Digambar had declared that it was the wheels of research that were taking the chemicals industries of the world ahead. What was modern today would be obsolete tomorrow. So HAC would have to participate in the stiff competition to make progress. The management had agreed. They had given Bonarjee the kind of freedom that was unbelievable in this age of government control. The members of the board were willing to provide whatever he wanted for research and development. And this was what troubled Digambar Bonarjee. He was afraid—was he worthy of their faith?

He had many dreams, Digambar Bonarjee. A day would come when India would shine the brighest on the international map of fertilisers. *If millions of tonnes of phosphate and ammonia and potash were required to feed India's billions, why should we depend on others?*

Some people had tried to inject Digambar Bonarjee with pessimism. They said nothing was possible in India, even if you tried you couldn't be successful here. So failure was written in Bonarjee's fate too.

But Digambar Bonarjee was aware of history. And the one man whose life's mission gave him hope and confidence was Nicolas Leblanc. When Leblanc killed himself in 1806, having no other option on finding himself penniless, did he know that one day the world would consider him the father of the modern chemicals industry? The Frenchman had wanted to manufacture chemicals useful to people at a low cost. What Leblanc did in France a hundred and seventy-five years ago was what Digambar Bonarjee wanted to do in India—he was looking for ways to manufacture fertiliser at even lower costs.

Digambar Bonarjee recalled that Leblanc's invention was inspired by a competition. The Royal Academy of Sciences in

Paris had announced an award of twelve thousand francs for the cheapest way to manufacture alkalis. Leblanc added sulphuric acid to sodium chloride to make sodium sulphate. Then he immersed chunks of this sodium sulphate in lime and roasted them on a coal fire. Black ash was produced, with a mixture of sodium carbonate and calcium sulphide in it. Leblanc dissolved the sodium carbonate in water, turned it into crystals, and gave the world the most important and revolutionary chemical process to manufacture soda ash or washing soda.

But Leblanc received no reward for inventing this process. The prize money didn't reach him, and his factory was ransacked and confiscated during the French Revolution. Napoleon eventually took pity on him and returned his factory to its owner, but Leblanc was unable to raise the cash needed to restart it.

The French, for whose benefit Leblanc had made his epochal invention, didn't spare him a glance. But cunning English businessmen took his process to their own country and began using it to manufacture soap.

Today's young men didn't know any of this, which was why Digambar Bonarjee kept telling the researchers in his laboratory, 'You must study history—immersing yourself in daily R&D and lab reports alone cannot expand the scientist's vision.'

The young scientists heard him but didn't do as he suggested. Once he was granted some more money, Digambar Bonarjee meant to hire an assistant to compile historical news about the chemicals industry. He had told his favourite student Nagen Basu of his plans. 'Living in an ivory tower will not further scientific research in today's world, Nagen. Scientists must have a historical perspective; they must know what their countrymen want. Only then can we realise the hopes and dreams of the country.'

'Scientific research is a kind of relay race, isn't it?' said Nagen.

'Of course,' said Digambar Bonarjee. 'Imagine how the methods of manufacturing alkalis in soap factories changed the face of the world in subsequent years. Coal, salt, lime, sulphur, air, water, petrol—all the mysteries nurtured safely by nature within these materials have been snatched away to manufacture thousands of things from paint to soap, from food to medicine, from plastic to clothes, from fertilisers to so much more.

Nagen Basu had listened attentively back then. But then he had dealt Digambar Bonarjee an unexpected blow, something that Bonarjee was not prepared for at all. He had trusted Nagen.

The car was probably back. He shouldn't hold the driver back any longer. Digambar Bonarjee left his office with his briefcase.

Waking down the long corridor, Dr Noel Digambar Bonarjee glanced at the closed glass doors on either side. An electron microscope in the physical research department had stopped working two days ago. Digambar had asked Rao to get it repaired quickly, but Rao had sent him a long note the next day. After reading the note, Bonarjee had considered sending for him, but on second thought had gone to the electron microscopy room himself with the note. Rao was talking to Khosla, the newly appointed officer of spectometry. He stood up on seeing Bonarjee. 'No need,' said Digambar Bonarjee and pulled up a stool next to Rao's. Holding out the note, he said, 'Considering I'm in the office next to yours, why not drop in instead of sending a note? When a machine breaks down, the first priority is to get it working. The other formalities can follow.'

'I wanted to put on record,' said Rao, 'government property, after all.'

'You're new to our laboratory, Rao,' said Digambar Bonarjee, 'so there are some things you must know. Many government laboratories do nothing but exchange notes.

But here at HAC, scientists are hired to do research, not write notes. I've told everyone, and I'm reminding you as well—there's no need to think of the machines under your supervision as government property. Think of each of them as your own and treat them with love and care accordingly. If there's any trouble because of this, if audit raises objections, tell them right away to contact the research director Digambar Bonarjee, because you're only following his orders.'

Rao was taken aback. 'I want all of you to pursue science fearlessly,' Bonarjee had said. 'I'll take care of the trivial things.'

He considered asking Rao to encourage the young scientists to learn a little bit of repair work for each of the instruments. *Many of the modern machines are more fragile than modern women—but that doesn't mean stopping your work out of fear. The large foreign companies are aware of this failing on the part of Indians, so once they have sold us their machines, they have us at their mercy when it comes to repairs and spare parts.*

Digambar Bonarjee had been to Russia some time ago. There he had seen the male scientists in every laboratory treating their machines like their girlfriends. The Russians had learnt the hard way that they couldn't send for the after-sales people from England or America or Germany at the drop of a hat. So, instead of sitting back, they had trained themselves in the primary maintenance and basic repair of their machines. Digambar Bonarjee liked the system very much and was thinking of following it in Chandanpur.

Bonarjee walked down the corridor. Sometimes he was taken by the desire to wander around this enormous building all by himself. Seven years ago, when he sat in his small chemical analysis office in Chandanpur dreaming of a research and development department, many had considered him mad.

He had said even then that a time would come when farmers in India would fight for chemical fertilisers. Just the one factory in Chandanpur couldn't possibly meet this demand. Two hundred nitrogen-manufacturing factories would be needed to produce millions of tonnes of fertilisers. But it wouldn't be possible to beg and borrow for the technology from foreign countries to set up these factories—India would have to develop its own expertise.

Many had laughed at Digambar Bonarjee. *Fertiliser technology doesn't hang like fruits from trees*, they said. *You can't manufacture ammonium nitrate or ammonium carbonate or urea with your own efforts just because you want to. There are no more than nine or ten companies in the entire world who have poured millions of pounds and dollars to perfect this technology.*

Digambar Bonarjee had just returned from abroad then. *If the UK or the US can do it, why can't we*, he had said. *Let the research begin immediately. It cannot be delayed any more.*

Acharya, the Indian Civil Service officer in charge of the Chandanpur project, had said, 'What you're talking about is impossible in any of the factories in this country. If we do need research, let me write to the government to set up a fertiliser research centre at a university.'

Digambar Bonarjee had said, 'University professors will never be able to make fertiliser. Our universities are woefully disconnected from reality. Information about the problems of our country or our joys and sorrows don't reach them. They live in a world of their own. I want the research to begin here at the Chandanpur project, let it move in tandem with the manufacturing.'

The authorities were not in favour of Digambar Bonarjee's ideas. They considered him a madman. *If wishes were horses, beggars would ride*, they said. *What is this Bengali arrogance that wants to compete with global giants like Dupont and ICI?* The general manager of the Chandanpur project said,

'Don't forget, Bonarjee, that the income of our company is not even one per cent of the amount these companies spend on R&D every year.'

Digambar Bonarjee would have had to withdraw had something out of the blue not happened. But because it did, he now stood in a laboratory which was not just a centre of chemicals research, but a confluence of physics, agronomy, botany, geology, engineering, and several other subjects.

Digambar Bonarjee walked out of the laboratory building. He was not in a cheerful frame of mind. The news about Nagen Basu was troubling him greatly.

3

Kamalesh went directly to his quarters from the station. Digambar Bonarjee's message was waiting for him. His heart filled with resentment as he left for the research director's bungalow after a wash. He simply couldn't accept being summoned back unceremonially to work straight after his wedding. His father had tried to calm him down. 'The job is everything for a man. Without a job all the joys of married life sour. Everyone else in the world wants to extract something from you—the only exception is your employer. So you have to adjust to these little difficulties with a smile.'

But the times had changed since Kamalesh's father's days as an employee. Even the merchant offices were not dictatorships anymore. And besides, Kamalesh worked in a government organisation, where everyone had some legal rights.

'Report sick,' Sutapa had advised in the morning. 'Even on annual leave anyone can fall ill. If you have a doctor's certificate, Digambar Bonarjee cannot harm a hair on your head.'

Kamalesh would never have returned had the telegram come from someone other than Digambar. None of the young scientists at the Chandanpur laboratory considered him their boss. He was actually their guru—unbelievable in this day and age, but true nevertheless. Digambar Bonarjee kept track of the minute details of the research that each of the three hundred and fifty scientists was engaged in.

He could reel off what every one of them was working on, and how much progress they had made, without looking at their files. Digambar Bonarjee didn't address anyone in the office formally, being on familiar terms with all of them. He kept a strict watch on everything and everyone. It was quite normal for him to tell one of the scientists, 'Get your paunch under control, Ajay. Your date of birth is such and such, you can hardly work if you get so fat at this age.'

To someone else he might say, 'You look like you're thinking very hard, Chintaharan. Don't let your thoughts about corrosion corrode you. You can't make a breakthrough when you're worried. Look up the history of the great discoveries. The ideas came quite simply and during lighter moments. Archimedes was in his bathtub, Newton was sitting under a tree.' When Chintaharan chuckled, Digambar Bonarjee said, 'I met the Hungarian biochemist Albert Szent-Györgyi once. He told me, "I'm embarrassed to go to scientific conferences—all those serious and contemplative expressions at lectures and seminars ruin my opinion of myself. I keep thinking about how much they know and ponder over all the time. I simply cannot believe none of them has won the Nobel Prize, while I have."'

It was Digambar Bonarjee who had persuaded Kamalesh Roychowdhury to join the Chandanpur project. He was one of the examiners of the doctoral thesis that Kamalesh had submitted at IIT. Kamalesh's research was on some of the problems of manufacturing catalysts. Digambar had grilled Kamalesh for an hour and a half during the viva voce. He was capable of intense cross-examination and seemed to have mastered all the mysteries of catalysts already. Only when he was satisfied with Kamalesh's responses did he relent. And then he rang Kamalesh that same night from the IIT guesthouse.

Passing on the good news that Kamalesh now had his PhD, he had said, 'So you can add a doctor to your name. But what happens thereafter?'

Kamalesh was dreaming of going abroad. 'I'm thinking of gathering some experience at a chemicals factory outside India,' he said.

Digambar Bonarjee had burst out laughing. Then, based on his own experience, he had said, 'Do you expect these factories abroad to teach you anything useful? Do you really think these white people will share their secret knowledge with an outsider? You're living in a world of dreams, Dr Roychowdhury. You'll realise after you've slaved for three years that they haven't even let you through the front door. Of course, they'll pay you enough to keep your mouth shut.'

A worried Kamalesh had asked Digambar Bonarjee if they could meet. In Room No. 2 of the IIT guesthouse, he had scanned Digambar Bonarjee carefully. The meeting had taken place several years ago, but Kamalesh remembered it well.

Digambar Bonarjee wore glasses with thick lenses even then. His eyes were magnetic, even though he never met anyone else's, always preferring to look away. Formally attired at most times, he was dressed for dinner. His skin was the colour of ebony, and he had an aquiline nose. His lower lip curled at times when he spoke.

'You have a fine record,' Digambar Bonarjee had told Kamalesh. 'So you're very likely to get a British Chemicals scholarship. But, and I cannot emphasise this enough, no chemicals company in England or Japan or Italy or France or America or Canada will allow you to learn the tricks of the trade. They have adopted the historical purdah system because they're perpetually terrified of their secret knowledge being disclosed. After all, that will mean losing their fat profits. For every step they take, they apply for a hundred patents. The next step comes only after that.'

Kamalesh had looked at him in silence. 'You know what's most interesting?' Digambar Bonarjee continued. 'The French revolutionaries took away the formula of the most important invention made by Nicolas Leblanc, the father of our modern chemicals industry, and distributed it free of cost to everyone for the benefit of the people. They didn't believe in patents. It was with this formula that England came to dominate the alkali-manufacturing industry. Then the Germans joined in. And the less said about the Americans the better.'

Digambar Bonarjee went on to air his opinion of American science. 'You cannot match them when it comes to buying inventions and discoveries made in other countries and luring away scientists to set up business. Look at the history of scientific inventions in the past seventy-five years. The motor car was developed by Europeans, but it was the Americans who turned it into a global enterprise. The major developments in steel technology were made in other countries, but American companies made use of them. I can give you dozens of examples from the chemicals industry. And everyone in the world knows America's nuclear science research is loaded with German names.'

Kamalesh was genuinely astonished that evening. Drawing on his pipe, Digambar Bonarjee said, 'I have nothing against the Americans. They have given many scientists a chance to pursue their mission. They're also unparalleled when it comes to using knowledge for the benefit of humans. But I feel our country can walk on the same path if it wishes to. And if we apply ourselves, no one in the world can match us. The Germans or the Japanese, the Americans or the English, they'll all throw their hands up in despair.'

'Do you really believe this?' Kamalesh had asked.

'Of course I do,' Digambar Bonarjee declared categorically. 'What is it that we lack? We have countless numbers of talented youngsters, millions of hardworking labourers, much more of natural resources compared to other countries, and none of the decrepit fifty-year-old factories that they have. We are about to start afresh. If we make sure to adopt only the most modern and efficient methods, who can compete with our manufacturing prowess?'

'But why hasn't any of this materialised?' Kamalesh was about to ask.

Digambar Bonarjee brought it up himself. 'It hasn't happened because we still expect people from other countries to set up our factories. Thousands of them are supposed to spring up overnight while we sleep soundly. The truth is that we haven't learnt to be self-reliant. But we cannot be free unless we stop depending on others.'

After a pause, he continued, 'There's still time. If we can get down to work with confidence, many arrogant countries will be forced to bow before us.'

Then Digambar Bonarjee began talking about his own experience. 'Take fertiliser catalysts. Three rupees out of every hundred spent in a fertiliser factory is on catalysts. The authorities at our Chandanpur factory didn't believe there was an alternative to importing these catalysts. All the imported catalysts went bad at Chandanpur on one occasion. They simply wouldn't work. Everyone was at their wits' end, because getting a fresh supply by ship would take a long time. So the authorities were forced to turn to us and say, the factory is about to close, see if you can do anything. After a hundred and twenty hours of straight labour in our tiny laboratory, God smiled on us. We found a way to revive the useless catalysts and make them work. That was the beginning. After this, you may have read in the papers, we developed several new catalysts. We can export these to world markets now if we want to.'

There was something brusque about Digambar Bonarjee, but also tremendously attractive at the same time. Eventually

Kamalesh Roychowdhury abandoned his plans of going abroad and applied for a job at HAC.

He would never have believed there was a research laboratory like this in an unknown place like Chandanpur unless he had seen it for himself. Digambar Bonarjee had said, 'This is just the beginning. I will expand it more. All I ask for is that all of you put your heart and soul into the work.'

Kamalesh was inspired and was soon caught up in the exhilaration of working in the laboratory. He made rapid strides and was quickly promoted from senior scientific officer to research manager.

One day Digambar Bonarjee sent for Kamalesh and told him, 'I'm thinking of moving you to a different role. Why should the citizens of this poor country tolerate the wastefulness of R&D that yields no practial outcomes. What the country needs now is that this scientific knowledge be used immediately for production in factories. So I want to focus on the process design department now—so that we can set up new plants at lower costs. We bought a foreign blueprint for the fertiliser factory coming up in Haripur. Even for the plant that our company built in Maharashtra we were dependent on others. We're paying large sums of money to foreign countries, but we don't have so much foreign exchange. The managing director took me to America in January. The way he had to bow and scrape before some third-class people for a little credit really annoyed me.'

'Do they humiliate us?' Kamalesh asked.

'Why should the world be cordial with a country that wants to buy things but cannot pay hard cash? I'm sure they laugh when they talk to us. They lend us money and charge interest for it, but the newspapers call it aid. And, besides, asking for credit means doubling your cost. They'll try to force ten-year-old technology on you, they'll charge you a hundred-and-fifty for what should cost a hundred, and you'll have no choice but to pay. As they say, beggars can't be choosers. After travelling abroad I've realised a borrowed meal is all but inedible.'

'I've made up my mind,' Digambar Bonarjee had told Kamalesh. 'We must use our own methods to set up one or two chemical fertiliser plants. I don't like the fact that three hundred and fifty of us will sit in air-conditioned rooms in the guise of doing R&D and collect our salaries while our managing director goes abroad and says, please set up our factories, gentlemen.'

That was when Kamalesh was transferred to the process design department. Sutapa had joked: 'What's going on, Kamalesh? Apparently you've become Krishna's Arjun?'

'What?' Kamalesh asked, laughing.

'It seems you're Digambar Bonarjee's top protégé. The man is besotted with Kamalesh Roychowdhury.'

'Oh Sutapa-di, change the subject,' Kamalesh had said. 'When I was a student I was told those who live in factory townships know nothing of the world outside, they only discuss their bosses.'

'In the office and in the lab, in bathrooms and homes, on the streets and in the markets, in drawing rooms and even in bed, it's nothing but the company,' Shubhashish had said.

'Let's talk about something else, in that case,' Kamalesh had said.

'A friend who's a physicist is researching kisses,' said Shubhashish. 'He says a kiss is no easy matter, it can weigh anywhere between fifty and twelve hundred grams.'

Sutapa ticked off her husband roundly for initiating a discussion on kisses with a bachelor. And so the conversation had veered round again to the laboratory. 'There are two people Digambar Bonarjee is pleased with,' Shubhashish had said. 'Nagen Basu and Kamalesh Roychowdhury. But I don't know which of them is his right hand and which the left.'

Kamalesh recalled fragments of all these conversations on his way to Digambar Bonarjee's bungalow. It was because of their affectionate relationship that he hadn't been able to ignore the telegram.

A small bungalow stood in the middle of an open expanse of land. Opening the gate and walking along the red gravel path, Kamalesh spotted Digambar Bonarjee. He was reclining in a wicker easy chair on the lawn. A table stood in front of him. A faint light glowed from a distance.

Many people in Chandanpur knew that Digambar Bonarjee often sat alone in the dark for a long time. Whatever time was left over from his busy working day was spent gazing into the darkness. Bonarjee's personal life was shrouded in mystery. Some said he was a committed bachelor. Others said, not at all, he used to be married to a Punjabi woman. Later, finding his lifestyle unbearable, she had divorced him. Digambar Bonarjee's mother used to live with him here. While she was alive, they would go to church on Sunday mornings. The church was nearly fifteen miles away. After his mother's death, however, Digambar Bonarjee was never seen in church. He spent as much time as he could in the laboratory, and after getting back, sat alone in an easy chair on the lawn in the dark.

Digambar Bonarjee had no deep understanding of the way Bengalis led their lives. Three generations of his family had lived in Punjab. He went to school in Delhi and then spent some time in the Army before disappearing abroad for a few years. Then he returned home for some unknown reason.

Delighted to see Kamalesh, Digambar Bonarjee said, 'Welcome. I was told your train was late.'

'Yes, sir,' Kamalesh answered stiffly but with professional courtesy. He wanted to maintain a distance. He was keen on letting the director know: you have summoned the person sitting opposite you from his wedding bed without notice.

Noel Digambar Bonarjee didn't take notice. 'I hope everything went off well,' he said.

'There were no mishaps,' said Kamalesh, maintaining civility with some difficulty.

'My very best wishes to both of you. I have even bought a gift for you.' His words didn't please Kamalesh.

'There was no need. Why did you bother?' he said coldly.

'I'd even bought a train ticket to attend the wedding, but ...'

Finally Kamalesh looked at Digambar Bonarjee.

'You have to know the full story, Kamalesh,' said Bonarjee. 'I was about to leave for the station when news came from the Krishinagar pilot project that Nagen Basu has had a minor heart attack. Nothing too serious, though, Dr Sen from the Krishinagar Hospital told me.'

Digambar Bonarjee stopped. Then he calmly said, 'You know how much I depended on Nagen. The honour and prestige of our research department depends on the Krishinagar plant.'

After pausing for a bit, Bonarjee delivered sensational news. 'What's most upsetting is that Nagen Basu has been in trouble for some time. The CBI is investigating him. I find it hard to believe, but a CBI officer has informed me they have irrefutable proof that the last time Nagen went to Europe, he took a bribe from a foreign company. They have asked me to remove him from Krishinagar. I was hesitant, but just then I learnt of his illness.'

'And so,' Digambar Bonarjee continued, 'I was forced to turn to you, Kamalesh. I'm sorry for spoiling your honeymoon, but who else can I trust with the entire responsibility for the Krishinagar project, tell me. Nagen is being taken to the hospital in Calcutta today. I have signed your posting order as project manager. You must leave tomorrow morning.'

Digambar Bonarjee rose to his feet. Grimly he said, 'Nagen has dashed my hopes. You must help me save face.' Taking his favourite protégé's hand in his own, he said, 'I wish you all the luck in the world, my dear friend.'

4

Kamalesh's jeep set off very early in the morning. Krishipur was a hundred miles away from Chandanpur. Digambar Bonarjee had chosen the location of his experimental factory with great care. The place used to be called Dariapur earlier. 'Who knows,' he said, 'this new project might turn into a memorable milestone in the history of the fertiliser industry. That's why after a great deal of thought I named it Krishinagar.'

Krishinagar was indeed turning into a full-fledged town. Kamalesh had been here for the first time about a year ago with Digambar Bonarjee, who had said, 'We could have conducted this experiment on the land next to the Chandanpur project. But I want to keep my boys at a distance from the bosses at the Chandanpur factory whose tendency is to depend on others. White people still have a good reputation in Chandanpur. They can't rely on the research department of HAC. They'd rather lean on someone else's stick than stand on their own two feet.'

The speedometer had crept up beyond forty and was about to touch fifty. A cool morning breeze washed over Kamalesh, soothing his body. He couldn't help recollecting the beautiful woman he had left behind in Calcutta. Poor Chandramallika must have tossed and turned in her bed all night. She must be up by now and thinking about her husband. She was supposed to go back to her parents' place this morning. He must ask after her as soon as he reached Krishinagar.

Kamalesh had quickly written a letter to his wife last night. 'My dearest wife,' he had said, 'those who don't believe that husbands prosper on the strength of their wives' fortunes should remember you. A promotion on the wedding night! Digambar Bonarjee is sending me to Krishipur with a new job, which means an increase not only in stature but also in responsibility. More on this when we meet. The first few weeks are crucial, because Mr Bonarjee is going to England for some time after that. I have to understand the Krishinagar project thoroughly while he's still in Chandanpur.'

The Krishinagar area was visible from a distance. An enormous signboard said: Restricted Zone, entry not allowed without permission under some security act or the other.

News of the new manager's arrival had already spread yesterday in Krishinagar. Another jeep approached from the opposite direction as soon as Kamalesh entered the HAC area. A man stepped out of the jeep and offered a long salute. 'I'm Haragobinda Das, security officer.'

Another security guard appeared and placed a garland around Kamalesh's neck.

Das said, 'Your secretary Sujata Das and our administrative officer Sudarshan Sen are following in the car behind.'

Sudarshan Sen was bald and rotund—his experience as an officer was evident at first glance. He rushed towards Kamalesh to greet the new manager. 'Welcome to Krishinagar. All our officers are waiting at the project office to welcome you.'

Sujata Das came up shyly behind Sudarshan Sen, greeting Kamalesh by joining her palms casually. The slim, dark Sujata's large eyes suddenly reminded Kamalesh of the woman the poet Jibanananda Das had named Bonolota Sen. 'Your secretary wanted very much to meet you here but was too embarrassed to ask. I made her come.'

Returning the greetings, Kamalesh said, 'Many thanks for taking the trouble to meet me early in the morning.'

Both Sudarshan and Kamalesh noticed that Sujata Das had looked a little surprised when she saw Kamalesh for the first time. Sujata didn't dare reveal the reason, which lay in her handbag—a wedding invitation that had arrived from Calcutta in the post a few days ago. Her friend Rajanigandha's sister Chandramallika was getting married to one Kamalesh Roychowdhury.

Sujata couldn't summon up the courage to ask Kamalesh about it. He was an important officer, after all, while Sujata was a mere shorthand typist. But as far as she could remember, the wedding night had been two days ago, in which case how had he arrived here today? Mallika must have married some other Kamalesh. Sujata was making a mistake. She didn't have the nerve to get the invitation out of her bag and check the date. If it was the right Kamalesh, she might have considered developing a light-hearted relationship with him by virtue of his being married to her friend's sister. But as a colleague in the workplace he might not care for such an equation. Sujata Das had no desire to invite humiliation on herself.

After another round of thanks, Kamalesh requested everyone to go back. Then he went back to his own jeep. From his seat next to the driver, he looked at the scene in front of him. The jeep was on high ground, and through a gap between two hillocks he could see the Krishinagar factory. A demon king had set up a playroom of steel for himself under the open sky, configuring metal pillars of strange colours and shapes according to his fancy. Despite his knowledge of various secrets of chemical engineering and of the minutiae of fertiliser plants, Kamalesh felt he was viewing an open-air exhibition of works by a renowned but impenetrable modern artist. The creator's carefully nurtured aesthetic of rhythm was somehow evident in the circular, tall, squat, slim, or thick pillars.

After taking charge at the project office, Kamalesh rushed over to meet Nagen Basu's wife. But the family had already vacated the bungalow. Nabanita Basu had accompanied her husband to Calcutta, while the others had returned to Chandanpur with their belongings. They had not vacated the quarters there, for Nagen Basu had moved only temporarily.

Kamalesh spent the day inspecting the work at the project. It wasn't particularly large—it could be said to be an experimental plant. But even this needed several millions of rupees. Nothing was possible at a low cost in the world today, which was why, Kamalesh reflected, the rich countries were marching ahead. Those who didn't have the resources couldn't keep pace in the competition to spend money.

It wouldn't take Kamalesh very long to grasp the work going on at the Krishinagar pilot project. For when Digambar Bonarjee was drawing up the plans for it, Kamalesh was always by his side. Every employee of the process design department had worked late into the night at that time. All of them were fired up by enthusiasm.

'If what we're trying to do with the production of synthetic ammonia and urea is successful,' Digambar Bonarjee had said, 'there'll be a minor explosion in the world of fertilisers. Half a dozen companies have erected walls with their patents to create a situation where every hungry human being in the world has to rely on their benevolence. No one can think of manufacturing chemical fertilisers without handing over fat sums of money to these companies as royalties and buying their machinery at high prices. If India can develop its own technology, we can be self-reliant in at least one respect. And if we're lucky, we might even be able to sell our technology to them.'

Digambar Bonarjee had been to the head office with all the design-related documents that Kamalesh had prepared.

He told Kamalesh before leaving, 'My problem is that Hindustan Agro-Chemicals trusts me implicitly. They agree to whatever I want.' This time they had suggested that Digambar Bonarjee test his plan for manufacturing urea in a small pilot plant. If the homegrown process proved successful, all the new factories under the next Five-Year Plan could be set up accordingly. And if it turned out that the method wasn't flawless, enquiries would have to begin immediately in the international markets for what methods their companies could offer.

The managing director took only two weeks before sending a telex message to Bonarjee: Go ahead. The head office also accepted Digambar Bonarjee's cost estimates without demur.

That was the beginning of the Krishinagar project. The plan was not publicised greatly. It was only announced that the pilot project would test the efficacy of various global production processes. In addition, there would be some R&D around the new compound fertiliser that had been named Urvara. But the plan envisaged some production too, so that the Krishinagar project would not have to be maintained with government money—its costs would be met from its own earnings.

Digambar Bonarjee had sent for Nagen Basu as soon as he got permission from Delhi. His favourite disciple had just returned from a trip to five European countries. He had been there to meet the big companies to figure out which of them to tie up with for technology, so that the next set of factories in India could be set up at lower costs. Bubbling with excitement, Digambar Bonarjee told Nagen Basu, 'We've got a huge opportunity, Nagen. Now you can demonstrate what the boys of the HAC research department can achieve for the nation.'

Nagen Basu was personally involved in setting up the Krishinagar project. The first to arrive at the spot were giant bulldozers, which brashly flattened the uneven land of Krishinagar in a matter of weeks. The contractor even hired a team to get rid of a hillock with dynamite. Then several groups of people came, some of them HAC employees, others day labourers and the contractor's representatives. Several small buildings came up, and a number of camps were set up. Everyone could see the plant beginning to rise towards the sky. Offices and testing laboratories were constructed around it, along with an enormous warehouse to store the fertiliser that would be produced. For now it was being used for cement, iron, and other construction material.

The project hospital came up further away, next to the river. Besides everyday treatment, there were facilities for surgery, since there was always the fear of labourers being injured while the factory was being built.

Work on laying railway tracks had progressed too, and much of the material was already being transported in wagons. Earlier it could only travel as far as the station five miles away, after which it had to be loaded on trucks for the rest of the journey. Now the raw material would be delivered right inside the factory.

These were the external aspects of the project. Kamalesh wanted to send a report to the director about the process design within a day or two. He held long discussions with the project officers to gather all the information he needed. Sujata proved very efficient, typing up several letters swiftly for Kamalesh. She asked if he'd like some tea.

An exhausted Kamalesh returned to his quarters at the end of a long day of work. There was an attendant to look after his needs there. There was a bed. And a telephone.

After a shower Kamalesh was thinking of writing his wife a letter when the phone rang. It was Sutapa from Calcutta. 'Hello, Kamalesh, what's this? First you run away from your wife, and then there's no news from you.'

'But I posted a letter this morning,' said Kamalesh.

'What use is a letter—you should have sent a telegram, though you can hardly declare your love for your wife in a telegram.'

'How did you know I'm here?' Kamalesh was surprised.

'I rang Chandanpur to summon a smile to your wife's wan face. That's how I got the good news. Then she couldn't wait anymore, so I had to ring you here. Talk to her now. We're moving away so that we don't overhear anything.'

Chandramallika came on the line. 'Listen, don't believe anything Sutapa-mashi tells you. I hope the train ride was comfortable.'

'Not at all, but who do I explain that to?' Kamalesh was all sweetness.

'Take care of yourself, all right?' Only a few hours had passed and already Chandramallika was concerned about her husband's well-being.

'You stay happy too. Don't fall sick worrying about me,' Kamalesh told her.

'I'll go now, all right?' Kamalesh was about to disconnect the call but Sutapa was on the line again. 'Listen to me, mister, while you're in exile, call your wife every day.'

'My God, do you know what making a trunk call every day means? Where's the money in a government job?'

'I don't care. Do you think our girl has no feelings? Call her every day, or else take her to live with you.' Sutapa ended the call.

The phone rang again soon afterwards. It was Sudarshan Sen, the administrative officer of the project. 'Dr Roychowdhury, my wife's very keen that you eat with us tonight. If you have no objections I'll come over to fetch you.'

Kamalesh didn't protest. Sudarshan Sen arrived soon afterwards. A jovial man, he said, 'Although you're a very important officer, you're my son's age. Don't hesitate to ask me for anything you need.'

His wife was a sociable woman. She greeted Kamalesh warmly.

Sudarshan Sen said, 'We are what you might describe as unencumbered. Both our daughters are married and have had their first child. So our warranty period is over. Our son completed his education and got a job. I've got him married and settled in company quarters in Rourkela. Now all I need is to secure the retirement letter from HAC before my wife becomes a widow.'

'Enough. Ever since we got married all I've heard is you're losing your job any day,' Sudarshan Sen's wife admonished her husband.

Undaunted, Sudarshan Sen told Kamalesh, 'What can I tell you, sir? There's no job more dangerous than managing money. Even military service is safer. There you can lose your life but not your wealth. But here our labourers might be killed in the line of duty anytime and the company will grab the provident fund given half a chance.'

Kamalesh laughed at this. 'We were told independent India began with the rule of the lawyers, and then came the rule of the managers,' he said. 'Now the biggest companies are headed by accountants. Those who invent or manufacture things, or sell them or repair them, are not being allowed to rise to the top. All power is in the hands of the bookkeepers.'

'That's just a joke for all of you,' Sudarshan Sen said. 'Our line of work is the punishment for mountains of sin. The moment I hear there's a new factory coming up I tell my wife, now yet another wretched administrative officer like your husband has been robbed of sleep. New projects don't mean progress for the nation—they only mean windfalls for criminals and the downfall of the manager. The contractor will try to cheat you, the suppliers will provide sub-standard material, the employees will turn in fake travel bills, there will be theft in the warehouse, tallying the accounts will be impossible—that's a new project for you. You can consider me out of my mind. But I have six months to go—the retirement letter should be coming any day. I don't have to mince my words anymore.'

'You can be so funny, Mr Sen,' Kamalesh said.

'This is how he talks,' Sudarshan Sen's wife said. 'At home, outside, at the office—his views are always the wrong way up.'

'I admit I was born the wrong way up. I make a living from a job in a fertiliser company; but sir, let me say it bluntly: I don't know why you're making this futile attempt to grow more crops on India's soil.'

Kamalesh laughed. 'What do you mean, Mr Sen? India's not going to have more land, so we have to increase productivity to make sure everyone has enough to eat.'

'It won't work, sir,' Sudarshan Sen said tragically. 'Doesn't matter how hard you and our director Digambar Bonarjee try, you'll lose. You have no idea of the rate at which children are being born. Our problem is in the basics, sir. We couldn't implement birth control, but the government has instituted death control. Those who used to succumb to cholera, smallpox, typhoid, malaria or black fever by the time they were eight or ten now reach adulthood, get married, and become parents. They don't budge from the world until they're fifty or sixty, having seen the faces of a couple of dozen grandchildren.'

'Is that so bad, Mr Sen?' asked Kamalesh.

'Not at all,' Sudarshan Sen said with a show of contrition. 'But watch your step a little. No need to indulge the goddess Shashthi so much. If the deity in charge of reproduction acts according to her whims, not even Digambar Bonarjee can do anything for the country. You men will keep fathering sons and daughters without a care, and Sudarshan Sen will have to bear the brunt in his old age by setting up camp in a jungle and supervising a fertiliser factory—is that fair?'

Kamalesh couldn't keep himself from laughing. Ignoring his wife's glares, Sudarshan Sen continued, 'No matter how confident you are as a scientist, sir, you can't do it. I read somewhere there were three hundred million people on earth when Jesus Christ was born. When hunger forced Columbus to set off to discover India fifteen hundred years later, the population of the world was five hundred million. And then in just four hundred and fifty years the number has turned to three billion. India alone has increased its population by eighty million between 1951 and 1961. The headache that the government has created by popularising the use of DDT, penicillin and soap will now need hundreds of fertiliser plants to be resolved.'

'Do the people who work here know of the gigantic cause to which they're contributing?' Kamalesh asked.

Sudarshan Sen burst into laughter. 'They know nothing. They're not interested in knowing anything either. All of them are here either to make a living or to make some extra money. Try talking to the workers here. The man who digs earth every day for his wages has no interest in the reason it must be done. All he wants is money to buy his rice. The Punjabi contractor who's constructing the buildings couldn't care less who'll occupy them or why. All he wants to know is when his bills will be settled and when a fresh tender will be floated. The clerks in my office want to know why the dearness allowance isn't going up. Whether your factory produces fertiliser or not is not their concern. The world is a tough place, sir. What you and Digambar Bonarjee aspire after cannot be found in India except in novels.'

Kamalesh listened to Sudarshan Sen in silence. 'Where's your mind wandered to, sir?' Sen asked. 'What are you thinking about?'

'I'm wondering whether I'll be able to fulfil my responsibility. Will I manage to get everything compeleted on time and have the factory running by the deadline?'

'Don't worry about it, sir,' Sudarshan Sen consoled him. 'What will be, will be. Has anything ever been achieved on time in India? There's a clerk in my department who talks too much. When I scolded him the other day he said, never mind humans, God himself cannot complete his tasks on time these days. Children are not born at the appointed hour, the monsoon doesn't arrive in the appointed week, trees don't flower in the appointed season, so how do you expect the work at the office to be carried out on the appointed day?'

What Sudarshan Sen said made Kamalesh worry even more. 'Our director cannot think beyond the deadline. I have more or less given my word to him.'

Back in his own quarters, Kamalesh found himself thinking about his wife again. He had given her his word too—that they would meet as soon as possible. All she could do right now was to pass lonely nights in her old bed in her parents' home. How strange the ways of the almighty were. Someone Kamalesh had no responsibility for even a week ago now occupied his entire mind and heart. Gobindo-babu from the catalyst department in Chandanpur used to say, 'Let scientists discover all the catalysts they can, remember that no catalyst like marriage has been invented yet. All it takes is a few rituals and incantations to make a pair of living humans come together in a chemical reaction.'

Kamalesh had written to Chandramallika about this form of catalysis in some detail. In reply, Chandramallika had written, 'Sutapa-mashi has read your letter. She has instructed me to tell you to write about romance without bringing science into it. Apparently love cares nothing for catalysts. Listen, I hate it here. The days just won't pass. I try to read, and my husband's face floats up in front of my eyes. I start listening to music, and all I recall are my husband's words. And that's just by day, so you can imagine the situation at night. Everyone says I'm withering away and growing darker. When will you come?'

He wished he could go. Krishinagar wasn't very far from Calcutta. And there was even a fast train from the station a few miles away. But there was no question of leaving Krishinagar now. Work was going on at full steam. Representatives of the Japanese company from which some machinery had been bought were here to install it. Two Germans had also begun work. A couple of machines for the urea plant had been bought from them, machines that weren't yet manufactured in India. The engineers were hard at work too. Leaving Krishinagar even for a day would need Digambar Bonarjee's permission. He would have rung Dr Bonarjee in other circumstances, but the man was bound to jump to conclusions if Kamalesh asked for leave now. Going to Calcutta was almost impossible.

A month later Kamalesh's impatient wife wrote, 'Don't you have business in Calcutta? So many people have meetings here. My friend Bakul got married six months ago. She was with her husband all this time. It's only been a fortnight since she's come to her parents' home, and her husband's already been to Calcutta twice for conferences.'

Poor Chandramallika, who had no idea about a corporate employee's life before her marriage, was forced to enquire about these things now. In his letters Kamalesh sent her news about his work. Chandramallika was not unaware of Sudarshan Sen. By now she had also come to know the ammonia plant supervisor Ghanashyam Das, the vigilance officer Narahari Patra, and the medical officer Dr Sen. About the vigilance officer, Kamalesh had written, 'I've never seen anyone whose work is so closely related to his name. He's always nearby, in a hurry to catch anone who takes a bribe or a commission. He knows your father. He's worked under him at some point in the past.'

In the next letter, Kamalesh wrote, 'I haven't told you about my secretary. Sujata Das. Very efficient. Considering there are so many openings for personal assistants in big cities, I have no idea why she's chosen to work in this godforsaken place.'

Chandramallika's reply came swiftly. 'I'm quite worried by the hints Sutapa-mashi has been dropping ever since I told her about your secretary. From your letter I assumed secretaries type letters and arrange their boss's papers, but now I hear many a secretary makes their boss forget about his wife. What's even more worrying is that you have written so much about your personal assistant, but you haven't mentioned whether she's married or not.'

Sujata Das came to a sudden halt as she was about to enter Kamalesh's office carrying documents. The boss was busy reading a letter on blue notepaper, which he had drawn out of a blue envelope. Sujata saw his face brightening as he read, with a quiet, private smile appearing on his lips now and then. Sujata realised he was immersed in epistolary love with his absent wife. Sujata was quite familiar with the lady's handwriting by now, since two or three letters for Kamalesh arrived at her desk every week. Her boss was always dying to read them at once and got rid of her on some pretext or the other.

Still unmarried, Sujata Das had not had this particular experience yet, which was probably why her curiosity was higher than usual. She was in charge of keeping Kamalesh's confidential correspondence safe, but he never left these letters on his desk even by mistake. He read each letter two or three times and then put it in his pocket. This behaviour from a newlywed man made Sujata smile.

Kamalesh had a mountain of work every day—sometimes he didn't even have time for lunch. But Sujata could bet that he would stay up tonight to write his wife a love letter. And at eight-thirty tomorrow morning Kamalesh would give her a heavy blue envelope with the address written in his own hand. Her job was only to add a stamp and send it to the post office.

Once in a while Sujata was tempted to open the envelope and read the letter, but she had eventually resisted the urge. She only scanned the name on the envelope several times. Chandramallika Roychowdhury.

Not that Sujata Das would have seen anything exciting had she opened the envelope. She'd have found the factory being referred to. And herself as well. Kamalesh had written, 'It's exactly as Sutapa-di and you fear. When the cat is away, the mice are at play. Sujata Das is unmarried. And of a dangerous age, not even thirty yet. She lives alone here, has the sweetest temperament, and looks like Bonolota Sen, lifting her bird's-nest eyes to speak in wonder. She's from Serampore.'

At this Mallika wrote, 'Sujata Das and Serampore sound familiar. Ask her if she went to St. John's Diocesan.'

A few days later Kamalesh wrote again, 'The work on the factory is progressing well. I've settled down in my small quarters here. But some people tell me a home without its goddess is no home at all. It's so odd to imagine three months have gone by since we got married. It's time to do or die. Digambar Bonarjee will be here for an inspection. I'll bring it up. I simply have to get leave. Yes, Sujata Das was astonished when I asked about Diocesan. Fixing a surprised gaze on me Bonolota Sen-style, she said, "You're right, how did you know?" I said, my wife told me. Then, excited, she burst out: "Chandramallika Chatterjee is your wife! She was three years my junior in school. I was even invited to your wedding; I didn't know then you were the same Kamalesh Roychowdhury. Look how small the world is." Sujata Das pays extra attention now to whether I'm eating properly. My teacup in the office shone the very next day. The bearers get a scolding from madam when they don't clean my office properly.'

Kamalesh reread his letter after finishing it. His wife wrote beautifully, so he had to be careful when he picked up his pen. He had already told her, 'I don't have a dictionary at hand, so don't laugh at my spelling mistakes.'

5

Finishing breakfast, Kamalesh stepped out of the house armed with the letter. The sparkling light on this autumn morning had lent Krishinagar a rare grace. Although he was not into literature, being far away from his wife reminded Kamalesh of Tagore's lines on the light in this season. He climbed into his jeep. In the mornings, he didn't rely on the driver.

The wide black road wound its way down as it pleased, first to the river and then, turning to the right, to the project site. A left turn at this point led to the railway station, and then the national highway. The big town of Dharmapur stood another thirty miles away.

Driving down the hillock, Kamalesh slowed his jeep upon spotting an unfamiliar car approaching from the opposite direction. Someone seemed to be waving at him to catch his attention.

The jeep and the Ambassador came to a stop more or less face to face. The owner and driver of the car, a man of pleasant appearance, opened his door and jumped out. Greeting Kamalesh, he said, 'We nearly missed you.'

By then Chandramallika had emerged from the back seat. She was glistening like the petals of freshly dew-soaked jasmine.

Kamalesh was startled. Although he had glanced at the passengers he hadn't recognised Chandramallika. How would he, since her being here was unimaginable.

Another well-dressed and beautiful married woman emrged from the car. Looking saucily at Kamalesh, she said, 'How do you like this suprise?'

Kamalesh realised she was both lively and bold. Going up close to him, she said, 'I'm Chandramallika's cousin Kanaklata. And this is Samarendra Roy, the man in my life. We couldn't go to your wedding, we were abroad at the time. We live nearby. My husband is a manager at British Explosives in Dharmapur.'

Kamalesh's unexpected joy had claimed his tongue. After a few moments he asked Mallika, 'Why didn't you wire me?'

Before she could answer Kanaklata glared at Kamalesh. 'Why should she? Considering you've kept your wife in exile for three months, why should she bother to inform you?'

Samarendra, who was smiling all this while, finally spoke. 'You could call it a well-hatched conspiracy, Kamalesh-babu,' he said. 'We had driven to Calcutta. On the way back from Kanak's parents' place we learnt you live close by. So we plotted a surprise for you.'

'This is what you call manna from heaven, sir,' said Kanaklata. 'I'm sure you'd assumed your helpless wife couldn't possibly embark on an adventure on her own, which meant you could do as you please here. Serves you right! Both you and this gentleman should remember India is under the control of women now.' Mallika's cousin warned her own husband too with a wagging finger.

'Jhumu was extremely worried that we might take her elsewhere and not to her husband,' said Samarendra, injecting more levity into the proceedings. 'Never mind all that. We have to inform her mother and your father immediately. But first, please sign the delivery voucher: Received one wife in intact condition.'

'Yes, Samarendra-da. Make sure he puts down the entire clause, like when goods are transported by rail.' Chandramallika joined forces with her husband's adversaries with a smile.

'In that case, please add: Received with full and final satisfaction,' Samarendra commented.

'The satisfaction is evident on his face,' Mallika's cousin said, seemingly to embarrass Kamalesh. After some thought, she added, 'But no, we're not delivering your wife to you. She was so downcast we thought we'd give her a glimpse of her husband. We'll take her to Dharmapur now and then back to Calcutta.'

Still radiating happiness, Kamalesh said, 'Since there's so much confusion and divergence of opinion, why don't we all go to my place instead?'

Chandramallika was about to get back into the Ambassador, but Kanaklata told Kamalesh with a serious expression, 'I allow you to drive your wife in your car this short distance.'

Chandramallika went and sat next to her husband. Kamalesh turned the jeep, and both vehicles proceeded towards the hillock.

Kamalesh would have kissed his wife on the spot had the other car not been following them. He only touched Mallika's hand lightly, and she gripped his tightly. Calming down after a few moments, she said, 'I've got you into trouble, haven't I?'

'Any husband would be ready to be in such trouble every single day. I couldn't have imagined that something like this could happen,' Kamalesh said.

'I couldn't work up the nerve, so I went to your place,' Chandramallika said. 'Baba encouraged me. He said, since the wretched fellow couldn't find his way to come and see you, you go and teach him a lesson.'

'You've got him eating out of your hands,' said Kamalesh.

'Considering my husband's been out of my hands since the wedding night, what am I supposed to do?' Chandramallika was emboldened now and had her repartee ready.

Taking the luggage out of the Ambassador, Kamalesh said, 'My attendant is at the market.'

Kanaklata asked bluntly, 'How large a domestic staff does your company give you?'

'Not even one. But you can hire as many as you like with your own money,' Kamalesh told her.

Disconcerted by his wife's question, Samarendra said, 'Never mind all that. Why don't both of you quickly make some tea for your husbands?'

Feigning anger, Kanaklata said, 'Is this my reward for bringing your wife to you?'

'It'll take you some time to use the equipment here, so I'll make the first round of tea,' Kamalesh said.

They objected, but he had lit the gas stove and quickly put on the kettle.

Sipping her tea, Kanaklata threw a barb at her husband, 'This is how to look after your wife.' Turning to Kamalesh, Kanaklata asked, 'How did you learn to make tea so well?'

Kamalesh laughed. 'Thanks to our director, Digambar Bonarjee. He's always ordering me around in the laboratory, "Kamalesh, make some tea".'

Kankalata was shocked. 'What! This is allowed in your company? The director ordering you to make tea? Why? Don't you have bearers?'

Kamalesh didn't take Kanaklata's gibe to heart. 'We often have to work late into the night at the lab,' he said. 'The bearers have long left by then. It's just a few of us and Dr Bonarjee. He says anyone who hasn't mastered the chemistry of making tea cannot possibly grasp the complex chemistry of fertilisers.'

Kamalesh rang his office. 'I'll be a little late today, Miss Das. Please postpone the ammonia plant coordination meeting by an hour. The peon must take his cycle and inform them, or else they will stop work and wait in the project office.'

'Why not get the meeting out of the way?' Chandramallika said. 'We'll chat here meanwhile.'

'Oh, please,' the ever-humorous Kanaklata gave her cousin a mock scolding. 'Is a meeting more important than a wife's visit after three months? My husband has meetings too—useless things. Endless pots of coffee, unending packets of cigarettes, jokes and laughter, all under the guise of discussions. There's no difference between office meetings and ladies' coffee meets.'

Everyone laughed. Kamalesh rang Sudarshan Sen. 'I want to rent a couple of beds, Mr Sen.'

'Nothing's available to rent, sir. I'll send you a pair of iron cots,' Sen said.

'Listen to me, Dr Roychowdhury,' Kanaklata said. 'Jhumu and I are the same age. Our grandfather was a flower-lover, so he named us after them. I've been married a year already, so I'll have to take on the responsibility of getting your wife started on setting up her household.'

Kamalesh quite liked the idea of his new wife getting started. 'We have similar contracts with those who sell us machines for our projects,' he told Kanaklata. 'The responsibility for getting the machines started is theirs.'

Kamalesh explained things to his retainer when he returned from the market. Then, with his guests' permission, he left for his office. There was a series of meetings. He had instituted the practice of meeting the department heads twice every week, so that all problems could be addressed immediately, and everyone was aware of the progress being made. They had all come to know that, like Digambar Bonarjee, Kamalesh Roychowdhury was also not a believer in writing letters.

'As all of you know, we have promised Dr Bonarjee to begin full operations at the factory on the seventh of December.

Dr Bonarjee has also given his word accordingly to the head office and elsewhere. If even one of us lags behind, everyone else's work will go to waste, which is why I want all of us to complete our allocated tasks well before the deadline. Keep a strict watch on the contractors working for you. Remember that daily supervision can prevent major lapses.'

After a pause, Kamalesh continued, 'Mr Hajra, how's the installation of the pipeline coming along?'

'I'll send you the progress report today,' Hajra replied.

'Don't forget, pipes are the arteries and veins of a chemical factory—the plant won't survive thrombosis.'

'The synthetic ammonia pipes have been laid,' Hajra said. 'We're checking the joints now.'

'You're aware how difficult it is to please Dr Bonarjee when it comes to welding sections of pipes together,' Kamlesh said. 'There'll be deep trouble if the welding isn't perfect.'

'You're right, sir,' said Hajra. 'Moreover, the contractor is an Indian one. With a foreign company there'd be no cause for concern. Overseas Pipes from Holland laid the pipes at Haryana Fertiliser. Their work was picture-perfect. The white men said, go to sleep peacefully, you'll have your pipeline in the morning.'

Kamalesh smiled and said, 'That's exactly what Dr Bonarjee objects to. He won't allow those days to continue, when the white men would put us to bed and do all the work themselves. So it has to be done by one of our homegrown pipe companies. You'd better make arrangements for X-rays of all the major joints in the pipes. Mr Iyer runs the X-ray department at the Chandanpur laboratory. Talk to him on the phone at once.'

The person in charge of the pipes in the urea plant was Pandey, whose wife was pregnant. Kamalesh asked after her before saying, 'Don't worry, Mr Pandey. Dr Sengupta, head of obstetrics at the Chandanpur hospital, is a friend of mine. I've had a word with him. Now tell me how the work is going.'

'We're slightly behind our target,' said Pandey. 'Singh, the contractor, was ready to work this weekend and make up for it. But we haven't received the pipes yet, sir.'

'What?' Kamalesh looked at Sudarshan Sen, who said, 'I've wired Jamshedpur twice. They tell me every day that the pipes will be here any moment.'

'Mr Sundaram in Jamshedpur is a close friend of Dr Bonarjee's. Send someone to meet him. We'll review the situation again the day after tomorrow.'

Kamalesh rang home after the second meeting. His retainer answered. When he asked to talk to 'Maiji' he was told memsaab was bathing. The phone was passed to Samarendra, who said, 'Don't worry. Everything is fine. The aroma from the kitchen suggests lunch won't be disappointing.'

Kamalesh dictated a number of letters to his secretary before walking over to meet Sudarshan Sen. 'Can you give me some suggestions, Mr Sen, I need to buy some glass crockery quickly.'

'If only it were Calcutta, sir, where money can buy you anything. We'll have to send someone to Dharmapur.' Sudarshan Sen began to grow a little curious. His questioning revealed that Mrs Roychowdhury had arrived suddenly without notice.

'A little bit of a crisis, therefore. I doubt there's enough crockery at home,' Kamalesh said.

'These situations are created to ensure a crisis, sir. I'm used to it, vigilance officers sometimes pay us these surprise visits.' Refusing to take no for an answer, Sudarshan Sen said, 'I'll send you some crockery from my home. Even though it's just the two of us, my wife has enough to entertain Ravana's extended family. That's her hobby—porcelain, brass, gunmetal, copper, aluminium, enamel, stainless steel, hind aluminium, nothing's been left out.'

Kamalesh was astonished when he returned home with the borrowed crockery. Several dishes were laid out on the table.

At the sight of the crockery, Kanaklata asked impishly, 'Oh, you were buying plates and dishes, instead of holding meetings?'

Poor Kamalesh was in a spot now, which made Chandramallika laugh.

'Your parents have packed an entire set of things to ensure their daughter-in-law doesn't have to suffer because of their son's incompetence,' said Kanaklata. 'What do you think all those trunks and packing boxes that were unloaded have in them?'

Everyone sat down to eat in a noisy bustle. Kamalesh declared that the food tasted different today, creating an opportunity that Kanaklata seized immediately. 'Naturally,' she said. 'We put a bit of turmeric on your wife's fingers and after she rinsed it off we added the water to the food. Obviously it's delicious.'

'Don't believe a word of what Rinki says,' said Chandramallika. 'She's cooked everything.'

Kamalesh was astonished on entering the bedroom. Chandramallika had already rearranged everything and made it pretty. The bedclothes were no longer rumpled. A new bedcover was spread over the bed perfectly. The books were neatly arranged on the shelf at the head of the bed. The pen and writing pad had been given pride of place where they belonged on the desk. The ashtray was clean. There was a glass of water, too, carefully covered with an upside-down saucer.

Kanaklata was reading a magazine in the drawing room. Chandramallika brought her to the bedroom, and at once she smiled and attacked Kamalesh. 'I'm told you're working round the clock to make the country self-reliant, even abandoning your wife on the wedding night for this noble cause. But the moment I set foot here I realised you have no option but to be wife-dependent. I wanted to take pictures to show the state of the house before and after the arrival of the wife. Now you can see for yourself the role wives play in your lives.' Kanaklata was fearless in her diatribe.

'I accept everything you're saying without protest,' Kamalesh gave in with a smile.

'It's not enough to accept it. Men must give more responsibility to their wives, understand, Mr Roychowdhury?'

'We would like to give them all of it,' Kamalesh said.

Widening her beautiful eyes even further, Kanaklata said, 'Oh, please. Men in this country want their wives to be nothing but cooks and partners in bed. They don't give them the chance to be partners in life.'

'Why don't you sit,' said Kamalesh. 'Use the bed.'

'Why should I?' Kanaklata curled her lips. 'I have my own husband, don't I? He's languishing alone outside.'

'Why don't both of you rest here?' Kamalesh requested her.

Curling her lips again and signalling meaningfully with her eyes, Kanaklata said, 'You're barely surviving here in exile, but you've got a double bed in your room in the hope that your wife will join you any day now. I don't see arrangements for anyone else.'

'This one is, in fact, for guests,' Kamalesh said with a smile. 'A pair of single beds will be here in half an hour.' Glancing at his watch, he added, 'I must go to the factory site once more. Why don't you rest, meanwhile? Once I'm back, we can chat late into the night.'

Kanaklata knitted her arched brows again. 'You can, but with her, not with me. My husband and I will be in our quarters in Dharmapur by then.'

Kamalesh coaxed and cajoled them to stay, but to no avail. They insisted on leaving after a cup of tea in the afternoon, so that they could be home by six or six-thirty in the evening.

'I'll be back from the factory site in no time, Samar-babu,' said Kamalesh. 'You can savour the hospitality of your wife and sister-in-law till then.'

6

In the silent afternoon the cousins lay in bed side by side. Mallika said, 'You're not being fair to Samar-babu. Why don't you call him in here, I'll go lie down on the sofa.'

'Don't talk rubbish, Jhumu,' Kanaklata snapped at her. 'Let him suffer a little now. It'll work in his favour afterwards.'

'You're very wicked, Rinki.' Chandramallika pinched Kanaklata.

Smiling archly and letting her hair loose, Kanaklata said, 'Once you're married, there's no such thing as being wicked or not wicked, you fool. For all the history you've memorised, you know nothing of psychology.'

Mallika grabbed her cousin's right hand and cracked the knuckles of two fingers. 'Forget my hand. In a few hours you can massage the fingers of the one who matters.'

'Uff, Rinki! You were never so explicit before you got married,' said Mallika, trying in vain to hide her embarrassment.

A little later, shaking her feet, Kanak said, 'Jhumu!'

'What?'

'How do you feel right now?' Kanak asked.

'I can't quite explain to you, Rinki,' said Mallika. 'But it feels soooo wonderful.'

'You know, Jhumu, this feeling is everything that matters when you're married. The day thinking of your husband doesn't make your heart flutter, the day you no longer find yourself interested in the useless details of the household, that's the day you'll know your married life has turned as foul as twice-boiled tea leaves.'

'I can't even think of these things now, Rinki, honestly. I just feel soooo happy.'

A while later Rinki asked, 'Asleep, Jhumu? Preparing for the night show?'

Jhumu was indeed thinking of the night. She blushed with embarrassment at being caught out. Without looking at her cousin, she somehow managed to say, 'Not at all, I'm awake.'

'You had only one night alone with him and yet he's made you lose yourself completely. How?' It was Rinki's turn to pinch her cousin.

'I know, Rinki! How do these things happen?' Mallika said softly.

Gazing at the ceiling, Kanaklata said, 'Look how our silly hearts go thump-thump for men, yet look how detached they are. Your husband happily abandoned his wife to give the cattle their feed.'

'Unless he gives the cattle their feed how'll he give me what I need?' Mallika spoke up in her husband's defence. 'The poor thing's only just got his promotion.'

'What's his designation now?'

'Project manager.'

'How much does your husband earn?'

'I don't know.'

Mallika's answer shocked Kanak. 'What on earth did you do in bed all night?'

'Come on, how can anyone ask about these things on the first night?'

'You don't have to ask. The husbands tell you themselves. Mine did.'

Mallika felt nervous. Then she said, 'He did bring up his work. Something about his mission—trying to invent something.'

'And you melted under the impression you've married Einstein,' Rinki snapped.

'Digambar Bonarjee their research director really loves him.'

'All directors love their employees when their targets are met,' Kanaklata said disbelievingly.

'You seem to know a lot,' Mallika said.

'Do you think being married is nothing but gluing lips with your husband like birds? Guiding our husbands properly is one of the biggest responsibilities for educated girls like us.'

'My goodness!'

'Nothing to do with goodness,' Kanaklata pinched Mallika again. 'Many of these men are just dimwits. They give their lives to their companies, the owners cheat them.'

'Private firms have owners,' Mallika said. 'This is a public-sector company.'

Rinki went off into peals of laughter. 'Private sector or public, all company owners are the same. You think the government cannot cheat anyone? Even God will cheat you given half a chance. Anyway. Take a nap, or the husband will be annoyed at night.'

7

Kamalesh woke up early in the morning and went out to sit in the garden. Mallika appeared too, standing barefoot on the grass. When he noticed, Kamalesh quickly got a pair of rubber slippers. 'Put them on,' he said. 'The dew on the grass can easily give you a cold.'

The sun had reported for duty in the eastern sky at the crack of dawn. In the morning light almost all of Krishinagar was visible from this height. There were no other habitations nearby. The five hundred acres of land on which Krishinagar stood was surrounded by a fence of sal wood and barbed wire. A row of single-storeyed residential quarters stood close to the fence. There were some larger buildings to the west, where the supervisors lived. Next to them was the officers' colony and, a little further, the guest house. The town was meant to grow in a circular pattern with the main factory in the middle and a ring road running around it. Several other broad streets met this road at various points.

Digambar Bonarjee had decided to name the roads of Krishinagar after flowers. Golap Sarani would have only rose bushes, no one would have trouble identifying it. Similarly, Krishnachura Sarani would be lined with royal poincianas, and Palash Sarani with flame of the forest. And then Rajanigandha Sarani with nothing but tuberose grown on it.

Kamalesh saw beautiful Mallika gazing into the distance like a figure in a painting. The factory stood like an unfinished canvas created by nature. Kamalesh kept looking at Mallika, as fresh and sacred as a flower. She was dressed in a thin teri cotton sari, and a red blouse on which the gentle light of dawn had fallen. On her wrists were a bangle of gold and one of red shell. She had made no attempt to gather her hair perfectly at this hour, most of it hung loose. A couple of curly strands had strayed past her forehead like tendrils on to her face.

Kamalesh picked up his packet of cigarettes and lighter from the table. He'd have certainly captured this special moment in a photograph if a camera were handy.

Widening her lovely doe-like eyes, Chandramallika asked, 'You're the boss of everything we can see from here?'

Kamalesh nodded.

'And everyone who works here has to follow your orders?' she asked in even greater surprise.

'About a thousand people are at work here right now.' Kamalesh paused. Turning his eyes towards the factory, he said, 'That's the cause for concern. I have to make all of them work together and get the plant operational by the deadline.'

There was no end to Chandramallika's astonishment. 'Do you know what each and every one of them is doing?'

'Of course. All the details are included in our plans and project report, which have been created in the Chandanpur research lab under Digambar Bonarjee's instructions. What we're about to do here hasn't been accomplished anywhere in the world.'

'Nowhere in the world? My God! Doesn't it scare you?' Chandramallika asked, draping the end of her sari around herself.

Resting his elbow on the table and his chin in his palm, Kamalesh said, 'It should. But Digambar Bonarjee isn't afraid of anything. He has personally developed a new method for recovering ammonia and urea artificially.'

'His name will be part of the history of science then, won't it?' like a little girl full of wonder Chandramallika asked.

Looking at his wife, a pleased Kamalesh said, 'How many have their names in history anyway? Hundreds of applications for inventions of all kinds reach the patent office every day. But our wretched country will benefit if Digambar Bonarjee's dream comes true. We will no longer be dependent on others, in this one aspect, at least.'

Mallika had already put the kettle on. Now she brought the teapot to the table. Kamalesh tried to help her, but she warned him: the wife's work must be done by the wife. The teaspoons clinked in sweet harmony with her bangles.

'I'll take you to the factory site,' Kamalesh said. 'You're a student of history, you can gather the material for writing a new history of India.'

'Oh goodness, even the thought of anything academic makes me yawn. My father's friend Dr Sinha has suggested I work for a PhD under his supervision. He's even fixed the subject: Mir Jafar and contemporary Bengali society.

Kamalesh smiled. 'The scientists regret that historians busy themselves only with kings and emperors and heads of state. But it is scientists who bring about the greatest changes in society. Even the country's sovereignty and security depend on science now. But the common people know nothing of its indomitable power. You could start work on this theme. Your dissertation can be on Kamalesh Roychowdhury and contemporary scientific society.'

'Baba has a weakness for scientists. One son-in-law is a doctor, one an IAS officer, one a chartered accountant. So he jumped at Sutapa-mashi's proposal for a scientist as the fourth one. He said yes at once.'

'What about Baba's youngest daughter?' asked Kamalesh laughing.

'I don't understand these things. I used to think being a scientist meant standing day and night wearing spectacles behind a high table with hundreds of glass jars and a perpetually lit bunsen burner. A man obsessed with mixing chemicals of various colours in test tubes.'

'And now you can see it's nothing like that. Scientists do their work and love their wives too.'

They laughed in unison, the sound resonating tenderly among the birdsong and spreading the headiness of romance all around.

Mallika scanned her husband's face closely. 'I'd never have married you if you had a shaggy moustache like Einstein's, though,' she said.

'And would you have married me if I had a crew cut like Oppenheimer's?' Kamalesh countered.

Mallika shook her head vehemently. 'I'll show you a photograph of the Nobel Prize winner Richard Feynman,' Kamalesh said. 'Looks like a film star. No college girl would object to marrying him, although he too had a hand in the harmful act of making the atom bomb.'

Glancing at his watch, Kamalesh shot to his feet. He would have to run. Work on the reactor in the urea plant was going to start any moment.

'Give me half an hour to make you some breakfast,' Chandramallika requested.

Kamalesh wasn't willing. 'Even if I drive at breakneck speed I'll be three minutes late,' he explained to his wife. 'But you must have breakfast. You can also go back to bed if you like. I'll eat at the plant.'

Putting on his work shirt and putting on a steel helmet, Kamalesh folded his wife in a quick embrace before heading out.

Mallika gazed at the car vanishing in the distance. She was very happy. Kamalesh's dedication to his work had evoked her respect. Mallika decided to involve herself closely with her husband's mission as well as his hopes and dreams.

Chandramallika's hours passed staring at the clock. The small hand was so lazy it simply refused to move. It took a great deal of effort to get it to go past the 1 on the dial. Only as it was about to touch 2 was the sound of a jeep heard outside. Mallika had bathed and was waiting for Kamalesh with her hair cascading over her back.

Kamalesh dashed into the bathroom with military speed and returned in five minutes after his bath. 'Looks like I simply have to get a camera,' he told his wife. Then he whispered a line from a Tagore poem in her ear, 'In the sea she has bathed, she sits now on the shore with her hair wet.'

Pleased, his wife said, 'Strictly in your imagination.'

'Half woman, half fantasy,' Kamalesh responded.

The very first bite of the food made it clear to Kamalesh that his wife had cooked today. Praising her, he said, 'Dr Bonarjee believes anyone who has unlocked the mystery of cooking will find it easy to be a chemical scientist.'

Kamalesh couldn't sit for a moment after lunch. 'I've kept poor Gurnam Singh waiting at the site. He won't go home till I get there,' he said, and vanished like a puff of air. The reluctant clock went back to limping forward painfully slowly.

Going out into the lawn, Chandramallika sat there for some time. Several jeeps and lorries could be seen moving about the factory site in the distance. A platform rose rapidly up a tower and then descended noisily. The scene bored Chandramallika after a while.

She went and sat in the bedroom. A framed photograph of Mallika was up on the wall at the head of the bed. She replaced it with one of both of them. Then Mallika lay on the bed and let her mind wander.

With thoughts of her husband running through her head, Chandramallika fell asleep. She was nudged awake with a soft, 'Jhumu, Jhumu.'

Mallka jumped to her feet to discover Kamalesh was back. The sun had set outside. It was evening. Stroking his wife's brow, Kamalesh asked, 'Are you unwell?'

'No,' said Mallika, adjusting her sari quickly.

They went out into the lawn again. The retainer brought tea. The bluish HPL lights at the factory site in the distance had come on. They did not get along with the night. The moment they saw darkness they chased it away like a ferocious German Shepherd.

Mallika was a little cold. The air was damp. Refilling her husband's cup, she said, 'What does everyone who lives here do in the evening?'

Kamalesh considered her question, exhaling smoke from his cigarette, as though this was his answer. He didn't want to scare his wife so soon. After some thought, he said, 'People from various parts of India are gathered here. They're immersed in work during the day, but it's difficult to say what they do afterwards.'

Mallika gazed at Kamalesh. He could tell that a young woman surrounded by friends and family in Calcutta was not used to this lifestyle.

He decided to elucidate. 'Take those giant Sikhs who're setting up the pipeline. When they're working you'd think they know nothing but welding pipes together with electrodes. But as soon as evening falls they go off in a group to Dharamapur on a truck to get drunk and have fun together, not returning to Krishinagar till late in the night.'

'Don't they have families?' Mallika asked.

'I'm sure they do, but who knows where they are? These workers behave as though they were born inside thirty-two-inch diameter pipes and will become pipes themselves as they weld them together.'

'Poor things,' Mallika said with compassion. 'Why don't you ask them to bring their wives too?'

'They're the contractor's workforce. Bengal today, Bihar tomorrow, Maharashtra or Tamil Nadu the day after, there's no knowing where they'll be welding pipes next. We cannot take the responsibility of deciding where their wives should be.'

The answer didn't please Mallika. 'It's not as though they're not entitled to personal lives just because they've been hired by a contractor. '

'I know what you're trying to say, Jhumu,' Kamalesh said gravely. 'But we'll never get this factory built if we have to fulfil everyone's wishes.'

Mallika asked about the other workers. 'The local labourers have begun walking home now that the work for the day is done,' Kamalesh said. 'They walk eleven or twelve miles every day for these casual labourers' jobs. I don't know how much time they spend at home, considering they have to leave at four in the morning and don't get back till ten at night. They carry their food in little bundles.'

'Many of the clerks play cards in the evening,' Kamalesh continued. 'Now they're even rehearsing a play, even though it might never be staged, because they have no female actors. Still the rehersals go on. The supervisors go back home and chat with their wives, maybe play cards. I'm told there's whiskey sometimes.'

'Which means none of them knows what to do in their spare time. They only wait to go back to work the next day.' Mallika's observation revealed her discomfort.

'Something like that,' said Kamalesh. 'There's an officers' club too. They've made some arrangements for sports. Want to go?'

Mallika wasn't willing. She wanted to be alone with her husband.

8

There was a thick layer of fog in the morning. Experienced and skilful at his work, the sun god dispersed it with the flames from his welding set. The half-built factory was faintly visible on the horizon again.

Mallika had got back her cheer. In the afternoon the tide of her joy had run low, but it was high again at night. Close intimacy had allowed her to begin disovering her husband in different ways. Now she was brimming like an overflowing river.

After she had made tea she roused her husband from sleep. 'Don't stay in bed anymore. Otherwise you'll have to run to work without breakfast again.'

They went out to the lawn on the south. Mallika handed a cup of tea to Kamalesh, who was gazing intently at the factory. She felt this must have been how Emperor Shah Jahan must have contemplated a piece of his heart, the Taj Mahal, when it was being constructed.

'Don't you have any books on fertilisers here?' asked Mallika.

'We have innumerable books, but all of them are in the Chandanpur library. Are you thinking of reading up on fertilisers?' Kamalesh asked curiously.

'Naturally one half of a couple wishes to know what the other half worships day and night,' Mallika said.

'Simply put,' said Kamalesh, 'we're trying to feed the soil that keeps everyone on earth alive.'

'What will the soil eat?' Mallika expressed her scepticism.

'Aren't mothers allowed to feel hungry?' Kamalesh smiled. 'Two thousand years ago, too, people knew the soil needs fertiliser. But there was no way to find out how to make trees grow taller. Four hundred years ago an eccentric named Jan Baptist van Helmont conducted some very strange research over five years. He planted a five-pound willow in two hundred pounds of soil, keeping a strict watch for five years on the sapling as it grew into a tree. Then he made measurements and discovered the tree weighed a hundred and sixty-nine pounds, but the soil was only two ounces lighter. From this he concluded that water is what provides plants and trees their food and their life. Totally incorrect. But it began a new era in the history of science.'

Patting her hair into place, Mallika said, 'Didn't his wife scold him?'

Kamalesh laughed. 'The willow sapling would never have grown for five years if his wife had been annoyed.'

After a pause he continued, 'Then an Englishman named John Woodward planted seeds in different kinds of water, such as rainwater, water from the Thames, water from Hyde Park drains, and so on. He found that plants grew quicker when there was mud in the water. Finally, after two hundred years of dedicated effort, the secrets of the soil were revealed to mankind towards the end of the nineteenth century. It was discovered that of the ninety unique substances found in the earth and the air, sixteen are indispensable for plants and trees. Three of these come from the air—carbon, hydrogen, and oxygen—while the other thirteen come from the earth. And of these, three—nitrogen, phosphorus, and potash—are the most important.'

Kamalesh lit a cigarette. 'I'm sure it sounds like a college lecture,' he said with a smile.

Mallika encouraged him. 'Go on. Do you think I don't listen to the radio? On Krishikatha they shout about the same three things every day. Nitrogen, phosphorus, potash. I never paid any attention earlier—who knew I was going to marry a fertiliser-maker?'

Kamalesh laughed. 'I feel terrible when I think of how little the people in our country know about agriculture. We're a farming country. One bad harvest means millions starve to death. And yet the educated young have no idea about how plants get their nutrition. Our experiments at the Chandanpur laboratory have shown us that growing wheat just once on one acre of land depletes it of fifty pounds of nitrogen, twenty-one of phosphorus, and sixty of potash. If jute is grown instead of wheat, the soil loses sixty pounds each of nitrogen and potash. For tobacco, it's eighty-four pounds of nitrogen. Which means ...'

'Which means stop smoking,' Mallika interrupted with mock gravity. 'If everyone smokes there'll be no nitrogen left in the soil.' She giggled.

'Oh but that's what we're here for. To replenish the nitrogen,' Kamalesh protested. 'Earlier people used cow dung as manure, even cow urine. Digambar Bonarjee has a report on this practice too. One cow yields an average of fifteen tonnes of dung and nine hundred gallons of urine every year. And only point three per cent of cow dung is nitrogen.'

Mallika wrinkled her nose at the imagined stink. 'What! Is this what you call research? My father would never have let me marry you if he'd known. I detest cow dung.'

Kamalesh laughed. 'All right. That's why we're asking everyone to leave the cows alone and move to chemical fertilisers. Let us return the millions of tonnes of chemicals we're sucking out of the soil every year. That's our demand.'

'And if we don't?'

'Then the land won't give us crops either. Our colleagues only have to look at a tree to tell you what the soil beneath it lacks by way of food. If there's a nitrogen deficiency, the tree won't grow, the leaves will turn yellow, branches won't sprout. If it's potash, the leaves will have streaks, their edges will wither.'

'So all of you are tree doctors?' Mallika asked.

'Other people are doctors. We are pharmacists. Massive research is underway to identify the fertilisers needed to grow any given variety of crops on a particular expanse of land. Our job is to manufacture the fertilisers they will ask for. Among all the chemicals, the demand for nitrogen is growing the fastest.'

'What's the way out, then?' Mallika looked concerned.

'Scientists are turning the world upside down in their search for nitrogen. Fortunately there's an abundant supply of it, since eighty per cent of the air is nitrogen. That means there's two million tonnes of nitrogen in the atmosphere above just this small township of ours.'

'Then what are you worried about? Why does Digambar Bonarjee have to write so many reports?' Mallika asked bluntly.

Kamalesh smiled. 'Mr Nitrogen is in the sky. He has to be captured and put away in a sack and taken to the soil, doesn't he? That's what keeps us so busy.'

'Imagine being so harried to get hold of something that can be found everywhere,' said Mallika.

'Nature plays hide and seek with us, Mallika,' Kamalesh said. 'We don't create anything. We only discover what already exists and then mix and meld and cut and trim to shape it the way we need it. This is all our mission is—and it's enough to make us sweat in despair. If nature does turn away from us one day, none of us will survive.'

Kamalesh continued after a pause. 'We make different kinds of nitro-fertilisers from ammonia, using various methods. From the Chandanpur factory we get ammonium sulphate and ammonium nitrate. In Krishinagar we'll make urea, which has a high concentration of nitrogen. Forty-five per cent.'

Mallika listened attentively. Then she said, 'Why do you people work so hard? Once the ammonia is made, you persuade it to change to urea.'

Kamalesh chuckled. 'Do you suppose it can be done so easily? We take baby steps to proceed. Ammonia is supposed to be nothing but a chemical marriage between nitrogen and hydrogen. But even when you bring them face to face they refuse to get married. So we appoint a matchmaker, the catalyst. In normal conditions ammonia is a kind of gas, but under high pressure and in very low temperatures, it's willing to condense. We use the name liquid ammonia.'

'No one melts under pressure; they get angrier,' Mallika protested.

'Thankfully ammonia doesn't have the same temperament as humans,' said Kamalesh with a smile and lit another cigarette. 'No one knew how to make artificial ammonia before 1913, Jhumu. The Germans developed a method, but it was to make bombs, not ammonia. When there was no demand for bombs after the war, the same process began to be used to make ammonia for farming. You'll find many explosives companies manufacturing fertilisers, like Samarbabu's British Explosives.'

Mallika fetched her husband's shaving equipment and asked, 'Once you've turned the ammonia into a liquid, what do you do with it?'

Lathering his face, Kamalesh said, 'What we're supposed to do, which is to get it married.'

'Oh my god! How immoral you people are—it's married already.'

'That was the first marriage, hydrogen and nitrogen. Now the second marriage, liquid ammonia with carbon dioxide.

But both parties are reluctant. So the bride and groom will not react with each other unless there is tremendous heat and equally tremendous pressure. This is a very difficult wedding to pull off. There are seven different incantations, which are all held in secret behind the veil of patents by seven separate foreign companies. You'll hear Digambar Bonarjee mention them when he's here, the Dupont process, the Montecatini method, the Inventa sequence, the Mitsui methodology, and so on. Some of these companies are American, some Italian, some Swiss, some Japanese. Now we're also trying to get in with our own new incantation. It should be called the Bonarjee blueprint. But Dr Bonarjee doesn't want publicity for himself, so we refer to it as the HAC process. Our Sudarshan-babu jokes that we should call it the Digambar mantra, and ourselves the Digambar community.'

'And what will Digambar Bonarjee gain from it?' asked Mallika.

'What can the priest gain? Ammonia will get married and take the title of urea, India will stand on its own two feet, and we won't have to deliver sackfuls of cash to other countries.'

'What about the priest's fees?' Mallika asked. But the alarm clock began to ring loudly, and Kamalesh rushed into the bathroom.

9

The same damp, soggy loneliness descended again like thick fog in the afternoon. Chandramallika's life slowed to a near standstill. Some clinking could be heard from the kitchen when the retainer was at work, but that too had stopped. Only the table clock ticked away routinely.

Chandramallika had nothing to do except wait for her husband. He was away extracting the lifeblood of ammonia from coal and naphtha, but Mallika had begun to fret that she might begin to wither away in her prime. Not in body, but in her heart. And yet it was the honeymoon period, the freshest and greenest time of conjugal life, when no fertiliser should be required.

Mallika was terrified at times when she glanced at the clock. How many days more, how many months more, how many years more like this, when her spirited, virile husband would be busy unveiling the secrets of fertiliser in his office and laboratory, in fields and factories, while she, a prisoner, languished waiting for her beloved to come home? When would they sit down face to face with their food and exchange a few words? In half an hour the jeep would roar down the black asphalt road again and disappear, while Mallika would renew her vigil.

Even at night Kamalesh couldn't stop brooding about work. He told Mallika the story of the famous project where it was found a year later that Pritam Singh, the manager, had fertilised nothing but his office secretary. Mallika had laughed very hard, but Kamalesh had looked grim again in a moment. The deadline for the factory was just three months away. The seventh of December was approaching far too quickly.

Kamalesh had promised they would go for a drive this evening. They would take sleeping bags. Mallika could lie down wherever she wanted. Her husband might be a scientific genius, but he lacked common sense. How could a woman lie down wherever she wanted? *So what*, Kamalesh had said, *I'll be on guard*. But she didn't trust him, for he was a deep sleeper. She had told him she had no intention of sleeping in the open. She only wanted to hold his hand and walk around.

Like an aged goods train the hands of the clock trundled into the junction of one-thirty. But Kamalesh was nowhere to be seen. Mallika was thinking of calling him when he entered.

Kamalesh didn't even want to give her the chance to close the door. He practically lifted his wife in his arms and took her to the drawing room.

Releasing herself with great difficulty, Mallika unbuttoned her husband's shirt. After a five-minute bath, he emerged from the bathroom.

'There was a crisis of sorts today, I thought I'd have to skip lunch,' he said.

'Oh dear,' Mallika said apprehensively. 'Some chemistry problem rearing its head? But what's the problem, didn't you say two million tonnes of nitrogen are floating overhead?'

Kamalesh laughed. 'A human problem, not a chemical one.' Mallika was reassured; so there were human beings here after all. She was under the impression that constant cohabition with machines had turned everyone into machines themselves.

Serving his wife some dal, Kamalesh said, 'You could call it a primal human crisis. But it's caused serious trouble. Some of the employees here have become involved with adivasi women. They have been here since the inception of Krishinagar. The adivasis are simple, unfamiliar with the ways of the so-called civilised world. Having given their all, the young women are in tears after being deceived.'

'What now?' asked a worried Mallika.

'Here I am worrying constantly about the seventh of December, and then I'm landed with horrible problems like these. The adivasis are furious, apparently. There might even be violence. The district magistrate is here. He's threatening to put our employees in prison. If that happens I will have to dismiss them temporarily. Can you imagine the scandal? I've left the DM Dipak Sanyal, IAS, with Sudarshan-babu in the guesthouse and come home to grab a bite. The meetings will resume when I go back. The loverboys have been summoned too. The DM wants to take action today. Sudarshan Sen and I are at our wits' end.'

'What are you thinking of doing?' asked Mallika.

'Sudarshan-babu says our hands are tied. We have no choice but to dismiss them temporarily. The boys are begging us not to. Work on the urea reactor will stop.'

After a few moments of thought Mallika said with a smile, 'Don't let this trouble grow. Get them married to the adivasi girls.'

Kamalesh thought it was an excellent idea. Patting Mallika on the back, he said in elation, 'Eureka! A wonderful suggestion, Jhumu! None of us considered such a simple solution. Sudarshan might say we cannot compel an employee to marry anyone, but the DM can help. Marry, or go to jail.'

Later in the afternoon Mallika was woken up by a phone call from Kamalesh, who sounded happy and excited. 'Your idea worked! Five of the six have agreed to get married.

The sixth one is hesitant, but the DM and Sudarshan-babu are talking to him in private. Everyone is amazed, and the adivasi leader is pleased with me.'

But the plan to go out in the evening was foiled. Mallika was getting dressed with great expectations, but Sudarshan Sen rang to say Digambar Bonarjee had arrived unexpectedly. He had returned to India yesterday after being abroad for a week and had driven straight to Krishinagar. He was inspecting the factory site with Kamalesh now and would have dinner at their place.

Mallika quickly did up the house in anticipation. Getting some flowers from the garden, she arranged them in vases and brought one of her own paintings from the bedroom to put up on a wall in the drawing room. The image of Digambar Bonarjee she held in her head was one of respect.

But he disappointed her greatly. A very disgruntled-looking Digambar Bonarjee entered the house with Kamalesh On being introduced to Mallika, he greeted her coldly. 'When did you bring your wife here?' he asked Kamalesh. 'You didn't tell me.'

'Just a few days ago, sir,' Kamalesh replied.

Digambar Bonarjee paid no attention to his response. He said with some irritation, 'Don't forget that our trial by fire is coming up over the next few months. Do you know why the Germans and the Japanese have marched ahead? They took their work seriously. Each project was like a battle. Even though they lost the war they have brought the same mentality to their work, you know. We use the term "war footing", but we don't know what it really means.'

Digambar Bonarjee didn't even acknowledge the presence of another person in the room. Mallika brought him a cup of tea. Offering a listless 'Thanks', he immersed himself again in discussions with Kamalesh. 'I've got some new information on the decay of the reactor tank. We've been using zirconium linings—we'll move to titanium alloy linings now. The Mitsui-Toatsu process is much cheaper.'

Digambar Bonarjee didn' seem to like the idea of anyone else listening to the conversation. Turning to Mallika, he said, 'How long are you thinking of staying here?'

Mallika wasn't prepared for this question. Kamalesh jumped in to save her, saying, 'We haven't decided yet.'

After this Digambar Bonarjee immersed himself in complicated and seemingly meaningless English words. Mixer, heater, reactor, condenser, feed-pump, solution tank, crystalliser, blower, re-melter, priller ... Mallika felt he was hurling the words at her like bricks.

Unsure of what to do, Mallika went into the kitchen for some time. But Digambar Bonarjee seemed to set more words loose behind her. Coal, hydrocarbons, naphtha, feed ammonia, ammonia synthesis, and a lot more.

When she went to call them to dinner after laying the food on the table, it appeared Digambar Bonarjee had no interest in eating. He wasn't going to let go till he had made India self-reliant in the chemical industries this very instant. 'Get the factory going on the thirtieth of November instead of the seventh of December,' Digambar Bonarjee told Kamalesh. 'The synthetic ammonia plant will be operational in a week,' said Kamalesh, 'but I still don't know about the urea plant, sir.'

Digambar Bonarjee merely pecked at his dinner. 'Whom have you made such elaborate arrangements for, Mrs Roychowdhury?' After a few spoonfuls of soup, he went back to talking about the factory. Throwing a cursory 'Thanks' again at Mallika, he got into his car. He was going back to Chandanpur the same night.

Locking the front door, Kamalesh found Mallika sitting on the bed with a grim expression. 'What're you thinking about?' he asked.

'Does your company need you to take permission to have your wife live with you?' Mallika asked, her voice choked.

'Of course not. Are you mad?' Kamalesh answered at once.

'Why did your director ask me how long I'm staying?' Mallika looked like she was about to cry.

'Because he loves us. We're like a family at Chandanpur Research Laboratory. Dr Bonarjee is the head of the family.'

'Is the head of the family supposed to ask someone's wife how long she'll stay with her husband?' Mallika couldn't forget her humiliation.

'Please don't mind, Jhumu,' Kamalesh said, trying to placate his wife and apologising to her.

Mallika didn't chat with Kamalesh in bed tonight. She had fallen asleep. Kamalesh was aware that young, educated women today had a great deal of self-respect. Digambar Bonarjee had said as much many times, and yet today he had behaved unnecessarily badly with Jhumu.

The director looked thinner than before. He seemed to have changed a lot since he had returned from England. He was never so testy earlier. And now he wanted the date to make the factory operational brought forward by a week.

Kamalesh respected and loved Digambar Bonarjee. He was ready to do anything for him. But he also felt sorry for the man's constant pre-occupation with work.

Kamalesh couldn't sleep. The discussions with Digambar Bonarjee kept going round in his head. Now the director had created a fresh crisis with his revised deadline of thirtieth November, without considering the possibility that Kamalesh might have a view on this. Why hadn't Kamalesh protested if he was so irked? Then again, how was he to protest? Kamalesh could see Digambar Bonarjee appear on stage, dressed in a peculiar costume like Sir Walter Raleigh's from the Elizabethan Age. He had a small stick. The audience cheered his entrance. Holding his stick in both his hands like Charlie Chaplin, Digambar Bonarjee began to declaim, 'Urea is a white odourless prismatic crystalline solid containing 46.1per cent of nitrogen with a cool saline taste.'

Now Bonarjee went very close to Kamalesh and, casting his gaze like searchlights on Kamalesh's face, asked, 'Specific gravity?'

Kamalesh stood with his head bowed. How strange! Kamalesh Roychowdhury, the brightest star of the Chandanpur Research Laboratory, couldn't for the life of him recall the specific gravity of urea. An annoyed Digambar Bonarjee screamed, as though he was giving Kamalesh one final chance, 'Specific gravity?'

Kamalesh woke up suddenly and heaved a sigh of relief. His body was covered in sweat. Mallika turned over, and, shifting closer to her husband, said, 'Not asleep yet?'

'I did go off to sleep, but suddenly I dreamt I couldn't recollect the specific gravity of urea. Although everyone knows it's 1.335.'

'Do you see urea even in your sleep?' asked Mallika.

'Never. But everything went awry today,' Kamalesh answered calmly. Then he closed his eyes again.

10

'The jeep's going to Dharmapur to get some things. Do you want to go and meet Kanaklata?' asked Kamalesh.

'What about you?' Mallika wanted to go with her husband.

'Another day. I have several crucial meetings today. We have a handover from the Japanese team that's here to install machines. The Germans are working on the prilling tower. There are some things to be done there too.'

Kamalesh rang Samarendra at the British Explosives office. Excitedly he assured Kamalesh, 'No problem. Rinki will jump with joy when she hears. By the way, send a photograph of Jhumu's and yours. Rinki needs it.'

Ending the call, Kamalesh told his wife about the photograph.

Mallika smiled. 'Why does Rinki want a photograph of ours?'

'To put in her album, I suppose,' Kamalesh said.

Mallika wasn't convinced. 'I'll take it because Samar-da has ordered it, but I won't hand it over unless I get one of theirs.'

'The car will go pick you up after work around four,' Kamalesh reminded her.

Dropping Kamalesh at his office, Mallika went on to Dharmapur.

Kamalesh walked towards the factory site instead of entering the building. Even at this hour of the morning work was in full flow. A few of the workers were gathered in a group, but they went back to work on spotting the boss. Many of the managers said 'good morning' to Kamalesh, and he walked on after returning their greetings.

Kamalesh saw the Japanese team near the urea reactor. Dressed in khaki shorts and white singlets, they were working like machines. Sudarshan Sen was standing nearby. 'I wonder what God used to make these people. They know nothing but work. They turn up at dawn, don't talk to anyone, not even amongst themselves. You can see their gold-capped teeth glittering when they smoke from time to time. You know, sir, many of these blasted local supervisors hover around them in the hope of getting foreign cigarettes, but no such luck. The Japanese also smoke Scissors or Charminars to save money. But I've seen their papers. The Japanese company pays for their entire stay here. I'd asked one of the younger men, why do you have to be such misers when the company's footing all your bills? He tells me in broken English, "If I spend less, the compamy will make more profits. And if the company makes more money, I'll get a larger bonus. You follow?" Imagine their psychology.'

Kamalesh laughed. 'It's this dedication that's enabled Japanese nation-building.'

'The Germans have built their nation too, sir,' Sudarshan Sen said, 'but they skimp on neither work nor play. I've seen the way they live. They can't do without expensive food and alcohol and cigarettes. Being caught in two wars within a span of twenty years has taught them that their time on earth is limited. They don't give up on any opportunity to enjoy life when they're not working.'

'Where have you put them up?' asked Kamalesh.

'In the guesthouse. The east wing's for the Japanese and the west wing for the Germans.'

'Make sure they're looked after well. They're guests of ours, after all.'

Sudarshan Sen chuckled. 'Don't worry, sir. Taking care of a dozen foreigners is child's play for yours truly. I had to look after two hundred and fifty of them when Chandanpur was coming up. And such demanding characters they were too, they'd kick up a row at the slighest of lapses. They wanted to have those pigeon coops installed in each of their rooms at four days' notice.'

'Air-coolers?' asked Kamalesh.

'That's right, sir,' Sudarshan Sen laughed.

'One thing, though,' said Kamalesh. 'Make sure the Japanese are involved only with their own work. They shouldn't have a chance to observe what's going on elsewhere.'

'You don't have to remind me,' said the wise Sudarshan Sen, narrowing his eyes. 'Don't think I don't know that no one compares to the Japanese when it comes to copying scientific processes. The Germans don't have these tendencies. But they can work hard, sir. Their handiwork is as fine as their godlike looks.'

Edging closer to Kamalesh, he whispered, 'I've planted a couple of security people as helpers for the Japanese. They didn't want them, but I didn't agree. I've warned the security men not to reveal their identities in any circumstances.'

Kamalesh was about to leave when Sudarshan Sen said, 'I have something to discuss with you urgently, sir.'

'Tell me,' said Kamalesh.

'This responsibility you've given me for matchmaking between the adivasi women and our staff is the most dangerous work I've ever done in my life.'

'But why? Haven't all of them agreed to get married?' Kamalesh tried to reassure Sudarshan Sen.

'Yes, sir. But the DM says the sooner the better. If they change their minds we won't be able to pressurise anyone to get married.'

'What's the problem with getting them married at once?' Kamalesh asked.

'I have only three inspectors. I've sent one to Jamshedpur. A second one has gone to Dhanbad to locate a wagon of pipes that seems to be lost. And the third is in Dharmapur for a court case, one of those blasted casual labourers stole three kilos of cement from stores; the case is being heard. How do I get them married in this situation?'

Kamalesh laughed. 'You're not the one getting them married.'

'You're new to this line, sir. You don't know these people. The gentlemen have had their fun. Now they've agreed to get married for fear of being jailed, but they want loans from the company.'

'Give them some advance pay. What option do we have?' Kamalesh gave permission with a smile.

'Very well, since you're authorising it. But let me tell you what's coming next. They'll demand quarters so that they can live with their wives. And those wretched women who used to live in huts will send written petitions claiming they cannot survive a moment without electric lights and fans.'

Sudarshan Sen went off in the direction of his office. But once he was seated in his jeep, he told his driver, 'Take me home first. I need some ghol. Can't keep a cool head without a cool stomach.'

When his wife saw him she said, 'You went off to the office leaving the bottle at home? You're becoming impossible.'

'Things are becoming impossible at work,' administrative manager Sudarshan Sen said ruefully.

'But it's the engineers who do the work. What keeps you so busy?' his wife shot back.

'How can you make such a claim? You think the engineers can build a factory without the administration department?' Sudarshan Sen said with great self-confidence, 'Let me tell you, my dear wife, without yours truly, your Digambar

Bonarjee and Kamalesh Roychowdhury's Taj Mahal will remain a dream.'

Taking a long sip of the ghol his wife offered him, the administrative manager said, 'But now I'm beginning to wonder whether the boat will be guided to the shore even with Sudarshan Sen present at the spot.'

'Oh? Why?' his wife asked anxiously.

Sudarshan Sen blurted out what he wouldn't dare say in the office. 'We had white men in charge of these things back then. You could relax once they had shouldered the responsibility. They'd set up the factory, get it running, and hand over the keys—here you are, a turnkey job done. But now Digambar Bonarjee keeps bragging and incites these young men: build your factory yourself.'

'What's wrong with that,' Sudarshan Sen's wife said, 'these boys are gems.'

'That's easy for you to say. It's all very well for Kamalesh Roychowdhury to consult the director and follow the blueprint and build this iron Taj Mahal. But what if no urea comes out of it?'

'What!' Sudarshan Sen's wife was taken aback.

'I don't tell you about all the problems at work, it will only frighten you. But we're spending recklessly. Each and every cheque goes through me, the millions of rupees that have flown out already just for this small pilot plant make my head reel. Maybe the white men would have taken a few millions more. It would have meant more work for me, but I could have managed it. Country first, personal pleasures afterwards.'

'You wouldn't even have had a job in that case,' Sudarshan Sen's wife said sceptically.

'Really? You have no idea of the fuss the white men make about everything. Seventy-five of them were here when the Chandanpur factory was being constructed. But the project was about to collapse because there was no toilet paper in the bathrooms. What a row! Eventually yours truly had to go to Calcutta and get the sahibs their toilet paper.'

'You've never told me this before.' Sudarshan Sen's wife wrinkled her nose in imagined disgust.

'Can't tell you everything, you know. Some things are top secret.'

Draining his glass, Sudarshan Sen rose to his feet, muttering to himself, 'I have to do so much of the work. But when the factory is operational, all credit will go to the engineers. The scientists will have their photographs published. Thakuma used to say having children is one thing but bringing them up is another matter altogether.'

Peeping into Sujata Das's room, Sudarshan Sen asked, 'Where have you sent your boss?' Miss Das's serious face broke into a smile onseeing Sudarshan Sen. Pausing in her typing, Sujata said, 'You think I decide where he goes? He's wheeling about like a spinning top without anyone having to tell him.'

Both of them knew why Kamalesh had to do this. Sujata said, 'Things were going well enough, but Dr Bonarjee seems possessed after his return from England. He's asked for the factory to be made operational a week earlier.'

Twenty-eight-year-old Sujata Das was slim and lively. Her appearance was graceful but not excessively youthful. She evoked affection at first sight—it was obvious she was from a middle-class family, forced into employment for some reason. Sudarshan Sen had told her the very first day, 'Krishinagar of all places, ma? Couldn't you get a job anywhere else?'

Sujata Das didn't answer at first. Then she said, 'I'm too old to get a permanent job, so I have to chase temporary positions.'

With some effort Sudarshan Sen had secured quarters for her next to where the nurses lived. How could a woman live here alone?

Getting hold of quarters is no easy matter, Sudarshan Sen had told his wife then. 'Look at those three nurses from Kerala. You can't call them beautiful, but it took them no time to find husbands. Their husbands were clever enough to realise that in normal course they wouldn't get a place to stay in soon, so why not pick readymade quarters with a readymade wife.' Sudarshan Sen would have written about these things if he had the ability. He had told Kamalesh these stories too, but Kamalesh didn't believe any of them, only offering smiles.

'In that case, Sujata, too, should have been married by now,' Kamalesh said.

But then Miss Das alone knew why she wasn't married. She had no faith in Indian men. She was full of contempt for them. Moreover, she had a slight defect in her heart, and had only got this job because the health check at HAC was perfunctory.

Sudarshan Sen and Sujata often exchanged notes on their respective lives. Sudarshan Sen knew it was necessary to keep a line of communication open with the boss's secretary, so he dropped in whenever he could.

Typing an address on an envelope, Sujata said, 'Krishinagar would have been transformed if the white men were here, Mr Sen.'

'Of course,' Sudarshan Sen echoed. 'To tell you the truth, they inspire you to work.'

'And they know how to take responsibility for things,' Sujata added.

'That's true. You won't find them blaming others for their own mistakes.'

'They know their work too,' said Sujata. 'Look at these Germans slaving all day, but always with a smile.'

'You're right. Both of them smile all the time.'

Sujata stopped typing and asked Sudarshan Sen, 'Do you know why these white nations have achieved greatness?'

A very important question, but Sudarshan Sen had never concerned himself with it. So he couldn't provide an instant answer, as he usually did. Rubbing his bald pate, he said, 'A race of emperors is bound to be great.'

'The Germans weren't emperors,' Sujata reminded him.

'Oh they were. The Kaiser was closely related to the British king—they were cousins or something.' Sudarshan Sen couldn't quite remember.

'I don't know about that, but they're great because they know how to respect women,' said Sujata.

'We too refer to women as our mothers,' Sudarshan Sen protested mildly.

Sujata looked offended. She said with clear annoyance, 'Lip service. Observe Mr Remark or Mr Schiller when they're here. See for yourself how perfect their behaviour is. Indians will never learn it, even if they try through seven incarnations.'

Sudarshan Sen glanced at his watch. 'Our boss doesn't concern himself with anything but scientific problems,' he said regretfully. 'The office has many problems that need to be dealt with, but I just can't get hold of him.'

'Anything you'd like me to tell him?' Sujata asked.

Scratching his hairless head, Sudarshan Sen said, 'I have to discuss something with him face to face. Too sensitive for a note. About those adivasi women.'

'About those evil men, you mean,' Sujata Das protested. 'They were about to escape after ruining the lives of those innocent girls. And the less said of the girls the better. Imagine marrying these same men!'

'Dr Roychowdhury has put me in a spot,' Sudarshan Sen lamented. 'What if the audit department objects afterwards? He's sending those scoundrels to their wedding beds instead of jail. And knowing that they are being treated with indulgence, the honoured sons-in-law are now demanding advance salary. The boss has agreed. Now they want leave too. Not one of the scoundrels has even casual leave due to them. They will lose pay if they don't show up for work. Their only recourse is sick leave, which they dare not ask for. They're only getting married because of pressure from the company.'

They spotted Kamalesh returning to his office. He was dripping with perspiration. And was carrying several blueprints and documents.

'What should we do?' said Kamalesh after hearing out Sudarshan Sen.

'In the olden days I wouldn't even have had to turn to you,' Sudarshan Sen said. 'To tell the truth, my own wedding took place by bending the rules. The office records said I had a severe stomach problem, but actually I was getting married. Though when I come to think of it, I don't think it was much of a lie—marriage is, in fact, a form of serious diarrhoea.'

As he signed other documents, Kamalesh said, 'Give them special leave with pay. Then after that we'll see.'

Sudarshan Sen looked worried. 'What if the audit department objects?'

'Let them. Our director says let the audit people write a thousand letters; as long as your conscience doesn't object, go ahead.'

11

The door opened as soon as Kamalesh's jeep stopped on the hillock on which his house stood. After thanking the driver, Mallika emerged, accompanied by Kanaklata.

Swishing her hair and swivelling her hips, Kanaklata glared at Kamalesh. 'You're perfectly capable of murdering people, Kamalesh-babu.'

'Oh, why do you say that?' Kamalesh smiled, unable to find a reason for such an observation.

'Never heard of letting someone go off alone during the honyemoon,' Kankalata told him to his face. 'Jhumu's a softie, she doesn't speak up. So I'm here to fight on my cousin's behalf.'

'I'm glad you are. I hope you've brought your husband along,' Kamalesh said.

'Samar-da doesn't work Saturdays, so I brought both of them,' said Mallika.

'Isn't Saturday a half-holiday for you too?' Samarendra said, sitting down on the sofa.

'What holiday? Work is going on at full steam,' Kamalesh said sadly.

Kanak said, 'The British Explosives factory doesn't close down because the officers have a holiday. The work is done by labourers. What do the officers have to do with it? Working with your hands and working with your head are not the same.'

Kamalesh smiled. Offering Samarendra a cigarette and lighting one himself, he said, 'We did all the head-work in the Chandanpur laboratory. Now all of us work with our hands. You can certainly call your cousin's husband a labourer.'

Kanaklata wasn't one to give up so easily. She gave her brother-in-law a piece of her mind at once. 'Never mind all this talk of dainty labour,' she said ruthlessly. 'Please don't mind, but everyone knows government organisations do no work. In spite of making losses that run into millions, the shameless bosses of public enterprises strut about with their chests puffed out. They're serving the nation, they claim.'

Sipping his tea, Kamalesh said, 'That's an interesting thought. From private companies to public enterprises, from the honest to the dishonest, and even those who are infamous in the country for cheating and fraud claim they're serving the nation. Dr Bonarjee was amazed to see the Independence Day supplements in the newspapers. Even a company that swindles everyone, which we have reported to the CBI for duping consumers, boasted in an advertisement that it was working in the service of the nation.'

'You can serve the nation as much as you like,' Kanaklata said, 'but you mustn't forget my cousin. You made all those sacred vows only the other day.'

'We have to be careful from now on, Kamalesh-babu,' Samarendra said, laughing. 'The women in our country have awakened.'

Paying no attention to her husband, Kanaklata continued, 'They haven't awakened yet, but they're waking up. Don't expect to mutter a few incantations and enjoy the services of an unpaid maid by day and a partner in bed at night forever.'

Even Mallika was astonished by her cousin's plain speaking. Smiling covertly, she said, 'We'll send you to the Lok Sabha as our representative, Rinki.'

Kanaklata told her husband and brother-in-law, 'I'll make both of you read professor Sulochona Sanyal's latest novel. Many readers are stunned by what she's written, but she's a hundred and ten per cent right.'

'Reading Bengali novels is a tall order these days, Rinki. Why not just tell us what Sulochona-debi has written?' Samarendra pleaded.

'She shows us that there's no difference between a woman in prostitution and an ordinary housewife nowadays,' his wife said. 'One of them offers her body in return for money and the other, like millions in this country, pawns her body with her husband in return for financial support.'

'My god, this is revolutionary—' Kamalesh began, but the phone interrupted him.

It was Digambar Bonarjee from Chandanpur. The guests could hear Kamalesh say, 'Yes sir, don't worry. X-ray testing revealed flaws in some of the joints. They're being tested again. No, we won't proceed without hydraulic testing ... All right, we'll test at one-and-a-half times the normal pressure.'

Mallika heard several more fragments of the conversation, with the dates seventh December and thirtieth November being mentioned frequently. She could tell that Digambar Bonarjee was determined to advance the deadline for making the factory operational. Kamalesh was to blame, too. He could easily have said it wasn't possible. But he had a great weakness for Digambar Bonarjee, and this had become evident to Mallika.

The two couples were in bed in adjoining rooms that night. The moon lit up Mallika and Kamalesh's bed through the window. 'Should I draw the curtains?' Mallika asked.

'Let it be,' said Kamalesh. 'Every country has a legend about the intimate relationship between the moon and a newly married couple.' But Mallika didn't seem interested.

She seemed to have changed quite a bit since her return from Dharmapur.

'I have to send some money to Calcutta,' Kamalesh said. 'Will you remind me?'

Mallika said she would. Then she asked, 'By the way, how much do you earn?'

The figure wasn't as much as she had expected. And then there were deductions for tax and provident fund.

Mallika was upset. Considering the responsibilities her husband had, and the number of people who worked under him, his pay was rather low.

'But they make you work so hard,' she said softly.

'The pay isn't much at government companies, Mallika. Digambar Bonarjee himself earns less than three thousand a month,' he said.

'Rinki's under the impression you earn a lot,' Mallika told him.

'Salaries in private companies are confidential, but not here. Anyone can find out,' said Kamalesh.

'Samar-babu has wonderful taste. Their bungalow is beautifully done up.'

'I want to see it too,' Kamalesh said eagerly.

'As pretty as a picture,' Mallika continued. 'Apparently the curtains were specially ordered from Bombay.'

'Maybe that's the practice in foreign companies,' Kamalesh tried to explain to his wife. 'Why would Europeans leave their own country for this rustic place unless they can live in luxury?'

'But Samar-babu isn't an Englishman,' said Mallika. 'I'm talking about Rinki's flat.'

'If they're the same rank as the Englismen they won't live like slaves just because they're Indian. No government will tolerate this in independent India, Jhumu.'

In the next room Rinki moved closer to her husband and whispered, 'You're uncomfortable, aren't you?'

'Not particularly,' Samarendra said. 'I remember our Sudarshan Chopra went home on a month's leave but came running back after a week. They couldn't sleep nights without an air-cooler.'

'Why blame Chopra?' Rinki said. 'I've got so used to a foam mattress that I find it difficult to sleep anywhere else.'

'Imagine you're on a picnic,' Samarendra consoled her.

'The government sets its sights too low,' said Rinki. 'Jhumu's husband is so bright, he works so hard, still the Indian government doesn't try to give such people a comfortable life.'

'Digambar Bonarjee is cheating him under the pretext of idealism,' Samarendra said. 'A peculiar man.'

'Oh, you know him?'

'Apparently he tried to get a job with our company once, but the Englishmen didn't select him because he didn't seem smart enough. He's been full of bitterness about foreign companies since then. Mr Dev, our resident director in Delhi, refers to him as Swadeshi Digambar Bonarjee ever since. He's so arrogant that he actually claims British Explosives will have to purchase engineering technology from Chandanpur one day.'

Nestling against her husband, Kanaklata said, 'And what does your company say?'

Savouring the warm and tender intimacy, Samarendra said, 'British Explosives doesn't give a damn about India. If they find too many obstacles thrown their way they'll move to Singapore and set up a factory in Brazil.'

'My goodness, really?' This frightened Kanaklata.

'Don't worry. Nothing like that will happen,' Samarendra assured his bedmate. 'British Explosives will continue to operate in Dharmapur as it does now. We're not stealing or cheating anyone. We work hard to earn a living. These big shots in public-sector companies can talk endlessly but they do nothing. Still, it's dangerous to give people responsibility but not a comfortable life.'

'Why?' asked Rinki, held in her husband's embrace and rubbing his back.

'Kamalesh's predecessor here was a man named Nagen Basu. He'd been to our Dharmapur Club a few times. Digambar Bonarjee's right hand. Slaved like a demon but earned very little. Couldn't resist the temptation; took a bribe, and got caught.'

'What!' Rinki was taken aback. 'Everyone takes bribes in government offices. Does anyone actually get caught?'

'The CBI does catch some people now,' Samarendra said. 'Mr Basu took money from a European company abroad. He couldn't refrain from having some fun with hostesses in luxury hotels. Officers in private companies are no less when it comes to taking money and other benefits from contractors, but it's the public-sector employees who get caught. The rumour is that in this case the foreign company was so annoyed at not getting the contract that it tipped off the CBI.'

In the next room Mallika said, 'Dharmapur's a nice place. The officers of British Explosives have good lives.'

Placing his hand on his wife's back, Kamalesh said, 'Krishinagar may also grow into a mid-sized town one day. If our inventions work eventually.'

'You've contributed a lot to them,' Mallika said.

'You could say that,' Kamalesh answered. 'But these days inventions are usually made by teams. And, like conductors of symphony orchestras, they have leaders.'

Mallika's mood soured at the thought of the mustachioed Digambar Bonarjee. She had not forgiven him yet for his behaviour that evening. Bonarjee had insinuated that wives came between their husbands and their work. He looked as though he'd be happier if Kamalesh Roychowdhury's newly wedded wife weren't living with him in Krishinagar.

Kamalesh could tell how Mallika was feeling. Even though she hadn't said it explicitly, their marital life wasn't as happy as they had expected—the harmony was missing; imperfections had crept in. And yet Mallika was so sweet, she had no demands, she didn't want to control her husband like a puppet on a string.

The house was lively again in the morning. Rubbing her eyes, Kanaklata told her cousin, 'How do you expect me to sleep when lovebirds are billing and cooing all night in the next room?'

Mallika was embarrassed. But she refused to admit defeat. 'Just the opposite. Your buzzing didn't let me shut my eyes.'

'That's a terrible thing to say, Jhumu. We're your guests,' Samarendra reminded her laughingly.

'You're my guest. I didn't say anything to you. But I won't spare my cousin.'

Setting the table for tea, Mallika said, 'Rinki's always been a chatterbox. When we went to Mama's place she'd babble on in bed all night.'

Giving her a hand, Rinki said, 'Someone was crying her heart out after sending her husband into exile. I was the one who brought about a reunion. Naturally you'll bad-mouth me now.'

'We'll have to run away from home if this bickering goes on,' Samarendra said.

The cousins came to a compromise at once, and Kanaklata turned into a warrior queen to confront her husband. 'Just you try and break the rope. You don't know me yet,' she warned Samarendra. Mallika said, 'My husband nurtures the same wish in his heart. Many of the people in his company have relationships with adivasi women.'

'Ceasefire! Stop the bombing! We apologise.' Samarendra's unconditional surrender pacified the ladies.

The conversation and banter went on the rest of the day, but Kamalesh couldn't be present. He went to the factory site, then to the office and, from there, back to the site where the two Germans were at work. Sujata Das had informed him that Schiller was waiting to meet Kamalesh.

Young Schiller dropped in on Sujata once every day. The letters for the Germans came to the project manager's address and Sujata put the airmail envelopes with Ludwig Remark's name on them in bold letters on one side of her desk. Max Schiller didn't get much mail, but it was he who came to collect the correspondence.

Max looked like a fairytale prince. Not more than twenty-seven or twenty-eight, he was six-and-a-half feet tall, had the complexion of Italian marble and the immaculate figure of an Olympic athlete sculpted from stone.

Sujata knew that these white men knew how to show respect to women. They met now in the corridor, and Schiller promptly said, 'Good morning,' bowing his head in respect, then strode across to her office and held the door open for her.

Running her eye across the pile of letters, Sujata picked up a single airmail envelope. With a sweet and sympathetic smile, she said, 'Sorry, just the one letter. And it's for your friend Remark.'

Schiller wasn't fluent in English. What he said amounted to something like *can't be helped, not everyone is as fortunate as Ludwig*. The poor man had come from a distant land to this godforsaken Krishinagar to install his company's machinery. These people knew neither the local language nor how to socialise with the inhabitants. 'I hope for you to get lots of lovely letters from your homeland, Mr Schiller,' said Sujata.

Max understood her easily. With a smile, he replied, 'Many thanks, beautiful Miss Das. You must get a lot of letters even without asking. And so you should. For a charming young Indian woman like you deserves a letterbox full of mail every day.'

Sujata truly appreciated the natural courtesy that white men displayed towards women. Indians would need another century to learn this behaviour. They might never do it, in fact. Bengali men were getting increasingly arrogant. They might grant equal rights to women on paper, but they didn't really acknowledge women's independence. All that mattered to them where women were concerned was complexion, beauty, and paternal wealth. The Sujata Dases who had none of these felt the contempt and humiliation that men heaped on them. And if a beautiful Bengali woman were to have both self-respect and a personality, there was no end to her suffering.

The white men didn't blow their trumpets claiming to have done important things for women, but respect and courtesy were included in the way they addressed and conducted themselves with women.

The nurses in the medical quarters, desperate to get married, didn't believe Sujata. They were delighted to snare any Tom, Dick or Harry as a husband with the promise of their salary and free living quarters. They may be modern, educated women, but their mentality was still medieval. A husband was all they needed for their lives as well as afterlives to be complete. Sujata had met cultured Englishmen and Englishwomen, she had read some English literature too, and she couldn't imagine agreeing to a relationship where there was no mutual love and respect.

She often told the nurses, who were desperate to marry, about foreigners. 'I've worked a lot with men from other countries. They're not burning with lust for women all the time like Indian men. They consider women their equals. Not that they have a choice, because women in their countries don't need men to provide them with food and clothing.' Sujata Das had seen enough to be fed up of it all. The brash young men in this country were always ready to get into bed with the kind of women they wouldn't ever consider marrying. She didn't feel any desire to even talk to these men.

Returning to his office, Kamalesh went over various files and documents. Then he spoke on the phone with Chandanpur for about ten minutes. This was the time he usually had a detailed discussion with Digambar Bonarjee.

Sujata had no complaints about Kamalesh. He was an idealist and knew what he had to do. He worked himself to the bone, but this didn't put him in a foul mood—his smile was always intact. With all her heart Sujata wanted him to prosper, to get this factory operational, and to do even better in his professional life.

She had realised that he was a generous man. He had even invited her home a couple of times after his wife's arrival, especially since Mallika and Sujata had gone to the same school. But Sujata had avoided the invitation. The same Mallika who was her juinor in school was now her senior by way of marriage. Sujata Das was a mere stenographer and Mallika was her boss's wife. The man who was her lord and master was himself held in bondage by this slip of a girl.

Sujata knew she couldn't be comfortable with Mallika anymore. And unless consorting with the upper echelons had dehumanised Mallika, she too would be embarrassed and uncomfortable.

The miraculous power of the vermilion streak in a woman's hair surpised Sujata sometimes. The same little girl whom she had admonished in school was now on a much higher pedestal than her thanks to this red mark in the parting of her hair. No wonder all the women in this country were besotted by it despite all the torment and humiliation they had to face.

Sujata heard Kamalesh speaking to her. 'Could you connect me to my residence, Ms Das?'

Sujata had tapped the line and eavesdropped once or twice on Kamalesh's conversation. But it was as she had guessed. Indian men had no sense of romance. Kamalesh Roychowdhury too wanted to placate his wife with hollow assurances.

Kamalesh told his wife on the phone that he'd been a little worried about the Germans, but that they were nearly done with their work. One of the Germans would stay behind and the other one, along with the five Japanese men, would leave Krishinagar in a few days. Kamalesh wanted to host them at home before they left.

Mallika agreed enthusiastically. Kamalesh asked whether they should also invite Sudarshan Sen and his wife, as well as Sujata Das.

'That will be nice, invite them too,' Mallika said.

12

Kanaklata and Samarendra went back to Dharmapur on Saturday night.

Mallika had had an enjoyable time, even if it was just the one day. No matter how garrulous Rinki was, she was always animated and lively, infecting everyone with her buouyant, youthful happiness. She knew how to seek out her own joys too. Before leaving she told her cousin, 'The era of good girls is over, Jhumu. It's no good being a Sarat Chandra heroine today. Don't hold back. Run your husband according to your own thinking and judgement.'

Inexperienced and uncertain when it came to controlling men, Mallika smiled tentatively. Chucking her under her chin, Kanaklata said, 'You can eat up any man with your looks. But you have to bare your fangs too. You have to extract what's your due. No one will hand it to you. Just tell your husband: doesn't matter if you're building the Taj Mahal or the pyramids in Krishinagar. You have to make time for your wife and give her plenty of love.'

Mallika did want to make the demand, but she simply couldn't bring herself to say it out loud like her cousin. Rinki's behaviour could be very sweet, but it also held the fizz of a freshly opened bottle of Coca-Cola. She energised everyone wherever she went. But poor Mallika was perpetually terrified. Unable to ask for even what was justly due to her.

What was more important, however, was that Mallika's ideas aboout marriage were changing. Many women drowned in happiness as soon as they got married, yet she couldn't. On lonely afternoons she wrote long letters to her parents, to Kamalesh's parents, to Sutapa. Her parents and Kamalesh's father sent short replies, while Sutapa wrote long, juicy letters back, asking various intimate and uncomfortable questions. Mallika had plenty of time on her hands even after satiating her aunt's curiosity. Reading all the magazines and books, finishing all the housework, and ruminating on everything under the sun still left her with plenty of hours to kill. All she could do was lie down in bed or sit on the sofa or stare at the clock. The clock probably understood, for as soon as it saw her turn impatient, it slowed down its movement, continuing to tick but not allowing its hands to advance. This endless vigil frightened Mallika to no end. Sutapa had written that the first year of married life disappears in the blink of an eye. For Mallika, however, even a month meant thirty days of waiting for her husband every afternoon. And a year would mean enduring twelve such months.

It didn't matter to Kamalesh. If the Krishinagar project was successful, he was supposed to move to Haldia or some such place. Or to Visakhapatnam, where a factory a hundred times as large was to be built. There would be no respite after Visakhapatnam either, for by then many more fertiliser factories would have been planned, and the workaholic Kamalesh Roychowdhury would be needed for all of them. Waiting endlessly for her husband, Mallika would discover one day that she had become an old woman—her very youthfulness, the source of all her longing and fervour and ardour having taken leave of her silently. Without even the owner of the body getting to know.

Kamalesh had no time to think about any of this. The complex responsibilities of Krishinagar were devouring him gradually. He had become bolder after making the ammonia plant operational. The launch was mathematically precise. Digambar Bonarjee himself revealed that what they had achieved in just twenty-one days had never been accomplished in India before.

Kamalesh had hoped Digambar Bonarjee would visit Krishinagar to inspect the ammonia plant of his dreams. But he didn't like leaving Chandanpur these days. The same person who would turn up without notice preferred to supervise everything over the phone.

Still, even the phone conversation with him invigorated Kamalesh. 'I don't expect anything from old people, Kamalesh. Only if the youth have hopes and dreams will this country stand on its own two feet. Processions and slogans cannot dispel the misery of a nation. Show everyone with your handiwork, Kamalesh, that to make the country great we have to manufacture products in our factories and grow crops on our fields.'

Kamalesh had heard that there had been a mild buzz of resentment when many senior officers were superseded to put him in charge of Krishinagar. They had brought up Kamalesh's youth. But Bonarjee had brushed them off, asking bluntly, 'How old was Leblanc when he developed the process of making alkalis? Why did Einstein begin work on the theory of relativity at twenty-six? Why was Darwin only twenty-seven when he was researching evolution? Why didn't anyone mention youth when James Watt started unravelling the mysteries of the steam engine? How did Samuel Colt patent the revolver at twenty-one?'

Bonarjee paid no attention to chronological age. All he said was, 'Don't consider this new march of science a job. Employment is associated with a servile mentality in our country. If the brightest of Indians only seek trouble-free jobs, science will not advance a single step.'

Kamalesh knew there was a great deal of truth in what Bonarjee said. Despite having thousands of scientists and scores of laboratories, the country was still shamelessly dependent on others. Bringing about an industrial revolution with the help of the technological leftovers of other countries was nothing but a pipe dream.

Kamalesh recalled Digambar Bonarjee flying into a rage one day while reading the newspaper in the Chandanpur laboratory. 'What's wrong with the country, Kamalesh?' he shouted. 'Even for shirts and underwear, cosmetics and writing ink, we import technology—and we proudly proclaim this in our advertisements.'

'These are small things,' Kamalesh said to calm down Digambar Bonarjee.

'They're not small things at all, Kamalesh.' An annoyed Digambar Bonarjee asked, 'Why don't our newspapers write detailed articles about the Japanese? They have neither natural resources nor big markets at home. They have to import their iron and their petrol, and still they trounce countries much more powerful than them.'

Digambar Bonarjee felt that what Japan could do, India could do ten times better—if only all the scientists were self-reliant, if only the young researchers spent ten years of their lives assuming they weren't doing a job but were retaliating for the contempt and insults meted out to their country.

He said after a pause, 'I know the term "serving the nation" has become very cheap in independent India. Very well, no need to serve the nation; serve science and technology instead. Let our youngsters show that it's possible to run the developed nations close in the olympics of science even with limited investments and experience.'

'The man has a screw loose,' Sutapa used to say. 'He worshipped self-reliance so much that his wife couldn't rely on him; she had to run away to free herself.'

Digambar Bonarjee brought up even larger issues sometimes. 'In some distant century we, the people of the East, gave a set of scientific truths to the world as gifts. Apparently the glory of discovering zero belongs to us. Chemistry originated with us. These discoveries travelled to the Arab world from our land. Look at the wonderful festival of fertile ideas that followed. Science was reborn in the Western world. And ever since then we have only been taking things. In brazen shamelessness we go on accepting the teachings of the West. If anyone asks us why, we say we were under a colonial power all this time, what can we do? We have no capital, no machinery, you see. I don't like hearing this anymore, Kamalesh. It's time for us to give the world something. Others may not understand, but the educated in our country have plenty of reason to be embarrassed.'

When he thinks about it, Kamalesh too feels repulsed. *On the pretext of poverty Indians will lag behind the rest of the world by two hundred years; increase in population, while we educated gentlemen in big cities will put our feet up and enjoy our comforts. At most we'll dabble in a bit of politics. And scientists abroad will solve problems of population, food shortage and health. This is bound to hurt our dignity. DDT was invented in a laboratory in another country, we became free of malaria. Penicillin was discovered elesewhere in the world, our lifespans were extended. Urea was developed in a distant land, we found a way to avoid starvation. How long will things go on this way? This shameless dependence on others cannot be healthy for any nation with self-respect.*

But who's going to do anything about it? It's the educated people of India who are the most eager to accept things from elsewhere They are the ones most dependent on others. They monopolise the benefits of science. Millions of villagers don't know what electricity is. Fertiliser for farming is the only thing they have heard of. They're only just beginning to realise the value of chemical fertilisers.

Kamalesh's chain of thought was interrupted. Mallika was staring at him. She hadn't disturbed him earlier on the assumption he was solving an abstruse scientific problem.

Rolling two or three pebble-like objects in his palm and on his wrist, Kamalesh looked at his wife. Poor Mallika never said anything explicitly. It would have been easier if she had been as expressive as Rinki; Kamalesh would have known what she was thinking. But she only sat quietly.

Kamalesh looked at her again. Then he said, 'What are you thinking about?'

'Me? You're the one thinking about something,' Mallika answered.

'I don't want these thoughts, Mallika,' said Kamalesh. 'But they never let me be.'

The phone rang. It was someone from the factory. This was the problem—Mallika couldn't have Kamalesh to herself even at home. The phone rang at all hours. It was as though Kamalesh didn't need any rest, as though the project manager couldn't possibly have a home and family.

After a fifteen-minute conversation Kamalesh returned and sat down again. 'A particular machine in the ammonia recovery department was supposed to have been test run,' he said in annoyance. 'But it's making a strange noise when it's turned on and even the foundations are shaking. I asked them to check the alignment with a dial gauge.'

Mallika had no interest in these tedious details. She controlled her irritation, but her grim expression didn't change. Sensing her state of mind, Kamalesh said, 'A couple of young engineers are installing the machine. No experience, so they panicked and rang me.'

No sooner had he stopped than the phone rang again. It was Mr Das, the person in charge of testing for leaks. They were conducting tests with the introduction of ammonia into various pressure circuits. Doubts had risen over one or two joints in the pipes. 'We were supposed to have tested them with hydrochloric acid beforehand,' Kamalesh said.

He apologised to his wife again. 'You know, there'll be less to do when it's time to make the plant operational because we're catching these minor flaws now.'

Mallika listened, but Kamalesh wasn't too sure whether she believed him.

'Don't you have any friends here?' asked Mallika. 'So many phone calls from so many people, but none of them seem to chat with you or anything.'

'You're the only friend I have here, Mallika. With everyone else it's either work or self-interest. They want to keep me informed about everything because I'm the manager. Not because I know more than them, but because mine is the seniormost post. And, besides, they're always afraid. Who will take the responsibility if there's a mistake?'

'So the entire responsibility is yours? If anything goes wrong you'll be blamed for it?' Mallika was alarmed. She didn't care at all for this situation.

'That's how it goes, Jhumu. Those who want to rise above the ordinary have to suffer more for it.' Kamalesh reminded his wife of a historical fact.

Mallika was thinking of Kanaklata and Samarendra's life in Dharmapur. The company had been manufacturing explosives there for a long time. They had also built an enomous fertiliser factory nearby. But there wasn't so much dependence there on a single person—people were much more independent and self-assured. The scientists there worked hard too, but they didn't abandon their families just to meet the deadline set by a temperamental company director.

Kamalesh had been to Kanaklata and Samarendra's home with Jhumu. Rinki had hosted her new brother-in-law with great care and attention. 'But what's the use of having you live so close by?' she had asked.

'Well, here we are in your home,' Kamalesh said.

'But think of how much I had to beg and plead. We've been to your place six or seven times already,' Rinki said.

'My goodness, you're actually keeping count,' Kamalesh had said in surprise.

'I'm a chartered accountant's wife. Obviously I'm going to keep an account,' Rinki answered.

'Don't bring up your husband's profession now, or your cousin will have to learn chemistry,' Kamalesh said.

'What do you mean "will"? I'm deafened by Jhumu's lectures everytime she gets me alone. I've heard of your catalysts, whom you love more than your wife. Jhumu has told me about Digambar Bonarjee's innovative way of manufacturing urea, which made his wife leave him.'

'That's not why she left him. There must have been trouble even earlier,' Jhumu corrected her cousin.

'Find out if you can,' Rinki told Kamalesh. 'I'm sure this is the reason. Before you got to hear about it, she must have had to bear the brunt of Digambar Bonarjee's invention.'

Kamalesh laughed. Rinki said, 'Digambar Bonarjee's wife was a brave Punjabi woman. You're overconfident because yours is a cowardly Bengali. You're under the impression she can't leave you.'

'Tell him,' said Mallika, supporting her cousin.

Sitting in the cool drawing room, Rinki told Kamalesh, 'Don't imagine you can manage your wife in this day and age with nothing but chemistry books, Dr Roychowdhury. You have to read a couple of psychology books and novels, too, and watch a film once in a while. You'll find out that wives who leave their husbands don't do it because of a lack of material comfort. In many cases the husbands give them all the luxuries in the world, but not companionship. Every time this problem arises there's an opportunity for a novel.'

'Are you planning to write a story about us, Rinki?' asked Mallika.

'The beginning will be superb,' said Kamalesh. 'The beautiful newlywed wife of a young scientist joins her husband at his work site for their honeymoon. Her husband loves her, but he loves his work even more. Then ...'

'Obviously you know how to construct a plot,' said Rinki. 'You'd better complete the novel yourself. Where do you take your wife after this?'

'I thought you were going to write it,' Mallika reminded her cousin.

'Whatever for? I have a husband of my own. I'm already at the end of my tether managing him. With a husband like mine even a prolific writer like Agatha Christie wouldn't have been able to complete a single novel.'

'Does Samar-da start flirting with you as soon as he gets home from work?' asked Mallika, smiling suggestively.

'It's not that. Just that he won't do anything for himself. Doesn't even know where to put away his clothes. And yet this same man lived in England by himself for five years studying to be a Chartered Accountant. Besides which he's a glutton. Never satisfied unless his wife's slaving in the kithen. There are also all these parties in Dharmapur.'

'Who looks after your household if you're at parties every evening?' Mallika asked.

'The company's given us no cause for complaint there,' said Rinki. 'They've provided an orderly, a gardener, a cook, and a sweeper.'

Mallika was astonished. Rinki said, 'Who's going to spend their life in the wilderness despite having a foreign degree unless you have these luxuries? The staff manager from their head office had come to Dharmapur. We told him to come see for himself how dusty it is here. How can a single sweeper keep the house clean? There are rumours that a second one might be sanctioned.'

'It would have happened by now,' said Samarendra, 'but the government comes in the way these days. Why not allow foreign companies to pay their staff as much as they like? Their profits will only go up further if you don't, and more money will be repatriated from the country. The people in Delhi to whom our cases are referred get heartburn. They don't like sanctioning tasty sandwiches for others while they have to eat plain bread and butter, so they block the proposals as much as possible. What we say is, why don't you also work honestly and have biryani for dinner—we won't be jealous; in fact, we'll be happy for you.'

Samarendra and Kanaklata's neighbour, the young scientist Amitava Sen, had dropped in. His wife was British, and he had lived abroad for years. Sounding worried, he said, 'The ICS and IAS socialists in Delhi won't rest till the country is in ruins. Since their own salaries won't rise, they won't let others live in comfort either. You can't even argue with them because they will point to the hundreds of millions of starving poor from Kashmir to Kanyakumari. For heaven's sake, if your heart bleeds so much for the poor, you shouldn't accept the salary you're taking. Socialism isn't harmed when you ride in your cars and live in those huge bungalows and pocket three and a half thousand every month or hold dinner seminars at Ashoka Hotel or go abroad at the drop of a hat. But who are the villains of the piece? Those who have been educated here and yet have mastered foreign technologies. Those who use their brains and brawn to manufacture new products but don't stuff black money in their bank vaults or don't have two bank accounts. Those who convince even the canniest of employers to pay them decently on the strength of their merit. If there's the slightest trouble here in Dharmapur today, British Explosives will kick all of us out. If the company's profits drop, half our people will lose their jobs. But there's a different arrangement for socialists in Delhi with guaranteed monthly incomes. Even if all the schools in the country were to close down, the education secretary's salary will increase; even if there isn't a single paise's worth of exports, the secretary of foreign trade will get a promotion.'

Pausing at the end of his tirade, Amitava Sen said, 'I hope you didn't mind.'

'Why should I mind?' Kamalesh said. 'The country belongs to all of us. We all have to work together to find a way.'

'We've reduced India to a peculiar mess, Dr Roychowdhury,' Amitava Sen said ruefully. 'As long as we're led by these ICS and IAS bureaucrats who stick their noses in everywhere we'll never be a Japan or West Germany, we won't even catch up with China or Russia. It's the poor and helpless people of India who are suffering the most because of this. It doesn't really affect technocrats like us. If we find it getting difficult here, Canada and Germany still have their doors open.'

Kamalesh discovered Amitava Sen had a hobby. On weekends he painted and, along with his wife, listened to Western classical music. And yet he held a responsible position similiar to Kamalesh. And it wasn't as though the British Explosives factory stopped operating when he wasn't working.

Mallika must have taken note of everything. She was bound to bring up Amitava Sen as an example as soon as she had the opportunity. How should Kamalesh respond? The only thing he could say was that the technology and plans for British Explosives came by airmail from London. In case of problems a telex message went out to the design office in England, and the solution also came by telex. Kamalesh and his team didn't have such conveniences. They had to find their own solutions.

'The three-thousand-rupees-a-month socialists in the capital act as though no one else does anything for the country,' said Amitava Sen. 'As though what we're doing here in Dharmapur is of no use to anyone. For heaven's sake, if you doubt these people so much, why did you invite us here in the first place? If you're brimming with patriotism, put yourself through what Mahatma Gandhi did, limit your income to the average level for Indians. Hoist your gamchha above your knees and go about bare-bodied.'

'But we can't forget ours is a poor country,' Rinki said.

'Of course we can't. But are we able to say we won't buy Boeing planes because the country is poor? Has the construction of five-star hotels stopped because of our poverty? I know you'll bring up the needs of foreign tourists. But are they the only ones who reserve all the hotel rooms in Calcutta, Bombay, Delhi and Madras?'

Kamalesh still didn't get Amitava Sen's point. What he wanted to say was, *it's all very well for technologists and bureaucrats to have ego battles and hurl invectives at one another, but that won't solve the problems of the poor people. The question is, when will we stand on our own two feet? Whether our factories are owned by the government or by someone else is not the point. What's important is whether our factories manufacture products that are genuinely useful to people.*

Dharmapur's well-planned and swanky appearance attracted Mallika. Amitava Sen's and Samarendra's lifestyle had given her reason for thought. The officers here didn't slack off at work, but that didn't mean they slacked off on life either on the pretext of responsibilities. Those who toiled hard also did their hair. They went on picnics, chatted with their friends in the evening, played cards, and had no qualms about spending some time at Dharmapur Club.

The authority at Dharmapur Club was entirely in the hands of British Explosives officers, but they had no objection to admitting outsiders. Many officers from the collieries nearby had joined the club. The district magistrate, assistant district magistrate and the police superintendent were honorary members. Kamalesh could become a member too, if he liked. He lived only thirty miles away. Members had many facilities. They could host their guests at the club inexpensively. The wives didn't have to pay separate subscription fees.

Many of the members were involved in sports these days. Rinki let the cat out of the bag. 'All of them had turned into lazy lumps. Not even their wives could get them to be physically active. Eventually the managing director paid a visit from the head office and told everyone that tennis and golf are part of modern executive life. He was worried about the way the officers at the Dharmapur factory had put on weight even though they were barely thirty.'

'Do they think about these things too?' Kamalesh was surprised.

'What choice do they have?' said Samarendra. 'Cases of high blood pressure and heart attacks are rising among managers. And there's this other peculiar thing, the officers' wives are only able to have babies through caesarian operations.'

Government employees did go to Dharmapur Club. But they seldom paid for their own food. There was no need to, either. For club members vied with each other to host them. This new industrial culture had great regard for State power and what it was capable of.

Everyone welcomed Kamalesh warmly at the club. It was no secret to many here that he was a talented scientist. The club secretary said, 'It's not as though we do nothing but entertain ourselves here. We also familiarise ourselves to the extent possible with the things that concern the country. We have a lecture on the first Friday of every month. Many honourable ministers have graced us with their presence. From the magician P.C. Sorcar to Mrs Amala Shankar, from the spiritual monk Adwaitanandaji to Brigadier Harbachan Singh, they've all spoken here. Why don't you address the members, too, one of these days? Speak on any subject you like. The club members don't wish to distance themselves from contemporary realities. We're even ready to listen to lectures by socialist, communist and extremist leaders, if we have the opportunity.'

Kamalesh listened with great wonder. The secretary said, 'Our members' wives drink, go to the races in Calcutta, play flash, and dance, just as they also raise funds for orphans and sacrifice their comforts to knit sweaters for our soldiers. Brigadier Harbachan Singh has praised us unstintingly for our support.'

Rinki said, 'Arrangements are being made for batik, ikebana and Chinese cooking classes. 'If you want to learn Japanese flower arrangement or how to make chow mein, let me know, Jhumu.'

On the way back from Dharmapur to Krishingar, Mallika asked whether it would be a good idea to join the Chinese cooking classes. But she was deflated on learning that Kamalesh would have to pay for the fuel for her to be driven thirty miles there and thirty miles back every day. 'You do so much for the company, but using the jeep a little is wrong,' Mallika told her husband with great sadness.

'In government organisations, jeeps have logbooks, Jhumu,' Kamalesh explained to her patiently. 'You have to write down the distance travelled, and whether it was for official business or personal. Passing off personal business as official is lying.'

Perhaps Jhumu did understand, but it only made her more furious with HAC. 'No one makes this argument when you use your personal time for official work.'

'Legally we have no personal time, Jhumu. We're employees of Hindustan Agro-Chemicals twenty-four hours a day.'

'These inhuman rules were in place in English factories during Dickens's time,' said Jhumu, 'they're defunct now.'

13

Kamalesh was caught up again in his passion for work, inspiring everyone around him. 'What we're doing here in Krishinagar is not merely our jobs but something much greater,' he declared.

He had found sympathy and support from most of the labourers and engineers. Three or four individuals had chosen to be lazy, some people even stood to earn more if the work was delayed, but they were in an ineffectual minority now. Every part of the project proceeded like a fast-paced play on stage.

But work has its limits. Digambar Bonarjee had obstinately advanced the deadline by seven days. No one was failing in their efforts, but Kamalesh hadn't been able to commit yet. There was always a quicksand lurking within complex work—something could go wrong any time. There had to be a margin for that.

Kamalesh checked with Sujata whether the Japanese and the Germans had accepted his invitation. 'All the Japanese are coming,' she answered. 'Mr Schiller and Mr Remark as well. I am coming too.'

'Don't worry about transport,' Kamalesh told her. 'A jeep will pick you and the Germans up. Mr Sen has made arrangements for the Japanese.'

Sujata was ready a little ahead of time for the party. The Germans arrived in the jeep outside the nurses' quarters. Sujata was in a glittering sari, which the Germans greeted with cheers.

'My English isn't good enough to praise your beautiful clothes, Miss Das,' said Remark.

Schiller said, 'You look lovelier than even the prilling tower we have built for the urea plant.'

'Many thanks,' said Sujata in delight.

'How long is this wonderful sari of yours?' asked Remark.

'Five metres.'

'Five metres! How do you Indian ladies manage such a long garment? You people are truly mysterious, you know magic.' Schiller was amazed.

'I'll be on a Lufthansa flight at this time tomorrow, Miss Das,' said Remark. 'If there's a letter for me please give it to my friend.'

'Certainly, provided your friend checks with me.'

'Oh Miss Das! Letter or not, any young German man will hike three miles every day for the rare opportunity of a conversation with a beauty in a sari like you,' Max Schiller, who was driving the jeep, said with a drag on his cigarette.

'All of you have honey on your tongues, but you don't mean a word of what you say,' Sujata approved and protested at the same time.

'Not at all,' said Max. 'If you ever visit our country, you'll see what a huge hit you'll be.'

Adjusting the end of her sari, Sujata asked Schiller, 'Your friend is leaving tomorrow. What about you?'

A saucy Remark replied on behalf of his friend, 'I have someone waiting for me, a suspicious blue-eyed girl who writes me a letter every forty-eight hours. But Max can stay as long as he likes, he has no such constraint.'

Max Schiller laughed. Then he said, 'My days here are drawing to a close too, another four weeks at most. Your company won't let me stay on even if I want to. I'm free once I've got the prilling tower going.'

'Where will you go after that?' Sujata asked.

'Home to begin with. Then wherever they send me next. Thailand, probably.'

'You people are very fond of Thailand,' Sujata observed.

'Not us, fräulein! The Americans—who believe throwing dollars can get them instant love from young girlfriends.'

The jeep stopped outside Kamalesh's house. Sudarshan Sen was standing at the front door. Mallika came out, dressed in a red Benaras silk sari. She had dressed up beautifully, Sujata noticed. 'They live in a doll's world,' she told herself. 'The upper class marry dolls and bring them home as soon as they set eyes on them. No one values any other qualities in a woman.'

The Japanese had arrived already. After the introductions were completed Sudarshan Sen said, 'Our Sujata is a wonderful girl, Mrs Roychowdhury.'

'My husband is full of praise for her,' Mallika said. 'I told him, earlier there used to be a good wife behind every successful man, now it's an efficient secretary.' Turning to Sujata, she continued, 'You went to Diocesan too, didn't you? I've seen you in school, you were a few years senior.'

'That's right, I remember,' said Sujata with a visible lack of interest. She didn't mention the fact that Kamalesh had already told her about this. Sujata had expected Mallika to have visited her by now and ask her over too.

It hadn't occurred to Mallika that she should be doing this. She had not yet learnt how class-conscious and sensitive people could be once they were employed. She went on chatting artlessly with Sujata. 'How do you live in this remote exile? I feel claustrophobic.'

Sudarshan Sen's dutiful wife said with a smile, 'Not accepting this, Ma. Your husband is a gem. For women, heaven is where their husbands are.'

'Spare me,' Mallika said. 'I may not have a choice,' she told Sujata, 'but you?'

Sujata felt a little awkward initially. But then she said without guile, 'Not everyone gets a job in Calcutta. And, besides, I know so many people there I was beginning to feel stifled. All of them have the same question, why don't you get married. As though single Bengali women can have no other objective.'

Handing Sujata a glass, Mallika smiled sweetly and said in a low voice, 'I see, matters of the heart.'

Sujata didn't protest. On the contrary, she liked the phrase. After all, it was because of the defect in her heart that she wasn't married—no Indian man would knowingly court such a problem. But she couldn't lie either. For if her revered husband found out that she had concealed her illness and got married, he would leave her in the lurch and disappear.

Kamalesh stood in a corner of the room, surrounded by the Japanese. Mrs Sen was arranging a buffet dinner table. Mallika nudged Sujata in the direction of the Germans.

The Japanese guests were dreadful at speaking English. But things had become complicated because they were under the impression that they knew the language quite well. Sudarshan Sen was exhausted by his efforts at exchanging pleasantries with them. In a low voice he told Kamalesh, 'We made a narrow escape, sir. If they'd won the Second World War, we Indians would have simply perished. How would we have worked under them? We would never have understood the bosses' instructions.'

Kamalesh was a little disappointed himself. This lot didn't have anything but work in their lives. He had observed them in the factory. There was no one to supervise them, no Digambar Bonarjee to harrass them on the phone, and yet they never slacked off. On the contrary, what the nine or ten of them were doing here would have required fifty Indians. None of them had a degree in engineering. They believed in practical work. They didn't need engineering graduates for every single task. The Japanese were not in the habit of using a sword to push a pencil across the desk.

But they seemed to have no life beyond their work, which worried Kamalesh sometimes. *Are these the kind of people we're looking for in India, who possess nothing but arms and eyes, arms that have become so adept with practice that each of their owners seems to have ten instead of two? Along with this there's the greed for production. The more the production grows, the more the earnings—besides bonus and overtime pay. Their wives have no control over these machine-like humans. They're addicted to alcohol too. They have no hopes and dreams other than delivering mammoth production and making hefty amounts of money. All the industrially advanced countries are filled with this kind of incomplete human machine. Still, no matter how much criticism there might be, India does need this kind of person in large numbers right now. On farms and fields, in factories and offices, these are the people who will bring about a revolution. They can be the new heroes and saviours of the country.*

Going up to Kamalesh, Sudarshan Sen said, 'I've been thinking of asking you a question. You say you've designed the factory by yourselves. But I see all these Germans and Japanese workers.'

Kamalesh smiled quietly. 'The design is ours all right, but Dr Bonarjee has never claimed we won't get the machines from other countries. There are many such machines which are still not manufactured in India. So HAC has had to import some of them.'

'They may be be foreigners, sir, but actually they're mechanics,' Sudarshan Sen whispered. 'Try discussing anything else with them and it'll be a waste of time. They don't even know anything about the fertiliser industry. All they know is how to tighten the nuts and bolts according to the design. But they can work inhumanly hard.'

'So can our people,' said Kamalesh. 'Think of the wretched labourers and porters and rickshaw-pullers and farmhands. But we educated people aren't able to show them an alternative. If only we could have used their physical labour for the cause of science, we would have also been a rich nation.'

'I'm so much older than you, sir,' said Sudarshan Sen, 'will you accept my advice? Don't weave dreams when it comes to work. It will destroy your life. Nobody will value what you do.'

Kamalesh smiled. 'I can see the kind of effort you're putting in to fulfil Digambar Bonarjee's desire,' Sudarshan Sen said. 'Your health will suffer, Dr Roychowdhury.'

'Responsibility is a troublesome thing, Mr Sen,' said Kamalesh.

'No one actually takes responsibility for anything in our country, sir. All they do is shout,' said Sudarshan Sen. 'By all means work as hard as you can, but don't bring ideals into it.'

'What are you trying to tell me?' Kamalesh asked.

'I've gathered enough experience. I saw the Chandanpur project come up early in my career. Then Haryana Fertiliser. After this it was yours truly who maintained all the accounts of the Assam project. And, finally, Krishinagar. The more effort you put in, the more responsibility Digambar Bonarjee piles on your shoulders. Things here would have been delayed by a year had someone else been the project manager. And now he wants you to advance the date for operationalising the plant. Why do you think?'

'You tell me,' said Kamalesh.

'Nothing but a whim. And along with that, the desire for fame. Pardon me for being out of line. "Splendid achievement, Bonarjee," the minister will say. Maybe he will be called to Delhi on twenty-sixth January for a Rai Bahadur title from the President.'

'The Rai Bahadur title and the Knighthood have been abolished in India, Sudarshan-babu.'

'Same thing—it's called Padmakumar or something like that now,' Sudarshan Sen replied.

Kamalesh said, 'Come, the Germans are standing in a corner, let's go over to them.'

Remark and Schiller were in a good mood. 'We're not feeling lonely at all. Miss India is personally looking after us.'

Sujata, Kamalesh, and Sudarshan Sen laughed in unison. 'We cannot believe your wife made all this food herself,' said Max.

'In technical collaboration with Mrs Sen,' said Kamalesh.

'You could sell the know-how for this food in Germany and make millions of Deutschmarks,' said Max.

After the party Sudarshan Sen asked, 'Sujata, should I drop you home?'

Sujata said, 'No need. I'll go back the way I came.'

Max drove on the way back, with Sujata next to him and Remark on the other side.

The winding road, going uphill and downhill, brought them to the factory. Moonlight fell on the prilling tower, which looked as tall as the Ochterlony Monument in Calcutta. A moist, viscous mass of urea was to be piped here and then propelled upwards to a great height. There it would be rotated at high speed with the help of a wheel and made to form solid particles. Once the water had evaporated from these particles, the warm urea would drop to the ground.

Max whistled, and then leapt out of the jeep and craned his neck to take in the tower. Sujata couldn't resist the temptation to view the prilling tower by moonlight. She had ignored the factory all these days. She worked in this industrial township strictly because she had to earn a living. She had no interest in this gigantic machinery. But suddenly it seemed to Sujata that the prilling tower looked beautiful beneath the moon. There appeared to be no intrinsic conflict between nature and industry, they too were made for each other.

'What do you think, Miss India?' asked Max.

Sujata was relaxed with the Germans now. 'Glorious,' she said with a tinkling laugh. The young German men were gratified by the Indian lady's remark.

All three of them got out of the car outside Sujata's quarters. She had meant to offer a formal goodbye and go in, but Ludwig Remark said in a solemn, sorrowful and sincere voice, 'This is probably the last time we're meeting, Miss Das. So, all the best.' He held out his hand and, despite a moment's hesitation at touching a young man she didn't really know, Sujata shed her inhibition and shook his hand. Max was hesitant too, but out of natural courtesy Sujata said, 'Come on.'

Her soft hand, unused to this form of greeting, was lost in a moment within Max's giant palm. Sujata felt a spark running through her body. Max completed the handshake and stepped back, after which they said good night and left.

As she went in Sujata found her palm moist with excitement, while perspiration trickled down her nose, chest and back.

14

Life had speeded up at Krishinagar. Kamalesh had energised workers at every level to work harder and was himself immersed in everything.

But he no longer enjoyed the phone call from Chandanpur every morning. Digambar Bonarjee lobbed hundreds of questions at him for fiteen minutes every day before asking again whether the factory would be operational by the thirtieth of November.

Everyone had more work than ever before. Only one person didn't know what do with all the time at her disposal. Krishinagar had gradually lost all its attractions for Mallika. Kamalesh was busy at the office and on the site, and all he did at home was answer phone calls. He even went to bed with the phone next to him. One night there was a call at one-thirty in the morning, waking Mallika.

There was an invitation one evening from Kanaklata and Samarendra. Mallika was dressed up and ready. Kamalesh came home from work and changed his clothes. Mallika was just spraying some eau de cologne on him when the phone rang. 'I'll be back soon,' said Kamalesh after answering the phone and drove off in his jeep. There was no sign of him after this. Mallika rang two or three places, but he was nowhere to be found.

Returning late at night, Kamalesh found Mallika sitting sullenly. She had taken off the clothes she had meant to go out in. A contrite Kamalesh tried to kiss her, but Mallika was so hurt that for the first time she brushed him away.

'I'm so sorry, Jhumu,' Kamalesh apologised. 'The temperature of the synthetic gas in the reforming chamber of the ammonia plant had started rising suddenly. It was about to cross the limits allowed by the design. The tank could have burst. I had to ring Dr Bonarjee.'

Mallika had tears in her eyes. 'You could ring Chandanpur, but you couldn't ring me? My cousin had cooked for us. You may not consider them human beings, but they work hard for a living too.'

Kamalesh hadn't imagined someone as soft-hearted as Mallika could say something like this. 'What's all this you're saying, Jhumu?' He apologised again, saying the dinner invitation had slipped from his mind because of the crisis.

Mallika calmed down after a great deal of coaxing and cajoling. They rang Dharmapur. 'Let me apologise personally,' said Kamalesh.

'No need to get into this,' said Mallika. 'Rinki already thinks you overdo things when it comes to work.'

'Are you cursing us?' Mallika asked her cousin on the phone.

'Don't talk to me, disconnect the call.' Rinki sounded furious.

'Listen to me, all right?' Mallika said. 'I was getting dressed when I suddenly began to feel queasy. I threw up a couple of times. I thought I'd be all right after a little rest, but your brother-in-law didn't want to risk it. He was about to ring you but I said wait a bit. That's how we got late.'

Rinki's mood changed like magic. Excitedly, she screamed, 'Throwing up? What's going on? Pass the phone to the gentleman, let me check with him. If he's so busy with his work why is his wife throwing up?'

'It's not what you think,' Mallika tried to convince her cousin. But Rinki refused to be convinced.

It was Mallika's turn to be embarrassed. 'New trouble,' she told her husband. 'Rinki's suspecting something else. She said she's coming over on Saturday.'

Kamalesh decided to be a warm host this time and entertain them lavishly. He would invite a few other colleagues to dinner too. He would make it clear to Jhumu that he too loved Rinki and Samrendra, that he too knew how to socialise.

Rinki stormed into the house and hugged and kissed her cousin. 'Here I was thinking my brother-in-law is a detached scientist who is intent only on his work and pays no attention to his wife.'

'He doesn't,' said Mallika.

'Then why all this throwing up?' Rinki nudged Mallika.

'Believe me, it's just acidity. I'd eaten late.' Mallika was trying her best to sound credible to her cousin.

'I was so angry that evening,' Rinki said. 'My husband had invited Mr Dickson, too, the director of their fertiliser project. They're going to hire two or three senior scientists. The pay's more than four thousand a month. And then there was no sign of you, we were so worried. Your brother-in-law said, Jhumu's husband has forgotten, for all you know. I said that's impossible, Jhumu will make sure he gets here, she knows we've made special arrangements. Your phone call allowed me to save face. What do men care, I said, you always do as you please. It's the women who get into trouble.'

Mallika smiled. And, left with no option, Kamalesh put up an act.

Rinki had brought imported cosmetics for her cousin. Handing them to Mallika, she said, 'I had them brought from London for you. People at Dharmapur keep going abroad.'

Kamalesh said, 'I'm told nail polish, lipstick and make-up, these are quite good in India nowadays?'

'For heaven's sake,' said Rinki. 'Stick to making your Indian fertiliser for farmers, but don't ask us to use these lumps of limestone on our face.'

'Can cosmetics be imported these days?' Kamalesh asked.

'Not officially, no, but unofficially … how much do you want? When we were coming back from London I proudly displayed everything I'd got at customs. One of the young officers there was about to ask me a question, so I said, are you married? He was flustered, and said no. So I immediately told him, when you're married you'll know that once a woman's skin becomes bad, it never recovers. The bachelor boy was too intimidated to say anything more.'

That evening, Kamalesh had let them down again. Sudarshan Sen, his wife, Rinki and Samarendra were all waiting for him to come home. Mallika would serve dinner as soon as he arrived. But where was Kamalesh? Around seven-thirty the driver of his jeep came with a note: 'Send a clean shirt, an undershirt and a pair of trousers. And some sandwiches if possible. Don't wait for me.'

Mallika's face fell. Noticing, Sudarshan Sen said, 'There was a problem in the boiler tube. Dr Roychowdhury was there with the engineer, Nilmani Pattanaik.'

'Will Kamalesh not come home today if the boiler tube problem isn't solved?' asked Rinki.

'You never know,' Sudarshan Sen answered. 'Dr Roychowdhury says this isn't a normal time. Even the slightest delay anywhere will mean the factory won't be operational on time. He's usually on the spot to suggest solutions. He often rings Dr Bonarjee for advice.'

'Why doesn't Dr Bonarjee live here then?' said Rinki in irritation.

'None of us will survive in that case,' Sudarshan Sen said in alarm. 'But I don't know why he doesn't visit the project site as frequently as he used to. There are rumours he isn't keeping well.'

Mallika had meant to send some food for her husband, but Sudarshan Sen dissuaded her. 'You know what he's like. He'll never eat before everyone else has eaten.'

Kamalesh returned very late that night. 'Even during the war Churchill had the time for an afternoon nap and dinner at night,' Rinki told him.

An embarrassed Kamalesh said, 'We had to open up the upper half of the secondary reformer eventually. I didn't dare leave them to do it by themselves. And, besides, it's Pattanaik's wedding anniversary. How could I have come away when I had insisted that he stay there?'

Samarendra said nothing. Mallika felt he was disappointed. She turned away from Kamalesh in bed. Exhausted from working all day, Kamalesh fell asleep almost immediately.

'This was the last time,' said Rinki before returning to Dharmapur. 'We won't disturb you anymore. I drag your poor brother-in-law here every time, but your husband pays him no attention.'

Kamalesh took their hands and apologised.

'Do you remember the couples' competition at our club?' Rinki said suddenly. 'I've entered you for it. We'd entered already. The first prize is a free trip to Kashmir.'

'Don't they need a photograph?' asked Mallika.

'Why do you think I asked you for one of yours? Make sure you don't let us down this time.'

Kamalesh couldn't understand what was going on. Mallika told him Rinki had entered them for the Made-for-Each-Other competition at Dharmapur Club. She had always wanted to be Made-for-Each-Other, even before her marriage. Kamalesh didn't let go of this golden opportunity to make his wife happy and agreed enthusiastically at once. 'Although we have no chance of winning with you there,' he told Rinki, 'we'll give you a fight. You'll see us in Dharmapur on the evening of the contest even if there's a cyclone.'

Drawing him aside, Samarendra said, 'Our fertiliser project director Mr Dickson is extremely interested in you. He wants to hire a keen scientist like you. There'll be six months of training in Edinburgh after you join. You can convince them to let you take your wife along. Then a few weeks of touring the Continent at company expense, after which you'll join the new project. It'll take three years for our new factory to be put up.'

Going up to Mallika, Rinki whispered, 'They'll pay Kamalesh even more than Digambar Bonarjee.'

'Why don't you apply,' Mallika requested her husband.

'You don't have to apply for these jobs,' Samarendra said. 'I know your particulars already. I can pass them on to Mr Dickson. And, besides, he's met you before.'

'Me? Where?' Kamalesh asked in surprise.

'At a fertiliser seminar in Delhi. He was there to represent British Explosives. Digambar Bonarjee and you presented a paper together.'

Samarendra added before leaving that Dickson would be in Dharmapur on the evening of the Made-for-Each-Other contest.

Lying in bed, Mallika was in the mood to chat with her husband late into the night. Rinki had told her she often had romantic conversations with her husband till four in the morning. But Kamalesh fell asleep instantly. He was snoring a little, though Mallika just couldn't sleep.

The attraction of married life had begun to dwindle for her already. Last night she had felt as though she was tethered constantly like cattle in a shed.

On top of that, Rinki had added to her worries. It seemed Jhumu was making no effort to rein in her husband. Docile wives apparently suffer all their lives. Apparently, men ignore and neglect quiet and soft-hearted women. They take their wives for granted. Rinki had said, 'Let him know you have desires too—or else you'll suffer for the rest of your life.'

Mallika had decided to test her husband a bit. To convey to him that his wife wasn't happy. But Kamalesh didn't give her the chance, agreeing voluntarily to take part in the contest for couples. Mallika was dead certain he didn't like these things, but he had shown his interest to please his wife.

Kamalesh turned over in his sleep. Rinki must still be whispering with her husband in Dharmapur. Mallika felt calmer now. Her cousin had told her nothing could be considered an everlasting arrangement—no matter how eternal the love between a husband and a wife might be, evidence was necessary occasionally. Kamalesh had proved it today, but before she left Rinki had said, 'No need to melt at once. Show your unhappiness to your husband sometimes, put on a grim expression, insist on extracting your small dues.'

Rinki wasn't entirely wrong. Mallika would demand confirmation from now on. Kamalesh would have to demonstrate that there was another person in his life besides Digambar Bonarjee.

15

The mammoth project at Krishingar was gradually falling into place. Even from her office Sujata Das could tell Dr Roychowdhury was happy with the progress. After reviewing the blueprints and reports at great length, he was whistling to himself.

Digambar Bonarjee was extremely fortunate to have an assistant like Kamalesh. Sujata had seen for herself how much Dr Roychowdhury respected Dr Bonarjee.

Sudarshan Sen entered Kamalesh's office with some files.

'Everyone's on their way for the general meeting on operationalising the factory,' Kamalesh said.

Sudarshan Sen tried to retreat immediately. 'What can I contribute to technical matters, sir?'

Kamalesh said, 'You have en enormous responsibility in technical matters. You're the one who says that when Shah Jahan built the Taj Mahal, someone must have had a very difficult time maintaining the accounts. And yet we're so ungrateful we don't even know that person's name.'

Sudarshan Sen realised the boss was in a good mood. 'It's the starting up of a new fertiliser plant that's the most interesting aspect,' Kamalesh told him. 'We've divided the factory into four sections. First, synthesis and ammonia recovery; second, recirculation and urea solution; third, urea crystallisation; and fourth, drying, re-melting and prilling.'

Sudarshan Sen usually felt dizzy when anyone reeled off technical terms. 'The entire factory has been divided into forty circuits to make it easier to start operations,' Kamalesh continued. 'Everyone has a specific responsibility. Machine testing is underway. Flashing will begin tomorrow.'

The room filled up with people and the meeting began.

Sujata had hoped to see Max Schiller among the participants. But then she recollected that the factory would be made operational by Indians alone, no help would be sought from foreigners.

Sujata had developed something of a weakness for the handsome Max since their encounter the other evening. He dropped by to pick up letters every morning and Sujata spent those five minutes in indescribable happiness.

But he hadn't come by today. Why should he come every day, though? There were never any letters for him, after all.

Still, Sujata was restless. How beautifully Max smiled. There was nothing lewd in his laughter, unlike the men of this country.

Sujata peeped into the room to find the meeting in full flow. Kamalesh had a long, thin pointer with which he identified various areas of a map on the wall and provided a commentary.

Dr Roychowdhury wanted each and every labourer and worker to know how the urea would be produced. Many supervisors had no wish to devote so much time to labourers, but Sujata heard what Kamalesh was saying. 'This is essential. Unless there's a picture of the entire factory in their heads, the work will become meaningless for individuals. That's when mistakes occur and fatigue sets in.

Sujata was uninterested. She rang the prilling tower, in case she could get Max on the line. Where was he? Sujata couldn't hear what the labourer who had answered the phone was telling her because of the fishmarket-like noise in the background. Eventually, with great difficulty, she gathered that Max had not reported for work today.

She grew more worried. Beads of perspiration gathered on her nose. She considered not checking on the young German any further—why should she, after all? But she simply couldn't concentrate on her work. As though under a spell, Sujata rang the guesthouse.

The phone was next to the dining room. Answering it, the cook-cum-bearer Abdul said, 'Schiller sahib? Yes, he's not well.' Max was sleeping, apparently. Abdul was ready to call him to the phone, but Sujata suddenly felt embarrassed and disconnected the call. As she began to wonder if she'd been right to do this, Kamalesh rang the bell for her.

'Can you take a short note, Miss Das? I want to describe the process of manufacturing urea in simple terms, so that every worker in Krishinagar can understand it.'

'It's extremely complicated, sir,' said Sudarshan Sen. 'I'm utterly confused. What was that you said now? Liquid ammonia and other solutions will be mixed with carbon dioxide and sent into a reactor. There the pressure of the steam will be reduced to do some things. And then the ingredients will go to the rectifying column.'

'See, that was easy,' Kamalesh encouraged him.

'To tell you the truth, sir,' said Sudarshan Sen, 'the workers are not interested in your heaters, separators, second rectifying tower, seventy-five per cent urea solution or any of those things.'

'Then what are they interested in?' asked Kamalesh.

'They want to know whether their wages will be increased when the plant starts running, how much of a bonus they will get, whether more quarters will be constructed. Things like these.'

Kamalesh chuckled. 'These will definitely happen once the factory starts running. But first the urea must be produced.'

After taking the dictation, Sujata left the room. Now Kamalesh booked a call to Digambar Bonarjee. He was thinking of getting a head start on the task of dissolving ammonia in water for the prilling tower. After all, the viscous urea would have to be lifted a hundred and fifty feet through a suction process, and then scattered for spray drying—no easy matter without several trial runs.

Digambar Bonarjee listened every time Kamalesh made such calls, but then he always went back to his pet theme. His only question these days was whether the urea plant would be operational on thirtieth November or not. He had changed quite a bit lately, ever since his return from England—like a broken gramophone record he only harped on whether everything would be ready by thirtieth November.

And yet Digambar Bonarjee hardly ever visited Krishingar. But there was an increasing number of telephone conversations. He no longer sounded pleasant. Was he unable to trust Kamalesh as he used to? Or had the CBI sent him a secret report about Kamalesh too?

In spite of all this Digambar Bonarjee was still ensconced in Kamalesh's heart in all his glory.

16

It was almost dusk. Arranging flowers in the dining room of the guesthouse, Abdul saw a well-dressed woman approaching. The guesthouse was empty. Apart from the German Mr Schiller, there was nobody else. Who on earth had this lady come to meet?

Abdul was a little old-fashioned. He grew nervous when he saw unaccompanied young women. From his experience in military officers' boarding houses during the World War, men were fine when they were by themselves. But in the presence of women, they deteriorated. Still, Abdul was a mere bearer, who was going to listen to him?

Sujata had a flower in her hair today. 'Which one is Schiller sahib's room?' she asked.

Normally Abdul wouldn't allow a well-dressed young woman alone into anyone's room in the evening, but he remembered seeing this lady in the boss's cabin at the head office. So he offered her a salute. Then pointed the way to Schiller sahib's room.

Sujata knocked lightly on the door twice and waited. A voice said, 'Come in.'

Max was expecting Abdul. He shot out of bed when he saw it was Sujata instead. His bare, hairy chest was visible. Apologising profusely, he quickly buttoned up his shirt. 'What a pleasant surprise,' he said, very pleased with the unannounced but delightful visit.

Sujata was a little shy at first, but she gathered strength and accused Max affecionately, without any stiffness, 'Why haven't you seen the doctor, if you're unwell?'

Max seemed to have forgotten English in the throes of this unexpected pleasure. 'Not serious enough to see the doctor,' he said. 'But I thank my illness for this current stroke of fortune.'

How beautiful his eyes were. His marble-white body seemed to have become even more attractive after a bout of fever.

The flower in Sujata's hair didn't escape Max's attention. Beautiful women from India looked like they had come down from heaven when they had flowers in their hair. 'Is that flower meant for the gods?' asked Max.

'I don't know about the gods, but many people put flowers in their hair—I do too,' Sujata said with a smile.

'Oh yes, your husbands are your gods,' said Max, as though he had just remembered.

'I don't have a husband to think of as a god,' said Sujata. 'There isn't any chance of having one either. So I don't waste my time thinking of these things.'

'Did you ring me in the afternoon?' said Max. 'The call was disconnected before I could go out and take it. Abdul said it was a lady, and I told myself, must be Miss India. But I didn't have the nerve to ring you and ask.'

'Don't call me Miss India, Max. People will laugh. I'm quite lacklustre compared to most Indian girls. I'm dark, for one thing.'

Max paid no attention. 'Black is beautiful,' he said.

Was he gazing at her? Sujata couldn't tell. She felt slightly giddy. She wasn't entirely able to control a body ruled for thirty years by continence.

Sujata knew she would never marry. But she hadn't been able to get rid of the eternal, primordial, endless curiosity about men. And yet she geuninely detested Indian men. They seemed filthy to her.

White men weren't hypocrites. Max had candidly said he was unmarried but not a virgin.

Indian men didn't have this honesty. All of them wanted to portray a morally upright image.

It was with this awareness that Sujata had begun to like Max. He told her Miss India's temporary friendship was invaluable and beyond his expectation.

And then?

Sujata Das couldn't remember what came afterwards. What seemed unlikely took place even though they knew everything perfectly well. Sujata couldn't blame Max. He had informed her clearly that he couldn't get married and settle down in India. Sujata too had told him that she wasn't willing even if he was ready. So what happened was difficult to explain. But on that intimate November evening, she didn't free her virginal body from Max's passionate embrace.

Sujata may have lost her consciousness briefly in the crescendo of pleasure during the climax. Max was worried to see her looking so consumed and took her soft hand in his to check her pulse. Then he poured a few drops of vermouth on her tongue to revive her. Later he told her with great affection, 'I'm really very sorry. Let me take you home.'

'No, I can go by myself.' Saying this, Sujata Das had left, enriched by, yet uneasy about, her new experience.

She finally felt she had returned to her senses. Had she lost her sanity for a while? What was this she had done in her madness? Sujata couldn't think about it anymore. But at the same time she felt a hitherto untasted serenity.

She headed home.

17

Sujata couldn't maintain her poise anymore. At first she had felt the joy of a tremendous victory. Then she realised herself that there had been an element of revenge in it too. She had avenged herself in the most spectacular way on all those selfish Indian grooms and their even more greedy families who had rejected Sujata Das because she was dark, thin, lanky, flat-chested, had a slight squint and a dilated heart.

But now an unknown fear had begun to grasp her body which had lost its virginity. She had been to the guesthouse without any thought or preparation. The Sujata who went in there was not the one who came back.

The more days that went by, the more her fears intensified. The thought of that time of the month made her feel she was being swallowed by an unfamiliar anxiety. What if something scandalous happened?

Walking through his secretary's cabin on his way to his own, Kamalesh found her looking dull and listless. She had dark circles under her eyes. 'Did you not sleep last night, Miss Das?' asked Kamalesh. 'You look absolutely exhausted.'

Sujata smiled. 'I have a headache,' she managed to tell Kamalesh.

'Keep large quantities of Saridon at hand,' Kamalesh advised her. 'You, I, and everyone else here will need a pill for headaches quite often.'

The project manager left for the factory site with a map and documents. Sujata felt herself losing her grip again. Would Max visit her today? Why should he? He was a man;

he had no need to come to her anymore. He had got what he wanted. The worry was entirely hers now. Sujata felt like weeping loudly. Her anger was centred on the Almighty. *Where was the need to place the entire burden of responsibility on the female of the species and yet make them such helpless creatures?*

She saw Max approaching her a little later. The familiar, pure, smiling face. At once Sujata was reassured. She was certain that if it had been one of those young Indians instead, they would not have come anywhere near her after the episode. Her faith in and respect for white men grew stronger.

Sujata looked at Max with doe-eyed wonder. He said good morning to her. How easily he was dealing with yesterday's misadventure. Without any guilt or shame. He began talking to her just like he did every day.

Sudarshan Sen came in. 'Mr Schiller, how's work progressing?' he asked.

Max said, 'My work here is done. The urea can be released in the prilling tower in three or four days. Then I'm free.'

'No wonder you look so happy,' observed Sudarshan Sen. 'You'll be back home in a week. And Dr Roychowdhury will have his factory running.'

Everyone laughed. Sudarshan Sen declared, 'I've pledged an entire goat to the goddess. As soon as the plant is operational I'll pack my case and leave this place.'

18

Mallika counted the days off the calendar. She didn't trust her husband at all to eventally make it to the contest for couples in Dharmapur. Kamalesh always had a thousand things to do, so how long could it take him to come up with an excuse? But Mallika had decided that this would be the acid test of their relationship. If Kamalesh let her down yet again, she would go away to Calcutta for some time. She still respected her husband's work ethic, *but that doesn't let you off the hook when it comes to proving your love. Save us, o lord, make Kamalesh keep his word.* Mallika had converted the opportunity into a challenge. She wouldn't stop till she had found out whether there was any space for her in her husband's heart after he had leased most of it out to Digambar Bonarjee.

The contest at Dharmapur Club was an unusual one. Made-for-Each-Other night. On the phone Rinki said, 'I have a feeling Kamalesh and you will win. One look is all it needs to know God has made you a couple.'

'What do you mean?' Kamalesh asked.

'Haven't you seen the ad? Filter and tobacco, made for each other.'

'Each other,' Kamalesh said. 'I feel those two words in my bones. In school Himanshu-babu made me stand on the bench for getting them wrong. When the relationship is between two people, it's each other; when it's among several people, it's one another.'

'Meaning?' asked Mallika.

'According to Sudarshan-babu, all husbands and wives today are made for each other—they don't know anyone else in the world besides themselves. In his youth, he says, it was made for one another. The world didn't consist only of the husband and the wife; it included parents, brothers and sisters, other relatives, even society at large.'

Mallika said, 'Rinki's very naughty. I asked her what we're supposed to do in the contest, and she said act with your husband as though you're lock-and-key or salt-and-pepper or fork-and-knife. One cannot exist without the other.'

'Like pen-and-ink, socks-and-shoes, bread-and-butter,' Kamalesh added to the list.

'Oh you're giving beautiful examples,' said a delighted Mallika. 'Please, some more.'

Scratching his head, Kamalesh said, 'Needle-and-thread, bottle-and-cap, cheek-and-beard, lips-and-moustache, boss-and-stenographer, coat-and-trousers, gin-and-tonic.'

Kamalesh appeared to be a in fine mood to please his wife, but in his head he was praying that the work in Krishinagar went ahead without a hitch. He was close to exhaustion himself. A little rest would be welcome.

Mallika said, 'The Dharmapur wives are rehearsing for made-for-each-other with their husbands every day. But you're never home for us to rehearse.'

'Don't worry, we'll beat everyone on stage,' Kamalesh told her.

'Our parents' generation would have been furious at the idea of such competitions,' said Mallika.

'You never know,' said Kamalesh, laughing. 'There was a dreadful phrase back then too: whore-and-client.'

'What today's couples mean by made for each other is different. In joy and in sorrow, in delight and in sacrifice, neither will surpass the other.'

Taking a drag of his cigarette, Kamalesh said, 'Shiva and Parvati, in other words. The ideal couple.'

'The husbands in all these filter cigarette ads are always handsome,' said Mallika. 'You can tell they lack nothing in life. The wife indulges the husband's manly habit of smoking. The husband too is full of self-confidence and there are signs of a strong romance between them. A love that is legitimate, a love in which no one plays hide-and-seek.'

Kamalesh was about to praise his wife's sharp vision. But the phone rang again.

Once again it was talk about the factory. The conversation was endless. It was as though these people had a conspiracy. The moment Mallika began chatting with her husband, they would start calling. It seemed to her that if any two people or things were made for each other, it was Kamalesh and the telephone.

Kamalesh himself was annoyed. But he didn't tell Mallika the reason. The phone call was from Digambar Bonarjee. Kamalesh was working so hard, but still it wasn't good enough for Digambar Bonarjee. He reminded Kamalesh again, thirtieth November and not seventh December.

Kamalesh had decided they would quietly leave for Dharmapur on the afternoon of the contest. He wouldn't let himself be stopped by anything whatsoever.

On the day of the competition, Kamalesh left home at six in the morning. Since he wouldn't be present in the late afternoon, he didn't return home for lunch. After a quick meal in his office, he toured the factory site. The preparations for the launch were going well. He didn't anticipate any problems.

But there was no respite even when he came home at three. The phone rang continuously. Mallika looked annoyed at the onslaught. She blurted out, 'You won't end up going. Why are you asking me to get dressed?'

Kamalesh didn't take his wife's barb to heart. Smiling, he said, 'Get ready quickly. We'll leave before anything comes in the way.'

'You want something to come in the way,' Mallika accused him.

'Really?' Kamalesh was not going to hurt his wife in any way today.

'You're acting as though you love your wife more than your work,' said Mallika.

The phone rang again. But Kamalesh did something he had never done before. Mallika saw Kamalesh disconnecting the call without speaking.

She wasn't prepared for this. No matter how often she complained or revealed her irritation, she had unknowingly begun to develop a respect for her husband's engrossment in his work. She had been apprehensive that Kamalesh wouldn't be able to go, after all, but even though she was pleased when he disconnected the phone, she didn't feel proud. It seemed to her that such behaviour didn't suit Kamalesh Roychowdhury. It was a strange state of mind she was in—she wanted her husband to devote his time to her, but she also wanted to be proud of him. Mallika reproached herself mentally.

Kamalesh drove the jeep faster. All of Krishinagar rolled past them like a captivating scene from a modern film. Evening was descending on the labourers' quarters. A few naked boys were playing on the road. Adivasi men and women, after an exhausting workday, were trudging back to their villages with their bundles hanging from the ends of the sticks balanced on their shoulders.

The jeep raced past the hospital and nurses' quarters. The guesthouse lay ahead of them. A tall young foreigner was walking across the grass, lost to the world.

'Isn't that your German?' Mallika asked.

'Yes,' said Kamalesh. 'Work-crazy Max Schiller completed his assignment this morning. That's probably why he's in a good mood, taking one last look around Krishinagar. He leaves tomorrow morning.'

But the more Kamalesh wanted to put Krishinagar away from his mind today, the more Mallika reminded him of it. Trying to control the end of her sari, which the wind was blowing all over the place, Mallika said, 'How's your secretary? She never visited us again.'

'Maybe she's avoiding you. The boss's wife, after all.'

'The boss's wife isn't going to bite her,' Mallika said, sounding hurt.

'Something's the matter with her,' said Kamalesh. 'She's been looking very worried of late. She didn't even come to work today, she's not well.'

'It's because of her illness that her parents didn't get her married,' said Mallika. 'She fainted in school once.'

Mallika had an urge to visit Sujata in her quarters, especially since the poor thing was unwell.

But Kamalesh had no desire to pay attention to anything concerning work. He didn't even glance at the Krishinagar factory. The sunlight in the western sky had fallen on the prilling tower, which was as white as pigeon feathers. It was exactly like a street vendor pouring red syrup on a cone of shaved ice.

Mallika wished they could stop for a few minutes to take in this breathtaking sight. But Kamalesh didn't slow down. Mallika felt he was determined to do nothing but keep his wife happy today.

Kamalesh tried to be exuberant. He sped along the open road and even hummed under his breath. Mallika had finally got what she had been seeking all this time, which should have made her happy. But she felt awkward instead, telling herself that she wasn't so self-centred as to disrupt her husband's mission.

Rinki shrieked with joy when she saw Kamalesh. 'You're here at last,' she said.

'Why shouldn't I be?' asked Kamalesh, settling down on the sofa.

'My cousin would have divorced you today if you hadn't come. You'd have been in the same state as Digambar Bonarjee after his wife left him.' Rinki's response made Mallika uncomfortable.

'Poor thing, he's having to work harder than ever,' she said on her husband's behalf.

Rinki curled her lips. 'I thought I was fighting for *you*. Let your husband leave you in exile and spend ten years in Tahiti building a factory, what do I care? I don't like it when people don't speak their minds.'

Mallika was embarrassed. What if Kamalesh thought she complained about her husband to Rinki every day?

Samarendra emerged from the bedroom and greeted Mallika. Smiling slyly, he said, 'I won't chat with you and Kamalesh too much today, Jhumu. You're our competitors, after all. We have to try to beat you in the contest. You should change your clothes now.'

'Whether you win the prize or not, my cousin and you are the perfect couple,' retorted Mallika. 'Even an hour of separation leads to fainting bouts. You've ensured Rinki doesn't lack for anything financially, and she's given you a beautiful home. This is what "made for each other" is.'

'It's all very well to flatter your brother-in-law and say he hasn't deprived me financially, but do you know how long I've been asking for a set of pearls? No answer. Says he doesn't have the money.' Everyone laughed at Rinki's repartee.

'Has the cigarette company decided what an ideal couple is?' asked Kamalesh.

'Only the judges know those secrets,' Rinki said. 'But you'll see a number of ideal couples today. Some of them fight constantly, some have thrown out their husband's parents or are having affairs with other women's husbands.

All of them will arrive at the party with make-up, holding their legally wedded husbands' hands.'

'Should we practise the flaming kiss once more?' Samarendra asked his wife.

'You and your jokes, really!' Rinki gave her a husband a mouthful. Turning to her cousin, she said, 'You'd better practise lighting your husband's cigarette, Jhumu. Rumour is that ten points have been allocated for it.'

Mallika jumped out of her skin. 'Are they going to ask us to do things like this?'

'They won't ask you to do anything. You can do whatever you please with your husband. But they will watch you, and give you points accordingly. How you walk together, how your sari matches your husband's clothes, how you talk to each other, smile at each other, they'll observe everything.'

Mallika was flustered. 'Actually, every woman has to be as seductive with their husband as someone else's wife might be,' added Samarendra. 'And the husband has to behave as though he's still courting her, as though marriage hasn't been mentioned yet.'

Serving everyone cups of tea, Rinki glanced at the clock. 'Our husbands look like factory labourers, Jhumu. Let's pack them off for their baths. We don't have much time.'

19

Max Schiller strode across the grass. He had just come out of Sujata Das's quarters. He had been to the office in the afternoon to look for her and then decided to visit her at home when he was told she hadn't come to work.

In Germany Max had been dating girls freely from the age of sixteen but had never found himself in this sort of trouble before. He had heard that India was mysterious, but he didn't know that in spite of their ancient wisdom and mystique the women in this country were so helpless. He had been told that Indian women were modern now, they were doctors, engineers, scientists, ambassadors to foreign countries. But what he had seen was that, like the machinery here, the women were not yet self-reliant.

Max wasn't embarrassed about his momentary weakness with Sujata. Why was she so worried? But something had happened after that evening, Sujata had completely fallen apart.

Schiller wasn't unfeeling. He had met Sujata at the office. When he heard she was unwell, he immediately rushed over to her house. Poor Sujata was in bed, covered by a sheet—she looked as ashen as a plant deprived of nitrogen.

Sujata gave no answer when Schiller asked what the matter was, though tears appeared in the corners of her eyes. Max was under the impression that independent women knew how to protect themselves from the dangers that intimacy with men could lead to. He hadn't imagined Sujata was an exception and completely inexperienced. Sujata still hadn't had any physical indication of danger, but was terrified by the possibility.

Some people laid traps of fatherhood to get their boyfriends into trouble. But Sujata wasn't one of them. She had no expectations of Max. But then Max wasn't irresponsible either; he knew he had more to do till Sujata was certain she was safe physically.

Sujata would know in four or five days. But by then Schiller wouldn't be in India. When she heard that his work here was done and a telegram had been sent to Germany to this effect, that even his plane ticket had been bought, the poor thing began to tremble like a leaf.

Sujata hadn't made an explicit demand, but it was easy for Max to fathom what she wanted, being alone and in trouble far away from home. She would be grateful if only Max could stay on a few days more.

But he had no way of doing this. Why would the company keep him here? And if he asked for it, the authorities here would suspect something. Sujata was aware of these things. Max Schiller grew restless. All the tests on the prilling section had been completed early this morning. The HAC engineers were happy. A trial would be conducted this afternoon, with the urea being sent up into the tower. Today, Max had attached a small plate with his German company's name to the bottom of the tower. Those who would come years later to see this tower would learn the name of the company.

Max looked at Sujata in silence. Sujata said nothing but a helpless fear and a desperate plea were visible in her impenetrable eyes.

Leaving Sujata's house, Max Schiller began walking across the grass. Sujata would know whether she was safe in a few days more, two weeks at most. Was there a way to stay on here a little longer?

Gazing at the Hindustan Agro-Chemicals factory in the distance gave Max Schiller a strange sensation. He regretted completing his assignment so quickly—it would have been useful to have let it drag on a few weeks longer. On the other hand, the man who had just driven past in a jeep with his wife, Kamalesh Roychowdhury, was working relentlessly to complete the project a week before schedule. A remarkable tug-of-war over time had begun in obscure Krishinagar—some wanted to stretch it, others wanted to squeeze it.

But Max had no time to immerse himself in philosophical musings. His objective was clear. He had to steal some days for Sujata's sake. But how? What could he do to stay a little longer?

Max Schiller saw the sun had climbed down the western sky. A royal festival of colour was in progress, much like the unlimited resources and wealth of India. Someone seemed to have spray painted one side of the silver tower red without Max's permission. Max had a thought. A plan seemed to have occurred to him. After thinking some more about it he dashed towards the guesthouse and emerged with his bag of tools. Then he drove his jeep towards gate no. 4 of the factory, the one closest to the prilling tower.

The Nepali security guard at HAC had seen this white man every day. Sahib didn't normally return at this hour, but then he was the one who had installed this enormous machine. He saluted Max without any suspicion.

20

Sujata Das had got out of bed to sit on a cane stool. There was no reason to be so dispirited. What had happened had happened. Now she only had to wait for the outcome. But neither her body nor her heart was willing to accept this.

Sujata poured some vermouth from the bottle and drank it. Max had given it to her, apparently it strengthened the nerves.

Sujata hadn't demanded anything from Max. She had told him bluntly she was an adult and had participated knowingly. If something untoward did happen, she wouldn't pin the responsibility on him. But Max wasn't a brute. He knew what a difference it would make if he could stay on for another fortnight. Once he reached Germany he would disappear somewhere. Perhaps he would't even remain there, maybe the company would send him to Thailand or Venezuela.

Sujata had no one of her own to consult in this hour of crisis. The only person she had known earlier was Mallika, but the boss's wife had made no attempt to reduce the distance between them. She hadn't enquired after Sujata even though she knew of her illness. Mallika was wrapped up in her husband's hopes and dreams—where was the generosity to look beyond that?

She heard a jeep stop outside. The doorbell rang. Was Max back? He was leaving the next morning.

It wasn't Max. Sujata was startled to find Sudarshan Sen instead.

Sudarshan Sen was clearly worried. Beads of perspiration had gathered on his hairless head.

Gasping for breath, he said, 'Please don't mind. I was forced to come to you without notice. Have you any idea where our project manager is?'

'I didn't even go to work today,' an equally worried Sujata answered.

Throwing his hands up in despair, Sudarshan Sen said, 'He never goes anywhere without informing us. Things always go wrong when you fear the worst.'

Sudarshan Sen and the other project officers were looking for Kamalesh desperately. They had tried calling him at home. Nobody had answered. Sudarshan Sen had even rushed over his house himself—there was no one there. He had looked for Kamalesh everywhere—in the office, in all the sections of the factory, everywhere.

Finally he had come to Sujata. Kamalesh had a brother-in-law in Dharmapur, might Sujata have his phone number? If it was to be found somewhere in the office, Sudarshan Sen would take her along and have the office opened. *No, it wasn't in the office—Kamalesh Roychowdhury had the number in his pocket diary.*

'What does this brother-in-law do in Dharmapur?' Sudarshan Sen had seen the man but hadn't asked for his name or where he worked.

Sujata couldn't remember with certainty either. 'I think he works at British Explosives. His wife's name is Rinki, I think.'

What was Sudarshan Sen to do with this information? 'Telephone enquiry doesn't record the wife's nickname. Can't you recollect the gentleman's name?' he asked Sujata.

Sujata could not. Giving up, he said, 'Let me check if his trunk call bill is in the office. There must be a phone call or two to Dharmapur.'

'What's the matter?' asked Sujata. 'So what if he has gone out for a day?'

'It's very serious, Ma. An accident at the prilling tower,' said Sudarshan Sen with deep concern.

'An accident! Is anyone injured or dead?'

'A narrow escape. We can't tell yet whether it was a flaw in Digambar Bonarjee's design or something else. We'll be in trouble if we can't locate Dr Roychowdhury.' Sudarshan Sen rushed out.

Where's Max? Sujata had the impulse to ask but she didn't dare. She was even a little scared.

Her fear was suddenly converted to fondness. At this moment she liked Max very much. He seemed to have a sense of responsibility, she felt she could depend on him.

21

The beautiful women in the homes of all the officers of British Explosives in Dharmapur were absorbed in doing their make-up. Rinki and Jhumu were very busy in front of the dressing table. Their husbands were bathing in the two bathrooms.

Rubbing foundation cream into her face, Mallika said, 'You can't imagine how difficult it was getting out of Krishinagar today. Eventually I took the telephone off the hook.' For some reason she drew back from pinning the responsibility for this act on her husband. She felt it would make Kamalesh look small.

'Well done,' Rinki said, applying steam to her face and cleansing the pores on her skin with the help of French lotion. 'This is how to control your husband. They need to enjoy themselves too. How are they going to work hard otherwise?'

'The poor thing has taken an irrevocable vow to get the factory operational by the deadline,' said Mallika. 'For the betterment of the nation.'

Rinki didn't believe her. Continuing with her make-up, she said, 'Explain to your husband that a week's delay will not mean the end of the world in a country where procrastination has been a way of life for three hundred years.'

When the phone rang, Rinki said, 'Can you answer it? Must be Mrs Saha asking about compatible colours. Old as the hills, still doesn't know how to pair a blouse with a sari!

Insists on badgering me on the phone. Tell her I'm in the bathroom.'

It seemed to Mallika that it wasn't Mrs Saha but someone from Krishinagar. 'Hello, hello, Dharmapur? We're looking for our project manager Kamalesh Roychowdhury. Is he there?'

Mallika was annoyed. They had chased Kamalesh here too. Couldn't get on with their work without him even for a minute? She didn't hesitate and calmly said, 'He isn't here.'

'Hello, hello ...' the man was about to say something more but Mallika disconnected the call before he could continue.

'That's quite a feat! Dressing Samarendra-babu in a groom's outfit for the Made-for-Each-Other contest,' Kamalesh joked with Kanaklata in the car.

'Once you get to the club you'll see not everyone's a Westerner here,' said Rinki, dabbing her nose with her hankerchief.

The air was heavy with the perfume used by the cousins. Samarendra told Kamalesh as he drove. 'It's good for us to be a bit swadeshi.'

Waving her Japanese fan slightly, Rinki said, 'Even at formal parties my husband wears a galabandh prince coat instead of a dinner jacket. But white men believe in being international with their courtesy. They don't mind at all.'

She turned her attention to her cousin. 'Jhumu, how well you've dressed your husband! I'm tempted to enter the competition with him.'

'If your club contest rules allow it, I have no objection.' Mallika gave blanket permission.

A little later Rinki said, 'But what's the matter with you? Who's going to give a prize to someone looking so grim?'

Mallika smiled but said nothing. She felt unsettled. She had guessed that her husband didn't care for such silly contests. Mallika had been looking forward to a carefree evening, but the phone call had spoilt her mood.

'The whole thing is childish,' Samarendra said. 'Comparing husband and wife to filter and tobacco is unrealistic. But life is hard enough, so why not allow an advertisement to let you escape for a while?'

Mallika recalled that people said the same thing about unrealistic Hindi films. But she wasn't up to an argument now. She only wanted to be done with the competition as quickly as possible and return with her husband to Krishinagar.

'Actually this is a modern puppet show,' Samarendra continued. In this capitalist society of ours the advertisers want to trap men and women in an illusory web of hopes and dreams. Every couple wants to believe they're made for each other.'

'What's that your boss says?' Mallika asked her husband.

Breaking his silence, Kamalesh said, 'Digambar Bonarjee believes that the educated people of India, like the shameless and selfish, are made for each other. But unless they're made for one another the country won't survive.'

'This is also another form of his madness,' Rinki laughed.

Mallika couldn't let go of this opportunity to vent her anger towards Digambar Bonarjee. Bluntly she said, 'His own wife has run away. So like the fox without a tail, he wants to snip the tails of all foxes.'

Kamalesh remained serious. He didn't respond.

The competition was in full swing. There were valuable prizes, and yet there was no unnecessary excitement in Dharmapur Club on that account. It was like a casual wedding evening in the club hall. Couples moved about as they pleased, smoking, dancing, chatting. The room was full of bright lights. There was music from the record player. Not just Western music, but also wedding tunes on the shehnai.

Each couple had their own table. Samrendra came over from his to tell Kamalesh, 'Take a look at those blouses, my brother—the ladies are moving swiftly towards going topless. Look at Mrs Sanyal's back—eliminating the fabric from the shoulders and waist has brought things to the point of crisis. One deep breath will lead to the garment bursting, followed by imminent danger.'

Kamalesh smiled, expecting a response from his wife. But Mallika said nothing.

'The writer Amitava Choudhuri has coined a term for these blouses. The bra-ouse.'

A delighted Samarendra said, 'Brilliant! A new word in both the English and Bengali languages.'

'What would you like to eat?' Kamalesh asked his wife. Mallika had no appetite. Her husband wanted to give her everything today, but she couldn't accept any of it with all her heart.

Why wasn't her scientist husband distracted tonight? Mallika wanted him to think about his project instead of paying so much attention to his wife. She had never wanted to mar his dedication to his work. Let Kamalesh be absorbed in his passion, let his talent and fame be known of everywhere, let his name be written in the history of the nation—this was Mallika's desire.

It would have been nice to forget these things and lose herself in this celebration of happy couples. But Mallika couldn't do it. The phone call from Krishinagar kept ringing in her ears.

'Are you feeling unwell?' asked Kamalesh.

'No, not unwell,' said Mallika.

'What is it then?'

Mallika couldn't hold herself back anymore. Touching her husband's hand with hers fearfully, she said, 'You know, when we were getting ready at Rinki's house I think someone rang from Krishinagar to look for you. I couldn't tell, exactly, the call got disconnected.'

Kamalesh was startled for a moment. Then his eyes began to regain their old lustre. Mallika could see the dedicated scientist in her husband again. Pushing away the glass of orange squash, Kamalesh shot out of the hall. He didn't seem to even see his wife. Then returning after having made a phone call, he whispered, 'We have no time, Mallika, let's go.'

Mallika was about to mention Rinki and Samarendra. And that the results would be declared in just half an hour. But Kamalesh wasn't ready to listen. He had already informed Samarendra that there was an urgent phone call and that they were leaving.

22

Kamalesh Roychowdhury's jeep flew through the darkness along the National Highway. Mallika was a little frightened. What if they had an accident? Kamalesh couldn't be bothered. He was determined to swim against the current of time.

Stopping at home to escort Mallika inside, Kamalesh leapt into his jeep again and disappeared in a flash.

There was a large crowd around the prilling tower, including Sudarshan Sen, who had a helmet on.

Everyone made way for Kamalesh. Worry was written large on their faces; they couldn't speak. Like an injured beast, the machine still kept emitting smoke from time to time.

'It's all very strange,' said the engineer Hajra. 'Everything was fine in the afternoon when Mr Schiller handed over the machine to us. Later in the day we were supposed to test it with an injection of seventy-five per cent urea mixture. As soon as the feed went in and the switch was pressed, there was a minor explosion. The tower shook uncontrollably.'

People had begun to run thinking it was a major accident. Unable to find Kamalesh anywhere, they had switched off the machine. Kamalesh realised that the urea mixture would coagulate and ruin the machine. 'Arrange to hose down the tower with water at once!' he shouted. 'It may be too late already. If the spray drying machine breaks down we'll be set back by three months.'

No one had climbed up the tower yet. Disregarding warnings, and without a thought for his own safety, Kamalesh climbed up the narrow spiral staircase. Like ants, several others followed him with tools. Mr Das tilted the floodlights.

Meanwhile Mallika sat in the lawn, awake. She could see the prilling tower, bright in the bluish light of the mercury lamps. But she didn't know of the drama being played out there.

And Kamalesh forgot everything, defying the force of gravity to climb even higher.

Hours passed one after the other. Mallika felt she was counting the minutes as she passed through a harsh test.

She couldn't recognise Kamalesh when he returned after four in the morning. His expensive new clothes were covered in soot. He had grease all over his face and arms. His hair was as white as an old man's because of the urea grains in it.

They had left it too late, felt Kamalesh. The spray drying machine probably wouldn't be saved. But there was no time to rest. The German would have to begin repairs at once. Fortunately Max Schiller was still in Krishinagar.

'What are you thinking about?' Mallika asked her husband, handing him a cup of tea.

'Nothing, Jhumu,' Kamalesh said in an ice-cold voice.

But Mallika didn't believe her husband. He was thinking, *this crisis could have been averted if I had been able to come back a few hours earlier.*

Mallika remembered seeing her father sitting in the same bewildered state at home a long time ago. The surgery her elder sister needed had been delayed. Returning home from the Medical College Hospital at three in the morning after the operation, her father had told her the same way, 'Jhumu, make some tea.'

Mallika felt guilty. She wanted to beat herself up for what had happened. Taking her husband's hand, she said,

'Come, let me clean this out with soap. The grease won't go, otherwise.'

Kamalesh sat in silence. He didn't say a word.

Mallika moved very close to him. Touching him, she said, 'Don't worry, everything will be all right.'

Everything becomes all right eventually. But time doesn't wait, Kamalesh thought to himself.

Although Kamalesh wouldn't admit it, Mallika could tell he was suffering from deep remorse. Kamalesh said, seemingly to himself, 'None of them had the basic sense to run a hosepipe from the top of the tower.'

'They're new to this,' said Mallika. 'And the machinery is expensive. They don't have your courage.'

Some more time passed. Still anguished, Kamalesh sat like a stone. Mallika clutched her husband's arm with her tender hands. 'Come and sleep,' she said, dragging him to bed. Kamalesh was still exuding the strong and unfamiliar smell of several chemicals. Not even soap had scrubbed it off. 'Should I put some eau de cologne on you?' Mallika asked.

'No need,' said Kamalesh, and sat on one side of the bed.

Mallika had no doubt about what her husband was thinking. *I wish we hadn't gone to Dharmapur*. But it was too late.

Mallika felt like crying. She considered herself a criminal. Burying her face in her husband's shoulders, she broke down. 'I'll never be so foolish again,' she said.

A grave Kamalesh patted her back lightly. Reassuringly he said, 'Why are you worrying? You did nothing wrong.'

Calming his wife down, Kamalesh looked at the calendar again. He had had great hopes of surprising Bonarjee with a phone call on the morning of thirtieth November, announcing: 'I have kept your request, sir.'

The telephone rang. Who on earth was calling at this hour? Kamalesh answered the phone. So as not to disturb

Mallika, he spoke as softly as possible. Mallika could now tell even if she wasn't close by when it was Digambar Bonarjee calling.

Contritely Kamalesh said, 'I rushed back as soon as I got the news. Yes, sir, you heard right, there was a party there this evening.' Digambar Bonarjee probably said something harsh. Kamalesh said, 'I just got home after a four-hour battle. I'll give you a report tomorrow.'

Kamalesh tiptoed back to bed. He checked to see whether his wife was asleep. Then he pressed the bed switch and turned off the light.

23

Sujata Das had never seen the project manager enter the office covered in grease and soot. It was obvious Kamalesh had come here after spending hours at the factory site.

Sudarshan Sen rushed in too and began secret confabulations with the boss. After that Kamalesh called Sujata inside. She noticed he had not lost his usual courtesy despite all his anxiety. With great sincerity he asked her, 'How are you, Miss Das? You weren't well yesterday.'

Sujata couldn't look Kamalesh in the eye. He seemed to have aged ten years overnight. 'Send for Mr Schiller at once, Miss Das,' said Kamalesh. 'Stop him from leaving. Given the state of the prilling tower, I don't know how long it will take to repair it. But a fortnight at least.'

'How much time do we have?' asked Sujata.

'Don't embarrass me, Miss Das. We're only three days away from thirtieth November.'

'Don't worry, Dr Roychowdhury,' Sujata said quietly.

'Are you consoling me, Miss Das?' smiled Kamalesh. 'That's all I deserve now. I don't know what foolishness it was that led me to leave Krishinagar yesterday of all days.'

Sujata stared at Kamalesh, mesmerised. 'People are spreading all kinds of rumours,' said Kamalesh. 'Some say the design of the prilling tower was faulty. But how can they say that when it's been designed by Digambar Bonarjee himself. Sudarshan-babu just came with a tall story of sabotage. Apparently last evening Mr Schiller was seen going to the tower all by himself. Mr Sen has gone mad.

What motive could Schiller possibly have to sabotage the machine? In fact, he'd be the one in trouble, since he would have to stay on without the German company paying him for the additional days and work. I'm not insane; I'm not sending this case to the CBI.'

After some thought, Kamalesh continued, 'I'm certain there's no flaw in the design. Now I have to turn to Mr Schiller to rescue us from this mess.'

24

Max Schiller's work on repairing the prilling power had been in full swing for the past few days. The cause of the unexpected explosion couldn't be ascertained. Maybe some gas had gathered somewhere. Schiller had said it wasn't clear yet how long it would take to make the prilling tower operational again.

Kamalesh sat grimly in his office. 'What are you worrying so much about?' asked Sujata Das.

Kamalesh looked at her. Poor Sujata was also downcast because of the situation. Kamalesh was embarrassed. Summoning a smile to his weary face, he said, 'None of you should be concerned, Miss Das. Please continue with your work. In war or politics or factories, those who shoulder the responsibility have to suffer a little more from time to time.'

Paying no attention to this, Sujata repeated, 'Please don't worry so much.'

'The spray dryer isn't entirely out of commission,' said Kamalesh. 'But its capacity has gone down. The prilling tower hasn't been damaged significantly. But I don't know how long the German will take to repair it.'

Sujata reeled for a moment. If anyone knew the answer, it was she. Schiller had come by privately even today to ask her. Sujata hadn't answered.

Locking the bathroom door behind her, Sujata took out the vanity mirror from her bag. Then she went into peals of laughter. She wanted to laugh loudly enough to shake all of Krishinagar. Was she going mad?

Sujata looked into the mirror again. The girl in the mirror reproached her. 'Aren't you ashamed of yourself, you demoness?'

The excitement made Sujata gasp for breath. She was afraid of this gasping. It often led to chest pain. At this moment she considered herself the proudest woman in the world. A new name had just been added to the list of women who had made history, the Sitas and Helens and Cleopatras of the world. The name was Sujata Das, whose wish had led this enormous complex in Krishinagar to suddenly come to a halt. A triumphant Sujata wanted to shower kisses on Max Schiller's lips. She wanted to scream. To declare haughtily, 'See for yourself what the ugly Sujata Das, whom you ignored and humiliated all these years, has won. Look at the huge risk Max Schiller has taken just to stay by her side.'

If she remained there by herself any longer Sujata felt she might actually go mad and scream. She got out of the bathroom fearfully. She went and sat in her own cabin. Sujata saw Kamalesh replacing the telephone receiver.

'Miss Das,' Kamalesh called for her. Then he said grimly, 'Dr Bonarjee is arriving in a few hours. He couldn't inform us earlier because the telephone lines were down. Please let the guesthouse know. He's not well at all. He'll only have a little milk for dinner.'

When Sujata returned after making arrangements at the guesthouse, she found Kamalesh still worrying. *At the time of trouble Digambar Bonarjee didn't come. Yet today is the thirtieth of November, he's coming at the right time to inspect Krishinagar. So that he can taunt the irresponsible and unsuccessful Kamalesh Roychowdhury.*

'Do you have any instructions for me?' Sujata asked Kamalesh.

'Yes,' Kamalesh paused. 'Would you please type a letter for me? It's very urgent.'

'Tell me,' said Sujata, opening her shorthand notebook.

Doodling on a sheet of paper, Kamalesh said, 'Yes, take this down, please. Resignation letter. Dear Sir, I hereby resign from ...'

Sujata wouldn't have been as startled if she'd been pushed off her chair. 'Dr Roychowdhury! I won't type this. What's all this you're saying?'

Kamalesh lifted his eyes to look affectionately at his secretary. Then he said, more to himself than to her, 'The director had made just the one request. I couldn't keep it. The factory couldn't be made operational on the thirtieth of November. Now I want to get it going within a month and then leave.'

'What's all this?' Sujata interrupted him. 'No one's said anything to you.' Kamalesh smiled. Then he said, 'Dr Bonarjee asked me on the phone at four in the morning whether I'd won the Made-for-Each-Other contest or not.'

Women are probably softer. Kamalesh saw tears falling from his secretary's eyes. So at least one person here would be sad about his defeat and departure. Sujata Das was still tender-hearted.

Sujata didn't dare disobey her boss. She had to type the letter and hand it to him. But she broke down crying and requested Kamalesh again to change his mind. 'Why should you let your life be ruined?' she said again. 'It wasn't your fault. There's no reason for you to resign.'

Looking forlorn as he tucked the resignation letter into his pocket, Kamalesh said gratefully, 'I'll remember your sympathy all my life, Miss Das.'

The moment he left, Sujata pressed her fingertips to her temples and sat down in her chair. She still couldn't imagine that her mistake could be responsible for such a catastrophe in Krishinagar.

The phone rang. It was Mallika. 'Hello, Sujata-di? How are you? You asked me so many times the other day to come to your house. I haven't seen you in such a long time,

Sujata-di. Can you please ask my husband to send the jeep? I'll come visit you.'

Sujata felt her head reeling again. Poor Mallika still didn't know that her husband was on his way to hand in his resignation. Sujata requested Mallika not to come today. All the anger and hurt she had felt towards Mallika had disappeared.

Sitting behind her desk, Sujata couldn't stop her tears. Suddenly she felt there wasn't a more selfish witch than her on earth! For her own happiness, she was about to ruin the lives of an innocent newly married couple.

Suddenly the calendar caught her eye. It was the long-awaited thirtieth of November. A date that could have been shining brightly because of Kamalesh Roychowdhury's dedication had been poisoned by Sujata Das's blemish.

Sujata rose from her chair in a trance. She had to meet Max.

Evening had descended. Kamalesh was waiting in the portico of the guesthouse for Digambar Bonarjee's car. It was late. A mixture of pique and remorse had put Kamalesh in a strange state of mind.

Digambar Bonarjee's car arrived and came to a halt. He emerged almost two minutes later.

Good god! When had he begun to look this way? Kamalesh was astonished. Digambar Bonarjee had shrunk to half his normal size.

Noel Digambar Bonarjee walked to his room on slow, uncertain steps and sat down. Then he asked Kamalesh, 'Has the plant survived?'

'It has,' said Kamalesh with his head bowed. 'But it might take longer to get it operational. We'll have to wait for some time.'

Kamalesh had expected to be mocked for his unnecessary devotion to his wife. He was prepared for this. He would offer his resignation letter at once and remind Dr Bonarjee that there was a limit to human capability. But he would accept his fault for being absent from Krishinagar that evening and beg pardon for it.

Kamalesh was ready for Digambar Bonarjee's response. But what was this? Dr Bonarjee didn't mock him at all. Putting his hand on Kamalesh's shoulder, he said, 'You can wait beyond the thirtieth of November, Kamalesh. Time is on your side. It's not on mine. I'm being admitted to a hospital in Calcutta on the first of December. They want to open up my stomach and examine the state of the cancer. I learnt of it during my last trip to London. I didn't tell any of you, but I begged for time till the thirtieth of November so that this project could be completed.'

Kamalesh found himself weeping. It finally dawned on him that not everyone has all the time in the world to wait. In his ignorance he had misunderstood Dr Bonarjee. As with a little boy, his tears took away his ability to speak, even to apologise. Grasping Bonarjee's emaciated hands, Kamalesh said tearfully, 'I'll never be late again, sir.'

Leaning on Kamalesh's shoulder, Digambar Bonarjee went out into the guesthouse lawn. From a distance he gazed at his unfinished Taj Mahal to his heart's content. Then he returned to his room with slow, mournful steps.

Digambar Bonarjee had no time to wait. He drank a little milk and then returned to his car, lying down with his head on a pillow and his legs folded on the seat. The car went back towards Chandanpur.

25

And Kamalesh. Bidding goodbye to Digambar Bonarjee, Kamalesh Roychowdhury, scientist, seemed to be reborn. He stood on a dark, lonely, silent expanse, where countless unheard voices addressed him, *there's no time to wait, no time*. A half-delirious Kamalesh could see strange scenes playing out before his eyes—the constellations of stars had crossed over the boundaries of time to spread across a space where no time existed. The very next moment, he felt as though eternal time was itself sick, that, just like Digambar Bonarjee, it too was suffering from incurable cancer.

Wracked by remorse, an exausted Kamalesh was about to switch on the ignition of his vehicle. Suddenly he spotted Sudarshan Sen's jeep approaching from the opposite direction. When he was closer, the administrative officer shouted, 'I've been looking everywhere for you, sir. I don't know where you disappear sometimes.' Coming up to Kamalesh, he continued, 'It's unbelievable, sir. Mr Schiller is looking for you. Absolute magic—the German has fixed the problem on the prilling tower like a magician. You can start operations tonight if you like. Everyone's ready.'

Kamalesh wanted to go to the site at once with Sudarshan Sen. But the administrative officer said regretfully, 'I wish I could, but I have to rush to the hospital now. Your secretary Sujata has been admitted there with severe chest pain. I don't know what's going on at Krishinagar. She was fine even a few hours ago. But after you left some madness overtook her and she went off to inspect the German's work on the prilling tower. Schiller was welding something at a height of thirty feet. Such a daredevil, that girl, she climbed up the ladder to talk to him. Schiller fixed the machine soon afterwards.'

On any other day Kamalesh would have gone to the hospital himself. But now he didn't have the time. All he said was, 'How strange, she was typing letters for me just a short while ago. I'll go to the hospital tomorrow, please take Mallika with you today.'

'Sujata became nervous when she saw the situation here,' said Sudarshan Sen. 'At the hospital she was delirious. She was telling you, please don't resign, it's all my fault.'

Kamalesh rang home some time later. 'Have dinner and go to bed, Mallika. Don't wait up for me.'

Mallika sounded tearful after her visit to the hospital. It was doubtful whether Sujata would live. Even in this condition she had been asking for forgiveness for all her faults. 'I feel like crying,' said Mallika. 'The poor thing has no idea who's responsible for your not being here that evening.'

Kamalesh spoke words of comfort to give his wife strength. 'I'll never disobey you again,' said Mallika. 'I'll never come between you and your work.'

Ending the call, Kamalesh went up to the prilling tower again. It was a magnificent sight. The German really did know magic—he had repaired the machinery perfectly.

There was no problem anywhere in the urea plant now. Jacob, the production supervisor, said, 'By God's grace we can begin now.'

Kamalesh gave his assent. A whistle was blown and Jacob gave instructions over the phone. Almost immediately the feed ammonia and carbon dioxide were introduced into the bowels of the static giant. Shattering the silence of the night, the monster awoke from its long sleep with a deafening roar.

Kamalesh and everyone else stood in the open field, listening to the sound with wonder.

Taking a long and circuitous route, through heat and through cold, catalysed in marvellous ways, the long-desired urea was born in the prilling tower. Going closer to the machine, Kamalesh saw its white grains falling in the chamber like snow on a winter night. Digambar Bonarjee's invention had been successful.

Everyone cheered. Jacob knelt to convey his gratitude to a merciful God. An ecstatic Sudarshan Sen shouted, 'Joy baba Taraknath-er joy!' And Kamalesh felt he had witnessed the birth of his own child. As though urea had been created for the first time on earth. Even primeval humans were not as wonderstruck on seeing the sun rise on the first day. Like a pilgrim at a shrine, Kamalesh Roychowdhury picked up a fistful of the sacred white powder. Digambar Bonarjee's mission was a success. Science had triumphed. Then Kamalesh began walking.

The sun hadn't risen yet. After giving Mallika the good news at home, Kamalesh would rush to Chandanpur. At ten this morning Digambar Bonarjee was going to take the train to Calcutta so that he could be admitted to hospital. Kamalesh would meet him at Chandanpur station.

Driving up the hillock, Kamalesh gazed in utter awe at this extraordinary world created by humans. It suddenly occurred to him that in times to come many train passengers would see this lighted factory and township in the night from a distance. But they would know nothing of the joys and sorrows, the laughter-and-tears-filled hopes and dreams of the people here today. They would only see a factory that manufactured fertiliser.

Author's Acknowledgements for *Unlimited*

A few years ago, I was travelling outside West Bengal on a holiday where I had the unexpected opportunity to meet several young scientists at a modern laboratory. That was the origin of this novel. I pray that those in our country who are working silently to create a paradise full of hopes and dreams are successful in establishing our motherland in all its glory.

1 January 1973

Author's Note

Before they appeared in public, the characters of *Limited* (*Seemabaddha*) lived incognito in my head for nearly ten years.

In this period, I had the opportunity to become familiar with the way an international business organisation did its work. A new chapter had begun in India's industrial revolution after independence. With their intelligence, education and diligence, Indians were beginning to claim their rights to the glass-covered cabins which were once reserved for white men. But a common complaint surfaced among labourers and other employees, which was that the captains of industry had not succeeded in providing what was expected of them. In some organisations things came to pass where employees openly said, 'White bosses were better than the brown bosses. Working and discussing things with them was much easier.'

Many grew to think of this new nobility of the industrial age as 'more evil than villains'. In shamelessly copying the lifestyle of white men and women, these newly minted captains of commerce invited all kinds of trouble upon their personal lives and voluntarily exiled themselves from the mainstream of everyday existence in this country. Despite being born in their motherland, they turned into expatriates living in India overnight. They dismissed the antipathy of lower-level employees for them as nothing but envy. The distance between people increased, and the walls separating them put even the barriers around prisons to shame.

These cracks in human relations are extremely attractive to any novelist. I felt a strong desire to work on the theme, without misunderstanding or judging this life of wealth and luxury. With the help of several well-wishers, I collected some material over the next few years. One fading afternoon in winter, Shyamalendu Chatterjee of *Limited* made a silent entrance into my head. Since he was the protagonist of my novel and I didn't want to turn him into a villain, his pretty, well-educated sister-in-law, Tutul, also appeared on the scene from Patna.

Why Patna of all places? Because I had to visit Patna from time to time on business, and, on one occasion in a train compartment, I had to assume temporary guardianship of a lively young woman who was on her way to Calcutta to visit her sister and brother-in-law. Needless to add, the brother-in-law was a young manager in a British company.

Despite all these preparations, however, the novel did not progress. When drawing up its framework I was in search of an incident where the ambitious protagonist would do something in a crisis that, while not exactly being illegal, would certainly be immoral. The sting of this unconscionable act was indispensable for the climax of my novel. I met many people, made numerous enquiries, but not discovering something that met my expectations hindered the writing. The following year I resumed my search, but still didn't find anything suitable. I recall preparing a long list of possible misdeeds with the help of secret sources, but what I needed was missing.

In the absence of this essential ingredient, I was on the verge of cancelling the plan for the novel when a telephone operator whom I used to know called me one day to enquire whether I knew of a job opening anywhere. I requested her to meet a friend of mine in another company. But before this I asked her why she wanted to resign from a well-paying job at a renowned company. She told me quietly that trouble was brewing at her workplace. The company would be unable to meet the terms set out in a major export contract, and out of fear of having to pay a large amount as compensation, an agitation at the factory might be instigated.

The lady cut the call, but unbeknownst to herself, she had rescued me from my predicament. In an instant I had the answer to the question I had been pursuing for three years. And amazingly a lock out was indeed declared at this company three weeks later on the grounds of 'labour unrest'. Let me acknowledge the lady once more and offer my gratitude. Unless she had come to meet me that afternoon, *Limited* might never have been written.

There was a diversity of reactions to the novel after it was published in a festival special number of a newspaper. Ordinary readers were delighted, but some trade union leaders as well as sons of Bengal who were proud of their corporate designations were not pleased at all. The union leaders were upset that I had not been sufficiently harsh with Shyamalendu Chatterjee—they said I had not correctly portrayed people like him as class enemies. And among the Westernised elite, many, along with their wives, suspected that I was part of a conspiracy to unfairly demean ambitious, well-educated, and hardworking young men from the new generation. The irate wife of a young, newly-appointed company director held me responsible for the fact that the congratulatory letter from her sister to her husband said, 'I'm keen to find out what secret misdeeds you've been up to, like Shyamalendu Chatterjee of *Limited*.'

Another highly efficient senior corporate manager complained at a public event that by writing openly about the competitive race between him and his colleague, I had subjected him to humiliation. Fortunately, several others at the gathering described similar competitions at their respective companies. I hear of so many such incidents that I fear every company has a Shyamalendu Chatterjee and a Runu Sanyal locked in a do-or-die battle.

I recall another middle-aged manager. He was particularly disappointed when *Limited* was referred to sarcastically during a bilateral discussion with factory workers in his company. He presented his personal grievance to me in a letter: 'Does every talented and ambitious person in the country live in a world of immorality and shameless luxury? You have offered the lives of those of limited vision and will to the world, but there are many who are engaged away from everyone's eyes in silently creating a new India in the plants and factories of our country, whose vision is unlimited despite the obstacles of history and their environment—who will write about them?'

This letter from a stranger affected me greatly. That was when I began to think about the novel titled *Unlimited* (*Asha Akankha*). I offer my deepest gratitude to this person of unknown address.

About the Author

SANKAR (Mani Sankar Mukherji) is among the most significant Indian novelists of the twentieth century. He writes fiction and non-fiction in Bengali. Two of his novels, *Seemabaddha* (*Company Limited*) and *Jana Aranya* (*The Middleman*), were turned into films by Satyajit Ray.

About the Translator

ARUNAVA SINHA translates classic, modern, and contemporary Bengali fiction and non-fiction from Bangladesh and India into English. He also translates fiction from English into Bengali. Over eighty of his translations have been published so far in India, the UK, and the USA. He teaches creative writing at Ashoka University, where he is also the co-director of the Ashoka Centre for Translation, and is the Books Editor at Scroll.in.